Intended Target
An Alexis Parker Novel

G.K. Parks

Copyright © 2015 G.K. Parks

A Modus Operandi imprint

All rights reserved.

ISBN: 194271002X
ISBN-13: 978-1-942710-02-8

Jim, you are greatly missed

BOOKS IN THE LIV DEMARCO SERIES:

Dangerous Stakes
Operation Stakeout
Unforeseen Danger
Deadly Dealings
High Risk
Fatal Mistake
Imminent Threat
Mistaken Identity
Malicious Intent

BOOKS IN THE ALEXIS PARKER SERIES:

Likely Suspects
The Warhol Incident
Mimicry of Banshees
Suspicion of Murder
Racing Through Darkness
Camels and Corpses
Lack of Jurisdiction
Dying for a Fix
Intended Target
Muffled Echoes
Crisis of Conscience
Misplaced Trust
Whitewashed Lies
On Tilt
Purview of Flashbulbs
The Long Game
Burning Embers
Thick Fog
Warning Signs
Past Crimes
Sinister Secret
Zero Sum
Buried Alive

BOOKS IN THE JULIAN MERCER SERIES:

Condemned
Betrayal
Subversion
Reparation
Retaliation
Hunting Grounds

BOOKS IN THE CROSS SECURITY INVESTIGATIONS SERIES:

Fallen Angel
Calculated Risk

ONE

I sat in the back row of the courtroom, staring straight ahead at the judge's bench. The jury box was to the right, along with half a dozen windows. The defense had been seated on the left, farthest from the jury, and I couldn't determine if that was common. Did the prosecutor and defendant have assigned sides? Pulling out my notepad, I jotted down the question for later consideration. Then I stood, scanning the room for anything that I might have missed.

"Agent Parker, are you finished yet?" the court clerk asked, entering from the oversized wooden doors at the back of the room. "The crime scene unit finished analyzing the area yesterday. We'd like to clean up and get back to business."

"Not yet." I squinted at the window closest to the back of the room. The glass contained a single hole. It didn't shatter because the bullet had traveled at such a high velocity that it merely punched a hole through the window pane before punching a hole through a man's skull. "After we check the surrounding area for possible vantage points, I'll give you the all clear."

The clerk muttered something under her breath, but I

pretended not to notice. Instead, I picked up my phone and dialed Supervisory Special Agent Mark Jablonsky. Mark was my boss and mentor. He had taken a few members of HRT, Hostage Rescue Team, to scout the area for a sniper's nest. My marksman skills were decent, but the only time I had used a sniper rifle had been at Quantico or on the range. Too many factors played a part, such as wind speed, temperature, the type of ammunition used, and the thickness of the window. That seemed far too mathematical for my taste. Aim and fire, that was more my speed.

Stepping over to the windows, I peered outside. The best spot would be from the building across the street on any level higher than this one. After I divulged these brilliant insights to Jablonsky over the phone, he said they were narrowing down possible locations.

"All done." I tucked my phone into my pocket and turned to the clerk. "Our crime techs will collect the window pane later in the afternoon, but you may inform maintenance they can begin the cleanup." The floor was covered in remnants of brain matter and dried blood.

"Thanks a lot."

"Any time."

Normally, I was more amenable to my fellow civil servants, but since my six a.m. arrival at the courthouse, the clerk had done nothing but hound me. She was like a terrier, nipping at my heels. Frankly, I didn't see any reason why she had to hover. I was capable of working well under pressure. After all, that was one of the requirements of working for the Office of International Operations, a branch of the FBI. Ever since my recent reinstatement, I'd been transitioning back into the much more polite and respectful manner of conducting an investigation rather than the devil may care methods I'd employed while in the private sector, although Mark would probably beg to differ. Had I still been a private investigator or security consultant, I might have grilled the astute court clerk on her whereabouts at the time of the shooting and her blatant lack of emotional outpouring over the two deaths, but that would have been a waste of my time and hers. And obviously, she was already behind schedule at 7:15 this morning.

"God, I need coffee." I listened to my footfalls echo in the high-ceilinged hallways.

"Ma'am," a voice said from behind, and I spun, despising that word, "what are you doing here?"

Pulling my credentials, I held them out to the man in the off-the-rack suit. Everything about his presence screamed law enforcement. He was either a city cop or with a government agency. The gun on his hip and the two star points visible beneath his jacket indicated U.S. Marshal Service.

"Investigating. What can you tell me about the shooting, Marshal?"

He raised an eyebrow. "Did they teach you that trick at Quantico?"

"No, I'm psychic."

"CIA's the only agency I know with psychics on the payroll. MKULTRA and all." He smiled. "But you're too young to have been involved in that, and the wrong letters are stamped on your ID. So I'm guessing you're not really psychic."

"Damn, you got me." I jerked my chin toward his hip. "Not too many agencies go with the Wild West motif when designing badges."

He laughed. "I guess not." He extended his hand, and we shook. "Lou Dobson."

"Alexis Parker, but if you point me in the direction of a coffee machine, you can call me Alex."

"Well, you're in luck. I know just the place." He headed for the staircase, and I followed him to the second floor, making a sharp left and entering a tiny office. "Is high-test okay?"

"You mean there are other kinds?"

"Not in my office." He filled a paper cup, handing it over before going behind the desk and unlocking the middle drawer. "The Bureau already picked up copies of the surveillance footage. I've reviewed it. My people have analyzed it. There's nothing on it. The threat didn't come from inside the courthouse. If it had, those two people would still be alive."

I took a sip, cringing at the bitterness. "You don't seem particularly worried about the potential ramifications this could have. How can you be sure no one screwed up?"

"Because we didn't."

"Courthouse security is tasked to the Marshal Service. A prosecutor and juror were killed inside the courtroom. Someone screwed up, and you're the marshal on duty."

"Do you have something to say, Agent Parker?"

"I need your records for any courthouse renovations and security measures your agency approved." I took another sip, hoping it had improved in the last minute. It didn't. "Also, I'll have to review potential threats, the corresponding threat assessments, and your routine and whereabouts. This isn't personal. My agency has been tasked to investigate. It has no bearing on your abilities, Marshal Dobson."

"The hell it doesn't." His friendly streak just went out the window. "Fine." He unlocked another drawer, lifting a few thick binders and slamming them on top of the desk. "If that isn't enough information for you, someone already came to collect the hard drives that store the interior camera surveillance feeds. I'm sure you'll be able to spot me easily enough."

"Thank you for cooperating." Internal reviews were the worst, but it was mandated government regulations that an agency couldn't review its own mishaps in order to avoid the look of impropriety. "And thanks for the coffee. We'll get this cleared up as quickly as possible."

He sighed. "Since you're psychic, can't you tell me what the verdict will be?"

I pressed my lips together. We weren't enemies, and clearing Marshal Dobson of any wrongdoing was only a small part of our investigation. But I didn't know what happened, and until we completed our assessment, I wasn't prepared to make a promise I couldn't keep.

"The jury's still out."

"As if I haven't heard that a million times."

"I'll work on my material if you learn how to make coffee."

"The grounds add an extra pick-me-up."

"Good day, sir." I nodded, lifting the binders off the desk. "Your review will take top priority, and someone will be in touch soon."

"Yeah." He sunk into the chair. "I've been here for ten years. This is the first time anything's ever happened. It's not my fault, and just so you know, I wouldn't have done anything differently."

"Okay." Balancing the binders in my arms and the paper cup between my teeth, I turned the doorknob and left the office.

Depositing the items inside the trunk of my vehicle, I scanned the exterior of the courthouse. The streets in this part of the city were extremely busy. Parking was next to impossible, which explained why attorneys' offices lined both sides of the street on either side of the courthouse. A number of closed circuit security cameras were posted around the courthouse and inside. At some point, one of them would have spotted the shooter. There's no way that shot would have been possible without preparation and careful planning. But I wasn't a ballistics expert or a professional shooter, so my time would be better spent delving into the evidence and determining who wanted to kill an Assistant U.S. Attorney. But the number had to be in the hundreds. This would require plenty of man-hours and actual coffee.

On my way back to the OIO building, I stopped at a coffee shop and ordered two drink carriers worth of assorted espresso-infused beverages. If that didn't demonstrate how much of a team player I was, I didn't know what would. After carrying the marshal's files and the drinks up to the main level, I entered the conference room to sort through this mess. Thankfully, no one else had returned from their outing yet.

The target, AUSA Stan Weaver, sustained a fatal gunshot wound to the back of his skull. The deceased had been in the middle of cross-examination when he was killed. The only solace his family had was his death had been instantaneous. From the witness statements that had already been collected, it took a few moments before anyone even realized what had happened. The shot sounded more like a clap of thunder than anything else. The judge and testifying witness had been covered in blood and brain spatter, but the rest of the courtroom was unaware of the reason for the prosecutor's sudden collapse.

Security immediately removed the judge and other potential high-value targets from the compromised area, but it had taken several minutes before anyone realized that juror number five, William Briscoe, had also been fatally wounded. Briscoe had been unfortunate enough to be seated between the shooter and the prosecutor. The bullet traveled through Briscoe's upper back, severing his aorta, before going through Weaver's head.

Pushing away from the table, I paced the empty conference room, studying the photos. Basic physics dictated the bullet would continue its descent. So how did it go through a person's back before going through a man's brain?

Flipping through the photos again, I realized the jury box was elevated. The first level was two steps above the floor. The second level was another step higher. Briscoe was seated on the lower level.

I pulled out the medical examiner's report, looking for heights. Something didn't sit right. The annoying mental twitch buzzed through my mind. Briscoe was barely over six feet tall. Weaver was five foot nine. Even calculating the approximate added height from the two steps, it still didn't make sense.

I decided to leave the crime scene analysis to the men with the red laser tripods and fancy computer software and shifted gears to reviewing the courthouse security measures. The federal courthouse had never dealt with a situation like this before, and like Dobson said, the threat didn't come from within. The security implementations and his plans appeared sound. His logs were complete. Not a single entry was missing. His routine checks were conducted timely, and the rest of the courthouse security team was on constant alert. The stringent security measures were the precise reason the killer resorted to using a long-range rifle. Apparently, Dobson performed his job a bit too well.

"Damn," Agent Eddie Lucca said, entering the conference room, "I'd hate to see how things look in your mind's eye."

"What?"

Lucca and I didn't exactly get along. He was a stickler for the rules and probably resented my recent reinstatement as a personal affront. After all, an agent with a questionable past who resigned, consulted, and attempted to make a comeback a time or two before gaining actual approval was clearly violating the very fabric of the OIO. Plus, SSA Mark Jablonsky had a soft spot for me. He always did. He taught me everything I knew and bugged the living daylights out of me until I finally returned to work. We had a shared history, complete with tragically losing two of our team in an explosion. Lucca was jealous. He didn't get it, and if he was lucky, he never would.

"That." He nodded to the whiteboard that I had covered with notes, questions, and crime scene photos. "How can you make sense out of that mess?" He picked up one of the coffee cups, shaking it gently. "How many of these did you drink?"

"It makes perfect sense. You would realize that if you were an investigator. Shouldn't you be analyzing something?"

"I already did." He placed a thick manila folder on the table. "Complete background on the murdered AUSA. The AG had to grant us special permission to examine his current caseload. I've determined a list of possible suspects." He pulled out a stack of stapled papers. "This is the case that was being heard at the time of the shooting. It should be your starting point."

"This is my starting point." I gestured to the board before picking up my coffee cup. It was empty, just like the two beside it. "Have Jablonsky and the team returned yet?"

"I'm not a messenger." Lucca lifted up another of the empty cups, putting it down and grabbing one from the other drink carrier. He smiled, finding an untouched cup. "But our tech team was sent to examine the sniper's nest, so Jablonsky isn't returning until they provide him with their preliminary findings."

"Great." Maybe the buzzing in my head was from too much caffeine and not some contradictory piece of evidence. I snatched the folder off the table, flipping through the pages. It looked like a lot of redacted legal bullshit. "Why don't you give me the condensed version?" I wheedled, but Lucca looked torn. "C'mon, boy scout, you know you want to."

Lucca snorted, shaking his head. "Really, Parker, do you think batting those beautiful blue eyes and flipping your dark brown hair will convince me to do the work for you?"

"You've already done the work." I consciously made the effort to stop running my hand through my hair. It was one of the things I did when I was anxious, just like pacing. The act was never meant to incite any type of response from my male counterparts. "We're on the same team." Narrowing my eyes at the coffee cup, I added, "And I brought you coffee. It's the least you can do since I didn't get so much as a thank you."

"You should thank me. From the looks of you, you're probably one cup away from a heart attack, which explains why the whiteboard is a jittery mess." He grabbed a marker. "I'm sure you'll fail to agree, but penmanship counts."

"Don't touch my board." I snatched the marker out of his hand. "If you try it again, I'll cuff you to the table."

"Fine, I'll give you the complete rundown and save you some time but only if you tell me what I did to piss you off?"

This was a conversation I didn't want to have. "You didn't do anything. I'm just a bitch."

He stifled a snicker. "Right. Well, I won't disagree, but it seems you're okay with everyone else in the office except me. What gives?"

I'd seen the writing on the wall. Jablonsky didn't say anything yet, but he didn't have to. Since my reinstatement, Lucca had been assisting in a support role on my cases. He was an analyst by trade. He worked a desk, helped on investigations, and compiled data. He was also one of the junior members of the team, and he wasn't partnered with anyone. He was still learning the ropes in the field, and I was two years behind on recent advancements in proper protocol and procedure. We were a match made in heaven, but after my last partner was killed in the line of duty, I made it abundantly clear I worked alone. And whenever the powers that be ordered us to work together, I knew Mark wouldn't see any merit to my protests, but if Lucca refused to work with me, that would solve the problem. Plus, he seemed like a good guy, so there was no reason he should risk physical peril by being in such close proximity to me and my bad luck.

"Let's call it a personality clash," I said. "Now, if you'd be so kind as to read me in, Agent Lucca."

TWO

The case being heard the day of the shooting involved numerous armed robberies that spanned the tri-state area. Because the defendant, Jeremy Hunter, had committed felonies across state lines, his case became a federal matter and one the federal prosecutor had to deal with. However, Hunter was small potatoes. He had priors for larceny, armed robbery, B&E, and assault charges, but nothing extreme enough to warrant intervention by an unknown shooter. Plus, Weaver's death did nothing to exonerate Hunter. More than likely, whoever pulled the trigger did so on his own accord and not to benefit Hunter.

"Weaver's schedule is easy to find," Lucca said. "Just look at the court docket. There's always a case being heard that involves a federal prosecutor since it is the federal courthouse. If someone hung around long enough, they could easily figure out which courtrooms and cases Weaver was trying."

"Are you sure the shooter wanted to kill Weaver specifically and not any AUSA he could find?"

"It's unlikely this was a random killing. There are easier ways to gun down federal prosecutors." Lucca made a fair point, and I decided now wasn't a good time to question the reasonableness that Weaver was the intended target. It made sense since he had enemies, and he was dead. "Our forensic accountants are digging through Hunter's financials. We've subpoenaed Hunter's phone records, but I don't expect either to point to a smoking gun, so to speak."

"What about Weaver's enemies?"

"You'll need a new pack of markers." Lucca flipped to the last few pages inside the folder. "These are the individuals he's put away. Keep in mind, that doesn't take into account their family members, friends, or associates." He pushed the stapled list closer. "Why don't you start with A?"

"Oh, I can tell you what starts with A."

"Aren't you clever?"

"Play nice boys and girls," Jablonsky said, entering the room and dropping additional files and photos on top of our growing pile of intel. He surveyed the room, recognizing my methodology scrawled across the whiteboard. "Come to any conclusions yet, Parker?"

"Courthouse security was never breached. Marshal Dobson's measures are tight."

"Okay, I want a report and your notes on my desk before the end of the day. The sooner we clear that off our plate, the faster we'll be able to focus on finding our killer." Mark grabbed a cup of coffee out of the carrier and took a seat across from Lucca. "How much progress have you made, Eddie?"

"I've compiled a list of Weaver's work-related enemies. Agent Parker was about to begin assessing the likelihood of each individual's involvement," Lucca said, satisfied with himself for passing off the grunt work. Glaring in his direction, I bit my tongue while he filled Mark in on everything he'd already told me. "I'll start digging into Weaver's personal life. Surely, that will result in a few more names to consider."

"Very good," Mark said, dismissing Lucca, who left the conference room and returned to his desk. "So," he swiveled sideways in the chair and folded his hands over his gut, "the tech team is searching every inch of the area for evidence. We might get lucky and find fingerprints or DNA. In the meantime, I've made a few calls to get access to the neighboring buildings' security cam footage. In a couple of hours, we should have the tapes, and hopefully, it'll lead to an ID."

"Why did you tell Lucca to continue working on a suspect list?"

"There's no guarantee any of these things will pan out. It's important to always be prepared. How many times have I told you that?"

"If I had a nickel." Sifting through the information, I found the facts overwhelming. Too many possible suspects, no clear motive, and a million unanswered questions remained. Putting my head in my hands, I took a few deep breaths. "What should I do first?"

"Start with the security assessment. Once that's completed, you can leave for the day. You've been at this since five a.m. Did you even go home last night?"

"Yes, I went home. You can call Martin and ask."

"God," Mark shook his head, "I keep forgetting you moved in with Marty. What's it been? Three weeks?"

"Something like that. But seriously, I have no problem working late."

"You never do."

Marshal Dobson was meticulous. His records were organized and tabbed, making my job a million times easier. Even copies of the maintenance and upkeep for the metal detectors were included. He didn't screw up. Unfortunately, even with superb planning and perfect execution, this still happened.

After copying the relevant information for our records, I typed out the rest of my report in favor of clearing Dobson of negligence and any wrongdoing and hit print. Jablonsky wasn't in his office when I went to drop off the paperwork, so I left the items and returned to my desk. It was barely after four o'clock. Surely, I could spend a few more hours assisting on identifying the shooter.

"Any new developments?" I rolled across the room to Lucca's workspace. He was situated directly across from me, another sign that the two of us would eventually partner up.

"You already ran backgrounds and alibis and checked off every name that I gave you?" His eyes darted briefly from the computer monitor to me. "Because I'd say whoever wanted Weaver dead is somewhere on that list. If it were personal, the killer would have found an easier venue to plan the strike."

"I don't disagree, but you'd rather rake me over the coals than give me a nudge in the right direction? This investigation isn't about either of us. It's about putting a man to rest and giving his family closure."

Lucca pulled his hands away from the keyboard and leaned back in the chair. Suddenly, I had his full and undivided attention.

"The more time we waste, the greater the chances are that this son of a bitch will elude us. Do you really want that to happen?" I asked.

"Wow," he sucked some air in between his teeth, "how did I miss that?"

"Miss what?"

"You." He shook his head and went back to typing something into the computer. "Check your inbox. I just sent you the updated list. It's color-coded based on threat potential."

I slid back across the walkway to my desk, keying in the password to access the online dropbox.

"You're welcome."

"Thanks," I said, distracted by the information.

As I accessed records for the Department of Corrections to rule out those currently incarcerated, I shot a brief glance at Lucca. He was studying me so intensely his forehead might become permanently creased. The polite thing to do would be for him to look away, but he continued to stare. Returning to work, I fought to ignore the weight of his gaze.

"Who would have thought you actually give a shit about the victims?" His words came as a surprise, but I didn't respond.

Instead, I pretended I didn't hear him and continued working through the names highlighted in red. A few were dead. Some were in prison, and the ones who weren't would need to provide a solid alibi. After knocking the red names down to a couple dozen, I stretched in the chair and reached for the phone.

"Don't even think about it, Parker," Jablonsky warned. "I took your assessment under advisement concerning Marshal Dobson. The courthouse appears secure. He and his team were careful. I'll pass our findings off to Director Kendall. He'll inform the Marshal Service in the morning. In the meantime, you're off-the-clock. Go home. Someone else can check into our ex-cons' alibis."

"Fine."

Collecting my belongings and a copy of the suspect list, I dutifully took the elevator to the underground parking garage, unlocked my car, and circled through the city, taking a different route home than any of the ones I had already used in the past week. Some called it paranoia. I called it careful. And now that I was living with James Martin, his safety was my top priority. I'd take every measure imaginable to be extra cautious.

Martin's compound was on the outskirts of the city. His four story estate came with a state-of-the-art security system, numerous guest suites, a wicked home gym, an Infinity pool, and all the premium channels a girl could ever want. Too bad I still wasn't certain I wanted to live here. There was always a downside, and this one was a doozy.

After resigning from the OIO two years ago, I endeavored to a life of security consulting and private investigation. My first job was as James Martin's bodyguard. That event culminated in exchanging fire with a team of mercenaries inside the very house in which I now lived. Although to be fair, my apartment, which I adamantly refused to give up, had been the location of some pretty horrific scenes as well. Maybe I was just cursed. Unfortunately, when I returned to my previous career, concessions had to be made in my private life, and one of those was cohabitation. However, if a particular assignment or investigation proved to be unreasonably risky, I'd stay at my old place for the duration. This was a new experience for us, and we still had a few kinks to work out.

Once the garage door closed and the security system was reactivated, I took my copy of the current case file upstairs to the second floor guest suite. The suite was practically as large as my one bedroom apartment, minus the kitchen and dining area. The closet and dresser were full of my clothing. The bathroom contained my toiletries. I noticed the addition of a desk in the corner and a corkboard and whiteboard mounted to the wall beside it. Martin must have spent the morning redecorating.

Slipping my credentials free from my belt, I placed them in the top desk drawer and shrugged out of my shoulder holster. Normally, I'd keep my firearm in the nightstand, but since my back-up nine millimeter now had a permanent place in Martin's bedroom, or rather our bedroom, this one could stay here and keep my notes and theories company. Realizing the time, I decided to review the current information on the case once more. For some reason, I worked better secluded from others. It gave the voices in my head free range without interruption by actual living people. Snickering at my own insanity, I spread the information across the surface of the desk, picked up a few pins, and organized the crime scene photos and my notes into a timeline on the board.

When I was through dissecting the file, I stepped back to admire my handiwork. Something didn't coalesce. What was it? Narrowing my eyes, I reached across for my laptop and sprawled out on the mattress. The facts didn't fit the crime. A double homicide due to a single bullet from a long-range sniper rifle sounded more like the Kennedy assassination than someone intent on murdering an Assistant U.S. Attorney. Too bad there was no grassy knoll that would lead straight to a modern day Oswald. Although, if conspiracy theorists were to be believed, then Oswald was framed, and I wasn't in the business of arresting innocent bystanders. Since Lucca and Jablonsky were narrowing the suspect list, I conducted a people search on Weaver, followed by an internet search. Deep dark secrets tended to surface at the most inopportune times, and with the advent of social networking and smart phones, a person's worst moments were often photographed or filmed and appeared on the internet for all to see.

Hundreds of pages worth of hits surfaced. I rubbed my eyes. Why did our dead AUSA have such a common name? Entering a few more terms to narrow the parameters, I tried again. The hours passed without me noticing as I skimmed law review articles, court dockets, pro bono cases, news stories, and op-ed pieces. None of it was useful. Weaver was a normal guy.

Just as I began to sort through public records for property and financials, my phone rang. "What do you want, Lucca?"

"Jeremy Hunter's not involved. The forensic accountants cleared his bank history, and I personally examined his recent correspondence. It wasn't him, like I said."

"So you called to gloat?"

"Why do you have to be so difficult? We're on the same team. I was simply informing you of our latest development."

"I'm off-the-clock. Leave a sticky note on my desk next time."

"Jablonsky said you couldn't comprehend what off-the-clock meant." Lucca's voice was practically a snarl. With any luck, my brilliant plan was working. "He asked that I phone and inform you that we've gained access to a ton of surveillance footage, and the tech department is analyzing it now."

"Okay. Were they hoping I'd volunteer to make a coffee run?"

"No," Lucca paused, taking in a breath in order to contain his animosity, "and don't expect any more favors." Before I could say another word, he hung up.

"Tomorrow's going to be so much fun." I dropped the phone on the nightstand and continued my research.

Unfortunately, now I was distracted. Eddie Lucca was a newcomer. He didn't know me, my history, or the reason for my reticence against working side by side with another member of the team. Furthermore, I didn't want to get to know him because once I did, things would change, and I was scared. My biggest fear was losing someone I was close to, and since Mark insisted that I couldn't control everything or stop bad things from happening, my only other option was to make sure I didn't get close to anyone, particularly on the job.

Rubbing my face, I shook off the pointless emotional musing and stared at the computer screen. "Who were you close to?" I asked Stan Weaver's photograph. It didn't respond, so I shifted gears and pulled up his marriage records.

He was divorced. His ex-wife remarried seven years ago. They didn't have any children. From the quick scan of his phone records and e-mail accounts, they didn't speak. That didn't mean she had anything to do with his death. His current wife was a dental hygienist. From what I'd gathered, they seemed happy. No outstanding debts, a lack of overt threats, and a nice house in the suburbs. It looked like he was living the American dream or would have been if he had a white picket fence and two and a half kids. His parents were elderly, in their late eighties, and resided in an assisted living community in southern Florida. He had two brothers and a sister. They were scattered across the country with their own careers and families. On paper, he didn't fit the profile for a murder victim. Then again, there wasn't a profile for murder victims.

Flopping onto my back, I stared at the upside down view of the information I'd stuck on the corkboard. Something was missing. The most obvious motive for killing Weaver was his job, but his work records were at the office. Due to the sensitive nature of court cases, a lot of information had been redacted. The OIO had been granted clearance to check into most of it but not all of it, and like Lucca pointed out, Weaver was killed in a courtroom. If the shooter had personal knowledge of Weaver in a more intimate setting, then anywhere else would have been an easier place to strike. If the motive had been personal, William Briscoe, the unlucky juror, would still be alive. Collateral damage was the worst. My stomach clenched at the thought.

Digging deeper into Weaver's personal life wouldn't get us any closer to identifying the murderer, so I opened a new tab and did a brief people search for William Briscoe. He was widowed and had two grown children. Closing my laptop, I couldn't read anymore. The government required law-abiding citizens to partake in the jury process, and that inevitably led to a man's death. Obviously, no one ever expected things like this to happen. It was just a fluke. Perhaps if he hadn't died in the jury box, he might have been struck by lightning, but I didn't buy into that fate mumbo-jumbo. The person responsible would be caught. Stan Weaver's and William Briscoe's relatives were counting on it. I was counting on it.

I shut my eyes and rested my forehead against my folded arms. I didn't enjoy feeling helpless, but the investigation was in its infancy. Until enough data and evidence were collected, there was little to do. Considering the only other piece of the puzzle, I inhaled deeply, lifted the lid of my laptop, and accessed the government employee database for Marshal Dobson. He looked clean. I didn't doubt the conclusions I reached in my assessment, but it never hurt to double-check.

Lou Dobson's record contained commendations, gushing personal references, and an airtight plan for the courthouse. Entering dates that corresponded to his previous work history, I waited for the page to load, but I suspected he had been just as meticulous at his prior posts. As he said this morning, nothing like this had ever happened before. None of his earlier postings were marked by security breaches or his shortcomings. The guy was a frigging star, just like that stupid badge.

THREE

"What do we have?" I asked. My eyes were trained on the updated boards in the conference room. It was eight a.m., and the team had spent a good portion of the night running down names and checking alibis.

Lucca tossed a disinterested glance in my direction and went back to reading Weaver's case file. The techs ignored me, continuing to scrub the surveillance feed. From the notes and printouts, our unsub was male, Caucasian, and looked like a Yankees fan, based on the cap he wore. Either that or he might have been an incognito movie star. He wore the baseball cap low on his head with the bill pulled down to cover his face. He donned a pair of dark sunglasses, a windbreaker, and jeans. He carried a gym bag which probably held his sniper rifle and scope, and he entered the adjacent office building like he owned the place.

The building itself contained offices for attorneys, accountants, brokers, and other professional types. It would have been easy enough to gain access to the building and exit on the appropriate floor, but he either needed a solid plan in order to have some alone time or he had an accomplice. I skimmed the list of potential suspects, but most of the names were crossed out.

Clearing my throat, I focused on the nearest agent. "Has our unknown subject been spotted on the footage prior to the day of the shooting?"

He held up a finger as if my question was too much of an inconvenience and I should wait. Rolling my shoulders, I glared at Lucca. Whatever he said to the rest of the team made me persona non grata. Resisting the urge to stoop to his level, I grabbed my copy of the information and left the conference room.

"How'd things go with the Marshal Service?" I asked Mark.

"Dobson's cleared as far as we're concerned, but Dobson's superiors are conducting their own assessment. It'll be a few days before the marshal is back at work." He scanned the paperwork that covered my desk. "Any particular reason Lucca's vying to get you removed from this case?"

"The boy scout doesn't like me." I keyed in a few names to get mug shots brought up for the remaining suspects on our list. Maybe I could match stats faster than the facial recognition software.

"You should probably stop calling him a boy scout." Mark shook his head. "I know what you're doing. You need to cut it out."

There was no point denying it, so I went with the next best response. "Prove it."

"I don't have to prove it. I gave you an order. You will follow it."

"When did the OIO get drafted into the military?"

"Watch yourself, Parker. I get it. But you are this close to being insubordinate, and I'm not above sticking a formal reprimand in your file. You don't have to make friends, but you have to be civil. The men and women in this office have to be willing to watch your back, and you're making that increasingly difficult. If this keeps up, I will have you chained to the desk while we wait for another psych eval. Do I make myself clear?"

"Crystal."

"Good. Now go apologize for whatever dumbass thing you said to Eddie, and let's get back to work. This isn't kindergarten. I'm not some schoolhouse marm." He jerked his head in the direction of the conference room, and I stood. "We are not having this conversation again."

Dutifully, I returned to work. Lucca was scribbling some information next to my notations on the board. Resting my hips against the table, I crossed my arms over my chest and stared at his perfectly formed letters. He probably had a merit badge for penmanship too. It took some effort to refrain from saying as much.

When he turned around, he looked surprised to see me back in the conference room. His eyes shifted to Jablonsky leaning over one of the technician's shoulders to study whatever was on the computer screen. Obviously, I wasn't benched, much to Lucca's disappointment.

"May I speak to you outside, Agent Lucca?" I asked.

"Really, Parker?" He blinked a few times. "Fine. Let's get this over with." He led the way out of the conference room and back to his desk. "What is it now?"

"Look, we both have a role to play in this investigation, so I'd like to apologize for coming off as less than professional. From here on out, I will show you the utmost respect."

"I don't want your respect. I just want to know why you left this job and how you were able to come back. You have a meritorious service award and a few commendations, but you've also been flagged for testing positive on a drug test. The last case we worked involved drugs. What am I missing? Have you been on the job the entire time but assigned to some deep cover thing? Did you fall down the rabbit hole and have to resign to get yourself cleaned up? Are you a liability?"

Normally, I'd brush off the accusations with a gruff response, but Jablonsky insisted I apologize. So the words poured out before I could think of what would happen once they were uttered. "I'm not an addict, and I've never been on drugs. I resigned because I couldn't stay here, but for some reason, I just can't stay away." I met his eyes. "And I am a liability, so you should keep your distance."

My gaze darted to my dead partner's old desk. The void in my chest ripped open, the pain fresh and debilitating just like it had been that horrible day two years ago. I thought I had moved past this, but Lucca's confrontation mixed with lack of sleep threatened to reduce me to a quivering, emotional wreck. Biting the inside of my lip, I covered my mouth to hide the trembling in my chin. *Pull it together*, the voice in my head insisted.

Lucca's eyes went wide, and he put a hand on my arm. I flinched at the contact, but he held firm. "Sit down, Alexis. Put your head between your knees and breathe deeply."

Oh, god. Why did I have to lose it in the middle of the office? He rubbed circles between my shoulder blades until my breathing stabilized. After a few deep breaths, I set my jaw and sat up straight. We made eye contact. I expected him to run off to report my unstable behavior to Jablonsky or Kendall in order to make sure I stayed benched. Instead, he knelt to my level and brushed a few loose strands of hair away from my face.

"Whatever secrets you have, I'll keep safe, just between you and me," he said. "I'm around if you need to talk it out." Then he scooped the file off the desk and returned to the conference room like nothing happened.

"Fuck." I pinched the bridge of my nose, took another deep breath, and went down the hallway to the elevator. I couldn't stay inside this horrible building for another minute.

I was halfway across town when I called Jablonsky. From his tone, it was apparent Lucca hadn't spilled the beans. I wasn't sure if I was thankful or alarmed. After telling Mark that I was checking out a lead and would update him by the end of the day, I rerouted to the courthouse and parked outside.

I couldn't afford to lose it again. I'd only been back on the job for three months, but I had been fine for those three months. What was causing this mental turmoil? Chalking it up to too many sleepless nights, an overdose of caffeine, and the shock of Lucca's questions, I forced the current investigation to take hold of my wayward thoughts. I needed a direction. Climbing out of the car, I set off toward the neighboring building. If our shooter could go inside like he owned the place, I could do the same damn thing.

Smiling at the security officer stationed in the lobby, I continued on a path to the elevator banks. According to HRT's report, the shooter had been on the twentieth floor. Jablonsky had already sent our crime scene unit to collect evidence, but it never hurt to check things out in person.

The elevator stopped twice on my ride up. The professionals in suits didn't even bat an eye in my direction. Would that have been different if I was dressed in casual wear? I'd left the office too quickly this morning to know if the gunman had taken the stairs or the elevator to his perch, so I had no way of knowing who he might have encountered on his way in and out of the building.

When the door opened on the proper level, I stepped out into a large, open expanse. A directory on the wall indicated an accountant's office, an insurance company, a chiropractor, and several empty slots. Common sense dictated one of these barren offices must have housed the sniper's nest. Glancing out the nearest window, I realized the courthouse wasn't in view, so I reversed direction, moving to the southeast corner.

The door to the vacant office space was sealed with crime scene tape. I sliced through the strip of tape and turned the knob. But the door didn't budge. Deciding that my credentials were good for something, I went down the hallway to the nearest occupied space. As I sauntered into the chiropractor's office, the receptionist smiled warmly.

"Do you have an appointment, miss?" she asked, ready to key my name into the computer.

"Actually," I held out my identification, "do you think you could get someone from building security to come up here with a key for that office down the hall?"

"I'm sorry, hun, but building security doesn't have access to the offices. They're privately owned."

"Who owns the one at the far end of the hall?"

"That used to be Clayton Financial, but they moved out ten months ago. No one's occupied it since." She rummaged through the drawer until she found a flyer. "The real estate agency had an open house to attract renters two weeks ago. As far as I know, no one was interested, but they had some great cookies. I snuck over during my break to check it out. They had a nice spread. Cold cut platter, finger sandwiches, cookies, cake. It was lovely."

A patient came in, and I stepped to the side so she could take his information while I considered her words. When she was finished, I flipped through the content on my phone, finding a photo of the unsub from the security footage.

"Do you recognize this man?" I asked.

She took the phone, narrowing her eyes at the screen. "I don't think so. I'm not sure." Her brow furrowed. "What's going on? The police have been crawling all over this building for the last few days. Did something happen?"

"Nothing to worry about." I took my phone back and gave her a reassuring look. "If you remember seeing anyone strange lurking around here, give me a call." I handed her my card and went to the door.

Since building security couldn't let me inside the office, I'd have to let myself in. After checking the doorknob again to make sure it wasn't stuck, I removed my lock picks and set to work. The cheap lock popped ten seconds later, and I cautiously entered the room.

Fingerprint powder coated a few areas of the room, and the tripods holding laser sights to calculate angles and trajectories remained. Other than that, the room was empty. It was nothing more than a large, rectangular space with half a dozen floor to ceiling windows. The window closest to the corner had a six inch circle cut out of the glass near the floor. The space had been boarded up by one of the techs in order to ensure outside elements didn't contaminate the scene. No one wanted a room full of pigeons or a swarm of bees taking up residence inside.

A clear view of the courthouse was visible from the window. I wished I had binoculars or a scope. Our shooter must have laid flat on the floor, his high velocity rifle propped up to steady the shot. How long did he wait for AUSA Weaver to step into his line of sight? Did he realize Briscoe would impede the shot? How certain could he have been that the bullet would travel this distance, punch through the courthouse window, and pass through a man before killing another one? There were a hundred other ways to plan a hit. This wouldn't have been the one I chose. The only clear advantage for using this location was the ability to make a clean getaway. No one inside the courtroom would have realized where the shot came from or think to stop anyone from leaving, at least not immediately.

Studying the slight scrapes on the tile, I took a few photos in case the crime techs were lazy. This had been our sniper's position. From the remnants of fingerprint powder that covered the floor, they attempted to find prints, but I didn't know if they did. I stepped backward, surveying the spot. Sneak inside, assemble the rifle, patiently wait hours or even days, pull the trigger, pack up, and escape. Leaving the room, I locked the door, took off my gloves, tucked them into my jacket pocket, and considered the accessibility of the stairwell. I had taken the elevator up, so I might as well take the stairs down.

The doorway opened into a cinderblock expanse. The paint was old and peeling. The air smelled stale. Just a typical unused stairwell. I didn't see any surveillance cameras as I descended flight after flight. About ten flights down, the elevator started to look much more appealing. By the time I reached the bottom, I decided the treadmill would be unnecessary this evening.

Opening the bottom door, I expected to come out in the lobby. Instead, I was in a narrow hallway. To the right was a door marked maintenance. To the left was the lobby. Deciding to perform my due diligence and check out the entire area, I went right and tugged on the thick door.

Circuit breakers, pipes, and other necessary mechanical functions for the building were inside. But something in the far corner caught my eye. I stepped deeper into the room. My hand automatically came to rest inside my opened jacket. I glanced down at the gym bag and nudged it with my shoe. After checking the area for signs of life, I put my gloves back on, knelt down, and unzipped the bag.

"Have you made any progress on identifying the weapon used?" I asked when Jablonsky answered my call.

"There wasn't much left of the bullet. Ballistics is

narrowing down possible makes based on caliber."

"You might want to send another team to finish cataloguing the evidence. I just found the gun." After giving him my location, I stepped away from the gym bag, cognizant of the surrounding area.

Our shooter must have taken the stairs down, deposited the weapon here in case he was stopped or questioned, and continued out of the building. For whatever the reason, no one bothered to look in here, and until someone arrived, I was stuck babysitting a murder weapon. How often did maintenance come into this room? Could the shooter work inside the building or have an accomplice who did? It would explain how he gained access to an empty office and entered and exited undetected.

Making a mental note to check into building employees and every individual and company that had an office within this high-rise, I resisted the urge to pace. Instead, I leaned against the wall, checked my watch a dozen times, and hoped the occasional scurrying sound I heard wasn't due to rats. My plan to avoid getting stuck inside my own head wasn't working now that I was stuck inside a maintenance room, but thankfully, I had more important things to occupy my mind.

"Agent Parker," Lucca called, leading our crime scene unit inside, "did you really find our smoking gun?"

"It's been a few days, so it isn't smoking anymore. But I think so."

He looked at me for a moment. "I can take it from here."

"Great." I went to the door. "Before you leave, send someone upstairs to reseal the door to the office our shooter used. I cut through the tape in order to look around."

"Anything else? Maybe I should pick up your dry cleaning while I'm at it." His words might have been snarky, but his tone was playful. Either Lucca was using kid gloves, or for some unbeknownst reason, my earlier meltdown had made him warm to me. Crap.

"My dry cleaning won't be ready until Tuesday but thanks anyway."

FOUR

I stared at the blinking cursor on the screen. We found our murder weapon, a Remington 700. It was eerily similar to the M24, the version the military and police used, and it caused a sinking feeling in my stomach. The weapon was devoid of prints. Our lab rats even went so far as to swab the sight and trigger for skin cells but found nothing conclusive. A few of our suspects that had recently been paroled were questioned, but so far, we'd hit nothing but dead ends.

My desk phone rang. I leaned away from the keyboard. After conducting background checks on the building's security personnel and the individuals and companies that owned office space inside the building, I had nothing new to report. No one who worked security had a criminal record. The most heinous crimes were a few nonviolent misdemeanors. So I remained at my desk, attempting to come up with a new angle and different parameters that would lead to the guilty party, but brilliance failed to strike. Nothing panned out.

"Parker," I answered, glancing around to see if any of my fellow agents looked like they might have a lead, but they looked as bored and clueless as I felt.

"Your victim's autopsy is complete. There are a few things you might want to see."

"I'm on my way." Disconnecting, I went to Mark's office and knocked. "The medical examiner's office just called. They found something strange. Do you want me to check it out?"

"Yeah, that's fine. We can spare you for a while." He glanced into the bullpen. "Where's Lucca? Did he come back yet?"

"I don't think so. I haven't seen him since he procured the weapon."

"Okay." He jerked his chin at the door. "It looks like you're on your own. Get to it, Parker."

When I arrived at the medical examiner's office, I was escorted into the morgue. Dead bodies were never a pleasant sight. It was difficult to discern if the sudden chill that traveled down my spine was from the refrigerated air or the smell of antiseptic and death that filled the room, clinging to my hair and clothing. Today wasn't the day to be reminded of mortality, but I forced my brain to focus. The doctor offered a friendly smile and went to the drawers, opening one on the second shelf and rolling out the body.

"When he first came in, the bruises weren't nearly as pronounced, and due to their position, it was hard to determine it wasn't from blood pooling internally on account of the gunshot wound. My assistant wasn't sure, so he ordered a complete panel of x-rays." Dr. Janice Cole pointed to the area beneath the bullet stippling. She flipped through the file, extracting a set of films and sticking them on the lightboard. "As you can see, these are just your victim's most recent set of injuries."

"What about Stan Weaver?" I asked, my mind reeling from the repeated beatings and remodeled injuries William Briscoe had sustained in the last six months, according to the ME's report.

"What about him?" She raised a confused eyebrow. "He died from a high velocity bullet to the head. His autopsy was simple. No surprises," she flipped through his chart to be thorough, "unless you're worried about his high cholesterol, but frankly, it's a little late in the game to worry about that now."

I was appalled by the humor, even though I'd been known to crack dark, scathing jokes at the worst times imaginable. Unfortunately, I wasn't in the mood for jokes.

"No, I'm not worried about his high cholesterol. Does he have any previous injuries or anything that could hint why someone wanted him dead?"

She shrugged, sliding the drawer closed on William Briscoe. "I only report what I find, and there was nothing to find on Weaver. Now, with your other vic, the bruises, hairline fractures, and slight remodeling on his intercostal, clavicle, and ulna bones indicate whoever beat him had done it before." She pulled the films off the screen and put up another set of x-rays of Briscoe's hands and arms. "It looks like he fought back." She pointed to his knuckles and wrists. "We typically see injuries like this when people first learn to box and aren't used to maintaining proper form."

"Or he fought back, and those are defensive wounds."

"Also possible."

"Thanks, Doc."

Now I was more confused than before. What did any of this have to do with our shooter and Weaver? One thought came to mind—jury tampering. But Lucca already determined the current defendant, Jeremy Hunter, wasn't involved. So who would want to beat up one of our jurors and execute the prosecutor? I signed out of the morgue and took a copy of the two autopsy files back to the federal building to add this confusing new piece to our puzzle.

After making copies for the rest of the team, I went into the conference room and placed the autopsy reports in front of each chair at the table before tacking the photos of William Briscoe's extensive injuries to the board. As I flipped through the files for additional information on Briscoe, it became apparent that aside from name and stats, no other information was available. Why didn't anyone look into the sniper's second victim?

I returned to my desk, keying in William Briscoe's name and social security number. In his lifetime, he'd received two dozen traffic violations, one drunk and disorderly charge that was dropped, and had reported his car stolen three years ago. Other than that, the government didn't spend much time worrying about him. He paid his taxes on time and generally played by the rules. If he had been more of a firebrand, he might have failed to report for jury duty and dodged a bullet. Then again, given his recent beatings, maybe he thought he'd be safer reporting to the courthouse every day. Boy, was he mistaken.

"Alex," Mark's voice sounded behind my shoulder, "what happened at the ME's office?"

"Briscoe's been enduring frequent beatings. He looks like he could be the intended target."

"Briscoe was a juror. The selection process is complicated, to say the least. The identities of the jury pool are concealed. It's difficult for anyone to determine who served on what jury. You know this. It's not quite anonymous, but it's supposed to be. What you're suggesting is someone gained access and used this as an opportunity to kill William Briscoe." Mark spun my chair around, so I was facing him. "Shake off the cobwebs. Those aren't reasonable conclusions. Briscoe's death was accidental. The bullet tore through his aorta. From what the techs have determined, he must have stood up for whatever the reason and ended up in front of Weaver. It's the only thing that explains the height differentiation involved in the trajectory of the shot, first through Briscoe's back before entering Weaver's skull. It was purely coincidental. If Briscoe was the intended target, the bullet would have been aimed at his head, not Weaver's."

"You've always said there are no such things as coincidences."

"This is the exception to the rule."

"C'mon, Jablonsky, look at the autopsy photos. Someone had an axe to grind. And this," I grabbed the list of suspects for Weaver's murder, "has yet to pan out. Sure, Weaver had a ton of enemies, but none of them are responsible."

"That list only deals with his professional life, not his personal one. There are still a million stones to overturn."

"You said a personal vendetta would have been carried

out elsewhere."

"Whoever's been using Briscoe as a punching bag would have killed him elsewhere too. Think about it," Mark insisted, ever the voice of reason. "We have the murder weapon. The location. Techs are scrubbing the footage from that office building and the courthouse. We'll get an ID, and we'll find him. You found that weapon today. Somehow, we missed checking the maintenance room. So why's a rain cloud hanging over your head?"

"Because the facts don't fit," I toyed with the hem of my jacket, "and no one else seems to notice the giant elephant in the room."

"Let me hear your theory."

"Briscoe pissed someone off. His wife died five years ago. Maybe he was having an affair with a married woman or a younger woman. Or he could have owed someone a lot of money. We don't have his financials, but it's possible. Whoever it is found him and made their point. Maybe they planned to kill him then, but he escaped. His wounds could have been defensive. He might have witnessed a crime, and the perpetrator threatened him. His frequent appearances at the courthouse this week for the case might have spooked the culprit, and he decided to permanently silence Briscoe."

"That's a hell of a lot of conjecture. When you hear hoofbeats, you're supposed to think horses."

"Occam's razor. Assume the simplest solution. But it hasn't provided any real leads. So maybe we're wrong."

"And you want to go on a safari."

"It couldn't hurt to explore the possibilities. Plus, Lucca's got it covered. I'm sure he's perfectly capable of analyzing Weaver's other threats, running backgrounds, and checking into alibis."

"You're not sticking him with that much work, even though he tried to do the same thing to you. Didn't we discuss childish behavior earlier today?"

"Fine. I'll continue on this course, but for the record, I believe we're looking at this wrong."

I returned to the conference room, forcing myself to focus on Stan Weaver as the intended target. During my earlier field trip, a couple of agents had spoken with the Department of Corrections and crossed a dozen names off the list. A few phone calls were made, and alibis had been checked. Whoever murdered Weaver wasn't on the list.

Eddie Lucca returned from the crime scene and was compiling a new list of suspects. Now that we had the murder weapon, he was searching for individuals who purchased ammunition or sniper rifles in the past who also had a strong connection to Weaver. A few names overlapped. Lucca believed we were getting closer.

"Nice job, locating our murder weapon, Agent Parker," Lucca said to the otherwise empty conference room. "Our crime scene techs just sent verification that the slug that went through Weaver matched the striations of the bullets test fired from that Remington 700." He squinted. "What made you look in the maintenance room?"

"I was being thorough." My bad mood was seeping into my words, and despite my promise to be nicer to Lucca, I was too drained to care. The smell of the morgue was still present in my nasal cavity, making the day that much worse. "Do you think you can manage this on your own?"

"Do you have something more pressing to do?"

"I want to follow up with the real estate agency that hosted the open house. Maybe the realtor can give us the names of the people who showed up. After all, jury selection began a month ago, and the court had Hunter's case scheduled for some time. The killer might have been planning this just as long."

"Okay. I'll see you tomorrow, but if you make any headway, call immediately. I don't care what time it is."

"Thanks." I collected the paperwork and went to the door.

"No quip about me being a boy scout?" Lucca asked, trying to goad me. "Shouldn't I be earning a kindness merit badge for letting you beg off the grunt work or something?"

"Good night, Lucca."

"Hey, Parker," he glanced out the open conference room door, "about earlier, are you okay?"

"Sure."

It was after five when I arrived at the real estate office.

The receptionist was packing up for the day. A few of the realtors were bustling around or making last minute phone calls, probably planning to meet with prospective buyers. Studying the closest print ad featuring a blown-up photo of Sylvia Britt, the top realtor for ten years running, I debated how to play this.

"Can I help you, ma'am?" the receptionist asked. "We're just about to close. Did you have an appointment?"

"I'm in the market for some office space. There was an open house last week." I dug through my purse. "No, it was the week before. It was inside that high-rise near the federal courthouse. Dammit," I flipped my bag upside down on top of the counter, glad my gun and credentials were concealed, "I know I have that card somewhere." Offering a conciliatory smile, I tried to appear frazzled. "It's been a long day. I can't even remember my name, let alone the realtor's name. I'm so sorry."

"No worries." She smiled and handed back my chapstick that had fallen onto the floor. "I know which property you're talking about. Mrs. Britt hosted the open house." She glanced at the large office behind her. "She has an appointment this evening, but if you give me your name and number, I'll have her call you first thing in the morning about that property."

"That sounds great, assuming no one is about to swoop in and steal it. There was some guy lingering around that day who seemed particularly interested. You wouldn't happen to know if anyone has inquired or made an offer, would you?"

The receptionist looked torn between helping and getting into trouble. Her shifty-eyed gaze landed on the closed office door. "I can check for you."

"Thanks so much." Letting out a dramatic sigh of relief, I continued to stuff the few remaining items back inside my bag. I always packed light. Aside from a minimal amount of makeup to cover any dark circles or injuries, my bag contained chapstick, my wallet, car keys, a knife, a few hair ties, and zip ties. Just the essentials. Luckily, she didn't scrutinize the questionable items. "Today's been insane. My boss has been nagging the hell out of me. I'm so ready to quit and start out on my own."

"Oh, tell me about," she muttered before she could stop herself. She blushed slightly and tried to hide the faux pas. "Promise not to let anyone know I showed you this." She handed over a sticky note with three names scrawled in barely legible writing. "They expressed an interest, and those are their bid amounts."

Quickly memorizing the three names, I nodded and added my own and my phone number to the bottom of the list with an amount a few thousand over the highest bidder. "Have Mrs. Britt call as soon as she gets a chance. If I have to deal with too many days like today, I might need that office space sooner than I thought."

She smiled, dropping the note on top of the desk before ushering me out the door. Once I was back inside the confines of my car, I pulled out my phone and passed the names off to Lucca. He was getting ready to call it quits for the night too, but the three names I passed along could be added as potential leads to the new suspect list they were building.

I doubted our killer would have been that sloppy, but maybe someone would remember seeing him at the open house. A few sketches had been made of the assailant based on the surveillance feed. Possibly one of the renditions would be close enough to his actual likeness to jog some memories. But I was off-the-clock. The agents unlucky enough to be working nights would continue to work the rifle angle. Lucca was confident we'd be knocking on our suspect's door in the morning, so who was I to rain on his parade?

FIVE

Driving home, I didn't bother taking as many precautions as usual. I wasn't coming from the federal building, and after conducting numerous turns, it was apparent no one was following me. Once I pulled into the garage, I parked my subcompact on the end, next to the dozen high-end sports cars. Martin's town car wasn't here. I suspected he wasn't home yet. As usual, it was a tossup to see which of us would work later.

Going up the stairs, I went to the master suite, dug out something clean to wear, and headed for the shower, stripping and leaving a trail of my clothing strewn across the bathroom floor. Maybe I should burn it. It might be the only way to get the smell of the morgue out. After washing my hair three times and scrubbing my skin raw, I leaned against the shower wall, letting the water cascade down my body. I wasn't sure how long I'd been in there when I heard a faint knocking at the door.

"Alex?" Martin called. "Can I come in?"

"Sure." I inhaled deeply, struggling to pull myself together. The door opened, and he glanced down at my clothes, picking them up and tossing them into the hamper. "Don't put them in there. They need to be incinerated or thrown out."

"Why?" He undid his tie and shed his suit jacket, leaving them bunched on the bathroom vanity. He pulled his belt free and kicked off his shoes and socks. Then he opened the glass shower door. "What's wrong?" His green eyes were clouded with a mix of concern and lust.

"They smell like death." Resisting the urge to reach for the shampoo again, I crossed my arms over my chest, feeling naked and exposed. "I had to make a trip to the morgue today. God, I keep smelling it on everything."

"Hey," he stepped underneath the water still in his dress shirt and suit pants, "what's going on?"

"Martin, you're getting all wet."

But he pulled me into his arms, even as the water soaked through his clothing. He chuckled into my hair, running his fingers through my tangled locks. "It's a bit of a role reversal. And the only thing I smell is coconut and vanilla." He kissed me, his thumb trailing across my cheek. "The water's getting cold. How long have you been in here?" He lifted my hand, examining the waterlogged flesh on my fingertips.

"I don't know. I'm having a bad day."

"Give me a chance to improve it." He kissed down the column of my neck. "It feels like we've been missing each other for the last two weeks." He reached behind me, turning the faucet farther to hot while I unbuttoned his shirt, skimming my hands up his washboard abs. He kept in incredible shape, and right now, I wasn't opposed to a sexy distraction. "Have you even come home this week? By the time I get up in the morning, you're already gone, unless you were never even here."

"My days don't seem to end. This case is a mess." I shook my head, unable to talk about the specifics of an ongoing investigation. "We're looking in the wrong direction, but Jablonsky doesn't agree."

Martin growled, brushing his dark brown hair backward to stop the water from dripping into his face. Mark was Martin's best friend, so I didn't understand why mentioning him had earned that type of response. But it didn't matter. The water was growing increasingly colder.

Martin shut it off.

Leaving the shower, I wrapped myself in a towel while he shed his soaking wet clothes and left them near the drain.

"So much for dry clean only," he mused. "So since my plans for showering turned into a bust, can I offer to warm you up instead?"

"Absolutely."

* * *

I pressed my palms against the bullet wound, hoping to slow the bleeding. This couldn't be happening. Screaming for help, I frantically glanced around the room, but no one was there. The shooter was dead. I killed him, but Martin was bleeding out. Pressing my hands more fervently against his shoulder, I begged him to live.

"Alex." His voice sounded thick with sleep.

"Stay with me."

"Alex," he repeated, hissing in pain. "Ouch. Sweetheart, let go." I clung tighter. "Shit, I'm sorry. I hate to do this."

Suddenly, the world pitched backward, and I felt like I was falling. I dug my fingers in deeper to anchor myself, and my eyes shot open. My heart was pounding in my ears. I was clinging to Martin's shoulder with everything I had. We were upright in bed. The world made little sense to my sleep-addled brain.

"It was a nightmare," he said soothingly, prying my hands off of him.

My fingers were cramped into gnarled claws. Once I steadied myself, he rubbed them between his hands until my locked muscles released and I could once again straighten my fingers.

Scooting backward, he sat with his back pressed against the headboard. "And you thought I splurged on a padded headboard for only sordid reasons." He stroked my back while my pulse and breathing stabilized. I buried my face in his neck, and he pulled the blankets up around my trembling body, not bothering to remove me from his lap. "I didn't mean to startle you awake, but you seemed pretty adamant about remaining trapped in that dream."

"I'm sorry."

"It's not your fault. Was it because of work? Did the morgue remind you of Michael?"

"It wasn't about him." My fingers traced the scar on Martin's shoulder.

He took my hand in his and kissed my knuckles, understanding what my nightmare had been about. "Should we talk about moving our bedroom to the second floor? Is this too close for comfort now that you live here?" He swallowed, unsure if I wanted to talk about these things ever, let alone at four a.m. "I changed the flooring and moved the walls around when the house was restructured after the shootout, but it still makes you uneasy."

"It probably won't make a difference where we sleep. I have nightmares. You know this."

"I also know that they get worse when you're under a lot of stress or when you haven't had much sleep. Your job makes them worse." He attempted to maintain a neutral tone, but there was an undercurrent of hostility below the surface. "Your job is the cause of most of them."

Sighing, I kissed him and climbed out of bed. "It wasn't about him," I murmured, repeating what I'd said but finding a completely different meaning for the words.

"I shouldn't have brought it up. I know you don't like to talk about your late partner." He arched an eyebrow as I dressed. "Where are you going?"

"To work on a lead. I'll be downstairs. Maybe now you'll actually be able to get some sleep, especially since you have to be up for work in two hours."

He blinked, obviously tired and knowing now wasn't the time for meaningful discussions or petty arguments. "I see you less than I did before you moved in. I'd be willing to give up a few hours of sleep if it meant we could spend that time together."

"I need to chase this down while it's fresh on my mind. Go back to sleep. We'll have breakfast before you leave for the office."

"I'm holding you to that. Am I cooking?"

"Only if you want something more substantial than cold

cereal." Slipping out the door, I returned to the guestroom I was using as an office. There was nothing like an adrenaline rush to start the day.

After ripping down all the hard work I'd pinned to the board the previous day, I started over. The victim was William Briscoe, forty-five years old with two children and a previously deceased wife. I sketched out the few facts I knew about him and his family, making a note to speak with his daughter, Laura, and his son, Will Jr.

Laura was twenty-two, currently interning at an internet startup company. Will was twenty and seemed to be struggling to find his path in life. He had dropped out of college and had taken a slew of odd jobs. Losing their dad wouldn't make life easier for either of them. Scribbling down their address and contact information, I would stop by and see them this afternoon. Surely, one of them could shed some light on who had an axe to grind with their father.

Closing my eyes, I visualized the interior of the courtroom. Briscoe was juror number five. The bullet went through his back and continued on its path. The shot hit Weaver straight on, as if he had a target painted on the back of his head. He was also the prosecutor and the intended victim, according to my colleagues, but I failed to agree. The position of the gunshot wound on Briscoe's body continued to nag at the recesses of my mind.

Grabbing a marker, I sketched out the scene. Our forensic experts would be able to prove or disprove my theory using their computer programs, but if Briscoe hadn't stood up, would the bullet have gone through his head instead? The shot seemed too high. It probably would have sailed over his head, meaning his death was accidental. Dammit. I threw the marker across the room. Why was I having so many issues accepting this fact as true?

I paced the room, wondering when I reached this insane conclusion. Yesterday started wrong and just got worse as the day progressed. After visiting the medical examiner, I decided we'd been turning over the wrong stones, but maybe it was just an excuse to explain why we hadn't made much progress up until that point. Someone shouldn't be able to shoot into a courtroom, kill two people, and walk away scot-free.

The possibilities were endless when it came to suspects who wanted AUSA Weaver dead, and I didn't want to think that someone was killed for doing his job. It made my own safety seem even more questionable, and that was something I didn't want to think about, even if that would explain my breakdown in the office concerning my last partner. Perhaps this case had nothing to do with Briscoe. The only problem with that was the substantial number of injuries present on his body. Could they be unrelated?

I was tired, frustrated, and annoyed by my own incompetence. Pulling a legal pad out of my desk drawer, I made a list of the things I needed to accomplish today. First, I had to follow up with the realtor about our suspect. Second, I would have a conversation with Laura and Will Briscoe, just to make sure it was purely a coincidence, and third, I'd pull it together and do whatever menial tasks Lucca and Jablonsky wanted. Sometimes, it was easier to take orders than to exercise free will and make decisions.

My head was already aching when I went into the kitchen to brew a pot of coffee. It was 5:30, which gave me another hour and a half until Martin would be ready for breakfast. He always stuck to a similar schedule during the week, up at six, a forty-five minute workout, showering and dressing for the day, breakfast, and off to work. Instead of slaving over the stove to cook a fantastic meal, I grabbed a blanket from the linen closet and curled up on the couch. I'd get up just as soon as the coffee was ready.

"Alex, what time do you have to be at work?" Martin asked.

"Eight." I opened my eyes and lifted my head off the pillow. "Damn couch. It has powers over me."

He glanced at the time. "I left a plate for you in the microwave. So much for breakfast together." He sounded agitated, but I wasn't coherent enough to figure out why. "You should probably get ready if you don't want to be late. Will I see you tonight?"

"You can count on it."

"Like breakfast?"

"Shit, I'm sorry. I don't know what's gotten into me." Rubbing my eyes, I stretched and got off the couch. "I feel like I'm drowning."

"Do you want to talk about it?" He looked torn between leaving for work and leaving me.

"Not now." I kissed him and headed for the stairs. "Thanks for breakfast."

"Stay safe, Alexis."

"Always."

He continued down the stairs, exchanging muffled greetings with his driver and bodyguard, Marcal and Bruiser. I'd have to remember to tell Rosemarie, his cleaning lady, that the second floor guestroom was off-limits since I was using it as an office and storage space. She'd always been great about tidying up, but the materials covering the desk and corkboard were sensitive.

Since the vast majority of my belongings were scattered throughout the master bedroom, the guest suite, and my apartment, I'd have to find time to organize and condense my crap into one workable space. While focusing on daily chores instead of the case, I prepared for the day, only to be torn from my musings by my ringing cell phone.

"Parker," I answered.

"Ms. Parker, this is Jack Fletcher, the junior attorney at Ackerman, Baze, and Clancy."

"I remember you, Mr. Fletcher." A smile crept onto my face. He worked for the firm that handled Martin's personal business. We'd crossed paths a time or two. "What can I do for you?"

"I am in need of your investigative services. You didn't seem too keen on working for the firm, but this is a personal matter, so I was hoping you might be open to hearing me out. Do you still have that P.I. office at the strip mall?"

"I do, but I'm not in a position to take on any new clients." Relenting on account of owing him a few favors, I said, "Actually, if you swing by around six, you can fill me in. Maybe I can recommend someone. How does that sound?"

"Great. I'll see you tonight."

After we disconnected, I remembered my promise to Martin and had the urge to slam my head into the wall in the hopes of knocking some sense into myself. I always had the habit of biting off more than I could chew. With any luck, it'd be a short meeting, and I'd be home at a decent hour.

Returning downstairs, I scarfed down the heart-shaped pancakes Martin had made. He could be nauseatingly sweet at times, but this morning, I chose to find that annoyance endearing. Then I added the items from my mental list to my actual list, grabbed my belongings, and went down the stairs to my car. By the time I got behind the wheel, my phone rang again.

"Parker, we've made some headway on identifying the shooter. Our suspect list is down to six possible subjects. Forensics is still working to clear up the camera angles, but I'm ready to knock on some doors if you're game," Lucca said.

"I'm on my way."

SIX

"That was fun. What do you plan to do for your next trick? Accuse a dead man of the murders?" My sarcasm was even more prevalent when I was tired. "For an analyst, you've done a stellar job of ensuring your information is up-to-date. Did you even make it through training at Quantico?"

"How was I supposed to know two of the names on my list were otherwise detained? They weren't processed into the system until this morning. That doesn't mean I don't know how to do my job." Lucca stared in my direction while I drove to Sylvia Britt's office. "We haven't finished fleshing out my leads."

"This is on the way." Parking at a metered space, I shed my jacket and divested myself of my shoulder holster and credentials. I stowed my nine millimeter and badge in my purse. Then I undid my braid and let my hair fall in loose waves. I put on a layer of lip gloss and unbuttoned my top two buttons. "Stay here. I'll be right back."

"Do you have a hot date with this realtor lady?" he asked, eyeing my change in appearance.

"Yes, seeing her face on every park bench has given me the hots for her."

Rolling my eyes and letting out an incredulous sigh, I

opened the car door and headed for the office. Going inside while dressed like a federal agent might make her suspicious, and before I could gain any insight into who was interested in the office our shooter used, she'd lawyer up. Then we'd have to petition the court for access to her files, and that would take too long. This way, she would be in selling mode and far less likely to conceal key facts.

"Good morning, Ms. Parker," the receptionist from last night greeted. "Mrs. Britt was thrilled you expressed an interest in that property. She's on the phone right now, but if you'll take a seat, she'll be with you shortly."

"Thanks." I offered a conspiratorial smile and lowered my voice. "Am I still the top bidder?"

She nodded and went back to performing her duties while I took a seat in an armchair and picked up a magazine. Today started out as a big disappointment. I hoped my meeting with the realtor would turn it around. The forensic team was unable to positively identify our shooter. The hat and glasses obscured too much of his face for facial recognition to match him with any statistical certainty to anyone in the database, and Lucca's leads weren't panning out either.

Of the six possible suspects, we had already ruled out three, and it was barely eleven a.m. Two had been arrested approximately thirty hours ago for grand theft auto and armed robbery. The police had taken them into custody, but from the statements we'd read and the information we'd obtained from the arresting officers, these two felons had been in the midst of a crime spree at the time of the shooting. The third suspect we'd gone to see was in the hospital and had been for the last five days. He was involved in a shootout and had sustained multiple gunshot wounds. The Remington 700 he purchased was in the trunk of his car, which ruled him out. It was my turn to follow a lead, even though Lucca didn't agree.

"Ms. Parker?" a forty-something woman asked. She wore a red skirt and black silk blouse. Her platinum hair was short and glued in place with enough hairspray to tear another hole in the ozone layer. "I'm Sylvia Britt. Please step into my office." I followed her inside and took a seat.

She shut the door behind me and went around the desk, offering her hand as she sat down. Her grip was firm, and I suspected everything about her was part of the 'sell, sell, sell' mentality. "I hear you're in the market for some office space."

"Absolutely." I smiled, playing along. "I was hoping for something in a more upscale building. The other day, I happened to be visiting my chiropractor and noticed a few empty offices on the twentieth floor."

"I'd be happy to show you the property." Her smile never faltered. "Unfortunately, that particular space is undergoing some minor cosmetic changes at the moment. If you can wait, I'm sure it'll be ready sometime next week." She was shrewd, skillfully leaving out the part about it being an active crime scene that was off-limits to the public. "However, there are plenty of properties on the market that are available to rent or buy. What size space were you considering?" Her smile remained as she tapped a few keys. "I can also narrow down locations by price range." She gave me her undivided attention. "Why don't you begin by telling me what business you're in and what you're looking for?"

"I'm a security consultant." I pulled out one of my old business cards from when I worked at Martin Technologies. "I'm hoping to branch out and start my own firm. At the present, I don't need that much space, but I was hoping to rent in order to upgrade as my business grows."

"That's fantastic." Her eyes stared at the card, the money question floating just beneath the surface. "Did you have a specific neighborhood in mind? The business district has the most options, but the price goes up substantially."

"Price isn't an issue. I have an investor willing to sink a substantial amount of money into this venture." I nodded at the card, never saying anything specific but letting her draw her own conclusions.

"Excellent." She keyed in a few more things and popped up a dozen locations. "I'll get you the information on a few other properties in the meantime. If something strikes your fancy, let me know, and we'll schedule a visit." She hit print and dug through her drawers for some pre-printed information.

"Mrs. Britt," I said, trying to get her back on track and knowing this was just the first step to getting information on the only property I had any interest in, "I really had my heart set on that one specific space." Before she could come up with another feasible excuse, I continued. "Is it still available? Did anyone seem overly interested in it during the open house?"

"It is available. A few people stopped by, but honestly, the fish weren't biting that day."

"Please," I held the smile, even though my mouth and cheeks were starting to hurt, "I'm sure you say that to all your clients, so no one gets disheartened."

"No, really." Her look dropped for a moment. "In all truthfulness, a lot of space in that building is empty. It isn't in a very good location. With the federal courthouse across the street and all the attorney offices nearby, parking is damn near impossible. It deters a lot of traffic and potential customers."

"What about the visitors at the open house?"

"They were mostly attorneys and some sorry saps who smelled the freshly baked treats."

"Really?" Now we were getting somewhere. "Just some random schlubs wandered in off the street?"

She snorted, covering her mouth and looking embarrassed by the unprofessional noise she just made. "One of them came into the room, stared out the window for twenty minutes, told me he was thinking about it, grabbed a handful of cookies, and left."

"Did he make a bid or leave his name?"

My question caused an uneasy thought to enter her mind based upon the odd look that flitted across her perfectly coifed features. "Don't worry, Ms. Parker, I'm sure if that's the spot you have your heart set on, it'll be yours, but one of these other buildings would be better suited for your needs."

I held the fake smile, taking the papers she offered. Making one last-ditch effort as she showed me to the door,

I said, "Are you afraid I'm going to scare away a potential buyer because I promise I won't. I just want to maintain the top bid, and your window gazer sounds extremely interested."

"He wasn't that interested. He never followed up." She ushered me into the lobby. "Call if you have any questions."

Sighing, I went out the door. The next time I called, I'd have to step up my game or have my credentials in hand. When I got back to the car, Lucca raised an eyebrow. Before he could gloat that my lead was just as worthless as his, the phone rang.

"Jablonsky checked into our remaining three suspects. He brought two of them in for questioning, but they've been cleared. The third has dropped off the grid," Lucca said, relaying the message.

"Do you think he's our shooter?"

"Perhaps." Lucca wasn't insisting on anything at this point. "Forensics used an acid wash on the rifle's serial number. They were only able to pull a partial. However, there aren't that many retailers in the area that sell Remington 700s, so we were told to drop by the gun shops and see if anyone recognizes the sketch of our suspect."

"Right," slamming my forehead into the steering wheel seemed like a better and better idea as the seconds ticked past, "because a white male, approximately five foot ten, a hundred and seventy pounds, with sunglasses and a baseball cap is going to stick out in anyone's mind."

"We have our orders," Lucca said. "Need I remind you, you hit a dead end faster than I did?"

"No, I didn't. Our shooter was at the open house. I just can't prove it yet. But I'll find a way to convince the realtor to give up a name."

"We'll get a court order." He was already dialing. "What did she say exactly?"

"That a guy in street clothes went inside, stared out the window for twenty minutes, and took a handful of cookies with him."

Lucca stared as if I were insane, hitting end call on his phone and shoving it into his pocket. "That's not a lead. That's circumstantial. It's a high-rise with floor to ceiling windows. Everyone looks out the window."

"It was him." There was no room to argue with my gut instinct. Unfortunately, gut instincts weren't permissible in court. "It'll just take some cajoling and creativity to get a name."

"If you're so sure, put your money where your mouth is."

"You want to make a bet?"

"Yeah, if you're right, I'll leave you alone and ask that we aren't assigned to work together in the future. But if you're wrong, you'll tell me the real reason you despise this arrangement." He gestured at the space between us. "Like I said, I'll keep your secret safe."

"How 'bout we put a hundred on the table and call it a day?"

"I thought you were positive."

"Fine. You can tell Director Kendall it wasn't you, it's me."

"You do know I'm married. I thought that meant I was done reciting that clichéd dating line."

Letting out an exasperated exhale, I tossed a scathing look at Lucca. "Keep your personal life personal. I don't need or want to know what you do outside the walls of the office."

Narrowing his eyes, he assessed me but refrained from saying anything else. However, the wheels in his head were turning. He had spent the last few weeks trying to figure me out, but after my breakdown in the office yesterday morning, I thought he had finally put that to rest. Obviously, I was wrong. That was starting to happen far too frequently.

The dozen gun shops proved to be a bust, like I knew they would, and feeling like my instincts might be back on track, we returned to the federal building to see what progress Jablonsky had made.

"Slater Christianson," Lucca poked at the last name on the list of suspects, "do we have any idea where he might be?"

Jablonsky glanced in my direction, resisting the urge to balk at Lucca's question. "Go find out, Eddie. In the meantime, we'll take another approach to solving Weaver's murder." He flicked his wrist, dismissing Lucca and swiveling in the chair to speak to a few members of the evidence collection team. When he was finished doling out a new set of assignments with updated parameters on how to proceed and orders to begin a thorough assessment of Weaver's friends, family, co-workers, and any vices he might have had, Jablonsky spun to face me. "What do you have, Parker? I know that look. It's time you share your lead."

"You need to get surveillance footage from the office building a week prior to the shooting. The shooter planned his kills and took some time to set up. I can't be sure, but he probably decided on that location the day the real estate agency hosted an open house for that office. Assuming he shopped around, you might be able to pull an ID from somewhere in that building or off one of the surrounding buildings. He would have been less careful that day." I reached into my pocket and pulled out a torn sheet of paper containing the names and phone numbers of the bidders from the open house. "One of these people might recognize him."

Jablonsky picked up the list and read the names. "Nice work." He glanced out the conference room door at Lucca, who was behind his desk, frantically typing things into the computer. "Have the two of you worked out your differences?"

"Sure."

"Do you want to try that again, but this time, make it sound convincing."

"You know what my issue is. It doesn't matter who you pair me with because I don't want to be assigned a partner. I'm back, but I don't want anyone depending on me."

"You weren't at fault. You promised me you were done blaming yourself," Mark said in a hushed tone. "Is this because the case hinges on the death of an attorney, just like the last case you and Carver worked?"

"No." Okay, maybe that had something to do with it, but regardless, I didn't want someone else's life to be my responsibility. "Put me behind a desk or whatever since I don't want to be in the field with anyone. I can watch my own back. I've been doing it long enough."

"Everyone needs help. Even you." He sighed. "Fine, I'll give you a free pass on this one case because it hits close to home. Don't deny it. I know it does because it's too close for me too. Work on your own leads, but as soon as you have something solid, bring it to me. We are not cutting corners. Everything is going through official channels. Weaver's office will fry our asses if we botch this. Don't screw up and don't play the hero."

"I'm not a hero. I'm just a working-class stiff."

"With creative ways of attacking problems." He held up the sheet of paper. "If Lucca tracks down the culprit before you do, should I assign someone else to make the arrest?"

"Do whatever you want, Jablonsky. You're in charge. I'm just here to work the investigation and follow your orders."

"Yeah, you might need to take a refresher course on that one." He jerked his chin at the door. "Dismissed."

"Aye, sir."

SEVEN

I spent the rest of the afternoon in the conference room, staring at the boards and twirling my pen. My actions didn't look particularly productive, but it gave me time to think. I called in a few favors with members of IT. The surveillance footage was being scrubbed from the date in question. It wasn't considered a top priority, but the work was getting done. I requested a copy for my personal perusal. It was delivered to my desk just as I was getting ready to call it a day.

"Anything?" I asked.

"Honestly, I don't know. It was put on the backburner as soon as the gun shops sent over their records and surveillance footage. The accountants are going through the transaction history, and that's added to the pile of information our computers have to process. Our best bet will likely be from comparing our composite sketch to the driver's license photos of our gun buyers, but that's just my guess. It's normally how things like this work," Agent Lawson, our resident technical expert, said.

"All right. Keep me in the loop."

Collecting my files, I took the elevator down to the

parking garage. Normally, I would have stayed in the building to review the footage, but I had a meeting with Jack Fletcher in an hour.

"Where are you going?" Lucca asked, stepping into the elevator as I was getting off.

"Home. This is nine to five. You should be more fiscally responsible, boy scout. The government is in enough debt without having to give us overtime."

"We're salaried. There is no overtime."

"Details."

"Parker," he pushed the elevator door open a second before it closed, "do you think the sniper was contracted to perform the hit?"

It was the question that had been floating around my mind since I sat in the back of the courtroom, studying the scene. It was a good shot but not great. Great wouldn't have resulted in collateral damage. At least one of our victims was an accidental casualty. If the hit was contracted, our killer could have been hired by anyone, thus making every alibi we'd checked completely pointless. "That would mean we have to start back at square one."

"Shit." He exhaled. "It's the only conclusion I can reach. AUSA Weaver's enemies, professional and personal, have alibied out. There are probably others, but unless we get a hit on a gun buyer, that's the most likely scenario."

"Start with the current wife's financials and ask the guys in IT to scan the message boards and chat rooms. They know where to look." I opened my car door and placed my belongings inside. "Hey, Lucca, are you positive Weaver was the intended victim?"

He rolled his eyes, letting the elevator doors close.

*   *   *

Meandering through the city streets, I let my mind process different possibilities and scenarios and dialed Kate Hartley, my longtime friend and one of the forensic accountants at the OIO, to have her check into the financial records for Stan Weaver and William Briscoe. There was no reason not to be thorough. Surprisingly, she said Lucca already asked her to do the same thing. Shaking off the theory that there was an alternate reality in which the two of us would actually make a good team, I disconnected and drove to my P.I. office at the strip mall.

When I arrived, I opened the door and scooped up the giant pile of mail that had collected over the last two months. After returning to the OIO, I closed my office. I hadn't had time to freelance or deal with any additional dilemmas on account of an undercover assignment and a few investigations. Even now, the only reason I agreed to show up was because Fletcher was a business acquaintance, and it never hurt to have the junior member of one of the best law firms in the city in your corner.

Jack Fletcher worked for Ackerman, Baze, and Clancy which specialized in corporate and civil law. They were Martin's attorneys. When he had been arrested, they had called me to investigate. That seemed like a lifetime ago. A lot had changed, but Jack Fletcher always seemed like a good guy. It wouldn't hurt to hear about his problem and pass him off to a capable investigator who had ample time to deal with his issue.

I finished discarding the junk mail just as the bell chimed and Fletcher stepped inside. He looked as exhausted as I felt, but he smiled, relieved to see me. Without invitation, he took a seat and opened his briefcase, extracting a legal-sized envelope.

"Thanks for doing this, Ms. Parker. How have you been?" he asked, attempting to be courteous even though it was obvious he wanted to get down to business.

"I can't complain. What's going on?"

"Someone's blackmailing me." He placed the envelope on the desk between us and sat back in the chair. For the most part, people in his position would be antsy, but he simply accepted this fact, resigned to dealing with it. "What should I do?"

"You're the lawyer." I couldn't help the quip, but I shot a smile at him to dull the blow. "Honestly, you should turn it over to the authorities and let them handle it. Blackmail is a punishable offense."

"Are you trying to lawyer the lawyer?" He held up his

hand. "Before you start citing the state penal code, you should know this isn't about money."

"What is it about?"

"I have a problem. One of the partners at the firm introduced me to the fight scene. Boxing, mixed martial arts, cage fights, things like that. There's an underground circuit that's particularly popular among the more affluent members of our community."

"That's nothing new. Powerful men enjoy watching other men beat the shit out of each other."

"The fights are unsanctioned. They exist in the grey area of the sport. The fighters are on the cusp of getting sponsored and breaking into the main fight scene. It's how a lot of them get noticed. The fights are scheduled and take place throughout the tri-state area, maybe even throughout the country. I'm not sure."

"Are you on the ticket or betting on the ticket?" I asked, wanting to cut through the explanation. "Tell me this isn't your personal version of Ed Norton versus Brad Pitt."

"I've bet on a few of the fights, but it's not what you think." He held up his hand. "I'm not indebted to a bookie. I haven't even wagered that much, less than a thousand dollars total."

"So someone caught on to your presence at these unsanctioned sporting events and is hoping to do something unsavory with this information?"

"Ms. Parker," he opened the envelope and placed a news article and a photo on my desk, "if I don't pay, they're threatening to report my involvement to the bar association and potentially have my license suspended."

Skimming the article, I didn't need to read the words to understand the gist. One of the fighters died in the emergency room from a brain bleed. It was most likely the result of an injury sustained at one of these events. Unfortunately for Fletcher, it was the same fighter he had bet on, stupidly using a torn business card to scrawl his wager on the back. Illegal betting was a crime, and criminal activity was prohibited by professional rules and ethics.

"Someone died, and you did nothing." My tone was neutral. Most bystanders did nothing. That fact wouldn't have surprised me.

"Actually, I got called away before the first bell. That's why I used my card to place the bet, so they'd have my phone number to get in touch if I won. It was stupid."

"The smart thing to do would be to turn in the people involved in the illegal gambling and admit you made a mistake."

"One of the partners is an avid fan. So is a judge. Do you see where this is going?"

"You can pay off the blackmailer and sweep this under the rug, or you could potentially face criminal charges and ethics violations."

"Not to mention the fallout at the office and in the courtroom, if I'm not disbarred. The partners would either fire me or find some way to prevent future promotions. I'd hit a glass ceiling, which would be almost as bad as having the bar association review my standing and suspend my license. As you're well aware, the moral standards I'm held to are a bit higher than the average citizen on account of my position as an officer of the court. Any illegal activity could jeopardize my career."

"Do you have any idea who's behind this? You've recognized a few affluent figures at these fights. Are you sure one of them isn't trying to scare you away?"

"That's precisely what is supposed to make these fights secure for the more affluent gamblers. We assume the same amount of risk because we all have something to lose."

"I find it hard to believe that no one else attends these fights when they serve as a backboard to future sporting careers." I gave Jack a skeptical look. "And everyone loves to roll the dice."

"Let's just say I was told it was fine, and I'd be a pussy not to get in on a piece of the action." He blew out a breath. "This is not my finest hour."

"It doesn't look like anyone's finest hour, particularly when Hector Santos died in an ER waiting room. Let me guess, a bunch of rich guys hang around and cheer while some struggling lower income individuals beat the crap out of each other, but it's okay because everyone's doing it."

The concept sickened me. I didn't bother to mask the disdain from my voice.

"It wasn't like that. These are the same men who pay thousands for ringside seats in Vegas and Atlantic City. They are the ones who pull strings and find agents and sponsors for these athletes. It's how the system works. It's no different than boxers getting scouted because their coach knows someone involved with the big-ticket fights."

"The difference is someone died and no one did anything about it. It's unsanctioned. There is no sports association or league to determine if the match should have been called sooner or if this was just a fluke. You said these matches take place across state lines?"

"Yeah, but what does that have to do with the blackmail letter I received?"

I opened my credentials and placed them on top of my desk. "Did I mention the reason I wasn't taking on any new clients was because of my reinstatement at the OIO?" The blood drained from his face. "The fact that it crossed state lines could make this a federal matter, but seeing as how you aren't certain of most of these facts, I'll look into it quietly. After all, I'd hate to take down the mayor and a few judges with unsubstantiated allegations."

"Thank you, Ms. Parker." He breathed a sigh of relief. "Agent Parker."

"Let's just go with Alex for now." I dug through my drawer for a pad of paper and a pen. "What were his demands?" I nodded at the envelope.

"Fifty thousand dollars. I have one week to get the cash and leave it inside a locker at a local gym."

"Okay." I handed him the paper and pen. "Write down everything you remember from the night in question and the instructions you were given. Do you have the envelope and blackmail letter you received?"

"The threat was sent via text. I had the number traced, but it linked back to a disposable cell phone. The article and photograph were delivered with the rest of the firm's mail. By the time I realized what it was, I had shredded the envelope."

"What did you hope to accomplish by hiring me? Even if

I identify the culprit, you can't take further action against him without facing the same repercussions you would if you turned this over to the police right now."

"I'm prepared to pay," he admitted, "but I thought if I knew who he was, I could take steps to ensure this was a onetime thing so he couldn't extort more money from me."

"I'll look into it, but if this turns into something that requires an official investigation, you'll most likely be implicated. Hopefully, it won't come to that. It depends on the circumstances surrounding this fighter's death," I flicked the news article, "and if there have been other similar incidents in the past. If this was just a freak occurrence and some asshole is hoping to take advantage of you because of it, perhaps we'll find another way to stop it. I'd hate to have to look for a new attorney, but I can't make any promises."

"That's okay. I know you're bound by a higher ethical standard too. I should have known better. It was a mistake. I've always been more of a follower than a trendsetter. When one of the partners invited me out for a night of drinking and entertainment, I thought it would put me on the fast track for a corner office and my name on the front door."

"We all make mistakes." I glanced at the time, realizing if I didn't leave in the next twenty minutes, I would be making one of my own. "I'll get started on this tonight," I promised, escorting Fletcher to the door.

Once he was gone, I resisted the urge to dig through the databases and lay the groundwork for a profile on Hector Santos, the dead fighter. Instead, I found an empty folder, tucked the information inside, and locked up. If Martin worked late, as was his norm, I'd be right on time for our dinner date.

When I arrived home, Martin's town car was parked in its usual spot in the garage. There was no sign of Marcal or Bruiser. Obviously, Martin had been home for at least ten minutes. It was that type of incredible deductive capability that made the OIO beg for my return. Snorting at the ludicrous notion, I went up the steps, balancing the Weaver case file, the information I'd received from Sylvia Britt, the facts on William Briscoe, and Fletcher's file in my arms.

I cursed, dropping half of them onto the floor as I manipulated the doorknob with my full hands. I knelt down, shoving everything into a messy heap only to trip on the top step and drop everything again before managing to make it inside and kick the door closed behind me.

"It sounds like you're having another bad day," Martin called from the kitchen. "Do you want a drink?"

"Yes. One for each hand. Or a straw might be better since my hands are full."

He laughed as I went past him into the guestroom, divested myself of the job-related paraphernalia, and returned to the kitchen. On the counter, he placed a lemon drop martini and a mostly full shaker. A few empty takeout containers were in the recycle bin. The oven beeped, indicating it was preheated.

"I ordered from Giovanni's since I wasn't sure how late I'd be working."

"So it's not because you thought I'd miss dinner?" I asked.

"Perhaps that thought crossed my mind."

"Well, if it makes you feel any better, I didn't know if I'd make it either." I took a sip, enjoying the crisp, tart bite. "Damn, that's good."

"Rough day?"

"What else is new?"

"Do you want to talk about last night?" he asked, but I remained silent. "You haven't slept through the night since moving in. Your nightmares are getting worse. I was under the impression it was because of the job, but you're dreaming about the shooting that happened upstairs. Should we move our bedroom to another floor? Would that help?"

Busying myself with setting the table, I ran through a few different responses in my head before opening my mouth. I wanted to be diplomatic. "Nothing helps. I'm not adjusting very well to this cohabitation thing. I'm used to late nights, takeout, and spending my downtime pacing the confines of my apartment, scribbling notes, tacking things to the wall, and tearing my hair out."

"I've never noticed any bald spots." He stepped away from the stove and ran his hands through my hair. "Nope. You're still gorgeous, but you'd be breathtaking regardless."

"I wasn't being literal on that last part." I surveyed the room. It was ridiculous to think I missed my one bedroom apartment, but I didn't have to hide my nightmares or work from anyone in my own apartment. "Thanks for moving the desk and hanging the boards on the wall in the guestroom."

"It's your room. Your office. Whatever you want it to be. We can try sleeping in there for a while to see if it makes a difference."

"Your bedroom is fine. I have bad dreams. Really, it's nothing."

"It didn't seem like nothing." He removed another takeout container from the fridge and emptied the large salad into a serving bowl, poured some dressing on top, and tossed the mixture. "Should I leave the bed in the guest suite now that it's your home office? There's still plenty of room to walk around, even with the furniture, but if you'd prefer a more practical workspace, just say the word and it's gone."

"Stop being so accommodating. I am not flipping your house upside down."

"It's your house too."

"Martin, I can't even offer to pay half the rent for this place."

"That's a relief, seeing as how I own it and have no plans to sublet." He held up his pointer finger. "I don't want to hear you mention anything about property taxes either. You're already paying rent for an apartment you don't live in anymore." The timer sounded, and he grabbed the oven mitts and pulled out the baking pan containing our dinner. "Are you working this weekend? I figured if we both had some time, I'd help you pack up whatever's left and we can rearrange the bedroom."

"The bedroom's fine."

"Really? Then how come most of your belongings are downstairs? We'll pick up another dresser and reorganize the walk-in closet. My suits don't need that much space."

I gulped down the rest of my martini and poured another. "Can we table this discussion for another day when I'm not bogged down with work and exhausted?"

"Okay." He stabbed at the food on his plate. "Would you mind giving me a ballpark figure for when you think that might be? I'm hoping for a date sometime this century, but I'm not holding my breath."

EIGHT

Despite the fact that I had wanted to speak with Laura and Will Briscoe yesterday, a million other things had gotten in the way, or I let them. I hated being around bereaved families. I understood grief and pain, but there wasn't a damn thing I could do to make it hurt any less. Truth be told, the questions I asked were likely to cause more pain, so I hated this part.

"When's the last time you spoke to your father?" I asked.

I was sitting in Laura's apartment. Will didn't have a place. He stayed with his sister whenever he couldn't find a friend's couch to sleep on.

"I talked to Daddy a week and a half ago." Laura brushed her hair behind her ear and stared at the rug. "I called to tell him I was being considered for permanent placement at my job. He was happy. Relieved, really." She rapidly blinked, fighting back tears. "Money's been a little tight. I have student loans, and an unpaid internship doesn't help with those."

"You can use his life insurance to pay them," Will choked out from his position in the kitchen. He hadn't stopped fidgeting since I arrived. His fist clenched around an apple.

"Stop it, Will. I love Dad. I'd live in a cardboard box for the rest of my life if it would bring him back."

"Yeah, and then he'd be just as disappointed in you as he was in me."

"Mr. Briscoe," I interjected, hoping to defuse the family argument, "when did you last see your father?"

"I don't know. It's been a while." He opened the fridge, white-knuckling the handle before slamming the door shut and rattling everything inside. "Are we done? I have more important things to do."

"Will, Agent Parker is trying to help. She wants to find the man responsible," she squeaked as the tears started to fall again.

"No," his dark eyes burned, "she wants to find the person who killed that federal prosecutor. *That's* her job. She couldn't care less about Dad or us." He stormed out of the apartment and slammed the door.

"I'm sorry," Laura said, but I waved her apology away.

"No. I'm sorry for your loss and for asking you these things. Did your dad have any enemies?"

"I don't know. I don't know anything anymore." She got up from the couch and went across the room to a lockbox. "These are my dad's records. Old tax returns, car titles, stuff like that. Anything important, he kept in this box." A brief smile crossed her face, followed by sobs. I got up and hugged her, unsure what else to do. When she was able to speak again, she handed me the key to the box. "I found some old family photos in there too. There are quite a few odds and ends. You can look through it, if you think it might help."

"Thank you."

I would have liked to take the box with me, but she wouldn't part with it. So I sat at her dining room table while she made phone calls and prepared for her father's funeral. Most of the information was irrelevant, but for the sake of being thorough, I quickly photographed any information we wouldn't be able to obtain through official channels, paying close attention to handwritten notes and photographs.

Thirty minutes later, I closed the box and handed her

the key. "I will find who did this. In the event you remember something or you just need to talk, you have my card."

She nodded, and I let myself out.

When I returned to the car, Agent Lucca was leaning against the door. "How'd it go?" he asked. "Did you break the case?"

Glaring, I threw the keys at him. They bounced off his chest and landed on the pavement. "Just drive the damn car."

"Someone's bitchy again."

He went around the front while I climbed into the passenger's seat, fastening the belt and pulling my legs to my chest. Will Briscoe's words had cut deep. It was true. There were two reasons why the OIO was investigating these murders. One, they occurred on federal property. Two, an AUSA was dead. If William Briscoe had been killed an inch from the courthouse steps, this would be a police matter, and the PD was better equipped to deal with homicides. They would investigate, and even if the percentage of closed cases wasn't particularly encouraging, it was a task they dealt with on a daily basis. They wouldn't leave a stone unturned or write William Briscoe off as collateral damage. It was probably why I refused to either. I'd consulted too often with the major crimes division to maintain the professional aloofness some of my fellow agents exhibited.

"Have we made any progress identifying who purchased the rifle?" I asked.

"It's being narrowed. All we know for certain is the sale did not occur within the last two months. We're digging deeper. That partial serial number might just come in handy."

"It could have been purchased out of state or in a private sale or from a pawn shop. The possibilities are endless."

"Is that a side of pessimism to go with the bitchy?" He glanced at me. "You were in Laura Briscoe's apartment for over an hour. You must have discovered something. Do you want to fill me in? We're on the same team. It might help if you have more eyes reviewing the info."

"The son is mad at the world. It sounds like he and his father had a few unresolved issues. The daughter is beside herself. And we aren't any closer to providing either of them with answers or finding justice for their dad. So what do you want me to say?"

"We'll figure it out." He offered a determined smile. "Trust me."

"I'm letting you drive. Don't push it."

He laughed, and we returned to the OIO building. Once inside, Lucca disappeared to check on the progress that had been made concerning his leads, and I went to my desk to check my messages and e-mail to see if something panned out. Nothing new had surfaced, so I logged into my private e-mail account and sent a message to Sylvia Britt, asking about one of the properties. I needed to get her on the hook in the hopes of plying her for more information on the open house. I pondered if flashing my credentials wouldn't gain compliance faster, but I was afraid she'd clam up. And since she had nothing to do with this investigation, it'd be hard to find a lenient judge who would grant a court order to access her records. The open house was such a minor event. It was unlikely our shooter signed in. So I doubted a judge would grant a sweeping search warrant or subpoena to gain access to every person she encountered in the past month.

Returning to the conference room, I scanned the information for updates from our crime techs and accountants, found nothing to be worthwhile, and came up with another idea. Dialing Marshal Dobson's number, I waited for him to answer. When his voicemail kicked on, I left my name and number and asked for a call back. He was free from suspicion as far as the OIO was concerned, so that meant he might be able to shed some light on the double homicide.

With no other distractions present, I returned to my desk, downloaded the photos I'd taken inside Laura Briscoe's apartment, and printed hard copies. Then I cleared my desk, spread them across the top, and sorted them from earliest to latest. The only helpful item inside the box was William Briscoe's weekly planner. I had spent most of my time photographing the fifty-two pages. Arranging them in order, I outlined his routine, noting the standing appointments and places he frequented, and typed the information and locations into the criminal databases. Twenty minutes later, I got a hit.

"Bingo." I circled the information. This might be our first and only solid lead, and it was all mine. Performing a quick internet search, I scribbled down the address and put my jacket on over my shoulder holster.

When I arrived at the recreational center, I scanned the area. It was in a less gentrified part of the city. A few skateboarders performed tricks half a block away. From the hard looks I got from a few of the neighborhood kids, I suspected the government-issued black SUV stuck out as much as my suit and sunglasses. So much for keeping a low profile.

"Can I help you?" a man asked from behind the desk. He bit off the end of a piece of beef jerky and chewed with his mouth open while he waited for me to say something.

"Special Agent Parker." I held out my credentials, and he stared at the insignia. "I just have a few questions to ask."

"Shoot." He smirked, narrowing his eyes. "And for the record, I didn't mean that literally."

"Do you know William Briscoe?"

"Hmm, I don't know." He was hoping to shake me down. The police probably came here often enough that he knew what the going rate for his helpfulness was. "A lot of people come through here."

Pulling out my wallet, I removed a twenty. "He was in his mid-forties. He came here a few times a week."

He scooped the money off the counter without even looking at it and shoved it into his pocket. "Willie hangs around in the late afternoons on Monday, Wednesday, and Friday. He helps out with one of the youth boxing classes."

"Anything else you can tell me?"

"Like what?" He eyed my wallet.

"When was the last time you saw him? Are you aware of any problems he might have had? Did he piss someone off recently?" I took another twenty out of my wallet and placed it on the counter, holding it down with my pointer finger so the helpful greeter couldn't snatch it away.

"It's been a couple of weeks. He said he had something to take care of and he'd be gone the rest of the month."

"Did he say what it was?"

"Nope." He grabbed the end of the bill and slid it out from underneath my finger. "He came straight from work, changed in the locker rooms, coached the class, packed up his crap, and left. Why are you trying to jam him up for doing a nice thing?"

"I'm not."

"Yeah, that's what the cops always say, and then they arrest the person they come here looking for."

"I won't be arresting Mr. Briscoe."

"Yeah?" He jerked his chin up. "Then why are you asking about him?"

"He's dead."

"No way." He sat up straight. His eyes darted around the room. "Do you think someone here did it? Because he never had a problem with nobody that I could tell."

"Can you show me his locker?"

"Sure." He stood, suddenly much more compliant than he had been. "Willie was always one of the nice ones. Brought the staff coffee or snacks when he came from work. Never had a negative thing to say about anyone. I can't imagine who would want to hurt him."

"I never said someone hurt him."

"Look, lady, this isn't the best neighborhood. When a cop comes sniffing around, asking about a dead guy, it's because someone killed him. That's just how it goes."

He led the way into the locker room. A few men quickly covered themselves when I entered. One whistled, but after meeting my cold stare, he decided to secure his towel and mind his business. The staff member led me to locker 312. There was no lock. He opened it to reveal empty space.

"He carried his stuff in a gym bag. I don't know that he ever left anything here overnight."

"Not even a lock?" I asked

The guy shrugged. My neck and shoulder muscles bunched due to the frustration of hitting another dead end.

I resisted the urge to question the naked men inside the locker room. Instead, I followed the staff member back to the desk.

He liked William Briscoe, and upon finding out that Briscoe was dead, his helpfulness had increased tenfold. He gave me the class roster and the name of the instructor, H. Santos. Given that it was a Thursday, I didn't see any reason to hang around longer than necessary, particularly since there was a good chance someone would jack my vehicle if I stayed here for another five minutes.

While en route to the federal building, my phone rang. Sylvia Britt had received my message and was hoping we could rendezvous. The property I asked about was in escrow, but she had another five similarly priced locations she thought I would love. Detouring to her office, I decided to make the most out of my outing. When I arrived, I performed another presto-chango inside the car.

"Ms. Parker, please come inside," Sylvia said. I cast a glance around the rest of the empty office. "Don't be shy. The other realtors are showing properties, and I sent our receptionist home for the night. Let me show you the other properties." She flicked off the overhead light, and a projection of one of the offices lit up the wall. "As you can see, this has an ample waiting area, three separate offices, and—"

"I'm gonna stop you right there. The only space I have an interest in is across from the federal courthouse." Before she could voice a protest, I said, "Mrs. Britt, I appreciate the trouble you've gone through to come up with alternatives, but why can't I see that space? Did something happen there?"

"The authorities believe it might be useful to one of their investigations, so until further notice, the building manager has banned any realtor from showing the space."

"Who owns the property?"

"It went back to the bank after the previous owner couldn't make payments. Each office inside that building is privately owned or the property of a corporation or bank. We're the premier real estate agency that deals with renting and selling the properties that this particular bank holds the notes to," she sat on the edge of her desk, "and they've put us on a three month time crunch before it goes to auction. That's why I held the open house a couple of weeks ago. It was a last-ditch effort, and that's why I'm thrilled that you're so adamant about taking it off my hands, especially with that offer you made. However, until the authorities clear out, I can't touch it, and I'd hate for you to go elsewhere while I make you wait."

"I see." I knew most of this, but since she was being so open and honest, I thought now would be a good time to ask a few questions. "Do you know William Briscoe?"

She thought for a moment and shook her head. "The name doesn't ring any bells."

"What about Stan Weaver?"

Her brows knit together, and she frowned. "Who are you really, Ms. Parker?"

"I'm just a woman looking to rent an office."

She continued to scrutinize me, probably smelling the federal agent scent pouring out of my skin and clothes. "Neither of those men were at the open house. Someone has already asked about them, and he didn't try to deceive me by hiding his identity." She pulled a card off the corner of her desk and handed it to me. "You should probably ask him whatever questions you want answered because I already told him everything I know." She gestured to the door. "Good day, Ms. Parker."

NINE

"I'm going to kill you. That was my lead, and you screwed it up."

"I asked questions, and she answered them," Lucca said. "There was no reason to perpetrate any deception. We have an obligation to follow the evidence and a duty to question individuals who might possess valuable information. You weren't doing either of those things."

"You don't know what I was doing. You weren't there when I spoke to Britt."

"That's right. And the reason I wasn't there was because you made me sit in the car, just like you did when you interviewed Briscoe's relatives."

"Don't you dare go near them. They've been through enough without you kicking up more dust."

"I'll do whatever this job requires. Clearly, you don't have a clue what that is. You've only been here for three months, and you were undercover for half that time."

"You have no idea what I know about this job. I was here for almost five years. I've done and seen more things than you can ever imagine. You've been on the job for a little over two years. You only had the training wheels taken off in the last six months. You don't know a thing, so stop acting like you have any clue what is going on."

"I know exactly what's going on." He slapped his palm against the board. "You're wasting time and resources while we should be focusing our efforts on finding the individual who purchased the rifle. You rather play house and dick around than perform any grunt work because that's beneath you. Just because Kendall asked you to be reinstated does not make you god's gift to the OIO. It just makes you a washed-up agent who couldn't hack it in the private sector." He was lucky the conference table separated us because I wasn't sure that I wouldn't haul off and hit him. "I tried to be nice. I wanted to understand you. To show you some compassion. I've given you every opportunity to open up to me and become a part of this team, but you refuse. So fuck it. I'll just follow up with your leads because you're incapable of doing it."

"Watch yourself," I warned, "because when push comes to shove, you better hope someone will still be standing in your corner because it damn well won't be me."

"That's the best news I've heard all day."

"Screw you, Lucca."

Storming back to my desk, I searched the drawers for my files. I had a few leads. Whether or not Agent Lucca believed they were leads was a different story. He was not in charge. Jablonsky was, and if Mark thought I was nothing more than a drain on our limited resources, then he could dress me down, not this freshly minted Special Agent who was stupid enough to believe he was a genius. After spending a few minutes composing myself, I collected my belongings, filed my paperwork for the day, and knocked on Jablonsky's office door.

"Come in," he called, not bothering to look up from his desk.

"Sir," I began, and his eyes shot to me, knowing I typically didn't do the 'sir' thing unless we were in a formal setting, I was being sarcastic, or I wanted something, "you gave me some leeway to investigate, so I was wondering if I could do that elsewhere."

"Fine, but if you stumble into a situation that requires backup, you will wait for them to arrive, and you will not do anything to jeopardize the veracity of this case, including collecting evidence or questioning witnesses or potential suspects. Is that clear?"

"Yep, and for the record, I didn't do anything to jeopardize the investigation when I spoke with the realtor. In fact, I gave you the heads-up. I don't appreciate someone else shitting where I eat."

"Lucca can be overzealous. The same way you used to be. Cut the kid some slack. This is his first homicide investigation. He wants a shiny gold star."

"Then he should have joined the U.S. Marshals instead of the FBI."

I needed to get my priorities in order. I was spinning out of control, but I couldn't stop it. After leaving the federal building, I drove to my apartment, let myself in, and dropped my belongings on the floor near the door. I walked through the living room into the attached kitchen, opened the fridge, stared inside at the meager foodstuffs, shut the door, repeated the process with the pantry and liquor cabinet, and then curled onto the couch. My first priority had been to determine if Marshal Dobson was at fault. Mission accomplished. Second, since we conducted the preliminary investigation, we were tasked to identify the assailant. While some progress had been made, it wasn't enough to satisfy any of us. My personal priority was to determine who the intended target was. This was where lines blurred and the spinning began.

Since Jablonsky gave me enough rope to hang myself, I decided to focus my efforts on William Briscoe. I already made a few strides on that front, and since Agent Lucca was adamant this was a waste of time and resources, he was less likely to swoop in and steal my thunder again. Or so I hoped. The only downside would be if I was wrong. Nothing in Briscoe's history indicated he should be targeted, but despite Weaver's numerous enemies, something just didn't feel right.

Getting up, I pulled the crime scene photos and the technicians' evaluations out of my bag. Why did Briscoe stand up at that inopportune time? What would have happened if he didn't? The other jurors on the panel had been questioned, but no one remembered anything. The most helpful recollections focused on Weaver dropping to the ground. A few remembered hearing a crack of thunder, which was the report from the sniper rifle. Unfortunately, no one noticed Briscoe. Apparently, he had stood, been hit immediately, and slumped back into his chair. It took seconds, maybe even minutes, before anyone noticed he was dead.

This was old information, but something was there. Shaking off the buzz that indicated the beginnings of a headache, I determined what it was. Regardless of anyone else's conclusion, I was certain if Briscoe hadn't stood up, the bullet would have gone through his head instead of his back. He was our primary target. Even if I couldn't quantitatively prove it, I knew it was true.

Phoning the forensic team, I asked them to run another simulation, accounting for the height difference on my recent theory and pass the findings along to Jablonsky. Mark always trusted my gut instincts. With any luck, his faith in me wasn't misplaced.

Deciding that I couldn't hide out here for the rest of the evening, I packed two boxes. One held as much food and liquor as I could shove inside, and the other contained my shoes. After loading them into my car, I returned to my new abode.

I unpacked the edible items, finding a few spots in his pantry and on top of Martin's well-stocked bar to house them. Lugging the box of shoes into the guestroom, I left them in the corner and plugged in my laptop, determined to make some progress on Jack Fletcher's problem while I had the house to myself.

Starting with the information he had given me, I searched for the underground fight scene. If these bouts were as popular as he made them out to be, they had to be publicized somewhere. The best place to start was the internet.

My first search resulted in hundreds of pages of entries. This was going to be more complicated than I imagined. Narrowing the results wasn't too difficult, but most of what I found were related news stories dealing with the dead fighter. As I skimmed the seventh story, I found mention of the gym where he trained. Making a note, I continued searching for venues.

An entire online community existed for the various circuits. There were scheduled matches for every martial art and boxing style imaginable. Some were sanctioned by the larger sports authorities. Those fighters were paid per match, often had sponsors, and occasionally advertising deals. They also had agents, trainers, and a team of handlers to deal with their issues. The lesser known matches were mostly coordinated through gyms and owners. After glimpsing an outdated schedule that was likely part of the same circuit Fletcher and his boss had frequented, I decided the easiest thing to do would be to pay the gym a visit during regular hours.

The fact that they were closed now did nothing to alleviate my natural curiosity, so I spent far too long stalking them through their social media channels. A few members had posted videos of matches, training sessions, and proper ways to execute a few techniques. The matches proved the most interesting. I replayed one a dozen times, focusing my attention on the crowd. It was one of the fights Fletcher had attended since I spotted him easily enough. I just didn't know where the fight was held.

Picking up my phone, I dialed, hoping he would provide some additional information. "Mr. Fletcher, I have a few more questions," I said.

"Ms. Parker, now's not a good time. Can it wait until morning?"

"That's fine." He was the one on the time crunch.

"Great. Good night."

He disconnected, and I rubbed my eyes, checking the time. It was after eleven. Martin wasn't home yet. Someone was a workaholic, and for once, it wasn't me. Okay, maybe it was still me, but no one was around to point it out.

Dobson hadn't returned my call. Fletcher was being evasive, and Lucca and I were no longer on speaking terms. With my current batting record, I phoned Mark's work number and left a message on his voicemail, telling him I wouldn't be coming in tomorrow. Due to my last undercover assignment, I had some personal time on the books, and there was no reason why I couldn't perform my due diligence without the overbearing annoyance that was Eddie Lucca.

Resisting the urge to read the same information over and over again, I went up to the fourth floor, changed into one of Martin's shirts, and crawled into bed. I stared at the ceiling for the next hour before the security system beeped. I practically jumped out of bed, assuming the worst. That type of behavior was ridiculous since the red light blinked back to green a moment later when the security system reactivated, and Martin came up the steps. He flipped the light on, and I rolled over, shielding my eyes from the sudden brightness.

"Hey," I said, sitting up, "you're home late."

"You're in bed early." He hung his jacket on a hanger and placed his tie over the chair. "Did I wake you?"

"No. And for the record, this room is sorely devoid of entertainment, so when I move the rest of my crap in, we should stick my TV in here."

"Don't you think you have enough sleep problems without the added stimulus of flashing lights and action movies?"

"I sleep just fine. Actually, I sleep much better when there's something to distract from the inner turmoil."

"I can distract you from the inner turmoil." He grinned, adding a swaying motion to his movements. "Experts say the bedroom is only supposed to be for two things." He continued to disrobe while I settled against the headboard, enjoying his mild striptease. "Sex and sleep."

"Well, in that case, you need to slow down. Slower. Slower."

He met my eyes, pulled his belt free, tossed it onto the chair, and went to work on the buttons of his shirt. "Is this better?"

"Y'know, if we had a TV in here, you could take lessons from those stripper workout videos." He made a face at my suggestion. "Fine, I'm all about compromise. We can occasionally watch something from your dirty movie collection. Happy?"

"I don't have a dirty movie collection, Alex." He smiled, pulling the tails of his shirt free and becoming distracted with rearranging his pile of dry cleaning. "Do you have anything that needs to go to the cleaners? Marcal's dropping my clothes off in the morning."

"I am capable of taking care of my own dry cleaning."

"It's stupid to make separate trips."

"Probably, but I'm not you. I don't want to use your staff. Why do you even have staff?"

"You insisted on the bodyguard. Marcal and Rosemarie are the only other staff I have. It makes sense to have a driver who runs errands, particularly when I have seventy meetings scheduled for the week and eighteen-hour workdays, which also explains the usefulness of a cleaning lady."

"Damn, why don't I have staff?"

"You can borrow mine any time you want."

He added his dress shirt to the pile, and something caught my eye. I scrutinized the dark blackish bruise that covered his shoulder. He turned away, entering the bathroom and closing the door. When he emerged, I was waiting on the other side of the door.

"How did that happen?" I asked, fearing I already knew the answer.

"It's nothing. I shouldn't have startled you awake the other night. I'll know better next time."

I took a breath, resisting the urge to place my hands over the bruises that would perfectly outline my fingers. "It's official. You're in an abusive relationship, and you're making the same excuses every battered person makes. It wasn't your fault. It was mine."

"Alex, you had a nightmare. You got a little handsy. It's nothing. Really." He smirked. "I was hoping to persuade you to add some scratch marks to my back to complete the look."

"That's not funny."

"It is a little." He pulled me into his arms. "It's okay. I promise."

"What if I had gone for your throat? Or my gun?" Rubbing a hand down my face, I tried to pull away, but he held tight.

"Stop." He stared into my eyes. "You weren't dreaming about killing me. You were dreaming about saving me."

"But—"

"You've never acted out any of your violent nightmares, so I'm not worried. You shouldn't be either." He walked us backward to the bed. "Where did we land on the scratch marks debate?"

TEN

"Alex?"

I opened my eyes and pulled my head off my arms. The computer screen had gone dark. I clicked a key while rubbing my neck. My session had expired, so I closed the browser before shutting down.

"What time is it?" I asked.

"A little after seven," Martin said. He ran a hand through my hair, untangling the long brown strands and offering a kiss. "Did you sleep down here last night? You were gone when I got up, and I didn't hear you leave in the middle of the night." His lips curved into a sly smile. "You really wore me out."

"I couldn't sleep, so I thought I'd get a jump on work."

He narrowed his eyes, knowing the real reason I snuck out of bed after he fell asleep, but he didn't voice his suspicions. Instead, he surveyed the room which was covered from floor to ceiling in paperwork and crime scene photos.

"You've been busy. I guess it's a good thing we didn't move the bed out of here after all." He watched me wince while I moved my neck from side to side. "Sit up." He gently massaged the crick out of my neck. "What time are you supposed to be at work?"

"I'm not going in today. I'm feeling off. I'll probably just putter around and take care of a few things."

"Why don't you go upstairs and get some sleep? I'll be home late again tonight, so don't wait on dinner."

"Do I really strike you as the domesticated, doting partner? Just so you know, I'm not planning to fetch your slippers or wash your socks either."

"That's why I have staff," he teased. "But you make a good point. No one would ever confuse you with being subservient."

"Tell that to Lucca." I climbed off the bed and went into the kitchen in search of coffee. "That jackass really thinks he's something. Mark doesn't necessarily trust Lucca's rationale either, but he still expects me to be nice to the boy scout."

Something dark passed across Martin's eyes. "Why do you call Lucca a boy scout?"

"He's all about following protocol and procedure to the letter. He's too fresh-faced to realize that sometimes you have to fudge a little." I sat down and took a long sip. "The job's a lot easier when you see things in black and white, but when the consequences could potentially be life or death and your only options are to wait for a warrant or bust through the door in order to save someone, you bust through the door. He just doesn't get it. Truthfully, I hope he never does."

Martin kissed my temple and picked up his briefcase. "Try not to bust through any doors today. I'll see you tonight." He went to the stairs while I watched from my perch at the kitchen table. "Y'know, I love that I can say that every day."

"Sap."

On the way upstairs, my cell phone rang. It was Dobson returning my call from yesterday. After agreeing to meet for breakfast to discuss things in person, I threw on some casual clothes. Making sure I had the gym address written down for later, I ran through my mental checklist, hoping Jack Fletcher would phone soon, and drove to a diner near the federal courthouse.

Lou Dobson was seated at the counter, sipping from a

steaming mug. I slid onto the stool next to him and eyed the menu hanging against the wall. After ordering and exchanging some basic pleasantries, I scanned the rest of the diner. The place was pretty empty. Two older men were seated at the other end of the counter. A couple sat in the back corner booth. Other than that, it was too late for the breakfast crowd and too early for lunchtime.

"Are you back on duty?" I asked, attempting to be polite.

"I've been cleared, but courthouse security is still being evaluated. While that happens, a group of bright-eyed and bushy-tailed youngsters is patrolling the premises." He made an aggravated groan, picking up his spoon and gulping down a mouthful of something that looked like the love child of oatmeal and cream of wheat.

"I'm sorry things are taking so long."

"What do you want, Agent Parker?" Dobson asked, dropping all pretenses. "You didn't want to meet just to have someone to share a meal."

"My agency has been tasked with tracking the shooter. From the intel we've collected, it's safe to assume he spent a bit of time planning this."

"How much time?"

"At least a week. He needed the time to pick his perch."

"And you think that I might have missed noticing him?" The accusatory, defensive tone crept into his words, and he slammed the spoon down. "I was cleared."

"Hold your horses, cowboy. What I'm asking is if you wouldn't mind going into a few more details about the past two weeks." He looked skeptical, so I added, "It's off-the-record. In fact, no one at my office even knows I'm here. They think my theory on the matter is farfetched."

"What's your theory?"

Hesitating briefly, I considered Dobson's position and status. The simple fact was he already knew the details surrounding the double homicide. Speaking about this to him wasn't violating any privilege, and hopefully, he'd be more willing to hear me out than Agent Lucca.

"I'm not convinced the prosecutor was the primary target. I believe the dead juror was."

He considered my words for a few minutes while he

aimlessly stirred the remaining porridge. "All right. If the killer was poking around during jury selection, you should check out the vantage points for that area." He pulled a napkin free from the holder and removed a pen from his shirt pocket. He drew a square and a few lines. "This is the courthouse." He added a compass in the corner. "Front steps are here." He pointed with his pen. "People who get called to show up for jury duty come in the front, go through the security checkpoints, and are ushered down the stairs." He frowned. "Have you pulled the records from that day? Maybe the killer tried to get inside the courthouse but couldn't get through security."

Grabbing a napkin of my own, I scribbled that down to check later. Our waitress came by, refilling my coffee and giving us both a strange look. It wasn't every day that two people sat at the counter and used the napkins to make lists and draw rudimentary blueprints. Thankfully, she didn't ask what we were doing.

"Do you remember someone being denied entry?" I asked.

"It happens all the time. People carry the damnedest things around with them." He continued working on his sketch. "As I was saying, they go down the stairs and wait to get called for the jury panels. That floor is slightly below street level, and the windows," he pointed with the tip of his pen, "are only partially blocked by the building's shrubbery. It's one of the weaknesses I've mentioned in my reports, but considering that area serves as a giant waiting room, no one in charge was ever concerned about it."

"Why didn't he take the shot then?"

"Come on," Dobson dropped some money on the counter, "we'll stop by and get the security footage from that day, and I'll show you the windows."

"Thanks, Marshal."

"I guess you aren't so bad, even if you were one of the federal agents assigned to sabotage my career."

"I told you it wasn't personal."

"I know." He shrugged into his jacket. "You also said you would get it done quickly, and you did. So far, you haven't promised anything you didn't deliver. I'm assuming that means you think things through before reaching your conclusions and theories. It won't hurt to check into the possibility that our shooter can be spotted on the courthouse footage." He lowered his voice. "However, if that's the case, maybe you could leave it out of the report or toss in a good word about my assistance."

"This won't bite you in the ass," I assured. "You're clear of any involvement or negligence. This won't blow back on you. That's just the pessimism talking."

He scrunched his brows together. "With this job, pessimism is second only to breathing."

As we made our way across the street, I scanned the area. Tall buildings flanked us from all sides, and traffic was ridiculous. At least the realtor hadn't been lying about everything. Dobson led us up the steps. I stopped at the top to check for possible vantage points. Whoever took the shot wanted to contain the scene. Killing someone inside a courtroom wouldn't lead to mass hysteria since it would take time for word to travel, units to scramble, and the shooter's position to be compromised. Great, the technical aspects were easily resolved, as was the where, if only we could determine who and why.

Dobson led us through security, making small talk with the guards at the checkpoint while we flashed our credentials to bypass the line of waiting visitors. From there, he took me down the steps. I studied the windows and the view of outside. It would have been difficult to make a clear shot. If our killer wasn't a professional, as the collateral damage indicated, he'd have to wait for the actual court proceedings since the courtroom windows provided a much better angle to open fire.

"How would he know which case William Briscoe was assigned?" I asked.

"That's confidential. We could have an internal leak," Dobson cringed at the thought, "or the killer came inside and hung out for the proceedings. It's like a lottery. He might have noted which panel the vic was assigned to, and then called the automated hotline to see when they were required to report for duty."

"But he wouldn't have known which courtroom the

panel was assigned until the case began."

"You're forgetting voir dire," Dobson chided. "The prosecutor and defense counsel would be present to question the jurors. It's possible he heard the attorneys' names, checked the cases, and found out when they were serving on the docket. Sure, there is attorney-client privilege, but the prosecutor's office has their own list because each AUSA tries so many cases there would be overlap and scheduling conflicts. Have you checked their office for a breach?"

"Maybe." I shrugged, unsure if Lucca had looked into it.

"It's something to consider." He led the way up a back staircase toward his office. "Do you wanna look at some footage?"

"Is there a possibility I can see a copy of the schedule for that week first?"

"Do you have a court order?" He chuckled at his own joke. "For the sake of my sanity, didn't your people already collect this stuff?"

"Yeah, but we had an information overload. It was analyzed, cross-referenced, and perhaps dismissed." Pulling out my phone, I shot a text to the tech department to have them scan the footage that I planned to review with Marshal Dobson. They had computers, but depending on how bogged down they were, they might get a hit faster than I would. Also, I hated staring at security cam footage. "If this pans out, will you have to modify your courthouse security plans?"

"I'd probably recommend they ID everyone who enters before allowing them access to the jury pool waiting area. Unfortunately, that would slow things down at the door, unless we were given funds to hire additional marshals or police personnel, so who knows if they would even hear a word I said. You know how funding works."

"Luckily, I don't have to think about it. I'm not much of an administrator."

I waited patiently while he went in search of the video footage. At least he seemed more amenable to working with me today than he had the first time we met; although, I suspected it had a lot to do with his currently benched status and the boredom that went along with it. On the bright side, he was cleared of any malfeasance.

When he returned, he logged onto his computer, pressed a few keys, and searched for the relevant dates and times that corresponded to the properly numbered security cam. Once the video began to play, he offered his chair. Fast-forwarding through the footage, I waited for people to be called, hoping to find Briscoe. Thirty minutes later, he was assigned to a panel. Continuing to speed up the footage, I watched for suspicious activity within the room. Two dozen people weren't assigned to jury duty and were free to go. Only one member of the unassigned mass stood out. He was a white male with a baseball cap, glasses, and a windbreaker. Unlike the rest of those relieved to be dismissed from having to perform their civic duties, he lingered, stepping into the men's room with two or three other people.

Five minutes later, when everyone else had vacated, he stepped out of the men's room still wearing the baseball cap and glasses. As he headed up the steps, he brushed into a few men in nice suits, apologizing and patting their jackets. Then he went on his way.

"Son of a bitch." I recorded the timestamp and dialed Lucca. "Check the basement courthouse footage at," I read off the time and date, "because I've found our guy."

"Where are you?" Lucca asked. "We tracked the rifle to a possible sale made from a hunting shop that specializes in long-range weapons. The owner thinks he remembers the guy. He has copies of driver's licenses from the sales. We're checking them now. We should know his name within the hour."

"Great, but check the footage when you get a chance to make sure it's the same guy. Guns are stolen and resold all the time."

"I must have missed the memo saying you're in charge." He disconnected, and I sighed dramatically.

"Trouble in paradise?" Dobson asked, and I shrugged. "It might help if you didn't tell your partner what to do. You're supposed to be on a level playing field, unless you're senior, but I don't see how that's possible, unless you started working for the Bureau when you were five."

"He's not my partner." The bitter tone hung from every word.

"Not to overstep, but a friendly word of advice, you'll have to accept his role at some point. The sooner you do, the easier it'll be."

"How do you know that?"

"I called in a favor and read your file." He didn't appear particularly apologetic. "You're not the only psychic around here, and since you were the agent assigned to investigate me, I thought I'd return the favor." He glanced around his tiny office. "Is there anything else I can do for you? I have a few more days off, and they shouldn't be spent here."

Taking that as my cue to leave, I collected my notes, checked the time, and decided since I was in the neighborhood, I'd pay Jack Fletcher a visit since he hadn't bothered to return my call.

ELEVEN

"Is Mr. Fletcher available?" I smiled warmly at the receptionist.

"Mr. Fletcher is in a meeting. Do you have an appointment?" She took her eyes off the computer screen for a split second to make sure I wasn't one of their more affluent clients, decided I was nobody important, and returned to performing her tasks.

"Just tell him Alex Parker is here to see him." I glanced at the mostly empty couches and chairs in the waiting area. "I'd be happy to wait."

Her eyes shot up with something akin to annoyance. "Ms. Parker, you'll have to make an appointment. Mr. Fletcher is very busy today. If this is some type of emergency, I might be able to convince one of the other associates to assess your case."

Adding a bit more saccharine to my smile, I placed my shield and ID on her desk. "It's Agent Parker, and I'm sure he can spare a moment or two in between meetings. Why don't you save us both some time and ask him?"

"Fine." She glared in my direction, probably wanting to inquire as to whether or not I had a warrant or subpoena but thought better of voicing her protests. "It might be a while."

"Not a problem. I haven't read this month's issue of *Gentlemen's Quarterly* yet."

She rolled her eyes, somehow failing to find my remark amusing, and clicked a few keys on her computer. I stepped away from her desk and took a seat in one of the chairs. I scanned the selection of magazines on the table, finding the titles boring, so I pulled out my notepad and scribbled random thoughts pertaining to the courthouse shooting. Just as I finished writing out what I knew of Briscoe's daily routine, someone cleared his throat.

"What are you doing here?" Fletcher asked. From the looks of him, I knew things had escalated in the last day and a half. "I said I'd call."

"May we speak in your office?"

"That would be a good idea." He led the way down the corridor and gestured to the leather chair. "Take a seat." He closed the door and went behind his desk. "Have you identified the party responsible?"

"I don't have enough to work with." I watched the way he dropped into the chair, sore and stiff. "What happened since the last time I saw you?"

"Nothing."

"Considering the fact you lie for a living, you should be better at it."

"I'm a lawyer. We don't lie. We manipulate the facts until they fit our needs." He chuckled, aware of my disdain for his profession. "Would you believe I fell down the stairs?"

"No."

"I went to visit the locker where I'm supposed to leave the money. I thought there might be some clue as to who was behind this, but I didn't find anything. I spoke to the gym owner and said I was an attorney. He wasn't impressed. He cursed and threw me out. A few of the fighters must have heard the argument and decided to demonstrate their skills. When you called last night, I was in the ER."

"Did you report the assault?"

"No. It wasn't that severe."

"You're being stupid, Jack. Failing to report these

crimes makes you look guilty. Not legally. But like you have a guilty conscience and feel you deserve to have these things happen to you. Not to mention, it's fucking stupid to perform your own recon. You hired me to investigate. What were you thinking?"

"I got myself into this mess. I should at least try to get myself out. I know how dumb that sounds. I spoke with counsel earlier today. More than likely, my involvement in illegal betting would result in nothing more than a slap on the wrist. Obviously, it depends on how the bar wants to interpret it, but I have no previous violations. There's no reason to think it'd have a lasting impact on my ability to practice law." The way he said those words made me think he didn't actually believe them.

"So why aren't you filing a police report?"

"Because the legal community is tightly knit. You're in the club, breaking into the club, or blackballed, and since one of the partners brought me in, he'd just as easily kick me out. I like this job and this city. I don't want to be forced to uproot because I didn't have the stones to persevere."

"You make this sound like a hazing ritual."

"In a way, it is."

Considering his words, I wondered how possible it was that someone with power and prestige might be using this to challenge Fletcher's position or loyalty. "Were any of the firm's clients present at the fights?"

"The more important ones have been invited, but I didn't recognize anyone at the events I attended." He thought back. "It's not like there is some secret knock or handshake to gain admittance. I'm sure the fight schedule is posted somewhere so people can just show up out of the blue, even though I was initially told it was one of the firm's best-kept secrets."

"I plan to find out." Flipping to a clean page in my notepad, I slid the paper in front of him. "Give me a list of venues you've visited with dates and times, if you remember. I'll perform my own recon. With any luck, I won't have to temporarily disable any prize fighters while I'm doing it."

After leaving the law offices of Ackerman, Baze, and Clancy, I detoured to the federal building. Even though I swore not to show up, I wanted to see if we knew the shooter's identity. The driver's license contained an outdated photo and incorrect address, but we had a name. Slater Christianson. It was the second time his name surfaced during the course of our investigation. He might be our guy. Lucca had phoned for an arrest warrant and was leading a team to Christianson's new address. Since we already had the murder weapon, I wondered how long it would take to place Christianson at the scene of the crime.

Phoning Sylvia Britt at the real estate agency, I spoke formally, not bothering to mention I was the same woman who had claimed an interest in that particular office space, and asked if she had any dealings with Christianson. The name didn't ring any bells, and I had no reason to think she was lying. However, that didn't keep me from sending a couple of probationary agents to show her the photo and ask a few innocent questions.

Once that was done, I updated Mark on my helpfulness and ducked into the elevator. I didn't need to hang around and step on Lucca's toes. He thought he knew what he was doing, so he should go ahead and do it. Personally, I would have gotten a search warrant for Christianson's apartment in order to find the clothing worn by the assailant on the security feeds or ammunition that went with the rifle, but supposedly, I was out of practice and had no idea how to do this job. My gut said one of us didn't know how to do the job. We'd find out soon enough who the incompetent agent was. But there was no reason why I had to stick around and wait.

Double-checking the gym address where Fletcher was supposed to leave the fifty thousand dollar bribe, I parked a few blocks away, concealed my gun and credentials inside my purse, and stuffed my empty shoulder holster into the glove box. Pulling my hair back into a ponytail, I went down the street and wandered into the gym.

The interior contained battered equipment. The heavy bags were duct-taped around the middle. The ring was stained with sweat, dirt, and blood. The only people present were trainers and fighters. This wasn't a swanky gym with a fancy juice bar and color coordinated workout gear. This was something out of *Rocky*, or it would have been if there were hanging hunks of meat that needed tenderizing.

"What can I do you for?" a short, older guy asked. He wore faded grey sweats and snapped his chewing gum. "I don't let any of my fighters have their girls here." He assessed me for a moment. "Unless you're looking to train." I hadn't even said a word, but he circled me. "We have a few lady fighters. Kickboxing mostly. Some of them are into that MMA shit. Whatever floats your boat, darling. I don't judge. Kicking ass and getting your ass kicked. That's what it's about."

"Where do I sign up?"

"No, it doesn't work like that. You meet the coaches. If they like you, then they sign you up. Not the other way around. If you think this is some get in shape thing, go check out the equal rights place down the street with the plastic front and sauna." He jerked his head toward the door. "The only people who come here and stay here are serious about the sport and serious about competing." The corner of his eyes crinkled in a silent laugh. "Real fighting will ruin that pretty face of yours, so think about it, cookie."

"Did you escape from some 1920s gangster flick? Because I'm not anyone's cookie, sweetie, or doll. I want to fight." Okay, where did that come from? I was supposed to be asking questions, not volunteering to have my jaw and nose broken. "I'm looking to make some cash. You have paid fights, right? I found this place mentioned online. It's part of the circuit. Recruiters, agents, shit like that?"

"How old are you? Most of our fighters are kids. You're already past your prime."

"Thirty-ish."

"A bit old-ish," he mocked. "You might not have that many good years left." But before he could reject me, another man stepped up behind him.

"Let's see what she's got before you turn her away, Tim." This new guy held out his hand. He wore basketball shorts and a ripped tank top. His muscles bunched and moved.

He was stocky with thick thighs from too much weightlifting. He was about twenty pounds away from bodybuilder status. "I'm Ron."

We shook, and he gave my hand a light squeeze, probably afraid that if he didn't take it easy, he'd crush my bones.

"Alex."

"Nice to meet you." He noted my lack of gym bag. "Our female fighters mostly train together. We don't have mixed matches, aside from the occasional sparring. The girls train in the evenings from six to nine. Why don't you come back in a few hours so I can see what you've got?"

"Is there a beginner's class?"

"No. People who show up at this gym and want to become fighters already know how to fight. I just hone techniques and help them focus and dedicate themselves to this path. Where do you work?"

"I'm a consultant."

"So you sit behind a desk all day and think you have what it takes to win a fight?"

"Hey, when you constantly deal with assholes, it's important to find a healthy outlet to release the pent-up hostility."

"We'll see." He tore a flyer off the wall and handed it to me. "Before this goes any further, these are the monthly fees. Personal sessions are charged by the hour. If it's too rich for your blood, don't waste your time showing up tonight because you should probably just check out the rec center instead. They offer free classes."

"I'll see you tonight." I folded the paper, stuck it in my pocket, and went out the door.

On the way home, I stopped at my office and ran through the gym's financial history, hoping to find last names for Ron and Tim. Tim was the owner, and the man responsible for the assault on Jack Fletcher. Tim Coker, fifty-one years old, arrest record for domestic abuse. The charges were dropped. He had been a fighter twenty years ago but not a very good one. He never hit it big, so he bought a gym. It was true what they say, if you can't do, teach. After a few more searches, I couldn't find a surname for Ron and called it quits.

Tonight would be an information gathering mission, so I didn't need to drive myself crazy in the meantime. Returning to Martin's, I rummaged through the kitchen, found a yogurt, and went into the guest suite to search for appropriate attire. After changing, I went downstairs, stretched, jogged an easy mile to loosen up, grabbed a few protein bars, water, and a sports drink, and drove back to the gym. Rush-hour traffic was horrendous, causing me to arrive twenty minutes late.

"I thought you changed your mind," Ron said when I entered. "I figured the price sheet scared you away."

"The fact that you don't have a beginner's class was more frightening."

"Linka," Ron called, and a woman who looked like she should have been on *American Gladiators* appeared behind him, "we have some fresh meat to test out."

Linka, last name unknown, must have been 5'10 and at least 160 pounds. We definitely wouldn't have been in the same weight class. Frankly, I wasn't entirely sure she was even female.

She sized me up, and I gulped. Sure, I knew how to fight. However, street fights and self-defense tactics were different from ring fights. First off, my tactics were often considered illegal inside the ring. Second, the goal wasn't to subdue in order to apprehend; it was to stay upright longer than the other person.

"Y'know, Mr. ... what's your name?" I hoped Ron would say something useful and I could be on my way.

"Ron." He shot a look in my direction. "Scared?"

"This isn't exactly how I thought things would go." I kept my eyes trained on the large beast of a woman. "Maybe this is a mistake. I didn't mean to waste your time."

Linka smiled, suddenly appearing much friendlier than before. "Don't go. I'm sorry. The intimidation thing is just something me and Ronnie like to do." She giggled, a sound I never expected to come from someone built like a muscular bear. "Tim's so old school with his training. He makes this place sound like a Russian prison camp." She frowned, making her voice deep. "Listen, cookie, this place is for real fighters. We wash the floor with your blood and drink your sweat." She and Ron laughed again.

"That's a pretty accurate depiction of how my encounter with him went earlier today," I said.

"Come on, let's see how your technique is on the bag. If you're up to speed, we'll try some light sparring," Linka insisted, heading toward an empty corner of the gym.

My eyes scanned the area, noting the other women who were jumping rope, doing sit-ups or push-ups, and taking turns holding pads. It was nothing like the way Tim and Ron made it sound. Ron must have sensed my unease because he fell into step beside me.

"Tim thinks the sweet science is a male-only sport. He tries to act like this is an equal opportunity gym, but he hopes to run off the women through intimidation and price hikes. He doesn't understand that women are just as capable and definitely more vicious in the ring. I run the show at night after he leaves. We have easy, laidback sessions. If you want to get on a ticket to fight, I can make it happen, but if you just want to hang out, spar a bit, and take out some aggression on the bags, that's cool too. The only thing you have to do is keep the act up in front of Tim. It's his gym. If he realized half the training fees are paid by women who want nothing more than to keep in shape or be able to defend themselves, he'd shit himself."

"My lips are sealed. I'm not ready yet, but at some point, I'd like to enter the ring and give the actual fight scene a try."

"Let's see how much work you'll have to do first." He stepped to the side, so he could watch as Linka held out a pair of fingerless training gloves. They were the same gloves most kickboxers and MMA fighters wore instead of the bulky all-encompassing boxing gloves. I slipped them on and tightened the Velcro around my wrists while she took a position behind the bag and instructed what combinations I should perform. By the time I worked up a sweat, Ron called a stop to the workout. "I thought you said you needed a beginner's class."

"I do," I replied.

"I want to see something." He put a pair of focus pads on his hands and made sure the area was clear. "Hit the pads. Right cross, left jab." He bounced on the balls of his feet, and we circled around as he called out instructions. If he kept this up for another minute, I'd feel like a trained monkey.

I swung with my right. He pulled his hand back, attempting to clock me with his other hand. Automatically, I sidestepped, negating some of the blow. "Beginner's luck," I muttered.

"You've trained before." It wasn't a question.

"I have a long history of self-defense classes in my past."

He swung again and again, attacking like a windmill and continuing to back us into the corner of the gym. His blows were landing with more of an impact. My face stung from where the pad hit my cheek. I blocked as best I could. Once I was backed against the wall, I blocked a hit and followed through with an uppercut. He stepped back for a second before coming at me again. The cushioned pads hit against my forearms and wrists as I ducked behind my arms, keeping them up and in front of my face. When he shifted downward to pummel my torso, I kicked him, forcing him away.

He rubbed his stomach. "If you want to try your luck in the ring, I can make that happen. You don't panic, and you can take a hit." He nodded to Linka to take over, discarded the pads, and went to watch a few of the other fighters spar.

"Let's get you weighed and figure out what class you're in." She led us toward the locker room. Since Tim was a sexist relic, there was only one locker room, and tonight's training session was proving rather enlightening. With the right questions, I might be able to give Fletcher a name by this evening.

TWELVE

"You're classified as a flyweight by women's boxing standards." Linka scribbled something down on a clipboard. "There aren't that many fighters in your category who work the circuits."

"What does that mean?"

"It means Ron could probably find you a match, but it's not one of the more popular events. So you should have a few months to train and prepare. He might talk with the other coaches about having a flyweight match as the opener for a lightweight or middleweight fight." She moved through the rows of lockers, and I noted the location for the blackmail drop.

"I'm not ready to fight. Sure, I want to step into the ring and maybe make some extra money, but I'm not up for this yet." I stopped our progression, hoping to broach the subject of locker ownership.

"If money's tight, how can you afford to train here?"

"I figure it's an investment."

She bit her lip, thinking. "Y'know, sometimes Ron and a few of the other coaches train fighters on a contingency basis. Instead of paying monthly, they take a cut of whatever you make from the ticket."

"How does any of this work? I've seen fights on TV, but are these bouts really part of that giant enterprise?"

"You know how baseball has the Triple-A teams and the minors?" I nodded, so she continued. "We're the equivalent of that. Think of us as the unofficial minors. From here, it's possible to move up to the minors and beyond. Each fight brings in some money, and the fighters and the coaches each get a cut."

"Where do these fights take place? Can anyone buy a ticket to watch the event?"

"Absolutely. The more, the merrier. Mostly, gyms host the matches. We utilize online and word-of-mouth advertising. Ticket sales aren't great, but money gets collected and divided up. Somehow, it works."

"Whatever brings in the dough, not that I have any intention of looking a gift horse in the mouth." I turned to stare at the row of lockers. "Hey, since I'll be hanging around, can I rent a locker or something?"

"The lockers are Tim's domain, but I'll check the roster and see if there are any spare ones. Ron can always say one of the daytime guys wanted it."

"You work here?" I asked, somehow missing this fact.

"Not exactly. Ron's my husband. We manage the female fighters together." She smiled conspiratorially. "Don't tell Tim."

"I wouldn't dream of it."

She led us back into the gym and forced me to run through some circuit training with the other fighters. By the end of it, I despised the concept of the medicine ball in relation to inverted sit-ups. Ron gave me some pointers on weightlifting techniques and exercises, deciding that I had plenty of stamina but not enough bulk or muscle mass for a fighter. Then Linka appeared with copies of diet recommendations. While I scanned the sheet, pretending to take these suggestions to heart, she checked the locker rental forms. I leaned over her shoulder but couldn't make heads or tails out of Tim's writing. Somehow, she understood the chicken scratch and found an unassigned locker I could use. Penciling in my first name, she hoped Tim wouldn't think too hard about it, but if he did, Ron would say there was a new guy who was looking to train. Sometimes, it was helpful having a unisex name. Then they wished me a good night, insisting that they would see me tomorrow.

With a day job, I didn't have the time or energy to devote to an in-depth investigation, but since the money was supposed to be left in the locker in less than a week, I was already on a time crunch. As I drove home, I considered Fletcher's strange attitude toward his threat. He was being blackmailed for money, but the real leverage the blackmailer had against him was the risk of career suicide. That seemed rather unrealistic since the crime of illegal betting wasn't that severe and never endangered any of his clients. Surely, the bar wouldn't take action, even though Hector Santos died after one of these fights. Therefore, Fletcher wasn't afraid of the bar. He was afraid of what his boss would do if their illicit activities turned into a police matter.

Arriving home, I went up the stairs to the master suite and took a long soak in the bathtub. Martin's bathroom was ridiculous. The shower had at least a dozen different jets that went along with the enormous showerhead, and the bathtub, which was large enough to seat four, had a million different settings and more buttons than I knew what to do with. No wonder I favored the guestroom. It was nicer than my apartment and didn't mock my technological incompetence at every turn. When my fingers were appropriately shriveled, I wrapped myself in a warm towel and studied the red blotches on my face left by the focus pads. The marks were similar to carpet burns, but they'd be gone by the morning.

I found some comfortable clothes, ate dinner, and began a more thorough investigation into the gym, Tim Coker, and the fight circuit. Now that I had the venues listed, it shouldn't take long to put two and two together. Sometime during the course of my research, Martin came home. He was on the phone and disappeared up the stairs to continue working. Thankfully, we both had trouble distancing ourselves from our addiction.

After diagramming the fight circuit, printing a list of the

upcoming matches, complete with times and locations, and running a background on Tim Coker, Ron Greenwood, and Linka, I felt confident none of them were responsible for the blackmail scheme, even if Tim had no problem assaulting Fletcher or telling someone else to do it. More than likely, whoever was pushing Fletcher's buttons was someone he was familiar with. Maybe this was just a hazing.

I called Fletcher and left a voicemail saying I needed more information. I didn't want to mention precisely what that was or indicate what we were working on in the event any of this got turned over to the authorities. Hopefully, he'd remember to call in the morning because I didn't have the time to drop by the ABC law offices again.

Besides exploring his clients and associates, my investigation had hit the wall. There was nothing else I could do tonight. Straining to hear if Martin was still on the phone, I went into the living room and found him watching the business report on one of the twenty-four hour news stations. He glanced in my direction and hit mute.

"I thought you weren't working today." He focused on my cheek. "Did you decide you needed your own set of bruises in order to convince me to leave scratch marks on your back?"

I pressed my fingers against my cheekbone, but it didn't hurt. "It's nothing. I was sparring and got hit with a pad." I sat next to him and stared at the scrolling DOW numbers at the bottom of the screen. "How was your day?"

"Long." He sighed. "I'm ready for the weekend." He turned off the TV. "Are you working? I can't remember what you said. Are we moving the rest of your stuff in this weekend? Or are we waiting? What's going on?"

"I don't know yet. I'm moonlighting, and who knows how the OIO investigation will take. An arrest warrant was issued, but it's too easy."

"Everything doesn't have to be complicated, sweetheart. A guy does something wrong. He messes up. He gets caught. See, it can be simple."

"Damn, I've been doing it wrong all these years. If things are that easy, how come you can't simplify your job?"

"Because I like complicated," he smirked and brushed a tendril of hair out of my face, "in case you haven't noticed."

"I've noticed, but that probably makes you a masochist."

He climbed off the couch and offered me his hand. "Let's go to bed so you can abuse me some more." His words weren't funny, and I hesitated to move from my spot. "It's too late to argue about the real reason you snuck out of bed last night, but I want to sleep with you. That's not a euphemism. I'm exhausted, and you look beat." He winked. "No pun intended." He took my hand and led us up the stairs.

I fought to remain awake. Regardless of what he wanted, I planned to sneak back downstairs as soon as he was in a deep sleep, but instead, my phone rang, jolting him upright.

"I'm sorry. That's for me." I grabbed my cell phone from the nightstand and read the display. *Lucca.* "What's up?"

"Hey, Parker, I hope I didn't wake you," Lucca said.

"No. Why would I be asleep at," I squinted at the clock, "3:20 in the morning?" I made a move to get out of bed, but Martin wrapped an arm around my middle, holding me in place and nuzzling my neck. "Speak, boy scout."

"Our lead didn't pan out. Christianson showed us his rifle. I guess the partial serial number wasn't enough for an accurate hit." Lucca blew out a breath. "Needless to say, Jablonsky wants you back in the office in the morning to brainstorm on better ways to flush out our killer." He paused, speaking to someone in the background before coming back on the line. "We're going back through everything pertaining to both victims. It's possible we missed something."

"You think?"

"Shit, Parker," he snapped, and I heard a whimper in the background. "Daddy's sorry, baby."

"What?" I shook my head, confused by that statement.

"I wasn't talking to you," he replied, and another squeal sounded in the distance. "Shh...quiet, honey. Daddy's talking on the phone. That's my good girl."

"Lucca, are you doing something that I don't want to

know about?"

"What? No. Forget it. We'll talk in the morning. I just wanted to make sure you were planning on coming to work."

"I'll see you in a few hours." Hanging up, I rubbed a hand down my face, knowing I needed to have a few suggestions on what to make of this investigation by our morning briefing.

"Is everything okay?" Martin asked, snuggling closer while I tried to edge out of his grasp.

"I think Lucca's with a prostitute, and he called to let me know I have more work to do. I'll see you at breakfast."

"You'll run out of excuses eventually," Martin said, rolling over.

*   *   *

During the morning briefing, I couldn't shake the infernal mental buzzing. It was like a swarm of bees had taken up residence in my brain. What was I missing? Lucca profiled AUSA Stan Weaver, dismissing our previous suspect list, clearing Slater Christianson of any wrongdoing, and assessing the progress that had been made on the list of potential renters that the realtor, Sylvia Britt, had handed over to our agents yesterday.

Next, Jablonsky stepped in to update the team on the other fatality, William Briscoe. The autopsy report listed the injuries sustained antemortem, and whatever wayward thought my subconscious had been chasing suddenly clicked into place. The rec center and youth boxing classes hadn't meant anything until now, but that was the connection that explained Briscoe's injuries. Pushing away from the table, I left the conference room and returned to my desk to research typical boxing injuries.

"Now you're too good to wait out the morning briefing?" Lucca asked, approaching my desk. "You're the one who was so insistent Briscoe was the target."

"Quiet." Narrowing my eyes, I focused on the screen, committed to maintaining my train of thought. "Briscoe was a fighter. MMA, kickboxing, boxing, something. It explains his previous injuries."

"William Briscoe was a sales rep for a wholesale produce company," Lucca stated, not listening to what I said. "He volunteered at some inner city recreational center and taught little kids to box. That doesn't make him Evander Holyfield or Mike Tyson."

"Look at his injuries." Tim Coker's words from yesterday rang through my head. *The rec center teaches classes for free.* "Out of my way." I pushed past Lucca and barged into Mark's office, closing the door behind me.

"Parker?" He looked up, identifying the look on my face as a break in our case. "What is it?"

"Briscoe might have been involved in an underground fight circuit."

"Okay, where's your proof?" Jablonsky asked.

"It's speculative for now." Inhaling, I sunk into a chair. "Hypothetically, the area gyms hold matches and tournaments to gain recognition for their fighters in the hopes of getting sponsorships and larger paydays. Some of the city's elite enjoy watching these events and betting on the winners. It's my understanding they occasionally encourage sports agents and sponsors to give these fighters a chance to break out onto the main stage. These events aren't sanctioned, and recently, Hector Santos died from complications due to injuries sustained while fighting in one of these matches."

"Santos." Mark frowned and rifled through the pages on his desk. "That sounds familiar." He continued searching, finally locating the piece of paper he was looking for. "He worked at the rec center with Briscoe, had a juvie record, was given community service instead of getting sent to a detention center, and turned it into a regular job after his state mandated hours were completed." He dropped the paper on the desk and stared at me. "He's dead?"

"Yeah. It happened less than a month ago."

"A few weeks before Briscoe and Weaver were gunned down. Huh." He chewed on a thumbnail and leaned back in his desk chair. "And you think the murders are related?"

"I don't know."

My brain was still reeling from the updated information

concerning Santos. H. Santos—the boxing instructor Briscoe assisted and who was tied to the impetus behind Fletcher's blackmail. I scanned the information. The kid was eighteen. He should have had his whole life ahead of him. I stood, itching to see what I could find out.

"Did I miss the hypothetical part?" Jablonsky asked, drawing me from my reverie before I could leave his office. "You said the matches were hypothetical, but this kid's death wasn't hypothetical. Where'd you get your information?"

"You don't want to know."

"Is Marty involved in something illegal?"

"God, no. He's your best friend. Where would you get an idea like that?"

Mark shrugged. "Maybe I don't know him that well." He blinked. "It doesn't matter. Who's your source?"

"Remember when I was reinstated and you mentioned I could hold onto my old job if I kept things under wraps?" I asked, and he nodded. "Well, a prominent client brought this to my attention."

"If your side project is related to our investigation, you need to divulge everything right now."

I thought about it for a moment, spinning the facts into different patterns, but I couldn't determine how the blackmail and murders were connected. I just knew they were. "Hector Santos is the only common factor. We don't know enough about William Briscoe's involvement in underground boxing to even connect the two outside of the rec center."

"They're already connected, Alex. The two men worked together, and they're both dead. Hell, look at Briscoe's injuries." Mark pushed the paperwork over. "Do you want to reconsider your earlier declaration?"

"Not yet. Give me some time."

"You have until the end of the day, and then I want to know everything."

THIRTEEN

"Mr. Fletcher, it's Alex. You need to call me back as soon as you get this. There have been complications we need to discuss in person." I hung up my desk phone.

Fletcher wasn't involved in the murders, but in the event his blackmailer was, we needed to figure this out now. Running through my limited resources, I performed my due diligence and would turn it over to the team before the end of the day. I didn't have the luxury to wait. Our victims' families deserved answers. If this screwed Fletcher in the process, so be it. I'd give him as much advanced notice as I could without compromising the murder investigation.

I grabbed my keys, a copy of the updated information, and drove to the rec center. When in doubt, it was important to start at square one. Someone new was working the front desk. Unclipping my badge from my hip, I opened my credentials and laid them flat in front of her. She was an older woman, in her fifties. From the way she took stock of the younger kids nearby, I suspected she was the motherly type.

"Hector Santos. Did you know him?" I asked.

"Yes." She looked around, maybe afraid someone would see her speaking to me.

"Do you get a break? The labor board requires workers to be given breaks."

"Yeah, I get a break." She sounded a bit uncertain, but hopefully, she'd comply with the proper amount of nudging.

"Good. Meet me outside. I need a cup of coffee." I walked out without giving her a chance to protest. If she didn't appear in the next ten minutes, I'd go back inside and make a scene, but I didn't think she wanted to risk drawing attention to my presence. At least, I was counting on it. I sat in the car, my gaze shifting from the entrance to the nearby foot traffic. Seven minutes later, she stepped out of the rec center, donning a baseball cap and slipping on a pair of sunglasses. I flashed my lights at her, and she climbed inside. "How well did you know Hector?"

"He's been coming here for years. He'd chat with me whenever he got the chance. He was always, 'Mrs. Reed look at this' or 'Mrs. Reed what do you think about that'." She stared pointedly out the windshield. "The kids that come here aren't comfortable with the heat. I don't want to discourage them from visiting. It's a safe place. It keeps them off the street." I started the engine and pulled away. "Hector was a good guy. He turned his life around. He was a real inspiration to the younger kids. He showed them that even if you mess up, it's still possible to fix things." She shook her head. "It's a shame what happened to him."

"I'm sorry for your loss. Mr. Santos sounds like he was quite the role model. I hate to ask, but do you know what happened to him? Where he was? What or who he might have been involved with?"

"Hector," she smiled sadly, "dreamed of being a prize fighter. He wanted to be champ. Y'know, pay-per-view fights and ring girls hanging all over him." She chuckled. "He thought he was a lot more grandiose than he really was. He's been training since he was fourteen, I think. He used to hang around the rec center and act like he was some tough street thug. The older boys used to knock him down a few pegs whenever he mouthed off, but as he got older, he got tougher. After he got himself into trouble, he changed for the better. I never thought that scared straight shit held any water, but it made him step up and become a man. He was a kind young man." She shook her head a few times. "It's a shame. He would have made something of himself. He would have made this world a better place."

"Do you know where he trained or who taught him to box?"

"Willie would work with him after they finished with the youth class. Every other night, I'd be locking up and hear them pounding the bags or jumping rope." She scrunched her face together, a thought hitting her. "I haven't seen Willie in a while either. Someone said something happened to him, but I thought it was just a rumor."

"William Briscoe?" I asked, not wanting to tell her he was also dead.

"Yeah, that's him." She grasped my arm as I continued to drive in circles around the neighborhood. "Is he okay?"

"Ma'am, let's just focus on Mr. Santos for the moment."

She covered her mouth with her hand and rocked slightly in the seat, mumbling a few quiet prayers. I waited, wishing there was something more I could say or do. When she collected herself, she spoke again about Hector. Apparently, he had been boasting about working his way up the circuit. His final match was his tenth fight. He had been told a few scouts would be there to watch the bout.

"Do you know what happened?" I asked.

"No. I didn't know anything about it. It was the weekend. Hector wasn't supposed to be coaching the youth until Monday. But when I saw Willie, I knew something horrible had happened. The man looked so distraught. He couldn't even function. He showed up to work, asked one of the other volunteers to take over the class, and cleared out. I saw the newspaper article a few days later. Hector died because of that fight. Are you investigating his death? A few cops have stopped by to ask questions, but they never told us anything."

"We'll get to the bottom of it," I said, unwilling to tell her I was tasked with investigating Briscoe's death instead. "Do you think Mr. Briscoe was somehow responsible or at fault?"

"God, no. Willie wouldn't hurt a fly. Hector's death hit

him hard. I think that's why he hasn't been back since. Poor Willie, he must have felt responsible since he was training Hector." She blinked, and a few silent tears rolled down her cheeks.

"Did Hector ever train anywhere else? Was Willie a professional boxer or something?"

"Hector started training at some gym a year ago. I don't know which one. He talked about it all the time, but I don't remember him mentioning a name. It's been six months or so since he talked about it. I remember it was expensive, and that's why Willie was helping him out. Hector had the techniques down. He just needed someone to help maintain his discipline and spar with him. I wish I'd told him to pursue a more realistic goal, but I didn't want him to get discouraged. From the things Willie said, I thought Hector really had a shot." She sniffled loudly. "The cost wasn't worth it. I should have said something."

"It's not your fault." I stopped the car in front of the rec center. "Are you okay? Do you want to call someone or something?"

She laughed between the tears. "I'm fine. These kids will break your heart, but I gotta focus on the ones who can still be saved." She opened the car door. "Thanks for respecting what this place is and how it works. Those cops don't understand the importance of finesse."

"Hey," I handed her my card, "if you remember anything else, give me a call."

"I will."

"What's your name?"

"Geraldine Reed." She closed the car door, wiped her eyes, slipped her sunglasses back on, and strode inside like she owned the place.

On the drive back, I dialed Lucca. "Do you have the file on Hector Santos?"

"No. It's a police matter, but we have a copy of the coroner's report."

"What about the progress that's being made on the investigation?"

"I just said we don't. Do you have a hearing problem? Or is it some type of comprehension issue?"

"Tell Jablonsky I'm on my way to the precinct to gather some additional information, but everyone needs to stay late tonight for an update on the courthouse shooting."

"For the record, I'm not your personal messaging service."

"Are you sure about that? Because one of the terms of my reinstatement included the promise of a personal assistant." Before he could say anything else, I hung up.

When I entered the precinct, I went straight to the major crimes division. I had spent a lot of time working with Detective Nick O'Connell in recent years. He and his wife, Jen, had become close friends, and one of the few couples Martin and I spent time with. Emerging from the stairwell, I scanned the room, spotting O'Connell sharing a story with his partner, Thompson.

"Boys," I greeted, casting a questioning look at the empty desk nearby. "Is Heathcliff still on sick leave?"

"He's milking it for all it's worth," Thompson said, downplaying the severity of the injuries Detective Derek Heathcliff sustained the last time we worked together. "He'll be back in a couple of weeks. He thought he'd use as many of those accumulated sick days as he could and enjoy a little vacation."

"Well, Derek deserves it," I said, "which means you guys are lucky enough to work with me."

"Joy," O'Connell deadpanned, tapping his pencil against the desk. "Let me start by asking in what capacity you are seeking our professional skills."

"Official OIO business," I flashed my credentials at him, "but in all seriousness, I need information on an ongoing homicide investigation and to speak with the detective in charge."

"Who's the DB?" O'Connell dropped the pen and clicked something on the computer.

"Hector Santos. Eighteen years old."

Thompson rubbed a hand down his face. "That's a tough one." He jerked his chin at Heathcliff's vacant desk. "You might as well get comfortable, Parker. You're gonna be here a while."

"Who caught the case?"

"You're looking at him." O'Connell hit print and searched through his desk drawers for his notepad. "Shouldn't I be asking for a warrant or some kind of official statement signed by Jablonsky or someone in charge of the OIO field office?"

"Jeez, you guys complain when I keep you in the dark, and you complain when I ask for help. Can you just cut the crap and get to it? I have to figure out if Santos' death is related to a double homicide, and you aren't making this easier."

"What double homicide?" Thompson asked.

"Did you hear about the federal prosecutor and juror who were gunned down inside the courthouse?"

"Damn," O'Connell frowned and retrieved a thick folder from the filing cabinet, "then you're not going to like what we've found or haven't found."

I read the sheets, but the investigation was mainly inconclusive. Santos died from blunt force trauma. The police were still in the midst of identifying the parties responsible. I scanned the evidence manifest, which mainly listed Santos' personal effects at the time of his death. A memory card and recording device were listed.

"What's on the tape?" I asked.

"The fight, but our IT guys are still piecing it together with online footage in order to put some names to the faces in the crowd," O'Connell said.

"I need to see it."

"Follow me." He led the way down the corridor and into the A/V room. "Take a break, guys. Special Agent Parker needs her breathing room." The few police officers snorted, muttering derogatory comments as they left the room.

"Was that really necessary?" I asked as he dialed up the proper file.

"You're back on the job, so I have to get my kicks somehow. How are they treating you? Are they letting you keep your clothes on these days, or are you infiltrating another drug and prostitution ring?"

"I'm investigating two murders, hence the need for your information."

"We're the police. We don't like to share with your

kind." His eyes twinkled. I knew he was only kidding. His words weren't meant to be malicious. We were practically family. "It would serve you right, after the last time your side failed to share with us, but I'm above that. And next time I need a favor, you're gonna owe me big."

"Fine, Nick. Whatever you want."

He hesitated to hit play and glanced at the slightly open door. Stepping closer, he lowered his voice as if we were plotting to overthrow the government. "Our double date night is coming up in two weeks, and Jen has her heart set on a fancy dinner and clubbing. But I promised Jacobs I'd cover for him, so I need you to cancel."

"Are you afraid of your own wife, Detective?"

"Parker, if you want my intel, you will cancel date night. Understand?"

"What if I get Martin to cancel instead? Does that work for you?"

He laughed. "Admit it. You're scared of Jenny too."

"Damn straight. She's a nurse. She knows exactly how to kill a person and get away with it. Now shut up and roll the film."

"It's digital, so no film and nothing to roll." He hit play on the computer, and the monitors lit up. "One of these days, you should update your references, and while you're at it, scratch my name off your list of phone-a-friends."

Chuckling, I took a seat in front of the monitors and pulled the cap off my pen. O'Connell opened the case file and pointed out people as we went. Some of the faces in the crowd that he hadn't placed I recognized from the blackmail investigation. I shared what I knew without implicating Fletcher and alluded to handing over a potential witness soon. While I waited for a copy of the video and the police files, I dialed Jack again.

FOURTEEN

"Ms. Parker," Fletcher said, "I've barely had a moment of peace. I don't have time to talk right now. I was planning to call you at the end of business today."

"Listen to me, what I'm about to say is very important. There's a chance that your current problem is related to a double homicide."

"What do you need me to do?"

"We need to talk about this in person. I won't impede the OIO's investigation for the sake of your privacy, but I wanted to meet to discuss this before I share my findings with them. The best chance for you to run damage control is by meeting with me now. I'm sorry. I hate to put you on the spot, but I don't have much of a choice."

"I'll make it work. There's a bar and lounge across the street from my office. Can you meet me there in thirty minutes?"

"I'll be there."

Disconnecting, I hit the lights and sped through traffic, ignoring the various stoplights along the way. Once I was within a reasonable distance, I killed the lights and parked at a hydrant, hoping the government tags would ward off any overzealous meter maids.

Jack Fletcher was sitting at a low table in the center of the room. The place was practically empty, but it was only three o'clock. A few businessmen were at the more scenic spots near the windows, and the functioning alcoholics were seated at the bar. Fletcher had a half-finished gin and tonic in front of him. I waved off the waitress as I slid into the seat across from him.

"Do you think the extortionist also killed that fighter?" Fletcher asked in lieu of a greeting.

"The police department and medical examiner's office will be checking into that." I took a deep breath. "Before I say anything more, you better bill me for this meeting because every word I'm about to divulge must be considered privileged or else my career's down the toilet."

"Should I mail the invoice to your P.I. office?"

"That's fine." After taking a moment to organize my thoughts, I spoke briefly about the death of the AUSA and juror. Then I mentioned the police investigation into the fight scene, the OIO's numerous failed attempts to identify a suspect, and my own inclination that Briscoe was the intended target. "The only common factor is the fight scene. It might not even play out, but that's where the investigation is leading. We've hit so many dead ends. We can't make heads or tails out of the AUSA's murder. The possible motives for killing that particular juror seem more plausible at this juncture. If he was killed because of the fight or because the fighter he helped train was killed, then the blackmail scheme will come to light."

"Shit." Fletcher picked up his glass and swallowed the remainder. "I get it. I do. But shit, I am so screwed."

"Look, if there's any way to mitigate your involvement, I'll do it. If I can leave your name out and still nail the asshole responsible, I will, but it doesn't seem particularly likely at this point. When are you supposed to make the drop?"

"In a few days." He pulled another envelope out of his pocket. "I received this in my office mailbox this morning. Wednesday, ten a.m., same locker number."

"This guy's an idiot." A thought crossed my mind. "How many ethics rules would you violate if you became a CI?"

"I can't speak out against a client."

"No, I know that. But you could identify quite a few people at that fight the day Santos died, right?"

"Parker," his voice held a warning, "that's a fine line." He looked at his watch. "I have to get back."

"Think about it, Jack. We might need an insider to assist."

He laid a twenty on the table and went to the door, not acknowledging my comment. Studying the room and the patrons, I figured this place and another dozen like it probably held plenty of secrets. The police should stick a few undercovers on the premises to bust tons of illegal activities. Shaking off the ingrained law enforcement mentality, I left the bar, no closer to coming up with a lead and unsure if sacrificing Fletcher was in anyone's best interest.

When I arrived at the OIO building, Jablonsky called me into his office. It was almost five o'clock. My day was up. I took a seat on the couch in the corner instead of in the chair across from his desk. It felt less formal, as if what I was about to say was off-the-record even though it wasn't.

"An associate from one of the city's high-powered law firms was present at the underground fight that resulted in Hector Santos' death. The police department has determined his death was the result of blunt force trauma. They have a tape of the fight, but from what I've heard, Santos' opponent hasn't been identified or arrested. Although, that makes little sense, seeing as how easily they could stumble upon this knowledge. Regardless, that's not our concern."

"You're rambling, Parker." Mark opened his bottom drawer and rested his foot against it. "Are you hoping I'll die of old age before you get to the relevant part?"

"Hector Santos trained at a gym, but it was too expensive. So William Briscoe would work with him after the youth boxing class they coached a few times a week at the rec center. My guess is Briscoe's injuries can probably be explained by his sparring matches with Santos."

"That's fascinating, but how does this lead back to a viable suspect in our two murders?"

"I'm not sure it does." I knew pieces of the puzzle were missing. "The lawyer I mentioned earlier is being extorted for betting on these underground fights." I fished out the custody form and the copy of the video recording from Santos' belongings. "Here's the video footage from the match. A lot of powerful people were there."

"So?"

"So my guess is whoever's responsible for organizing these shindigs wants to ensure everyone's silence by using blackmail, which means the blackmailer probably has more to hide than illegal gambling and racketeering charges."

"Without proof, that's just speculation."

"True," I pulled out copies of the blackmail information that Fletcher had given me, "but the legal associate went to check out the drop site for the extortion and had to visit the ER for his troubles. Someone's not fooling around."

"You think if they're resorting to extortion and violence, murder isn't beyond the scope of reason."

"It makes some sense. Honestly, I don't know what's going on. Unfortunately, this is the only connection I've found. Marshal Dobson showed me the footage from the jury selection process. One guy sticks out like a sore thumb. He wasn't there to keep tabs on Weaver, but he was paying a ton of attention to Briscoe."

"Okay. Who's your source?"

"Mark, don't you think we should look into this before we damage someone's reputation?"

"Just tell me who it is, and I'll see what I can do."

"Jack Fletcher." I slid Fletcher's business card across the desk. "He plans to pay the blackmailer because he believes his involvement would look poorly before the licensing board, and even if it doesn't, he's afraid the partners and other high-ranking public officials will get nervous and blackball his career."

"Powerful people always think they're above the system."

"Fletcher's not powerful. He's only an associate. He went along because he was invited and tried to fit in. He just wanted to make partner and get a piece of the pie."

"Like I said, I'll see what I can do." He shifted his gaze

to the exit. "Run the videos up to IT and tell them to focus on the courthouse tapes from a month ago. Their top priority should be coming up with the shooter's identity or possible witnesses. Then check into the gym where this dead drop is, run a complete business profile, and get a background on every employee listed. Maybe you can come up with some creative way to get names of their clients and start compiling their profiles too."

"There's one other thing," I said, moving closer to the door. "I already went to the gym and signed up. Getting locker records for that particular dead drop is a bit tricky since the records aren't exactly rock solid, but I have a few names I can start with."

"Parker, what the hell were you thinking?"

"That helping out Fletcher had nothing to do with our case."

"Fuck." He rubbed a heavy hand down his face. "I don't want to hear any more. Just go." He gestured to the door, and I walked out before I could be hit by shrapnel from his head exploding.

On my way to the IT department, I caught a glimpse of Lucca. His back was to me, and he was on the phone. Thankful to avoid dealing with him, I proceeded to follow the instructions I'd been given, returned to my desk, and was halfway through the business profile on Tim Coker's gym when Mark called us into the conference room. Six agents had initially been tasked with processing the courthouse shooting, but once the Marshal Service was cleared of negligence and wrongdoing, two of our team members were diverted to another issue. That left Lucca, the two tech guys, and me.

"All right, I want to start with progress reports from everyone. Where do we stand? Are we any closer on getting prints, DNA, or tracking who purchased the sniper rifle?" Mark asked, pacing in front of the blank monitor at the front of the room.

A chorus of negatives echoed, and Lucca sputtered out some type of excuse. Jablonsky brushed it away, asking a few other questions about traffic cam footage, the building surveillance feeds from the courthouse, and footage from the office across the street that housed the sniper's nest. There was nothing concrete, but the sketch artists had determined the man's build, and a rough profile had gone out over the wire for any information.

"Any other ideas?" Jablonsky asked, dropping into the chair.

"I've spoken to Weaver's friends, family, and colleagues. The few leads we've been given turned into dead ends. The gun is still our best bet. I'm conducting a search of weapon registries, checking into shooting ranges that have facilities for that type of weapon, and I think we're getting closer. Monday, I'll personally check them out and see if anyone recognizes our suspect," Lucca said.

"Okay, Eddie, you keep following that weapon. As soon as we can put it in our shooter's hand, this will be a slam dunk. In the meantime," Mark glanced at the forensic expert, "disassemble and check every inch of that weapon for something that will be admissible in court. I don't care that you've done it three times, keep doing it until we have something. And you," he pointed at Agent Lawson, our IT guy, "Parker brought you new footage. If you need additional help in order to make that a priority, pull someone off another project."

"Yes, sir," Lawson replied.

"Parker's brought a few things to my attention." Mark flipped open a manila folder and passed out the updated intel concerning Briscoe's connection to Santos and the gym. The blackmail was mentioned as a side note, but Fletcher's name wasn't on the page. "She's working that angle. If any of you stumble across a connection, we'll reconvene and devise a new strategy. Until then, let's divide and conquer, people."

"Rah, rah," I mumbled. Jablonsky would have made a great coach.

"Parker," Lucca called before I could escape the conference room, "why didn't you tell me about this last night when we spoke on the phone?"

"I didn't piece it together until this morning."

"You're so full of shit." He pointed to the page. "You signed up at that gym yesterday. What's going on? Are you covering something up?"

"And I thought I was paranoid. Stop being such a boy scout, Lucca. Jablonsky's in charge. You do what you have to, and I'll do what I have to. What makes you think I'm supposed to report to you?"

"You're not, but we're supposed to be working together since we're the only two field agents still assigned to this."

"Fine," I leaned back in the chair, "I'll tell you whatever you want to know. Go ahead. Ask a question."

"How long did you know the dead fighter was connected to one of our vics?"

"I didn't. It just happened that another matter I was investigating ended up being connected."

"What other matter?"

"It's off-the-books, or it was. It doesn't matter. That's not relevant to you or what you're supposed to be tracking."

"I knew you wouldn't clue me in. Just forget it. It's almost seven. I'm going home. We can continue this tomorrow."

"What? Daddy's got a standing date?" I challenged.

"What is your problem?"

"Look, I don't know what you were doing last night or who you were doing it with. Frankly, whatever kinks you have are your business, but don't call me again in the middle of the night if you're with an escort."

"Where would you get an idea like that?" He looked incredulous. "I was with my daughter. She's a year and a half and doesn't believe in sleeping through the night."

"A lot of that going around," I muttered. "Either way, don't talk about open cases in front of civilians."

Now ensuring Lucca's safety was more important than before. The last thing I wanted was to be in the field with him. I was a jinx, and he had a family depending on him. He had too much to lose to risk working with me.

"You're one crazy, complicated bitch."

"Yeah, but that was too long to fit on my business card, so I just went with Alexis Parker. They're synonymous though." Collecting my files, I grabbed my purse and keys. "Have a good night, Lucca."

Intended Target

"Friggin' crazy," he mumbled to my retreating back.

FIFTEEN

When I left the OIO, I dropped by the gym. I missed the training session for the evening, but I caught up with Ron and Linka as they were getting ready to leave. After I apologized profusely for my crazy work schedule, they said the weekends were optional anyway since that's when most of the bouts occurred. Monday, they'd introduce me to a few coaches, and if no one wanted to take me on, Ron would. Agreeing to meet Monday evening, I placed my bag on the counter to search for my planner to write down the schedule while I studied the sign-in sheet from that night. The only males listed were the coaches, and once I returned to the car, I wrote down the names and headed home.

The background checks proved useless. No one had a record except Tim Coker, the owner, and I wondered if the same was true of the men who trained at the gym. Surely, whoever assaulted Fletcher must have done something similar in the past and, more than likely, had been arrested for it. Unfortunately, Jack Fletcher was proving to be one of the least helpful clients I ever had. It was a good thing I was getting out of the private investigator business.

Hours later, I was still struggling to piece the case

together. "Follow the money," I mumbled to myself. It was late. I didn't even know how late. I'd been revising my theory, starting over and revamping, only to trash everything and begin again once I hit a dead end. The money I was attempting to follow was the winnings from the illegal betting. "Cash is liquid. No paper trail." I shoved everything off the desk and onto the floor in a fit of frustration.

Drumming my fingers against the cleared desktop, I wanted to scream. Instead, I left my room in dire need of a distraction. It was two a.m., so running a few miles didn't hold that much appeal when I was this exhausted. Instead, I opened and closed every cabinet in the kitchen, starting and ending with the fridge.

"Think, Parker, just stop and fucking think." I rubbed my eyes and sat at the kitchen table with a piece of paper and pen. Two murders. One extortionist. Countless numbers of bets placed. A dead fighter. Something pinged on the last part, but I struggled to grasp a hold of it. Where did Santos train before Briscoe took him under his wing? How did he afford it? Did he owe someone money? Fighters sometimes get trained on contingency, according to what Linka said. "Stupid." I shoved the paper away, wanting nothing more than to cry. If I were working angles on the Santos' case, I'd be doing great, but that wasn't my case.

Inhaling, I read through my scribbles. William Briscoe helped train Santos. He died soon after Santos did. Maybe the only way to solve the courthouse shooting was to solve the Santos murder. But was Santos murdered? He died as the result of complications from the match. Making a note to speak to Laura and Will Jr. about their father and anything he might have known about Hector Santos, I considered calling Lucca to ask what he thought. He wanted to be in the loop, but I wasn't going to phone in the middle of the night with nothing other than conjecture. One of us should have manners. Unfortunately, this also meant I shouldn't call Nick and ask him the million questions coursing through my brain.

Unsure of what else I could possibly do and still feeling

utterly incompetent, I went up the steps. Martin was in his office, speaking with the London branch of Martin Technologies. He sounded about as frustrated as I felt.

I returned to the second floor, deciding if I wasn't going to sleep, I might as well determine everything I could about Santos' last fight. An hour into the research, I had the specifics concerning the fight. Gavin Levere was the final opponent Hector Santos fought inside the ring. The match was brutal. Levere was fast and vicious. Santos had decent technique, but from the way the hits were delivered, one would think Gavin was a mind reader. Each time Santos dropped his guard, Levere pummeled him. Levere always seemed to know what combinations Santos would use. It was like they'd been trained together or had the same trainer.

Pausing the video, I opened the databases and started a search for Levere's records. Then I shot a text to O'Connell, providing him with information on Santos' final match. He didn't respond, which meant he'd deal with it sometime after the sun came up.

As the database search ran in the background, I resumed the fight, marking down names of individuals I recognized. The only time Jack Fletcher was caught in the video was before the first bell. When the camera panned again to that vicinity two minutes later, he was gone. Other notable characters were a federal judge I'd testified in front of, Alan Ackerman, a partner at Fletcher's firm, and enough Armani and Versace to ensure the spectators were prosperous moguls of some sort.

After rewinding and hitting pause, I recognized Tim Coker standing ringside. Ron Greenwood might have been next to him, but the shot only provided the bottom portion of his face, which wasn't enough to make a positive identification. Coker was shouting something, and upon closer inspection, it seemed apparent he was instructing the fighters what to do. Then again, almost every spectator was doing the same thing. Scanning the footage again, I hoped to determine if Coker was Levere's coach, but the video was limited.

The internet search on the Santos vs. Levere fight

resulted in a few pages of images and quite a few video clips. I bookmarked the data, forwarded the information to the IT department at the OIO, and e-mailed the same thing to O'Connell's work address. Then I compiled the videos into a single playlist and stared at the computer screen. By the end, the only relevant piece of information I gained was that Tim Coker was at the fight, and Gavin Levere was his fighter.

Picking up the phone, I dialed Lucca. He answered, sounding too awake for the hour, so I said, "I might have a lead. His name's Tim Coker. He owns the gym."

"That was in yesterday's briefing."

"He coaches the fighter who's at least partially responsible for Hector Santos' death. From the way the fight played out, I'm guessing he also coached Santos at some point because Levere knew exactly what Santos' weaknesses were, and in case he forgot, Coker called out the combinations."

"That's called a stellar strategy," Lucca replied. "What does this have to do with the courthouse shooting or finding the gun?"

"Just check out Coker and see if he's a gun aficionado or had access to that type of firepower."

"The gym's your angle. Shouldn't you be looking into it?"

"We're sharing intel, remember? Plus, you're all about the gun, so I'm offering up what I know."

"What's the catch?"

"There isn't one. You can look into it or not. That's your prerogative, Agent Lucca. I'm simply being a team player."

"Did you share this with anyone else?"

"I sent it along to our computer savvy buddies."

"If they make any progress on it and they happen to tell you first, let me know."

Resisting the urge to say I wasn't his assistant either, I forced a smile onto my face in case that nonsense about being able to hear a person's smile was true and said, "Sure. No problem. I'll see you later," and disconnected before he'd say something that would lead to an unfriendly response.

The kitchen clock read 6:15, so I stretched and made a pot of coffee. I found some eggs, separated out the yolks, chopped some fresh spinach and tomatoes, and made breakfast for two. Martin stepped into the kitchen looking almost as good as I felt and poured a cup of coffee.

"Did you sleep last night?" he asked.

"No. Did you?"

"I didn't finish with London until four, and then I wanted to get a jump on the notes while everything was fresh on my mind. By the time e-mails were sent, the freaking alarm clock was going off. What'd you do all night?"

"Watched a boxing match."

"Fun." He put the cup down and hugged me. "You didn't have to cook."

"I owe you a few breakfasts."

The toast popped, and he put it on a plate.

"Did you work out this morning?"

"Yeah. It gets the blood pumping and helps with the energy levels." He narrowed his eyes. "Why?"

"I didn't hear you hitting the heavy bag."

"That's because I put in five miles on the treadmill instead." He studied me for a moment. "I know that look. You're on to something."

"I need to call my client."

"After breakfast," Martin insisted, grabbing my cell phone off the counter and slipping it into his pants pocket.

"Fine," I scooped the scrambled eggs onto the plates, "but you know I'm not afraid to dig through your pockets. I bet I could get your blood pumping faster than any treadmill."

Before he could respond, my phone rang. He held it up, examining the caller ID. "It's O'Connell."

"I need to take that," I said. He handed it to me without comment. "Oh, can you call Jen this afternoon and cancel date night? If you have to reschedule, make sure she runs the dates by Nick first. Please and thank you."

Martin raised an eyebrow, but I stepped into the other room and shut the door so I could talk in private.

"Good morning, Parker. It looks like you've been busy

working on my case. You do understand that you aren't a homicide cop or assisting the police department, right?" O'Connell asked, stifling a yawn.

"Your case was in my way. It needs to be cleared before I can do my job, and you're taking too long."

"God, you're incorrigible. What do you need me to do?"

"Run through the leads I found, send a copy of whatever information you obtain over to my office, and meet for drinks later to determine who's going to take credit for the collar."

"You're that confident something will pan out?" Nick asked, but before I could answer, he snorted. "For a moment, I forgot who I was talking to." Someone in the background called his name. "I have to go. If you don't hear from me by lunchtime, give me a call back."

"Sure, no problem."

"And don't forget about that other agreement we made."

"Martin's supposed to call her this afternoon."

"Okay, I'll talk to you later."

We disconnected, and I returned to the kitchen. I placed my phone on the table, remembered I wanted to ask Fletcher about the fighters who had been at the gym the night he went to investigate the locker, and shot him a quick text. Then I drank my weight in coffee and ate a few pieces of toast with some eggs.

"It's Sunday morning. Shouldn't we be tangled in the sheets?" Martin asked, finishing his second cup of coffee.

"I hate to break it to you, but the honeymoon's over."

"How about we spend all next weekend in bed? We'll have breakfast in bed, champagne, strawberries, whatever you want." He gave me his most disarming smile, a confident, sexy look that always made my heart flutter.

"Pizza out of the box and TV?"

"Only if you agree to no cell phones, no computers, and no work." He could drive a hard bargain, but I doubted he'd be able to agree to those terms either.

"The same goes for you?" I asked, and he nodded. "Okay, you have a deal."

"Are we packing up your apartment and moving your TV in today?"

"Probably not. I emptied my fridge, pantry, and liquor cabinet. Plus, my shoes are here, so the necessities have been taken care of. My furniture can stay there, so whenever I do stay at my place, I'll still have somewhere to sit and sleep. Most of my clothes are already here, so I don't think there's anything left to move except the TV." I shifted my gaze toward his living room. "How do you have a ridiculously large four story estate with only two televisions? Hell, I'll splurge and buy one for the bedroom. It's the least I can do to contribute."

"You don't need to do that. I have four televisions, one on the first floor near the home gym, the big screen in the living room, and one in the upstairs and downstairs offices. That's plenty. My tablet is practically a portable TV, and frankly, I don't have the time or patience to waste when I could be doing something much more fulfilling."

"Pretentious snob," I teased. "So since you offered, is that your way of telling me you're free today?"

"No, but I could carve out some time for you," Martin said. My phone beeped, indicating Fletcher had actually responded in a timely fashion. "Or not." Martin cleared the plates while I texted a time to meet at my P.I. office. "I'll be at the MT building if you realize you need someone to help you pack the rest of your belongings which you've clearly overlooked."

He went up the stairs to change, and I went into the second floor suite, grabbed whatever I thought I'd need for the day, and headed out. Hopefully, next weekend would be less chaotic.

SIXTEEN

After I caught Fletcher up to speed on his case, which turned out to also be the OIO's case and the PD's case, he pulled out a few business cards. "Copy the information I've given you and staple this card to the top." He dug through his wallet. "That's my attorney. Please tell whatever investigator has a question to speak to him first."

"Jack, I'm not telling you that you shouldn't protect yourself, but time is of the essence. You're supposed to make the drop Wednesday evening. That's three days from now. By making the authorities jump through additional hoops, you'll slow down their work and the chance to catch this guy in the act."

"We'll see. In the meantime, why don't you show me those snapshots? I'll see if I recognize any of them from Thursday night."

I turned my computer monitor to an angle we could both see and clicked through a few photos of fighters and coaches from Tim Coker's gym. He identified Coker as the man he spoke to, but Fletcher didn't remember him from the fight circuit. Then again, I doubted he paid much attention to anyone except the fighters. He also pointed out Gavin Levere and another fighter, Elias Facini.

"Those two men put you in the emergency room? How severe were your injuries?"

"Mostly bruises. Nothing substantial enough to report."

"It's still assault, and we're reporting now. Were you aware Levere was the other fighter on the ticket the night Santos died?" I asked, and Fletcher nodded. "That's important. That's called a clue. That...," I paused, my brain narrowing in on the possibility Coker and Levere both had motive for blackmailing Fletcher, "might be our guy." I dialed O'Connell's number. As soon as he answered, I asked, "Do you have Levere in custody yet?"

"A couple of uniforms are bringing him in now. Do you want to drop by to watch the interview?" O'Connell asked.

"Yes, but more importantly, I'm with someone who would like to file assault charges against Levere and another boxer by the name of Elias Facini. He also has additional information to share, and since I'm being so generous, I need a guarantee that you'll work with the OIO and share your intel and copies of your interviews and evidence lists. Can I count on that?"

"The LT isn't going to like it."

"Tell Lieutenant Moretti to duke it out with Jablonsky. Our bosses can fight their own battles. You and I are on the same page, right?"

"Yeah, okay. It's not like you'd take no for an answer anyway," O'Connell said. "Be here in an hour."

Putting the phone back in its cradle, I eyed Fletcher. "Detective O'Connell is a good cop. He'll get to the bottom of this. He won't do anything to unnecessarily jeopardize your career or standing in the legal community. But if you want your attorney around, call him and have him meet us at the precinct within the hour. They're moving on this now."

"Now?"

"Yes. Do you really believe law enforcement spends Sunday afternoons golfing at the country club?" I picked up my keys and led him to the door, locking up my P.I. office. "I trust you will meet me there."

"Of course, Ms. Parker." He went to his car and drove away while I dialed Lucca to update him on what was going on.

When I arrived at the precinct, Lucca was waiting. He nodded in my direction and held the door for me. I led the way up the steps to the major crimes unit. Even though it was Sunday, he was dressed in regulation attire. Maybe he didn't own anything besides dark suits, white shirts, and skinny black ties.

O'Connell was speaking to Fletcher, and I didn't want to interrupt. Instead, I took a seat at Heathcliff's vacant desk and kicked a chair out for Lucca. He sat without a word, looking like the cat that swallowed the canary.

"How'd you get here so fast?" I asked, my eyes darting across the room to see if any of our suspects had been brought in.

"I was in the neighborhood." He spun in the chair, watching O'Connell. "I have a friend who works for ESU. I was asking him about the weapon you found, and we checked out a dozen shooting clubs and ranges this morning. Sunday's a popular day. He asked a few of his owner pals to voluntarily turn over their surveillance footage," Lucca patted his breast pocket, "but before I could take this back to the federal building, you called and said you were on your way here."

"Does any of that look promising?" I jerked my chin at the disks in his pocket.

"I don't know yet." He cocked his head to the side. "Weren't you wearing that yesterday?"

"So?"

He went to the coffeepot in the corner, filled a paper cup, and put it on the desk in front of me. "How many all-nighters do you pull in a typical month?"

"A couple. It depends on how intricate a case is or how many cases we might be working at any given time." I noticed O'Connell standing behind Lucca.

"Parker," O'Connell said, having heard Lucca's random question, "shit, she's practically a vampire. After all, she has the same degree as most bloodsuckers."

Glaring, I raised my middle finger.

"And the personality to match." O'Connell extended his hand to Lucca. "Nick O'Connell, her favorite detective."

"Eddie Lucca, her least favorite partner," he replied, shaking O'Connell's hand.

"We are not partners."

"I see what you mean." O'Connell chuckled. "Now if the two of you would be kind enough to follow me, I'd like a few words in private before I have to interview possible murder suspects."

O'Connell led us into the observation room that connected to the interrogation room and closed the door. He cocked a questioning eyebrow in my direction, unsure of how much information Lucca possessed on my extracurricular activities. I shook my head, hoping he'd understand my P.I. business was indeed private.

"Detective," I began, "Elias Facini and Gavin Levere both participated in the assault. Furthermore, it's my understanding that Tim Coker, the gym owner, instructed Facini and Levere to scare off Mr. Fletcher."

"And since Levere might be the fighter responsible for Hector Santos' death, that further complicates matters. Not to mention, the man he assaulted is also the victim of a blackmail scheme," O'Connell said. "Do I have that straight, Parker?"

"Yep."

"Okay." O'Connell shifted his gaze from Lucca back to me. "What I'm not entirely clear on is why the two of you are taking up space inside the precinct."

"Hector Santos has a direct connection to a murdered juror we're investigating," Lucca said, unwilling to reveal his cards.

"William Briscoe is our dead juror. From the intel I've gathered, he was training Hector Santos. But he wasn't always Santos' coach. Based upon the recording of Hector's final match, I'm confident Tim Coker coached Levere and Santos. It might go to motive for Levere being too aggressive, resulting in Santos' unfortunate death," I speculated.

"And it gives Levere a reason to blackmail a spectator and rough him up," O'Connell added, contemplating his own theory. "Or Coker could have been pissed Santos abandoned ship. Do you think one of these three men is your shooter?"

Lucca and I exchanged a look. "I hope so because we're out of leads," I admitted.

"We need something solid on them," Lucca said. "Right now, we don't have enough to get a warrant. Our accountants have looked through the public records, and I've fought tooth and nail to pull gun licenses and purchase orders. If you can make some charge stick, it'll open up a lot of information to further scrutiny. It could be the break we've been waiting for."

I stared at Lucca, wondering how he'd figured out precisely what my plan had been.

He met my gaze. "Oh, come on, Parker, you basically said as much on the phone. I do know how to read between the lines."

"Do you want to sit in on the interrogation?" O'Connell asked.

"I can't. The guys at the gym might recognize me. If this doesn't pan out, I need to maintain another method of gathering evidence."

Lucca considered it for a moment before shaking his head. "It'll make our investigation look like a fishing expedition. It'd probably be best if you pretended we weren't even here."

O'Connell laughed. "Sure, I'll give that a try."

He went into the interrogation room and stood in the corner, leaning against the wall with his arms folded across his chest. A minute later, a uniformed officer brought Gavin Levere into the room. The man wasn't even handcuffed since this was a courtesy visit before charges were actually filed. My guess was Fletcher was still on the fence about pressing charges.

"Stay here and take some notes," I said. "I'll be right back."

I returned to the bullpen to find Fletcher sitting at O'Connell's desk, whispering to a man I assumed was his attorney. His eyes met mine, and he offered a slight smile and introduced us.

"Are you waiting for an officer to take your statement, or did you forget the reason we came to the precinct?" I asked.

"Hopefully, none of that will be necessary," Fletcher's counsel responded. "The detective believes he can hold Mr. Levere on manslaughter charges, and as far as the other fighter, we'll see how things play out."

"Mr. Fletcher," I directed my comment to my client, "you know me. You know what we discussed, and you know exactly how many friends I have and who they are. Despite that, I can't make any rock solid assurances. You know I'll do whatever I can, but you need to cooperate." I glanced at Fletcher's attorney. "No offense," I said to the other man before focusing my attention back to Fletcher, "but this guy's an idiot."

"How is that not offensive, miss?"

"Fine, I'm sorry you're an idiot, but you don't understand what's going on or why this is important. Your priority is to your client, but there is more to the story." I spoke again to Fletcher, blocking out his attorney. "Look, if you end up being blackballed, I'm sure someone could be persuaded to hire you, but we need to stop this blackmailer. Since he went after you, I'd bet my badge he's doing the same thing to someone else."

"You're positive the only way you can stop him is by squeezing the men who assaulted me?" Fletcher asked, sounding resolved to this course of action.

I nodded. "And the gym owner too."

"Fine." Fletcher turned to his counsel. "Go find someone to take my statement. I have a lot of things to get off my chest." The other man looked at him like he was crazy, met my eyes which were full of cold determination, shook his head, and went to speak to the desk sergeant down the hall. Once he was gone, Fletcher focused on me. "I'm sorry, Ms. Parker. I've jerked you around quite a bit. I just haven't been able to figure out what the right move is, but since you say this is it, I'll accept it. I've seen you pull off a miracle or two. I'd appreciate it if you could do the same thing for me now."

"I'm working on it."

After an officer came to take Fletcher's statement and I made sure to insist this information went straight to Det.

O'Connell, I returned to the observation room. Lucca was watching through the two-way glass while he spoke on the phone to someone at the OIO. From his side of the conversation, it sounded like he wanted the forensic accountants to check Tim Coker's gym for any drastic monetary fluctuations in the last two years.

O'Connell asked Levere about the fight, his training regimen, and why he didn't come forward after news broke of Hector Santos' death inside the ER waiting room. Levere, as expected, insisted he was afraid the police would blame him. It would permanently stall his chances of becoming a professional boxer, and his coach told him to keep his mouth shut. At least the guy wasn't chivalrous enough to take the blame, probably since a voluntary manslaughter charge came with quite a few years, even if it was child's play compared to murder.

As soon as Levere admitted Tim Coker was his coach, the police had enough to bring him in. That was our cue to leave. I focused on Lucca who just concluded his call, practically chuckling.

"How did you pull this off?" he asked.

"I told you not to question my hunches or methods." Now that the evidence indicated I was no longer a raving lunatic, Lucca wanted to play nice again, but I was too tired to deal with him. "It's Sunday. Go back to the office, send out a few e-mails to update the team, drop off those surveillance tapes, and go home. Don't let this job consume you. The police are busy working on their own case and leads. They won't have anything concrete for us until tomorrow. So you should call it a day."

"Is that what you're planning to do?"

"What I do has no bearing on you, and frankly, it's none of your business. Now go."

"Damn, Parker, you're even more intolerable when you haven't slept, and that's really saying something." He went to the door, finally obeying one of my commands.

With Lucca gone, I returned to the bullpen, read the information Fletcher provided the police, made a photocopy for myself while O'Connell was distracted, took a seat at his desk, and propped my legs up. When Nick returned, he pushed me out of the way and clicked a few things on his computer.

"I'll put a rush on it, but until we get a handle on this situation and get a court order to search and confiscate some evidence, there's nothing else I can do to help the investigation along," O'Connell said.

"That's all right. You're doing what you can. I appreciate it."

"So that's your new partner?" O'Connell asked, resting his hips against the desk and facing me. "He doesn't seem so bad."

"He's not my partner. I don't do partners. You know that, but apparently, Jablonsky hasn't gotten the memo."

"Just like he didn't get the memo that you're moonlighting on the side?"

"No, he knows about that. Unofficially, anyway." I blew out a breath. "Try to keep Fletcher insulated from as much of this as you can." Reluctantly, I stood, feeling the fatigue setting in. "And feel free to work the blackmail angle in addition to Santos' death, if you're so inclined. As far as I know, those cases are out of my jurisdiction."

"I liked it better when you refused to share."

"I'll share Lucca with you too. Shit, you can have him." My eyes went to Detective Heathcliff's desk. "At least you know how to keep your people safe. It's when they get around me that they start having problems."

"Alex, it's not you." He noted the dark rings underneath my eyes. "We've talked about triggers and trauma before. Do you want to meet up for a drink and chat?"

"You're not my shrink. Now get back to work because I'd like to see some progress by tomorrow. If you'll excuse me, I'm going home and straight to bed."

He looked at his watch. "It's only two thirty."

"Damn. Now I have to come up with another plan, and that will probably involve packing and moving."

SEVENTEEN

My brain was fried. Too many sleepless nights and long hours had finally taken their toll. My concentration was shot to hell. After leaving the precinct, I stopped by my apartment, figuring I'd make some type of effort to pack something and make Martin happy, but instead, I took a seat at the island in my kitchen and stared at the wall. At some point, I must have brewed a pot of coffee because there was a steaming mug in front of me.

Deciding that I was useless, I went into my bedroom and climbed into bed. I wasn't much of a napper, but I hadn't slept in far too long. My thoughts were random, shifting from the fighters to Stan Weaver to moving my clothes upstairs to Martin's bedroom, but even though my mind was all over the place and I was physically and mentally exhausted, I couldn't fall asleep. Blaming it on the time of day, I scanned the items in my closet and dresser, feeling disconnected from my own life. This was my apartment. My bed. My belongings. But I couldn't find anything I wanted to bring to Martin's. In a last-ditch effort, I grabbed my pillow and coffee mug. Clearly, I was the least materialistic person in the world or the least adjusted.

When I made it back to Martin's that evening, I microwaved a frozen dinner that had come from my apartment on an earlier trip, stuck my now empty mug in the dishwasher, and went into the guestroom. Mentally, I tried to remind myself it was now my home office, but I didn't possess the brain power to retain the thought. Opening my laptop, I sprawled out on the bed and checked my e-mail, seeing messages from O'Connell and Lucca on the progress that had been made. I began a search on a list of names connected to Tim Coker and the gym and let my eyes close while the database search was conducted.

At some point, I felt a presence in the room and opened my eyes. Martin had closed my laptop and was placing it back on the desk. He realized I was awake and made a shhh sound before I could voice a protest that I needed to get back to work. Deciding it wasn't worth arguing, I rolled onto my side.

"Alex, lift up for a second," he insisted. When I complied, he tucked a pillow underneath my head.

When I opened my eyes again, I was on my stomach. Martin's hand was next to mine, and he had covered my body with his, trapping me between him and the mattress. We shared a single pillow, our legs tangled together. Someone had one hell of a learning curve. Lacing my fingers over his, I brought his hand to my lips and kissed his palm. He nuzzled against my neck as I shifted onto my side. He looped a leg over both of mine and tucked me tighter against his body.

"What are you doing?" I asked, realizing we were sleeping with our heads at the bottom of the bed, practically diagonal and on top of the covers.

"Making sure you can't escape." He kissed my temple, pulling me closer like a child with a favorite stuffed bear. "I'm tired of sleeping alone. If this is what it takes, then so be it." He closed his eyes. "Go back to sleep. It's five a.m. Neither of us needs to be at work before nine."

I flipped onto my back, but his grip remained firm. "What if I have another nightmare?"

"Relax. The only way you can hurt me is by leaving this bed." His green eyes opened, and he studied my expression. His uncertainty startled me.

I gave him a reassuring kiss. "Apparently, I'm not going anywhere."

We slept for another three hours until the obnoxious sound from his alarm clock ruined the peace and tranquility. He turned it off but didn't make a move to get out of bed. Instead, he surveyed the random half-unpacked boxes from his prone position.

"I'm clearing my schedule for this weekend. We're meeting the O'Connells for date night this Friday instead of next Friday, but after that, you and I are spending the rest of the weekend together. I don't care if it's in this bed or upstairs. It doesn't even have to be in bed. Just this once, I'll settle for the couch."

"I don't know if my case will be solved by then. We keep hitting dead ends."

"Then let someone else worry about it. I know your work is important, but I miss my girlfriend. If that makes me a selfish prick, I really don't care. You moved in because you wanted to prove you were just as committed to me as you are to your job, but I've barely seen you since you took up permanent residence here. I saw you more before we started living together. Don't deny it, Alex. You know it's true. And now that you're freaked out about sharing a bed, I've had to resort to some pretty drastic measures."

"Doubling as a blanket is pretty drastic," I joked, running my fingers along the muscles of his arm. "Next, you'll attempt to impersonate the throw pillows."

"You typically use me as a pillow anyway, so that wouldn't be nearly as drastic. Stop worrying so much. I'm okay. There's not a single doubt in my mind that we can cohabitate without you killing me."

"That makes one of us." I sighed. "Fine, I'll see what progress O'Connell and Lucca have made. If we haven't made an arrest by Friday, I'll leave it up to them." I climbed out of bed and opened my laptop. "You probably should have let me work last night."

"You needed sleep, and I needed you." He left the room as I restarted my computer to see what progress had been made while I prepared for another day at the office.

*   *   *

When I arrived at the OIO building, the room was abuzz with activity. It had been a while since the perception of progress had permeated the walls of the federal building. I couldn't help but absorb the optimistic attitude. The fact that I actually had a good night's sleep didn't hurt either.

"Where are we on the gun clubs?" I asked Lucca. "I got your e-mail. It sounds like things look rather promising."

"The ink is drying on a search warrant as we speak. Elias Facini has a membership to Stover's Gun Club. He trained at the police academy before getting bumped out on account of a busted eardrum. According to Mr. Stover, Facini spends hours on the exterior range every other week."

"What's his weapon of choice?"

"A M24."

"His own?"

"No, according to Stover, he always rents a gun for the day, pays for a box of ammunition, and refills it with his empty casings. I've searched the registry, but he doesn't have any legal firearms."

"What do you hope to find with the search warrant?"

"A box of ammunition, a scope or sight, a wind gauge, the realtor's business card. At this point, anything that will put him in that office building or tie him to the gun used works for me."

"Did you ask Sylvia Britt if she recognized him?" I thought back, but Facini wasn't one of the bidders. Flipping through the pages on Lucca's desk, I found Facini's driver's license photo. He could be the shooter, or he could be just an average Joe, if average Joe was in line to be the next big-time middleweight boxer.

"Britt didn't recall the name. After we conduct the search, I'll drop by her office and run his photo past her."

"Is he still in police custody?"

"I assume so," Lucca said, looking at me expectantly.

"Okay, I'll call O'Connell and find out what happened

with the fighters. If Facini's still being held, we might be able to ask a few unofficial questions before we request a custody transfer."

"Wow, you sound certain we have the guy. Does that mean I actually did something right?"

"Perhaps, but you should refrain from gloating until this is a slam dunk. We need to place Facini at the scene and come up with a motive."

Lucca gestured to the phone on my desk. "Then by all means, Parker, I'll let you get started on that."

Sliding over to my desk, I dialed O'Connell's work number. From the message he left last night, he had brought Coker, Facini, and Levere in for questioning, but the information Jack Fletcher gave him wasn't enough to hold Coker on anything. So once Tim decided he was tired of answering questions, he walked out of the police station.

Facini and Levere were another story. They were being held for assault and battery. Since they were brought in on a Sunday afternoon, the police had taken a creative license to avoid officially booking them until today. At the moment, they had legal counsel vying to get them an appearance before a judge and released on their own recognizance.

"The best way to deal with blackmail is to lay every card on the table in order to take back power," O'Connell said. "Fletcher's an attorney. He should know this. Why in the world did he want to keep it quiet?"

"So you think the blackmail and Santos' death are related?"

"Of course, they are. What we're working on now is determining if Santos' was allowed to continue the fight beyond a reasonable point in the hopes that something like this would happen. I watched the video of the fight. I'm not positive someone didn't rough Santos up after the match ended. The kid got the shit knocked out of him quite a few times, but he seemed coherent. Detective Thompson is reconstructing what happened after the match. I'm hopeful it might implicate at least one of the men we questioned."

"So in other words, you're working on it."

"Yeah. When I know more, I'll let you know."

I blew out a breath and swiveled my chair around to face Lucca. He was staring at me again, but this time, it wasn't nearly as disconcerting. He nodded at my phone, wanting to know what progress the police department had made.

"They'll get back to us," I said.

"And you're positive a dead fighter and a blackmailed corporate attorney are connected to the murders of an Assistant U.S. Attorney and a juror." From his facial expression, I was uncertain if Lucca was asking a question, recapping what we'd been over a hundred times, or just busting my balls.

"Do you have a better theory?"

He stood from his desk, going across to the conference room. Not bothering to wait for a formal invitation, I followed him inside. Hopping onto the table, I kicked my heel against the leg while he reread the notes.

"We haven't found any suspicious financial activity in the public record. Our court orders have been limited due to a lack of evidence, but it doesn't look like the shooter was hired. Facini looks good for the murders. The thing is," Lucca spun to face me, "he didn't have any reason to kill Stan Weaver. From what I've gathered, the two men have never met. Facini doesn't have a criminal record. No ties to gangs or drugs. He grew up in the 'burbs and wanted to be a cop."

"That's because Weaver wasn't the target. How many times do I have to say it before it sinks into your brain? William Briscoe was the target."

"Okay, so why would a perfectly upstanding citizen want to kill another upstanding citizen? Did the two men even know each other? Because I don't see a connection there either."

"The gym. Briscoe coached the youth boxing class with Hector Santos and helped Santos train."

"I know, but that doesn't explain a relationship between Briscoe and Facini. It could just be a coincidence."

"There is no such thing." Getting down from the table, I stared at the board again. "I have to talk to Laura and Will. They can tell us who their dad knew and who he crossed paths with."

"Facini's still our best bet. None of the surveillance footage I pulled showed anyone even closely resembling Tim Coker or Gavin Levere. None of the men have a registered weapon. No one has military training. The partial serial number we pulled off the Remington doesn't match sales to anyone. The experts were thinking it was a hot weapon that had a number re-etched over the previous one."

"How is that even possible?"

"Precision welding or metal works professionals could probably do the job. It requires patience and the proper equipment." His gaze shifted to the door. "I don't think it will lead to our killer. I think that's why the shooter left it behind. He knew it wouldn't trace back to him."

"So your plan to make a positive ID just went straight to the crapper?" I asked, and he shrugged. "Okay, so what's plan B?"

"Forensics is still scrubbing footage. The accountants are analyzing financials. I'm hoping you'll let me assist on your lead since it's now our only remaining course of action."

Considering my options, I sighed. "Fine, but you'll do what I say, when I say it. And you won't speak unless someone specifically asks you something, and even then, feel free to pretend you're mute."

"Any other rules?"

"Most importantly, don't get shot."

He cocked his head to the side, a question forming on his lips, but I strode out of the room, grabbing my jacket and keys off of my desk and heading for the elevator. Surprisingly, Lucca managed to squeeze inside before the doors closed. He remained silent while I drove to Laura Briscoe's apartment. The poor girl had enough on her plate without having to answer our questions, but it was the only way to find a connection.

"You're probably right," Lucca said when I pulled the car to a stop a few blocks from the apartment building. "It wouldn't make sense that two deaths weren't connected when the two decedents knew each other, but Weaver died from a headshot. And the venue makes no sense."

"Our killer's brilliant and wants to distract and throw us off the scent," I said, even though I lacked confidence in my own words.

"No," Lucca thought for a few moments, squinting into the distance and rubbing the tips of his fingers together, "something else is going on here. Could Weaver have been blackmailed too? Does he have any connection to this underground fight scene? He was a federal prosecutor which makes him a lawyer by default."

"Nothing supports it, and it makes our shooter seem like one of the best. If he was one of the best, I doubt two men would be dead. He would have taken a second shot and plugged Briscoe in the skull after he slumped back into his chair. It would have been too sloppy to walk away with a potential survivor."

"Which still makes me think Weaver was the target."

"The shooter panicked. He fired and took off. Did you check the timestamps at the office building? We can place him in the hallway at almost the same time the courthouse reports shots fired. He fired and freaked. He probably bolted down the stairs, dumped the bag, and took off out of the building."

"How did he get home?" Lucca asked, already formulating a new thought and grabbing his phone. "Pull transit records for the nearest subway and bus stops in the immediate vicinity and find out what cab companies generally hang out near the courthouse. It's a busy place, so see if you can find a hack that services the area. Our shooter had to escape somehow," Lucca said into the phone and disconnected. "Thanks for helping with plan B, Parker."

EIGHTEEN

I sat next to Laura Briscoe on the couch. She lifted her teacup to her lips and stared at the ceiling, willing the tears not to fall. We had made little progress on account of her upset state. The funeral was postponed since her father's homicide was still being investigated. In the meantime, she and Will had picked out a plot, ordered a headstone, and contacted whatever friends and extended family they had.

"Will should be back any minute. He went to book a block of rooms at a hotel," she said, sniffling. "He has my credit card, but it's been almost impossible to explain that we need the rooms but we don't know when we'll need them. At least we worked that out this morning with one of the nicer chains."

"It's good you can depend on each other at times like these," Lucca said, ignoring one of my rules.

"Would you mind telling us a bit more about your father's friends and hobbies?" I asked. "He volunteered at the rec center, right?"

"Yeah. Giving back was very important to him. He was helping this guy teach a class. I think they trained on the side too." She shook her head. "I can't remember what Daddy said." She rubbed her eyes and gripped her teacup tighter. "I should have paid more attention to his stories, but it was always something."

"Take your time," I said. "Anything that you might remember about his routine or who your father saw on a regular basis could help us determine what happened."

She fidgeted, sighing as her eyes darted back and forth as if she were watching a tennis match. "He traveled to a lot of grocery stores and supermarkets in the tri-state area as part of his job. Dad was a sales rep for a produce company. They prominently supported the area farmers with locally grown, organic items."

"Did he get along with everyone at work?" Lucca asked.

"Yeah, they were great. His boss sent over that fruit basket." She pointed to a large arrangement on the kitchen counter. "A couple of the ladies there called to find out when the service would be. They're just as devastated as we are."

"What about the people at the recreational center? Have any of them called?" I asked.

She shook her head. "I don't think they're even aware of what happened. Dad was just a volunteer." She sighed again and went into the kitchen. "Will might know more about that. Dad was always pestering him to volunteer somewhere. Since my brother couldn't be bothered to commit to a job, Dad thought he might find his way by helping others." A whimper escaped, and she blew her nose. "He was a really good father. But Will can be difficult at times, so Dad was trying a more tough love approach. He figured if Will saw how good he had it compared to a lot of less fortunate people, he'd go back to school and make something of himself."

"I take it they didn't see eye to eye," I said.

"That's why Will's taking this so hard. I can't even imagine what he's thinking. He took Dad for granted, and now, he can't fix it." She trembled, excusing herself and dashing into the other room and closing the door.

"Great way to clear a room, Parker," Lucca whispered.

"Shut it, boy scout. Why don't you do something helpful and get in contact with William Briscoe's boss and co-workers and see what you can find out?"

"Are you sure you can handle this situation alone?"

"Go."

Lucca went to the door, opening it just as Will attempted to unlock the door. They uttered a few cordial words, and then Will came inside. He took one look at me, and his face filled with anger.

"Where's my sister?" he asked.

"Bedroom." I jerked my chin toward the doorway. "Do you mind if I ask you a few questions? We didn't exactly get off on the right foot the other day."

"Did you find out who killed my dad?"

"Not yet."

"Then I don't have anything to say to you." He heard a muffled sob from the back hallway. "Get the fuck out of here. Can't you see that you are making this worse?"

"I apologize, but I want the person responsible to be caught just as badly as you do." My attempt to reason with him appeared to be working, so I forged ahead before he could change his mind. "Laura said you might know something about your father's volunteer work at the rec center. Maybe you can tell me if he had a problem with anyone there or what his schedule was like on a daily basis."

Will dropped onto the other end of the couch and rubbed his eyes. "Dad never had any problems from what I know. He wanted me to help out. He introduced me to some boxer one time. Um...," he frowned, thinking, "I don't know what the guy's name was. He was younger than me, but he and my dad were tight. Like best buds tight." The anger burned in his eyes. "Maybe you should ask him about it. He knew my dad better than I did."

I pulled out Hector Santos' driver's license photo and held it out to Will. "Is this the guy your father introduced you to?"

He looked at it, his fists clenching, and turned away. "Yeah, that's him."

"Would you mind taking a look at a few other photographs? Perhaps you might recognize someone else."

"If I do this, will you go away and leave us the hell alone?"

"Sure." I handed him the photos, and he flipped through them. I studied his expression as he sifted through the prints. Suddenly, Will looked alarmed. He swallowed, pulling himself unsteadily off the couch. "What is it?"

"Do you think one of these men killed my dad?"

"I don't know. We're following leads."

"That means these are the suspects. One of them did this?" He dropped the stack of photos on the table. "One of them did this," he repeated, bolting out the door.

"Will," I called after him. I grabbed my cell, dialing Lucca. "Will Briscoe took off. Don't let him get past you."

"Shit, Parker, you really are an expert at clearing a room. Why don't you pull the fire alarm and clear the whole damn building while you're at it?"

Disconnecting, I stared at the photo on the table. It was the same image that had shaken Will—the photo of Gavin Levere. While I collected the glossy prints, Laura returned from the bedroom. Her eyes were red, her cheeks blotchy.

"Where's Will? I heard his voice."

"He was upset. My...partner," I practically choked on the word, "will bring him back here." I shoved everything into the folder and tucked it underneath my arm. Laura had already reviewed the photos and had been unable to identify any of the men. "I'm sorry to put you through this. Like I said last time, if you remember anything, please give me a call. I should go, so you can grieve in peace. I am sorry for your loss."

I took the stairs down to the car. Slowing my pace as I opened the front door, I didn't want to cause another scene with Will Briscoe. Hopefully, Lucca was able to calm him down. Maybe he even got the kid to open up about why that photo caused such a reaction, but instead, the only person I found outside the building was Lucca.

"Where's Will? I thought you were going to stop him from leaving," I said.

"He didn't leave. He hasn't gone past me. Maybe he snuck out the back or something."

"And you call yourself an FBI agent."

"I'm not the one who scared him off." Lucca watched me shove the file into the back of the car. "Should we go find him?"

Will's expression right before he bolted left an uneasy feeling in the pit of my stomach. He knew more than he let on. "He might need to blow off some steam, but the kid's going to get himself into trouble. I showed him the photos, and Levere's mug freaked him out. He knows something, but he's not talking." Looking back at the building, I felt confident the side entrance and fire escapes both led to dead ends, but I wasn't positive. "Check around back. I'll go inside and see if he's hiding out somewhere in the building."

"Okay." Lucca gave the front door a final look and went around the side of the building.

As I went from floor to floor, my mind attempted to postulate the reason for Will Briscoe's outburst and errant behavior. He must know Levere, but I wasn't sure how. Will didn't recall Santos' name, and he didn't mention his father introducing him to any of the other fighters. Perhaps he had gone to a few of the matches. My phone rang as I continued up the steps.

"Parker, get to the roof now," Lucca said, "and whatever you do, don't act like your normal pain in the ass self. The police and fire department are on the way. I'll meet you up there."

"Shit." I ran up the stairs, taking them two at a time, and burst out the roof exit. Will Briscoe was on the edge of the roof. We were eleven stories high, and he was too close to the edge for my comfort. Startling him wasn't recommended, but I had to do something. "Hey, Will, nice view, huh?"

He looked over his shoulder at me but didn't say anything. With any luck, he had no intention of jumping, and Lucca was making a mountain out of a molehill. Will took a deep breath and stepped closer to the edge. Slowly, I approached him, making the conscious effort not to look down. Heights weren't my thing.

"Why shouldn't I do it?" he asked, far too calmly for someone who was acting on nothing more than impulse.

"It would hurt your sister and ruin everyone's day." Negotiating wasn't my forte either, and now I was negotiating on a rooftop. Clearly, I was the universe's punching bag. "You don't want to hurt Laura. She needs you. You're all she has left."

"I already hurt her." He turned sideways, stepping over the safety bar, so he could face me and be closer to the edge. "She'd be better off without me."

"That's not true."

"Bullshit." He leaned closer to the edge and peered down.

"Fine, let's talk about what happens when you jump. I'm aware of three possibilities. One, you survive, but you're a vegetable, dependent on her for the rest of your life because you didn't pick a high enough roof."

"Really?" His eyes shot to mine, pondering the truth of that statement.

I had no idea if it was humanly possible to survive an eleven story drop, but it was working to buy time. "Stranger things happen all the time. The human body is resilient." I shrugged, easing closer. "Is it really worth the risk?" He moved closer to the edge, and I resisted the urge to lunge for him. "Wait. At least tell me why you suddenly decided to do this."

"What were those other two possibilities?" he asked. "You said there were three. What were the other two?"

"Look, I'll make a deal with you. I'll tell you the other two if you tell me why you want to do this. Then if you still want to jump, I'll turn around and let you do it."

"You first," he insisted.

"Fine. Jumpers sometimes turn into human eggrolls. The outside looks fine, but your insides are pulverized into bloody, mangled pieces. The coroner will cut you open, and the gooey flows out. Your bones and organs and blood will pour right off the table and into the drain." Okay, so I was embellishing for dramatic effect. "I guess they could stuff you like a taxidermy project if you want an open casket at the funeral." I narrowed my eyes at him. "Laura will have to plan that one too, won't she?"

"Stop." He rubbed his eyes and put both hands on top of his head, trying to think.

"Three. You go splat. On impact, your body explodes.

Think of a water balloon filled with red paint. That would be you."

He looked queasy and teetered. I stepped closer, only ten feet away from him at this point.

"Don't do it," I said gently.

"I should."

"Why?"

"Because," he swallowed, leaning his calves against the outer side of the safety bar, "I'm the reason my dad is dead."

"Did you pull the trigger?" Adding some logic and rationale to the situation could only help, I hoped.

"No."

"Did you hire a contract killer to pull the trigger?"

"No." That time he sounded less certain.

"Then you aren't responsible."

"Yes, I am." He rubbed his eyes again. "One of those guys from the photos is another fighter. I told him about my dad and how he was training that other guy on the side, and he got really pissed. He said my dad would pay." Will scrunched up his face, fighting back his tears by gritting his teeth. "I wanted him to make my dad pay. I wanted him to hurt my dad. I just wanted Dad to stop spending all of his time with those losers. He always thought they were better than me. He...," Will made a choking sound and stepped onto the ledge, placing his toes at the end of the cement, "he's dead because of me."

"Will, look at me." My voice turned hard and forceful. He shifted his gaze from the street below to me. "It's not your fault. It sounds like you're the only one who can tell us exactly what happened. Without you, we'll never find the guy who killed your dad. We need you. Laura needs you. If you do this, she'll never forgive you. Do you really hate your sister so much to hurt her like this?"

"I don't hate her," he sniffled, rubbing his nose with the back of his hand, "but she'll hate me when she finds out."

"No, she won't. The only way she'll hate you is if you die and leave her alone. Trust me, I know that for a fact."

"How?"

"Because I lost someone, and it was my fault. At least it

felt like it." I lifted one leg over the safety bar, inching closer. Worst case, I'd handcuff myself to Will and hope he wouldn't swan dive and kill us both. A bitter laugh escaped my throat, and Will focused his attention on me, distracted by my story. "That stupid son of a bitch said it was okay. He said those exact words, that it was okay. He didn't blame me. He knew I would never do anything to hurt him, but shit happens. We're human, and we make mistakes. After he died, it destroyed me." I reached for Will's arm. Luckily, he didn't jerk away. "Maybe he could forgive me for making a mistake, but I can't forgive him for taking the easy way out and leaving me here. This is the hard part, figuring out how to survive alone. Don't chicken out on me, Will. Don't put Laura through that kind of torment."

"I...I..." Will seemed conflicted. He leaned forward again.

I had been so focused on Will that I didn't notice Lucca until he snuck up behind him, grabbing Will's shoulders and hauling him over the safety bar. Will tumbled backward, sprawling onto his back. Lucca flipped him onto his stomach and cuffed him, handing him off to a pair of uniformed police officers.

"Take it easy, guys," I called after them. "He's a material witness."

"Agent Parker?" Will sounded small and afraid, which made little sense now that he was actually safe and no longer staring his impending death straight in the eye. Then again, the thought of living could be more frightening than the alternative. "What's going to happen now?"

"We'll get this straightened out. We'll talk to your sister in the meantime. Everything's going to be fine," I promised as the door opened, and the cops hauled him out of view.

Lucca held out his hand, offering to help me over, and I realized I was straddling the safety bar. "Should I radio down to the fire department and tell them to hold off on removing the giant air bag?" he asked.

"Don't be ridiculous. Heights scare the shit out of me." I grasped his hand and stepped back onto slightly more stable ground. "Thanks for the assist."

"What were you planning to do?"

"Cuff him and hope and he didn't take a header off the side."

"That's not protocol."

"I never said it was." Taking a steadying breath, the seriousness of the situation sunk in, making my legs wobble. "Can we continue this conversation inside?"

"Sure, Parker, whatever you want."

NINETEEN

Lucca calmly explained the situation to Laura Briscoe while I answered the questions the responding officers asked and phoned Jablonsky to fill him in on what would become today's action report. Then I called Detective O'Connell and informed him of a potential witness and possible break in his case, hoping he could do something to get us access to Will while he was undergoing the mandatory psych hold and evaluation. Unfortunately, a detective's badge didn't trump a state-appointed psychiatrist.

"More than likely, we have a seventy-two hour moratorium on our hands," I said to Lucca.

"You did what you could. Did Will Briscoe say anything useful while you were on the roof?"

"He admitted to speaking to Levere about his dad and Santos, but he didn't go into detail."

"I'm surprised you managed to talk him down or at least delay him from jumping. I figured he would have gone over the edge just to get away from you." Lucca laughed, indicating it was a joke. "You did a decent job, keeping him distracted. I don't think he realized the fire department was set up below." I hadn't realized it either, but I kept my mouth shut. "Laura's beside herself, but she called a friend.

I don't think we need to worry about her."

Opening the car door, I climbed into the driver's seat and rested my forehead against the steering wheel. "Did I miss the warning signs with Will Briscoe?"

"He was clearly distraught over his father's murder, but that's understandable. He didn't seem particularly fond of you, but once again, completely understandable. So I don't think we missed anything." Lucca fastened his seatbelt. "It's okay."

Pulling my head from the wheel, I turned the key, uncomfortable with his final statement. I had said those exact words to Will on the roof, and now I was wondering how long Lucca had been up there. What did he hear?

On the drive back to the office, the question continued to nag at me. After I parked in the garage beneath the building, I turned to face Lucca. "How long were you out there?"

"Long enough to wonder if you might be considering jumping off the roof too."

"I don't like heights."

"Yeah, you mentioned that." He opened his car door. "The first step's a doozy, but it's the fastest way to ground level."

"That's not funny." The fact that he wasn't hounding me about following protocol didn't sit well either. I could handle Lucca when he was his normal obnoxious self, but when he was working this hard to crack jokes and get on my good side, it made me uneasy and suspicious.

"Whatever, Parker." He held the elevator, waiting for me to catch up. "After I finish my paperwork, I'll get started on plan B while you're getting your ass kicked for today."

"I thought you said I didn't do anything wrong."

"I said you didn't miss anything. There is a difference."

"I don't want to know what you're planning to write in your report. Just remember, you can't attest to anything that happened that you did not witness firsthand."

"There's that paranoia I've grown to despise. When are you going to learn to trust me?" He went to his desk while I went to Mark's office.

"Enter," Mark bellowed, so I stepped inside. He looked up, ready to berate. "You talked the kid down?"

"Sort of. Lucca cuffed him."

"Did you drag Will Briscoe up to the roof and threaten to throw him off unless he answered your questions?"

"No."

"Then you talked him down, saved his life, job well done, right?"

"Sure," I replied, hearing the company line loud and clear.

"Great. Write it up." Mark tore his eyes from the paperwork littering his desk. "Is there something else you want to say?" By his tone, I knew the correct answer was no, but I didn't exactly take the hint.

"What about Lucca's account?"

"Does he have a different story to tell?"

"I don't know."

"I suggest the two of you figure it out." He went back to work. "Out, Parker."

"Yes, sir."

After completing the paperwork, I swiveled in my chair, finding the rest of the bullpen empty. Lucca must be working on plan B, which meant I ought to work on my own plan B. Logging off the computer, I went to the locker room, changed out of my suit and into my workout gear, and returned to my desk to grab my purse and car keys. There was no reason to take a government vehicle to the gym and possibly blow my cover.

"You didn't happen to get anything else on the two fighters or the gym owner, did you?" I asked.

"No. The techs are scrubbing traffic cam footage from the day of the shooting. That was my plan B. Wasn't your detective pal supposed to be working the gym angle?" Lucca asked.

"He'll call when he knows something. In the meantime, I'll see what I can find out. I'll be back in two hours."

"I didn't think you believed in overtime." He shook his head and keyed a few things into the computer. "I'll be here when you get back."

"Before I go, I was wondering if you completed your

incident report yet."

His eyes shot up, and his expression turned smug. "Why? Afraid what I'll say? Don't worry, Parker. I only know that you managed to stall his swan dive long enough for help to arrive which is on par with basic negotiation guidelines. I don't have a problem with what happened. I'm just not sure why you're acting so squirrely about it." He looked around the room and lowered his voice. "Did you do something wrong?"

"I'll see you later." Turning on my heel, I hoisted my gym bag over my shoulder and headed for the elevator.

When I arrived at the gym, I was greeted by Linka Greenwood. She ushered me into the locker room where I stowed my gear before leading me to the mat. After a dozen introductions to the other female fighters, she instructed us on some warm-up exercises. Halfway through the routine, Ron and four other men entered the main gym area from one of the back offices. After five hundred reps with the jump rope, the women split up to work with a partner while the men circulated, calling out hit patterns.

Linka waved Ron and another man over. His name was Lawrence Caffrey, one of the trainers. After donning focus mitts, we circled one another, repeating the same sort of practice audition Ron had me perform a few nights ago. However, Caffrey didn't get nearly as aggressive with his hits, and he didn't seem particularly impressed by my skills. After quietly excusing himself, I caught sight of Linka and Ron exchanging whispers in the far corner of the room.

"I guess I failed," I said, ignoring the fact they didn't want to be interrupted. "Should I pack up and go?"

"No, work on a few combos with the heavy bag. I'll be with you in a minute," Ron said.

His words left little wiggle room, so I did as I was told. Positioning myself to watch the two, I noted there was something odd about their exchange. The hair at the back of my neck stood at attention. Had I been made? Or did something else happen at the gym? After a time, the two split up. Linka went to spar with a woman in her weight class, and Ron steadied the heavy bag.

"The last time a man held the bag for me, he asked me not to kick him in either head," I quipped, launching a kick at the duct-taped center of the bag. "Thankfully, my aim seems decent."

"Are you planning to become a kickboxer?" Ron asked, failing to find my story humorous. "Or were you leaning toward the sweet science?"

"I don't know. Which one pays better?" I pummeled the bag with a few left jabs and right crosses.

"Is money your only incentive for being here?"

"Mostly, I want to feel in control of something. If I know how to fight and how to control myself, that's enough. But money's good too. I could use it. The rent for my current office space is ridiculous. I'm looking to move into another building, but I'll need enough for first and last month's rent and a security deposit."

"What do you consult on?" Ron held up his palm, stopping my assault.

"Corporate security."

"That sounds impressive."

"It isn't. Does anyone really give a shit which type of security camera or biometric lock is used inside an office building?"

"Well, when you put it that way, it's no wonder you have so much pent-up aggression." He looked over his shoulder at the empty ring. "Have you ever been in a real fight?"

"With a referee and stuff?"

"No. A street fight."

"I fought off a mugger once, which all the self-defense classes I've ever taken strongly advise against, but it was my favorite purse and I just got a brand new cell phone. It was stupid, but that's just how it goes. And there was a thing that happened in a bar one time, but a lot of that is a blur."

"You're a lot more interesting than I imagined." Ron jerked his head toward the center of the ring. "Come on. I want to see what your go-to moves are. You kicked me the other day. Don't hold back this time. Just defend yourself. It'll give me a better idea of what direction you should take as a fighter."

"Okay, but take it easy. I'm not looking to have a nose job or get my jaw wired shut."

"No problem." He ducked between the two ropes. "I just want to test out your instincts."

I fought hard, making sure he'd want to coach me. The only way to discover how this underground fight scene worked was to get invited to play. I didn't pull my punches, and neither did Ron.

When his fist slammed into the side of my face, I saw stars. My eyes teared, and I stumbled backward. He came at me, hoping to use my moment of weakness to his advantage. I performed a double roundhouse kick. He ducked the first but didn't quite expect the second. I lunged forward, performing a three punch, two kick pattern until he grabbed my ankle, twisting and knocking me to the ground. After I leapt to my feet, he moved faster than I expected, knocking me back to the mat with an uppercut that nearly blacked out the world.

"Enough." He offered me his hand while I remained completely dazed. He leaned over me, holding up a finger. "Are you okay? Follow my finger." He moved it from left to right. I did as he asked, shaking off the stars and sitting up. "Sorry, I thought you'd block it. At least I know where to start your training."

"Does that mean you're my coach?" I asked, working my jaw and feeling the numb, tingly pain. At least I didn't lose a tooth.

"It looks like it. No one else wants you. You don't have the normal training or reaction we've come to expect, but that's a good thing. The other fighters won't know what moves to anticipate when they encounter you."

I rubbed my cheek and jaw. "It doesn't feel like a good thing."

"It is. The coaches here were trained by Tim, so we all use his methods of training. It's nice to have some fresh blood around." He lowered his voice. "Our fighters sometimes have problems when facing off against competitors with different training methodologies. Where did you say you trained?"

"I took a bunch of different self-defense classes and an

assortment of martial arts. I never stuck with any one too long." Wincing, I tilted my head from side to side. "I don't remember ever being hit that hard."

"Go grab a cold pack before your eye swells shut. We'll discuss your training in the office."

After doing as Ron said, I took a seat across the desk from him. The office was small with a few trophy cases and photos filling the two side walls. The back wall had a heavyweight belt, newspaper clippings, and a few old photographs of a much younger Tim Coker from his fighting days. Too bad there weren't a few blackmail letters or sniper rifle bullets anywhere in the room.

"Some fighters train on contingency, so instead of paying a flat fee for these sessions and letting me have the typical cut for the fight, I'll make life easier for you, Alex," Ron said, sounding oddly like a used car salesman. "You can train for free. Win or lose, we'll split what you get paid for a fight. How does that sound?"

"What if I decide not to fight?" I gestured to my face. "Or what if I can't fight? Then what happens?"

"That's never been the case before." He pulled a contract from the desk drawer and held it out. "This is very basic. You don't need to read it, just sign at the bottom."

I wasn't sure how legally binding any of this was, considering there was no mention of what happened when or if a fighter failed to perform at the levels required to reimburse the exorbitant training costs, but I signed an illegible fictitious name and slid the paper back. He could sue any time he wanted.

"This was much easier than what Mr. Coker made it sound like. He practically sent me to the rec center for their free classes," I mused.

"A couple of our guys have left us and gone there. Tim's never been a fan. Occasionally, we'll encounter the dropouts at a bout, but our gym is making a comeback. We train winners here. Don't let today get to you. You have to get knocked down in order to get back up. This will make you stronger and faster, and it'll teach you to block next time."

"It might also teach me to invest in headgear."

"That wouldn't be so bad either." He gestured toward the door. "Have you been sticking to the diet and workout regimen Linka gave you last week?"

"Not as much as I should."

"You'll need to commit to that if you want to be a serious contender. You definitely have what it takes, Alex." He sifted through a stack of forms and handed me another pamphlet on protein and carbs. "You need to pack on some pounds as soon as possible, so we can start converting that to muscle."

"Sure," I looked at the clock, realizing the session was wrapping up, "I was just about to grab some dinner."

"Good girl. I'll see you tomorrow."

TWENTY

Popping two ibuprofens, I leaned back in my desk chair and stared at the computer screen, making sure my vision wasn't impaired. Ron hadn't been joking when he said not to pull any punches. Glancing at the stupid recommended weekly diet, I balled it up and tossed it into the recycle bin. I had no desire to bulk up and become a professional fighter. In two days, the blackmail was expected to be paid. Detective O'Connell was working on that angle. Lucca had come up with a feasible alternative to identify our killer, but my money was on Will Briscoe coming through for us. Right now, Gavin Levere was number one on our suspect list.

"How's plan B going?" I asked when Lucca emerged from the elevator. He arched an eyebrow and knelt next to my desk, reaching out to touch my face. Immediately, I pulled away. "Any progress?"

"Did you try to knock a confession out of someone by smacking his fists with your face?" Lucca asked, detouring to his desk.

"No, especially since you would probably turn me in for brutality or unnecessary violence. My head hurts, so can you please stick with yes and no answers?"

"No, we haven't made any progress." He removed the lid from a Styrofoam cup, shook the contents, and pulled a microfiber cleaning towel from his bottom desk drawer. Flipping the cup upside down, he rolled the towel around the water and melted ice and pressed it against my eye. "Hold that there."

"I'm fine." But I did what he said. The last thing I wanted was to go home looking like this. Adding it to the list of drawbacks related to cohabitation, I skimmed the updated reports concerning the lack of progress on the sniper rifle. "Have they finished scrubbing the traffic cam footage from the day of the shooting?"

"Yep. Our suspect walked two blocks east of the courthouse before hopping into a cab. Due to the sun's glare, we had trouble identifying the plate, but we ran the medallion." He checked his watch. "Want to tag along?"

"Sure."

Lucca drove to the cab company's garage while I filled him in on the gym and how I came to resemble a panda bear. From the skeptical glances he tossed my way, I knew exactly what the former analyst was thinking. These were dangerous people. I shouldn't be screwing around with professionals who put people in the hospital for sport. Luckily, he had gotten to know exactly what type of reaction voicing such an opinion would elicit and kept his mouth shut.

I slipped on a pair of dark sunglasses, checked my reflection in the mirror, seeing the other darkened spot prominently featured along my jaw, from my ear to my chin, but there wasn't anything I could do to conceal that one without stage makeup. Instead, I took up a position two steps behind Lucca and let him do the talking.

Thirty minutes later, we were back inside the car. The cabbie didn't want any trouble and willingly turned over his records and receipts. While Lucca drove back to the OIO building, I skimmed the information, looking for a familiar name.

"He recalled the Yankees' cap and sunglasses, but he didn't remember anything else about the guy. He says he didn't recognize any of the men from the photos we showed him either," Lucca said, darting through traffic. "Do you believe that?"

"I believe he probably asked where the guy wanted to go and started the meter. It was a sunny day. The guy had a cap and glasses on. Would you have remembered anything else about him?"

"Yes."

"If you hadn't been trained to remember minute details, I doubt it." As I suspected, none of the names for credit card users matched any of our suspects. "Our guy must have paid cash." Checking the timestamps and location pick-ups, I found which suspect was ours. "Damn, we should have thought of this sooner. Weren't you an analyst before vying for a field assignment? Shouldn't you be conditioned to think of these things?"

"I've been busy, dealing with a particularly difficult agent. It must have slipped my mind," he retorted. "Where was he dropped off?"

"A few blocks from a residential area with half a dozen bus stops and a few subway terminals within walking distance. The location isn't even remotely close to Gavin Levere's known address, but since it's taken this long just to get to this point, I'm assuming he switched cabs or hopped onto public transportation to cover his tracks."

"How about you ask the computer techs to scrub the footage this time? Agent Lawson threatened to hack into my bank account and drain it if I asked him for another favor."

"And you didn't report him to Jablonsky for that type of insolence?" I pretended to be flabbergasted, opening my mouth wide in shock. "Ouch." I gently massaged my jaw.

"Serves you right, Parker." Lucca snickered.

Ignoring him, I sent a text to Lawson, requesting that he and his team track our suspect through additional traffic cam footage and the city's CCTV grid whenever they got the chance. Then I readjusted in the seat, attempting to get comfortable.

"It's almost nine. Are we calling it?" Lucca asked.

Checking my phone for a response, I read the message

from Lawson saying it would take at least twelve hours to access the footage and identify the unsub. "Yeah, I'm done for the night. It's been a hell of a day." My mind was reeling from talking Will Briscoe down from the roof and getting flattened on the mat. "Hopefully, tomorrow will be better."

"Want to grab a drink?" Lucca asked, pulling into the parking garage.

"No."

"C'mon, Parker, I'm buying. We'll share our leads."

"That's what we've been doing all day." I didn't want to socialize with him. That could lead to friendship, which could lead to disaster.

"I'll tell you what I wrote in my report from today's mishap."

"One drink, boy scout." I checked my watch. "I'll meet you there in twenty minutes."

"Why do I get the feeling you might stand me up?"

I shrugged. "It could happen." Closing the car door, I went around to the driver's side and leaned into the open window. "Lemon drop martini, and if you have a hankering for some type of appetizer, you better be prepared to share."

"Yes, ma'am."

"And the next time you call me ma'am, I'll let you smack my fists with your face a few times. Understand?"

"Yes," he restarted the engine while I headed for the elevator, "ma'am."

I went upstairs to grab the rest of my belongings and make sure the tech team couldn't put a rush on my request. After everything was completed for the day, I returned to the garage, climbed behind the wheel of my car, and went to the bar that my predecessors had claimed for the OIO years before I ever signed up to be a federal agent.

At one of the side booths, Lucca sat with an order of chips and salsa, an untouched lemon drop martini, and a Manhattan. I slid into the booth across from him, finding a bag of ice on the table. Holding it against my jaw, I took a sip of my drink.

"Were they out of Shirley Temples and near beer?" I asked, nodding at his drink.

"I didn't think to ask." He took a long sip from his glass, shutting his eyes briefly and sighing. "I heard you talking to Briscoe on the roof. Is that why you left the OIO? Because someone you loved died?"

"Wow." I gulped down the martini, ignoring the burning in the back of my throat. "Don't you think I've been beaten up enough today?" I snorted, playing it off as if it were a ludicrous statement. "You seriously believed that line of bullshit? Damn, I ought to be an actress."

"So it was a lie?"

"You were an analyst. Aren't you supposed to be able to read people? So read me, Lucca. This is a one-shot deal."

He drank the rest of his drink, remaining silent. "Whatever. I'm not playing this game with you. You'll tell me when you're ready." He glanced around, nodding at a man who just came inside. "I thought things would be different after today."

"What did you write in your report?"

"That Agent Parker displayed exemplary behavior in negotiating and calming the suspect until the situation could be safely deescalated." He picked up a chip and took a bite. "Why do you think I'm out to get you? What have I ever done to you?"

"You always point out my flaws and the rules that get bent. Clearly, you have an ulterior motive for doing that."

"I've seen missions get botched by overzealous field agents, and you definitely seem like one of them. It's just a habit I picked up when I was an analyst."

"How long did you do that?"

"A year. They had a shortage of analysts when I graduated from Quantico, and based on my aptitude, they altered my path. Two years training, one year analyzing, and then two years training to be a field agent. Frankly, we've been at this for almost the same amount of time, so don't treat me like a newbie."

I snatched a chip from the basket, biting down and regretting it. Soup would have been a better idea. However, it served its purpose of buying time. I washed the rest of the chip down with the martini and shifted the ice bag from my jaw to my eye.

"Thanks for having my back," I slid out of the booth, "and thanks for the drink."

He nodded, understanding this conversation was over for now, perhaps forever. "We'll get him tomorrow, Parker."

"I'm counting on it. I'm getting really sick and tired of having my ass kicked."

*　　*　　*

"I told you it's creepy when you watch me sleep," I murmured, forcing my eyes open. The room was bathed in a grey-blue that seeped in from behind the drapes. The sky was brightening, but the sun wasn't up yet. "Why are you awake this early?"

"I just came to bed," Martin whispered. He was propped up on one elbow, and his fingers played with the lock of hair that framed my face. "Are you enjoying my pillow and my side of the bed?"

Inhaling deeply, I smiled. "We don't have sides. We always end up in the middle. And I hate to admit it, but being close to you or something of yours helps me sleep. Maybe if I confuse your pillow for you, I'll be less likely to hurt you. The pillow might not make it, though."

Gently, he touched my bruised cheekbone. "Did you get into a pillow fight?"

I turned onto my side to face him, and he traced the sore spot on my jaw.

"Is this going to become a common occurrence?" he asked.

"This is nothing. You've seen me in worse shape."

"I have, but that doesn't make this any better." He looked around the room. "I should add a mini-fridge to the list of bedroom upgrades. That way, I won't have to go down to the second floor to get you an icepack every time this happens."

"If you weren't insistent on sharing a bed, I'd be asleep downstairs, that much closer to the kitchen." I ran my hand along his side. "I'm fine. Go to sleep."

"What happened this time, slugger?" He wasn't ready to

let it go, and I was too tired to fight.

"My sparring partner got carried away. I went to a gym under the pretense of becoming a fighter, and the coach socked me in the eye and followed through with an uppercut."

"Gloves wouldn't have left that kind of mark."

"He wore training gloves. Y'know, the fingerless ones. They aren't padded very well."

Martin sighed. "At least you came home and decided to give our bedroom a try."

"What's that supposed to mean?" I sat up and rubbed my good eye.

"Nothing. I just know how you are, and hiding away so I wouldn't notice you were hurt seems like something you might do." He wrapped an arm around my middle, urging me to lie back down.

"Well, the thought did cross my mind, but last night, I was reminded of how much better I sleep when you're around. Plus, I wasn't positive you wouldn't show up at my apartment or decide to sleep downstairs again. God, you're worse than the NSA, tracking my every move. You'd make a wonderful spy or a deranged stalker."

"Thanks, but since I own a tuxedo, I'm hoping that means I'm more spy than stalker."

"Spies don't watch their girlfriends sleep."

"Are you sure? They might just exercise more finesse or utilize state-of-the-art equipment. Infrared scanners and shit like that."

"Go to sleep, Mr. Bond." I pressed my body against his chest. "Before you embark on any other clandestine maneuvers, you should know I have to get up for work in forty-five minutes."

He kissed my forehead. "Alexis, how often should I expect you to come home injured?"

"Scrapes and bruises aren't a big deal. They're fairly common." It wasn't the answer he wanted.

"Have I seen the frequency of the major injuries firsthand?"

"Martin, I'm okay. Any day that doesn't involve an ER visit is a good day. The majority of my days are good days."

I felt an uneasy pang in my chest, probably a result of yesterday's drama. "But you know there are dangers. It's possible one day will be a very bad day."

"Don't say that, sweetheart."

"It could happen."

"No." His tone was hard, his hand gripped my side tighter. "Don't you dare put that out there."

"Yesterday, I tried to talk a kid out of committing suicide. I have no idea if I got through to him. Lucca cuffed him, but realistically, there's no way to stop that kid from finding a way to get what he wants. When he's released, if he decides to end it, he will. It won't matter what anyone says or does. It's out of our hands. That's just how it is."

"Why the hell are you this damn philosophical at five a.m.?"

"It has to do with my serotonin levels." I pulled myself away from his chest and kissed him. "You know I won't blame you if you want to walk away. This isn't exactly what you signed up for when we started dating. I told you then how dangerous and volatile my life was, but it's only gotten worse. Most of my stuff is still packed. I can load up the boxes and go home. Maybe give you some space to think about this."

"There's nothing to think about. I love you. I just wish that getting hurt didn't happen so frequently that you have a blasé attitude toward a black eye and bruised jaw. This is the second time in the past week that you've come home slightly disfigured. Should I hire a bodyguard to follow you around?"

"First, I'm not disfigured, and second, I don't think the federal government wants their agents to have private bodyguards. That scenario screams out lawsuit waiting to happen."

"Do you think I give a shit?"

"Not really. All you millionaires are alike, believing money can solve everything," I said dramatically. "And I love you too, which is why I moved in and do what I can to keep you safe, even if it means stealing your pillow."

"But you won't let me return the favor."

"You can have my pillow."

"That's not what I meant."

"I know, but you can't. It's a hazard of my job."

"And I can't persuade you to make a career change?" he asked, kissing that sensitive spot on my neck. "I can be very persuasive at times."

"Martin, I'm where I belong. It's taken a long time to piece myself back together in order to return to the life I left behind. The bruises will fade in a day or two, and we'll find our balance."

"I'm glad to hear you say that."

TWENTY-ONE

Traffic cam footage identified our shooter heading down the steps to the subway, but he was lost in the crowd. It would take a lot of time and money to figure out where he went from there. Frankly, he could have gone anywhere. It was another dead end.

"Any other brilliant ideas?" Lucca asked. Somehow, this was my fault.

"It's Tuesday. O'Connell should have something for me by now. We'll get access to Will by Thursday, and the blackmailer expects a drop to be made tomorrow evening." I tapped my fingernails against the desk, unable to come up with another angle. Had we really exhausted all leads? "Wait. Did anything helpful every turn up with Facini? We know he was a frequenter at the gun range. He resembles our shooter, and we can place him at the gym."

"I've dug through everything, but I haven't found a solid link between him and William Briscoe or Stan Weaver." Lucca shook his head. "No matter how hard I try, I can't wrap my head around someone deciding to commit a murder out of the blue. There were no warning signs or indications. The guy doesn't have a rap sheet or a history of violence."

"He's a boxer. Isn't that violent enough for you?" Picking up my desk phone, I dialed O'Connell. We needed to work this out. "Too bad Will Briscoe freaked out at Gavin Levere's photograph and not Elias Facini's." I listened to the ringing through the earpiece. "Go find out if there's any way we can speak with Will or have his doctor ask him a question."

"Parker, I don't even know how admissible that would be," Lucca warned, but I waved him off when Nick answered on the sixth ring.

"Hey, Nick, I thought you said you were going to call with an update. What's the verdict? You have two suspects in custody, or you did the last time I checked."

He exhaled audibly. "It's a clusterfuck."

"Okay, I'm gonna need you to elaborate."

"Gavin Levere is being held for manslaughter. Elias Facini on assault charges, and since they're against an officer of the court, his court appearance has been delayed, buying us a bit more time. Tim Coker is an accessory, accomplice, or something else that starts with an A."

"I'll agree with that."

"The problem is, aside from the assault and Levere contributing to the death of Hector Santos, we have nothing. A few uniforms are serving search warrants at the gym and our suspects' residences, but unless we find a smoking gun, they'll be cut loose, pending a hearing."

"There has to be something else you can do."

"The ME is reexamining Santos' remains, but the district attorney doesn't feel that a murder charge will stick. And he's not pushing for it. Santos played a contributory role in his own demise."

"Did you watch the video? The DA was probably at the fight and doesn't want to risk letting those facts come to light."

"Yeah, and the police commissioner might have been there to. The point is I can't do anything about it. I can investigate and make an arrest. They have my recommendation, but it's out of my hands."

"What about the two courthouse murders? Shouldn't they get justice?"

"Tie them together," O'Connell said, losing his patience. He took another breath. "Look, we're working different sides of the same street. You have to bring me something solid if you want me to meet you in the middle."

"I wish I had something for you, Detective. The shooter can't be identified through facial rec. He left his weapon at the crime scene, and every lead we've followed has turned into a wild goose chase. The gym is the only connection."

"Then you'll have to get someone to cooperate." I heard the doubt in his voice. "Alex, are you sure the crimes are connected?"

"I don't know anymore."

After disconnecting, I went in search of the man who some might consider my partner. Eddie Lucca was in the conference room, tearing down the notes and photos we had posted over the course of the investigation. When I entered, he didn't even bother to turn around. He was starting over. Once the boards were clear and the conference table was covered in the various items, he hung photos of Stan Weaver and William Briscoe in the center of the board.

"Pick a target," he said.

"Briscoe."

He glanced over his shoulder. "Pick again."

"I don't think Weaver—"

"How would you kill him?" Lucca asked, interrupting before I could perform another rendition of a broken record. "You have a sniper rifle. You went to the courthouse during jury selection and discovered what trial he was assigned. You determined which courtroom. You scoped out different vantage points."

"Did we ever identify our shooter prior to the open house?"

"No. He was probably there, but if he wasn't wearing the cap and glasses, we won't see him."

"What about our possible suspects? Have the techs run facial rec for one of them in the vicinity for the times and dates?"

"They're working on it." He tapped Weaver's photo. "Don't get distracted. You decide to kill him in court.

Why?"

"To make a statement, cover my tracks, or because I don't have anything else to do at that time of the morning." Grabbing my phone, I sent a text to O'Connell to check alibis of the three men for the time of the courthouse shooting, if he hadn't already.

"You take one shot. The mark goes down. You must know how to shoot."

"I trained. Practiced. And since I don't plan to take the weapon with me, I don't care about bullet striations or it being traced back to me."

"The gun isn't registered. You bought it hot or stole it." Lucca made a face, grabbing his own phone and dialing a number. After he asked for a full list of weapon thefts, he disconnected and continued with the theorizing. "It's done. You don't linger. You leave the building and hail a cab, but now you're getting nervous. You're afraid someone will catch on, so you run counter-maneuvers."

"Or I planned my escape ahead of time and knew how to avoid being tracked."

"Where are you going?"

"Home. Possibly work. Maybe out to meet a friend for lunch."

"If you were a professional, you'd be meeting your client to say the job's done and collect your fee," Lucca suggested.

"Except nothing indicates this was a contracted hit."

"So it's personal." He picked up a collection of pages and slammed them down. "Shit. We've come full circle." The stack of potential threats to Weaver slid across the desk. "Dammit." He met my eyes. "Don't say it."

"That's why I think Briscoe's the target."

He rubbed his face and slumped into a chair. "Run it."

"Everything still holds true, except targeting Briscoe at the courthouse makes no sense."

"I mentioned that," Lucca muttered.

"That's what makes it brilliant. That's the piece of the puzzle that says whoever did this is smart. The killing was meticulously planned. The location was scouted. Our shooter was careful, almost professional. He must be trained and aware of how investigations work."

"Facini." He nodded. "Okay, I'll bite. Facini's our shooter. He trains on the range with the military equivalent of the Remington. He doesn't own a gun, so we can't track weapon sales back to him. He went through most of the training at the police academy, and he falls within the physical parameters of our unsub." He met my eyes. "Why did he want to kill William Briscoe?"

"That's what we have to find out."

"Stop for a second." Lucca put his hand on my wrist before I could leave the conference room. "How would Facini know Briscoe was serving jury duty? The only people aware of this would be Briscoe's employers and his family and friends. We still have no connection between the two of them."

"Hector Santos."

"Why would Santos want to harm Briscoe? They were pals. Briscoe was helping Santos train."

"Santos is dead too." The buzz reverberated inside my brain. "They were killed weeks apart. I'll bet it was for the exact same reason." I scribbled our timeline back onto the whiteboard. "The shooter planned to eliminate Briscoe for at least a week prior to his death, but Santos' fight was already scheduled. Why would someone want to silence both of them?" We were getting closer. I could feel it.

"It has to do with the fight," Lucca surmised. He flipped through some paperwork, but the angles we had investigated didn't focus too heavily on Santos. "Briscoe must have been around quite a few of the fighters. His son recognized the men in the photos."

"Will Jr. said he was to blame. That's why he wanted to kill himself. Why the hell did you pass him off to the PD yesterday? We could have asked him a few questions before they took him away."

"It was out of our hands. The scene yesterday was a circus, and just so you know, we were denied clearance to ask him questions. Medical professional trumps federal agent every time."

"Not if you do it right." I pushed the door open. "Come on. We aren't going to solve anything by sitting inside this room."

"I will not be a part of some illegal questioning."

"We're not going to talk to Will. We need the police file on Hector Santos. Since Briscoe's family is familiar with the fighters, Santos' family should know a little something about Hector's assistant coach."

*　　*　　*

"Mrs. Santos, do you recognize this man?" Lucca passed a photo of William Briscoe across the kitchen table to the grieving mother.

"That's Coach Willie." She barely glanced at the photo. "He should have protected my son." She spat on the photo. "Trained him better. Made sure he was ready. If he had, Hector would still be alive."

"What can you tell us about Hector's training sessions?" O'Connell asked. Since this was considered official police business, I let him tag along as a courtesy. This was our middle ground.

"Hector trained every day. He worked at the rec center and used their equipment Monday through Friday, and on Sunday he used to go for a six mile run." Abruptly, she stood from the table, collecting a few items and bustling around the kitchen. "I never wanted him to fight. He was such a sweet little boy. He wouldn't hurt a fly, but then he made the wrong kinds of friends."

"Was Hector involved with a gang?" O'Connell asked.

"No." The look in her eyes would have killed a weaker man. "He wasn't in trouble. He wasn't involved with anyone in trouble. He straightened out, but it didn't make a damn bit of difference." She walked out of the room, leaving the three of us in her wake.

"Ma'am," Lucca called, following her into the living room, "we have a few more questions."

"Hector's dead. I can't bury my son until you finish your investigation, and I'm late for work. So go screw yourselves." A door slammed shut, and I imagined she must have closed herself inside the bedroom to change.

"Looks like that's our cue to leave," Lucca said from the doorway.

"Let me know when she comes back." I ignored the warning look on his face.

Lucca rolled his eyes and stood in the doorway between the kitchen and living room. Mrs. Santos' apartment was tiny. The kitchen held a table with three chairs and an opened ironing board. Other than that, there was barely enough room to walk from the doorway to the counter. However, on the wall were a few framed photos of her son. One, in particular, caught my eye.

Hector looked to be about fourteen and was surrounded by a group of six other boys. Removing my phone, I photographed the photo. O'Connell followed suit before going into the living room. Since Mrs. Santos didn't bother to throw us out, we were taking a few liberties with the items in plain sight. Nick found something of interest on the coffee table, and I joined him, pretending not to hear the gruff exhale from Lucca.

"Is that a yearbook?" I asked as Nick flipped through a few pages.

"No. Well, maybe." He held it out for me to see. "It's not from a school." The item was spiral-bound and appeared to be printed from one of those online photo services. "These are recent. It looks like something from the rec center." O'Connell flipped to the back, looking for some type of identifying information. "Recognize anyone?" He opened to the center page, a group shot of eight men.

"Facini, Levere, Briscoe, Santos, Coker, Greenwood." I scanned the bottom caption, unable to identify the other two men in the picture before Mrs. Santos returned.

"How dare you," she shrieked. "Get out."

"Ma'am," O'Connell began, but she practically pushed us toward the door, snatching the photobook from his hands, "we didn't mean to upset you. We're just looking for clues to help solve Hector's murder."

"Hector wasn't murdered. He died from getting hit in the head." Tears welled in her eyes, and she opened the front door. "This is harassment. Get out."

Lucca muttered an apology and followed Nick and me out of the apartment. "Is that how the two of you normally work?" he asked once we were away from the apartment.

"No, our lookout normally does a better job of looking out," I said.

"Do you want to take a crack at my suspects and ask about their connection with William Briscoe?" O'Connell asked.

"Absolutely. I'd say we have more than adequate reasons to question them," I said. "Care to give me a ride, Nick?"

"Does that mean you're not planning to take custody?" O'Connell asked.

"Not yet." I smiled, a devious gleam developing in my eye.

"Parker," Lucca growled, "what are you doing?"

"My job. Go ask Laura Briscoe about her father in connection with the other fighters. Ask her about her brother. Run names, profiles, whatever it takes. They seem like a tight-knit family, so she must know something. If anything, she might have some sixth sense about why her brother planned to take a dive off the building. You can ask if he has a history of depression, and while you're at it, get names and addresses of his buddies that he uses for couch surfing and follow up with them."

"You can't just tell me what to do," Lucca protested.

O'Connell snorted and clapped him on the shoulder. "I believe she just did."

TWENTY-TWO

"Mr. Facini," O'Connell said, "this is Agent Parker. Your name has surfaced in connection with an investigation she's working, and instead of making your life more difficult, we thought we'd save everyone some time and paperwork and partake in a joint interrogation. I trust you won't have any objections."

"Are you charging him with something?" Facini's attorney, Thomas Harper, asked.

"Not at the present," I replied.

"Then you have no right to question him," Harper said.

"Well, I do." O'Connell took a seat at the table while I hovered in the corner of the room, watching the exchange. "What can you tell me about William Briscoe?"

"He's a trainer. He helps out at the rec center." Facini squinted at O'Connell.

"Did he ever train you?"

"No, but he used to come around from time to time. He worked exclusively with Hector."

"What does this have to do with my client's assault charges?" Harper asked.

"Why did you assault Jack Fletcher?" I piped up, moving to the table and taking a seat next to O'Connell.

"Don't answer that." Harper looked at me. "We are contesting those facts."

I snorted. "Assault is the least of your client's worries. He's looking at blackmail, conspiracy, and probably murder."

"What?" Facini's eyes widened. "That lawyer guy is dead?"

"Shut up," Harper hissed. He shifted his gaze to O'Connell. "I'd like to speak to my client alone, and I'd like her removed from this interview."

"Fine." O'Connell went to the door. I gave Facini and his counsel a final hard glare before making my way out of the room. "I'd say that counts as an admission of his guilt for assaulting Fletcher," O'Connell said as we went back to his desk.

"Too many lawyers." I sucked in a breath. "Do you think we could twist it and make it sound like he was asking about the well-being of AUSA Weaver?"

"That's a stretch, even for you."

"Yeah, well, I'm scraping the bottom of the barrel. Are there any reasons you can think of why Harper wouldn't want me to sit in on the interrogation?"

"He must not be a fan of your glowing personality. Realistically, it doesn't matter what he wants. As long as you keep quiet, you can stay in the room. It's my interrogation. It's my prerogative what information is passed along to other members of the law enforcement community."

"Someone's been reading the regulation book again. Have you been spending time with Lucca behind my back?"

The detective scoffed and read the sticky notes on his desk. Pretending to mind my own business, I went to the coffeepot and poured a cup, returning to a position behind Nick so I could surreptitiously read over his shoulder. Fletcher had phoned to reschedule a follow-up for later in the afternoon. The ME's office found extensive internal damage on Santos' body, but it was unclear if the damage was due to the match or injuries sustained afterward. While I waited, Nick phoned the crime lab to ask what progress they were making.

When he disconnected, I smiled sweetly. "If you ask nicely, I'm sure our forensic experts could take a look at Santos' autopsy and compare it to the video shot of the fight and help make a determination," I said.

"You just want to get a hold of our evidence, which would be one less thing on my plate, and if you happened to discover a crime or evidence related to another crime that just so happens to fall under federal jurisdiction, that would be purely coincidental."

"Precisely."

"Fine. I'll call Jablonsky and ask if your office can help us out." He glanced at his partner who had just entered the bullpen. "Hey, do me a favor and see if Mr. Harper is ready for us to continue our conversation."

"With which suspect?" Thompson asked.

"Facini," O'Connell replied, already dialing.

"Okay, sure." Thompson made a face. Something about his attitude made me wonder what provoked that question.

"I'll walk with you," I offered, following after the detective. "Is Harper representing someone else?"

"He's representing all of them." Thompson poked his head into the observation room, making sure Harper was still inside before continuing down the hall in order to provide the attorney with privacy. "Facini, Levere, and Coker. It's privileged who's footing the bill, but my guess is Tim Coker or his gym is paying the fee."

"Isn't that a conflict of interest?"

"Not my problem. These are grown men. They ought to know they're entitled to fire their counsel or seek new counsel if they choose. My guess would be they can't afford someone of Harper's caliber." He knocked on the door to the interrogation room, waited a polite five seconds, and turned the doorknob. "Let us know when you're ready to continue, sir," Thompson said, doing that respectful thing required of police officers. After he shut the door, he leaned against the wall. "How is it that we got roped into helping you on another investigation?"

"You're just lucky, I guess. Have you made any progress identifying the blackmailer?"

"Not yet. We've been trying to determine the motivation for the blackmail. Is Fletcher on the level? He seems like small fries compared to a few of the faces I spotted in the crowd at that fight. I'd bet he saw something or did something else that night and that's why he's being targeted."

"He had to leave the fight to meet a client."

"Does the client have a name?" Thompson asked.

"It's privileged, so he didn't share it."

"He left early." Thompson frowned, his eyes darting back and forth as if he were watching a ping-pong tournament. "Did he see anything strange on his way out? Perhaps a bunch of guys waiting to pound Santos into the ground?"

"Not that I'm aware, but I didn't necessarily think to ask. That would change everything though. A new motive might tie the blackmail to the double homicide."

While I contemplated the possibilities that Fletcher might be an unaware witness to some other crime, I dialed the ABC law firm and left a message for Jack to call me back. Since I was no longer working on his case, it seemed unlikely he would comply, but it was worth a shot. Worst case, O'Connell could question him about it this afternoon.

Harper opened the door to interrogation and glanced at the two of us. It was obvious he didn't relish the idea that I was hanging around, but he kept his mouth shut. Thompson disappeared to get O'Connell, and I remained outside, offering a friendly smile to the officer on duty.

"Are you ready to continue?" O'Connell asked. Harper nodded, and we returned to the interrogation room. "Mr. Facini, were you at the unsanctioned boxing match between Hector Santos and Gavin Levere?"

Facini looked at his attorney, who nodded. "Yes."

"Why were you there? Were you on the ticket that night?" O'Connell asked.

"No, but our coach thought it'd be a good way to improve our techniques and analyze our competition."

"Was the match filmed?" I asked, earning a glare from every man in the room.

"My client wouldn't be privy to that kind of

information," Harper icily replied.

"Did you film the match for later study, Mr. Facini?" O'Connell asked.

"No."

"Were you friends with Hector Santos?"

"I knew him. It's not a large circuit. We all know one another."

"Is that why Hector's mother has a photobook containing a group shot of you, Hector, and numerous other fighters and coaches?" O'Connell asked. Harper nudged Facini, and neither man spoke. "Y'see, it appears you knew Hector rather well. You also know Gavin Levere. After all, the two of you have the same coach and attend the same gym. You were at the fight that resulted in Hector's death. You didn't do anything to stop it, and then you knocked around some guy who showed up at the gym who was also at the fight. It looks like you know something, and you're afraid your secret is out. Things will go much easier for you if you tell me what happened."

"You wanted to be a cop," I interjected. "You went through the training. You wanted to protect innocent people, but what you're doing right now flies in the face of that. Do the right thing, Elias." I shot a pointed look at Harper. "You are aware you can ask for a different attorney, or you can decide you don't want to be represented. You don't have to let the party pulling the purse strings control your future."

"Agent, that is completely uncalled for. I want the name of your supervisor, so I can launch a formal complaint." Harper turned his focus to O'Connell. "I should file a complaint against you and this department too."

"Be my guest. It isn't against the law to remind your client of his legal rights," O'Connell replied.

Facini looked torn. My statement triggered something in his brain. "Can I have a minute?"

"Take as much time as you need," O'Connell said, moving toward the door. "An officer will be outside when you're ready to continue."

This was turning into a ridiculous version of musical chairs, but I stood, placing my card on the table in front of the attorney. He could phone in a complaint any time he wanted. It wouldn't go over too well at the office, but Jablonsky should be used to that by now.

"You too," Facini said to Harper when the attorney failed to leave. "I want a moment alone. I don't need you here to threaten me with what will happen if I don't do what you say."

My eyes shot to O'Connell. The rabbit hole was getting deeper. Soon, we'd end up burrowing our way to China.

Harper waited for us to leave the room before whispering something to Facini. When he joined us in the hallway, he stalked past without even looking in our direction.

"You really know how to clear a room," O'Connell said. "What do you think that's about?"

"Facini's the closest physical match to our suspect, but based on his reaction, I'm having doubts he's a killer."

"He's been trained in the basics. Granted, the shit we learn in the academy does little to prepare us for most situations, but basic investigation techniques and weapons training and tactics go a long way. They're the most useful things we get out of the academy, and from what I've heard, your killer is well-versed on both of those fronts."

"Still, we're only breaching the surface. Until you found that photograph, I couldn't connect Facini with Briscoe." My mind raced. "Will Briscoe Jr., the son of one of the vics, freaked at the sight of Gavin Levere's photo. It's why he wanted to take a dive off the roof. I need to determine how tight Facini and Levere are. They train together. Coker coaches them, and now I find out they have the same sleazebag attorney. What the hell is going on?"

"Not that some lowly detective knows much of anything," O'Connell eyed me, "but I'd start with the common denominator."

"Yeah, the only problem with that plan is you no longer have Coker in custody."

"I'm not getting paid to do your job for you."

Before I could dial my colleagues and ask if they could have a chat with Tim Coker, Facini beckoned. He didn't ask for Harper, and we weren't about to suggest it. He took a deep breath, leaned back in the chair, and said with a straight face, "I assaulted that man at the gym."

"Okay," O'Connell slid a legal pad across the table with a pen, "do you mind telling me why?"

"Honestly, I have no clue." Facini picked up the pen, twirling it between his fingers. "I wasn't the only one. Gavin Levere did too. We didn't hit him that hard. The lawyer guy," he looked at me, "what did you say his name was?"

"Jack Fletcher," I replied, wondering if Facini was playing us now.

"We were supposed to scare him away. Neither of us had any intention of causing severe or permanent damage, and we definitely had no way of knowing that our attack would kill him."

O'Connell nudged my leg under the table. There was no reason to correct Facini's assumptions when they might prove useful.

"So I want to confess," Facini said.

"Who decided you should assault Mr. Fletcher?" O'Connell asked. "Was it your pal, Gavin?"

"He's the one who grabbed a hold of me. He said the lawyer was asking questions about the match, and he planned to shut the gym down." He inhaled deeply, rubbing his eyes with the back of his hand. "It was stupid. So stupid. But boxing is my life. I couldn't imagine someone shutting us down. If what happened at the match came to light, especially after Hector's death, my career would be over before it even started."

"Did Coker want you to scare off Mr. Fletcher too?" I asked.

"I don't know," Facini said.

"Think about it," O'Connell said. "Coker owns the gym. He gets paid to train you guys, and some asshat attorney comes in and wants to cause problems. Wouldn't he want to protect himself, his livelihood, and his fighters?"

Facini blinked a few times, rubbing his eyes again.

O'Connell leaned back. "Take a moment and think about that night. Do you remember Coach Coker speaking to Levere or anyone else before the two of you went outside to rough up Mr. Fletcher?"

Facini sighed. "I don't know. Maybe. I wasn't paying attention to what happened before. I was sparring with Coach Greenwood, running through some combos. My mind was focused more on my footwork than what was going on around me."

"Did Gavin Levere kill Hector Santos?" I asked.

"No, I don't think so. They fought hard during the match, but Hector seemed okay. We have referees at these bouts. No one called it. When it was over, Hector was fine. A little bruised, but he was up and talking. The next day, I heard what happened. Hector was a good guy and a good fighter. He would have made it big. Accidents happen, even with the big-ticket fights. It was probably just a fluke, which is why I couldn't understand why that attorney wanted to shut down the gym."

"So you were scared, pissed, and the testosterone levels were already through the roof," O'Connell chimed in, "which made it that much easier for you and your buddy, Levere, to take matters into your own hands."

"I never meant to hurt him. I just wanted to scare him away."

"Well, good news," O'Connell said, "the man you assaulted is alive and well."

"What?" Facini's mouth dropped open. "You said he was dead." He looked straight in my eyes.

"I said a lawyer was dead. I didn't specify which one." I stared at him. "William Briscoe trained Hector Santos. Do you know anything about what happened to him?"

Facini swore, glowering at me. "This is bullshit. What we just discussed was entrapment. I want my attorney back."

"Which one?" O'Connell asked. "The one that was hired to save the skin on your coach's ass or a different one that will work to get your felony charges reduced to a misdemeanor? A double homicide did occur, along with a lot of other horrible things. If you cooperate and tell us what you know, Agent Parker will try to have the assault charges dropped. What do you say?"

TWENTY-THREE

"Maybe you should have been a prosecutor," I whispered as O'Connell and I left the interrogation room. The officer who had been stationed outside escorted Mr. Facini back to a holding cell. Now, I had to convince Jack to drop his complaint against one of the men who roughed him up. "I'll need Facini transferred to the federal building as soon as you're finished with him."

"Do you really think he has anything valuable left to give you?"

"I don't know, but he seems willing to talk about the fight scene. It might lead to a few individuals we haven't investigated. Perhaps one of them will even be our shooter."

"Since when did you become an optimist? Are extreme mood swings what being back on the job does to you?"

"Apparently."

Facini provided Detective O'Connell with information on the fight that resulted in Santos' death. He named the parties involved, the coaches, the sponsors, the promoters, where the event was held, the cleanup crews and medical staff, and pretty much everything else he knew. However, he claimed to be unaware of most of the high profile spectators, except for those looking to sign fighters, and the illegal betting. I didn't necessarily believe him, but until I had proof to contradict his story, there was nothing I could do.

"Since I'm already here, can I take a crack at Gavin Levere too? I'll even throw in a pretty please." I batted my eyelashes.

"God, now I'm thinking those mood swings are a result of moving in with Martin."

"I always said they were catching. So Levere, yea or nay?"

"He's downstairs in holding. If I have to formally question him, I have to drag Harper back here, and frankly, I don't want to."

Reading between the lines, I thanked Nick for his help and went down to holding. Questioning a suspect in this fashion wasn't exactly legal, so I'd have to get creative. Thankfully, Lucca wasn't around to berate or report me.

I flashed my credentials at the officer manning the desk and followed up with a killer smile. "Do you have Gavin Levere in custody?"

"Yes, ma'am."

"Agent," I corrected, adding more dazzle to my smile. "I just need a quick minute. I need to eyeball him to make sure it's the same guy and ensure he has the information I need."

"Do you have paperwork on this?" the officer asked, reaching for his desk phone.

"My partner's bringing it. Seriously, it won't take any time at all. I just need to verify the guy matches our profile, and I'll be done."

He nodded down the corridor, distracting himself with filling out a form. Hopefully, neither of us would get in trouble for this. After all, speaking to suspects in police custody was one of my many talents, right next to being placed in lockup.

"Mr. Levere, I'm Agent Parker with the Office of International Operations."

"The what?" He scrunched his face together, creasing his forehead.

"A division of the FBI."

"Why didn't you just say that instead?" He shook his head. "Fancy jackholes."

"Yeah, anyway, Will Briscoe mentioned you by name. I thought it was only fair to hear your side of things."

He sucked in his top lip and glared, rising to stand. "What did that worthless punk say?"

"How close were you with his father?" I was toeing the line of impropriety. The information could potentially become inadmissible, and I wanted to gather just enough to warrant a court order without compromising the investigation.

"Closer than the idiot kid was to his pops." His eyes narrowed. "FBI? Are you asking what happened to Willie?"

"Not yet, but we'll get to that." Without elaborating further, I marched back to the desk, smiled at the officer, and left the precinct. By this afternoon, we'd be requesting two prisoner transfers. With any luck, the killer would be under arrest by dinnertime.

*   *   *

"How'd your day go?" I asked.

Lucca rolled his eyes. "You mean after I spent an hour talking Laura Briscoe out of filing a complaint against you? Or how she claims she doesn't know any of the men her father knew from the rec center? She even went so far to say that she didn't know he was coaching boxers."

"Do you believe her?"

"No, but we don't have anything compelling to use to encourage her to open up. She's rightfully pissed. Every time she talks to us, something in her life gets exponentially worse."

"What about her brother?"

Lucca pulled a piece of paper out of his breast pocket. "I was just about to run some backgrounds. His ex-girlfriend would probably be the best place to start. They broke up a few weeks ago, right around the time Santos died."

"Does he have a history of mental illness or depression?"

"Laura wasn't very forthcoming. It's up for debate whether Will ever thought to take a flying leap or if this was a reaction to the sudden stress and guilt."

"You don't honestly believe he's our shooter."

"We need to find out if he has an alibi. He was probably aware of his dad's jury duty. He might have known which courtroom they were using for the trial." He studied my face for a moment. "You don't think it's him, even though he basically told you he killed his dad."

"He didn't pull the trigger. He didn't make the connection until he looked through the photos. If he had, it wouldn't have come as such a shock."

After informing Lucca of the few facts I had uncovered, I waited patiently for Levere and Facini to be brought to the federal building. In the meantime, Lucca ran background checks and made a couple of calls. The last thing I wanted to do was return to the gym tonight. I was tired of getting knocked around, particularly when it wasn't serving any real purpose.

"I'm gonna speak to the girlfriend. Do you want to come?" Lucca asked, patting his pockets for a set of car keys.

"No, I want to see what Humpty and Dumpty have to say whenever they get here." I wondered why the transfer was taking so long. Facini's assault charges were being dropped, and while Levere might be facing manslaughter, the PD ought to realize we didn't plan to keep him indefinitely unless we had him on two counts of murder.

"Good," Lucca smirked, "I didn't want to ask the fire department to remain on standby."

"Bite me." My eyes flicked to him, and he chuckled before heading down to the garage.

Jablonsky watched Lucca leave before approaching my desk. Folding his arms across his chest, he towered over me. "It looks like the two of you worked out your differences."

"We're coexisting. It probably won't last." I checked the time again. "What's the holdup? I thought the PD was transferring our suspects."

"They did." Mark let out a lengthy exhale. "Why'd you

have to piss off the attorney?"

"He isn't acting in either man's best interest. O'Connell thinks Tim Coker is paying him, which means Harper's protecting Coker and allowing the other two to become sacrificial lambs." I leaned back in my chair. "Levere has valuable information for us. I need to talk to him."

"No, you need to learn to color inside the lines. Director Kendall is pissed. Harper's claiming harassment and mistreatment, so you're out. I will conduct the interviews. You don't need any black marks in your file, especially when you're still on probation." Before I could voice a protest, Mark grabbed Lucca's chair and dragged it to my desk. He sat, snatching a pen from atop my desk and flipping to a clean page in his notebook. "I need a rundown of this morning's interviews that took place at the police station." He looked up. "No conjecture. Just solid facts." Once he was up to speed, he tore off the sheet of notes and tucked it inside his pocket. "I'll let you know what I learn. In the meantime, go see what you can get out of Coker. It's normal gym hours so mingle."

"Should I also let him try to knock some sense into me?" I asked, cocking an eyebrow.

"Seriously, be careful, Alex. Any one of those steroid-addled bodybuilders could be our killer, or they might know who is. Don't screw around. The next time one of them puts a hand on you, show them you're not to be messed with. They'll respect it, and it could lead to some answers."

"We've seen the footage. The big, bulky muscleheads don't fit the build of the shooter. He appeared relatively average. A normal height and probably 170 pounds."

"Then you already know who's a waste of time."

Going downstairs to the locker room, I changed into some workout gear and loosened up on the gym equipment the federal government provided. Once I was warm enough to throw a few punches and kicks without pulling anything, I climbed into my car and drove to Coker's gym. On the way, I dialed Fletcher. Surprisingly, he answered.

"You suck at returning calls," I said in lieu of a greeting. "Did you speak to Detective O'Connell?"

"Yes, Ms. Parker." He sounded like a reprimanded child. "At his insistence, I dropped the charges. Although, I'd like to point out that you insisted I file a report in the first place."

Ignoring the remark, I asked, "Can you recall exactly what happened when you left the fight that unfortunate evening?"

"The police wanted to know the same thing. Honestly, I wasn't paying a bit of attention."

"Thanks for the sugarcoating." I sighed. "By any chance, did you happen to meet your client outside the arena and maybe this unnamed party could shed some light on possible illegal activity that might relate directly back to the blackmail threats you received?"

"You know I can't answer that."

"Explain to me what you think the motive for the blackmail is."

"I'm an easy target that will gladly pay."

"How would anyone know this? Have you been stalked? Did you receive previous threats? Why you? What makes you special?"

"I've been asking myself the same thing."

"Since we know where the fight was held, can you at least tell me which exit you took and approximately what time you left?"

The sound of papers shuffling filled the air. "I still have my parking stub."

"Great. Text me the information. I don't have a pen handy at the moment. The drop is supposed to go down tomorrow night. We'll do what we can to catch the guy and keep you protected. From where I stand, you didn't do anything wrong, and if you did, so did every other lawyer, judge, and politician at that fight. If the shit hits the fan, I'd suggest you speak to the partner who brought you to the fight and let him know any action he takes against you will result in his destruction as well."

"You're suggesting I blackmail a partner at the firm?" Fletcher sounded aghast and a little amused.

"It's not blackmail. It's just a friendly suggestion from one colleague to another."

"Will you call tomorrow evening with the verdict?"

"Absolutely."

As soon as we disconnected, I parked a few blocks from the gym and read the waiting text message. Then I dialed O'Connell and suggested he request security cam footage from the parking garage Fletcher used. It might lead to identifying a blackmailer and possibly a killer, so the city could afford to go through the expense and trouble. Worst case, I'd pass it off to Lucca and hope the boy scout had some strings he could pull.

Taking a deep breath, I left the car and went to the gym. Tim would not be pleased to see me again, and Ron might be pissed I was showing up early. Too bad. Someone inside was guilty of something, and I planned to find out precisely what that something was.

TWENTY-FOUR

After stepping foot inside the gym, I continued around the desk and passed the center ring, hoping not to be noticed. Linka Greenwood was in the back corner, seated in a folding chair and writing something in a notebook. She didn't spot me as I ducked into the locker room. It was too early for any of the men to be inside, so I headed straight for the dead drop location.

Today, the unit wasn't locked. I carefully lifted the handle and opened the door. The inside smelled like sweaty socks. Crinkling my nose, I felt around for a false back or loose side. Anything that might be used to further conceal the blackmailer's identity during the pick-up. But the metal walls were solid, as was the top and bottom. Whoever intended to blackmail Fletcher was stupid enough to think he'd get away with it.

"What the hell are you doing in here?" Coker covered the distance between us faster than I thought possible and slammed the locker shut, narrowly missing my fingers in his haste. "This is the men's locker room. I doubt you have something dangling between your legs."

"My mistake. I must have missed the sign. Where's the women's locker room?"

"At the rec center or one of those fancy ass gyms. The

same place you ought to be." He glowered, stepping closer. "What are you doing here?"

"Training."

He gritted his teeth and stepped even closer, placing us practically nose to nose. "I'd snap you in half in a second. One blow and you'd be down for the count, doll."

"Tim," Linka suddenly appeared behind him, "Alex signed up for the evening class. Ron's still assessing her. You don't want to scare off a paying customer, do you? That wouldn't be good for business, and you could use the business." She gave him a pointed look.

"Dammit, cookie," he said to her, "when did dames decide they needed to bash the shit out of one another?"

"It's because you men make it look like so much fun," I said.

Coker fixed me with another icy stare and slammed his palm against the locker. "This is off-limits. If I have to tell you again, you're gone." He turned to Linka. "Make sure Ron knows that too."

"Sure, Tim. I'll let him know." She guided me out of the locker room and into the corner where she had been writing furiously. "When did you get here? Class doesn't begin for another hour and a half."

"I know. I'm sorry. I just," I shook my head and sat in the chair next to her, "had a bad day and needed to escape. I forgot the men train every day. I just wanted to get some extra time in on the bags. You said I could have that locker, but when I went to leave my water bottle inside, Tim caught me."

"It's okay. He's a pain in the ass, but it's his gym. When he's around, you have to follow his rules."

"What are you doing here so early?" I asked, remembering Tim didn't let the fighter's girlfriends hang around.

She giggled. "Mr. Big-Time Gym Owner can't get his books to balance, mostly because Ron's training quite a few women on contingency and Tim doesn't know, so I offered to take a look. Tim thinks this is secretarial work, which means women's work."

"Sexist pig."

"Yeah, but at least he's predictable." She went back to work, and I tried not to appear overly interested, even though I was. "I end up correcting the problem every few months. Ron tosses in the extra funds whenever Tim notices, and I make sure it looks like an accounting error."

"That sounds sneaky." Or illegal.

"No one gets hurt, and this way, Tim makes more money and we women are more empowered."

"For a second, I thought Tim was actually breaking his own rule and letting the wives and girlfriends hang around and watch their men train."

"He hasn't done that in a long time." She thought back. "The last time, one of the guys got popped real good in the eye. He had a mouse. Tim lanced it to get the blood out from beneath the skin. The guy bled all over the mat, and Cynthia freaked out."

"Cynthia?"

"The fighter's girlfriend." Linka shook her head. "She was spouting out how the protective gear was subpar, and the owner shouldn't allow injuries like that to happen. She wanted to find a lawyer to sue and shut the whole place down. After that, women weren't allowed to hang around anymore."

"I thought scars were supposed to be sexy," I said.

"Yeah, just as long as they're healed and not bleeding all over the ring."

While Linka continued to work on Tim's net earnings, my eyes roamed over the fighters. Our shooter wasn't the bulky bodybuilder type, so Ron and half the guys were immediately ruled out. Unfortunately, no one was wearing a cap and sunglasses while they ran through drills and pad rounds, making identification that much more difficult. I snuck a sideways glance at Tim. He was too short and stocky to be our shooter.

When a sheet of paper fell free from the stack Linka was working on, I bent down to retrieve it, noting the exorbitant loss Tim had suffered the previous month. She took the paper from my grasp and continued to work. Money troubles were an excellent reason to resort to blackmail, and the drop was inside Tim's gym. Was he that stupid? Probably.

Wondering if pressing Tim's buttons might result in something solid for our case or at least O'Connell's, I sauntered to the front desk where Tim was watching two men spar in the ring. I stepped directly into his line of sight. Automatically, he shifted to the side, ignoring me.

"It seems we got off on the wrong foot earlier." I pretended not to notice his attention was focused elsewhere. "I'm sorry. I didn't mean to cross any lines."

"S'okay." His eyes snapped to my face for half a second. "Don't do it again."

"I heard you coach a lot of guys who fight on the circuit. Were you at the Santos versus Levere bout?"

"Levere's my guy." He was watching the match again. With enough finesse, I could probably get him to confess to something while he was distracted. "Santos used to be too until that asshole swooped in and stole him."

"Willie?"

"Yeah, that damn do-gooder." He coughed and stared at me for a moment. "Do you mind? I'm working here."

So am I. "Do you ever coach girls?"

He laughed, a deep, contemptuous sound. "Listen up, dollface, this is a real sport for real athletes. It was never intended for some former cheerleader."

"Do I look like a cheerleader to you?"

"Yeah, now run along and find your pom-poms. I have more important things to do." He waved his hand in my face, dismissing me.

"Perhaps your attitude is the reason Santos found himself another coach," I said. Tim reacted as if he'd been sucker-punched. "I bet that pissed you off when he left. My guess is you've lost a lot of fighters over the years. Is that why you made sure Levere destroyed Santos in the ring?" I looked at him with disdain. "You realize the kid died because of that fight."

"How dare you?" He came around the desk and backed me against the wall. "You come into my gym and accuse me of killing a fighter. Get the hell outta here."

"I didn't say you killed Santos. I said you let Levere ring his bell beyond what was appropriate. Did you pay off the refs to delay calling the match?"

"Get out, or so help me god."

"No? Okay. Then maybe you made sure some of your guys roughed up Hector even more after the fight."

He pulled his arm back to hit me, and I sidestepped. His fist made contact with the wall and drew the attention of the majority of the gym. He adjusted his legs into a fighting stance, muscle memory taking over, but I had no desire to fight him if I didn't have to.

"Who told you this?"

"I have some friends in the police department," I replied as we warily circled one another. I resisted the urge to raise my fists in front of my face in a defensive position. "Did you blackmail the lawyer you told Levere and Facini to beat up?"

Tim bent over and charged like a bull, hitting me dead center in the chest with his shoulder and ramming me into the wall with a thud that knocked the breath from my lungs. I gasped. When he straightened, he hauled back to hit me, so I dropped to my knees, feeling his knuckle graze my temple.

"You psycho bitch," he snarled. Two fighters dragged him backward before he could kick me. "Get out of my gym, and don't you ever come back."

"Just so you know, I will be filing assault charges, and everyone here is a witness."

"They didn't see nothing." Tim threw the two men off of him, but he didn't make another move toward me. "You're trespassing on private property." He pointed to the door. "Out, or I'll call the cops."

Linka stood in the back corner, shaking her head. Briefly, I spotted Ron amongst the crowd. He jerked his chin at the door. It was clear Tim had the final say. At least there was no doubt who was calling the shots.

I went to the door. "I guess I'll just find another coach and take you down where it'll really hurt, right in the old purse strings." I watched the few remaining fighters scatter to make a path. The sooner I was gone, the happier they would be.

Once I was back inside my car, I dialed Jablonsky and

said, "I just blew my ability to get inside the gym, but I think Tim Coker is involved or knows who might be. The reason he wanted Briscoe dead was because he was losing a lot of fighters and a lot of money on the fights. I can file charges against him for assault, but my guess is his fighters will cover for him. What do you want me to do, boss?"

"I probably shouldn't have told you to knock the fighters around," Mark muttered. "I should have realized you only know how to play dirty."

"Tim's a chauvinistic asshole. The only way he'd respect me is if I had something dangling between my legs, or so he said."

"I'll dig out some Christmas ornaments and a candy cane."

"I doubt that would work." I watched out my windshield as a few of the men started to leave the gym. "Should I make another approach?" Two of the larger bodybuilders went down the steps to the subway. "Someone must know something."

"Just be careful. Since Coker's in charge, he probably sourced out a hit on you," Mark semi-joked.

"That would make identifying the killer so much easier." I disconnected, grabbed my credentials, and strapped on my shoulder holster before zipping a hooded sweatshirt over it.

Taking off at a light jog, I rounded the corner, looking like someone determined to get a good workout regardless of what Tim had to say. I stopped a block and a half from the gym and leaned against a lamp post to stretch. A few more men left the gym, but I wasn't sure who to question.

When a lightweight stepped out of the gym, popping earbuds into his ears and tucking his mp3 player into his pocket, I found my opening. Since he was oblivious to his surroundings, I waited until he was a block away from the gym and sprinted after him.

"On your left," I announced. It was the polite thing most runners and bikers did, but with his music blaring, he didn't notice. I ran into his back, knocking him slightly off balance. He faltered, but once he recovered, he spun around. "Sorry," I mouthed, forcing him to remove his earbuds. "Sorry," I repeated, seeing recognition dawn on his face.

"Are you still itching for a fight?" He had an amused look in his eye.

"What?" I crinkled my brow, pretending I had no clue who he was. Then I made an exaggerated face. "You're from the gym?"

"Yeah." His eyes traveled down my legs and back up, assessing me. "That was pretty stupid of you to stand up to Coach Coker like that." He cocked his head to the side and smiled. "Kinda hot though."

"Yeah?"

"Yeah." He tilted his chin up. "Were you planning to be a fighter or something?"

"Or something." I held out my hand. "Alex."

"Brad." We shook hands, and he squeezed firmly. I squeezed back, and he laughed. "Now that you're blackballed, are you gonna go to the rec center like everyone else?"

"Maybe. Is that my best bet?"

He continued to hold my hand, rubbing his thumb across my knuckles. "It used to be, but that was before the shit with Hector and Willie went down." He inhaled, meeting my eyes. "How about we go someplace a little more private, and I can tell you who's good in the circuits?" He pulled me closer. "Maybe I could train you. I'm not a coach or anything, but if you're looking for a sparring partner, I'd be willing to take you down to the mat."

"What would your coach think of that?" I brushed a loose strand of hair behind my ear with my free hand.

"He doesn't have to know everything." He smiled again. "My place is right over there." He pointed to an apartment building on an adjacent street. "I'd hate for him to see us conspiring."

"Oh, that's what we're doing? I didn't realize we had to hold hands to conspire."

He practically blushed, embarrassed that I called him out on his flirtation.

"Well, lead the way." I gestured toward the building he indicated.

TWENTY-FIVE

Brad last name unknown opened the door to his apartment, a third floor walk-up, and kicked a gym bag and a pile of dirty clothes out of the way. A furry cat bounded out of the pile and rubbed against my legs, weaving a figure eight around my ankles. Brad continued past, stuffing some things into a closet.

"Sorry, my roommates are slobs." He glanced down at the cat that had followed him into the kitchen and was now meowing. "Mr. Whiskers isn't mine either."

"Okay." I spotted a bong on the window sill near the fire escape. "That's not yours either, right?" I snorted, playing it off as a joke.

"Of course not." He grinned. "Do you want a Gatorade or beer or something?"

"No, I'm good."

While Brad sifted through the fridge, I crossed the room, noting the free-standing punching bag in the corner, a couple pairs of handwraps, and some other boxing gear. Mounted on the wall were throwing stars, nunchuks, and a katana or some type of Japanese sword. From the living room, I could glimpse into one of the three back bedrooms. Magazines littered the floor, the bed was unmade, and I hoped the opened pizza box was empty.

"I caught some of what you were saying to Coach Coker," Brad said, coming up behind me. "Why were you saying those things? Are you a reporter or something?"

"I'm just a girl looking to fight."

"Did you know Hector or Coach Willie?"

"No, but I heard what happened. It's been in the newspapers. It's a shame when someone with such a promising future dies out of the blue. It makes no sense. I found a recording of the fight, and…" My voice trailed off. "Did you see Santos' last fight? Were you there?"

"No," Brad finished his drink, tossing the empty bottle into the recycle bin, "but I heard it was brutal."

"It looked like Coker had an axe to grind, and it's obvious he doesn't like women very much. We got off on the wrong foot today because I showed up a little too early. Needless to say, I probably should have kept my mouth shut."

"Why didn't you?" He leaned against the arm of the couch, clearing some papers and magazines out of the way.

"I don't know." I eyed him curiously, wondering if I'd been made. "Clearly, I'm trouble in capital letters. It's probably not safe to be in my presence." After all, I might arrest you.

"I'll take my chances since I like getting into trouble." The innuendo was not lost on me, but I giggled as if it were witty and flirty. "How long have you been training?"

"Ron just took me under his wing last week. Before that, I bounced around from place to place." I shifted my gaze to the wall. "Are you into martial arts too?"

"I like weaponry, but I only box. That kung fu crap isn't really my thing."

"That's cool." Making a snap decision which line of questioning to pursue, I decided to breach the subject of guns. Since Brad potentially fit the description of our shooter, it didn't hurt to find out some facts. "My ex-boyfriend was a gun collector. Vintage muskets, pearl-handled revolvers, crazy shit." I gave him a sexy smile. "Are you into any heavy artillery?"

"Will that earn me some extra brownie points?"

"Maybe."

He snickered. "Damn, I'm guessing motorcycles turn you on too."

"Only the fast ones." Okay, this wasn't heading in the direction I wanted. He stepped closer, looping his arms around my waist. "Whoa, buddy," I planted a firm hand against his chest, "I like fast bikes, not men that move too fast. You were gonna tell me about the coaches and the circuit, remember?"

"What if you show me some moves first?" he asked, raising an eyebrow suggestively.

Placing my other palm against his chest, I looked up at him. "Are you sure? You've already had a pretty tough workout at the gym. I don't know if you're in any condition to handle this."

"I rehydrated." He smiled. "We're good to go."

"Open-handed hits, agreed?" I asked, not wanting to risk getting punched in the face again.

Before he could respond, I knocked his hands off of me by hitting his forearms with the sides of my palms. Using his surprise to my advantage, I immediately slapped him on both sides of the face before stepping backward and placing my hands in front of me while I bounced on the balls of my feet.

"Agreed," he responded, unnerved by my brashness, "but I usually don't hit girls."

"Not a problem." We danced around each other, practically shadowboxing. "Did you ever train with Hector?"

"No. When I joined the gym, he was already on his way out. Coach knew he was getting extra fight time in on the side. Hector taught a class at the rec center. That was his place. He couldn't exactly afford to train with Coach Coker, and once Willie started helping him out, he up and left."

"Coker was getting contingency fees on Hector's fights?" I asked, incorrectly guessing Brad's next move and feeling a rush of air against my neck as he slapped my upper arm.

"Yeah. I heard a few of the guys talking about it. Coach Coker thought his gym might go under if he kept losing the bouts. A loss on the circuit didn't pull in enough cash to let the losing fighters train on a contingency basis, so everyone started training more often. It was a three strikes rule. After three losses, we have to pay the monthly gym fee or hit the road."

I slapped his chest and his ribcage on the lower right side before stepping out of his striking range. "Did Coker ever bet on the fights?"

"That would be against the rules." Brad hit my side hard enough that I winced. "I'm sorry." He made a timeout gesture. "Are you injured or something?"

"No, it just stung. Are we done playing around?" If this kept up, he'd discover my shoulder holster and handgun in no time.

"Yeah," he chuckled, "I wanted to make sure you weren't a reporter or lawyer or something."

"Have they been snooping around?" At least we were getting back on track.

"A lawyer stopped by last week. Coker had a few guys run him off." He must have seen the question on my lips. "I don't know why he was there, but it couldn't have been good. Maybe he was going to serve Coach with papers or threaten to sue or something. I don't know. I try to mind my own business. To each his own, right?"

"Sure."

"Come with me," he reached for my hand again, and I let him grasp my fingers in his palm, "I have a list of other gyms in my room. I tried out half a dozen. The only downfall is they have invitation-only fight teams, so you have to prove yourself before you get invited to compete on the circuit. On the plus side, they're far less sexist. Some of them even have mixed matches, if that's something you're interested in."

I followed him down the hallway, relieved the messy room wasn't his. He opened the door across from that room and ushered me inside. Apparently, he was telling the truth. The mess in the common areas must have been due to his roommates because his room was pristine. The bed was made. The top of the dresser was devoid of everything, and the closet was closed.

"Wow, how can you live with such polar opposites?"

"We balance each other out. Have a seat. Relax. This might take a minute." He went to the desk and opened the drawer, removing a folder. He flipped through some papers and a stack of business cards before removing half a dozen with various gym logos and handing them to me. "I thought I should hold on to these in case I struck out with Coker, but I can always get more if need be. Actually, if I get kicked out, I'll start going to whichever gym you pick."

"Are you really that sure of yourself?" I asked, still wanting to ask about Briscoe, betting, and blackmail.

"You said you had an ex-boyfriend, and you agreed to come to my apartment. You don't even know me, so there had to be a reason for it. Plus, I let you slap me in the face a few times. In some countries, I believe that makes us married."

"You don't have a girlfriend?"

"I don't have anyone special." Which meant he had a few girlfriends. "You seem like you could be special."

"Weren't you going to show me some guns and bikes?"

He rolled up his sleeves and posed like a bodybuilder, flexing his biceps. "What do you think of these guns? Too cheesy?"

"Definitely."

Before I could say anything else, another guy appeared in the doorway. "Hey, Brad." He stopped midsentence. "Sorry, I didn't realize you had company. Who's the babe?"

"Alex," Brad said, "meet one of the two pigs who lives in this place. Philip this is Alex."

"Nice to meet you." Philip yanked the backward baseball cap off his head. "I'll let you two get back to whatever it was you were doing. I just wanted to give your cap back." He tossed it onto the desk and pulled the door closed behind him to give us some privacy.

My eyes focused on the Yankees' emblem. Those baseball caps were highly popular, but it looked identical to the one our shooter wore. I scanned the rest of the room. It no longer seemed neat and tidy. It looked clinically cold. Perhaps even surgical.

"What's a matter? Are you a Sox fan?"

"No. I don't follow baseball." I unzipped my sweatshirt a

little and fanned my face. "I just got a little dizzy. Is that offer for a Gatorade still on the table?"

"Sure, I'll be right back."

As soon as he left the room, I took full advantage, opening his closet door, looking under his bed, and quickly checking each of his desk drawers while he was in the kitchen, talking to Philip. A moment later, their conversation ended. I closed the drawer, barely making it back to the bed before he came into the room.

"Is lemon-lime okay?"

"That's great. Thanks." I took a sip from the bottle.

"You never said why you were interested in boxing." He leaned against the headboard. "Sure, there are a dozen girls who show up at night, but most of them look like escapees from the Soviet Olympic team."

"How old are you?" I retorted.

"Thirty-two. I'm just saying. Linka's sweet, and she's an awesome fighter. I'm pretty sure she could kick my ass seven ways from Sunday, but she's built like a man. If she cut her hair and layered up on top, Coach Coker would probably let her train during the day with the rest of the guys."

"Now who's being sexist?" But his observation held some merit. Making a show of looking at the clock, I took another sip from the bottle and stood up. "It's getting late. I really should go. Thanks for the information and the slap fight." Taking a step backward toward the door, I added, "Maybe we could go to a fight sometime together or something."

"That sounds good." He picked up his phone and scrolled through the calendar. "There's one this weekend. Are you up for it?"

"I'll have to check and make sure I don't have to work. Why don't you give me your number?" I suggested. He rattled off his digits, and I scribbled them onto the back of one of the business cards. "Since the coach doesn't bet on the fights, does that mean the fighters don't either?"

"I can't tell you what other people do, but if things like that ever came to light, it could end a career."

"But these aren't sanctioned matches."

"Maybe not, but whenever someone gets signed and starts performing for the league and behavior like that comes to light, he could easily get cut. It's not worth the risk." He narrowed his eyes. "Why are you obsessed with betting? You've already been kicked out of one gym today."

"I have a few degenerate gamblers as friends. Sometimes, they'll blow a few grand on the stupidest shit imaginable. Once, they even bet how long a commercial would last. It makes me see gambling addicts everywhere I go."

"Well, it's a sport, so there are always bookies and betters hanging around." He walked me to the front door. "Are you sure you don't want to stay a while longer? We could go another round." Philip's eyes darted from the television to us, and I suspected Brad said it just to make it seem like he was a bigger player than he was.

"Thanks, anyway. Maybe next time I'll let you go out on top." I tossed a look toward Philip, playing along. "Hey, was all that talk about guns just bullshit?"

"Yeah. I've never even held a gun, but don't hold that against me."

"I'll try not to."

TWENTY-SIX

"Wonders never cease to amaze," Lucca said when I entered the conference room, dressed in my workout gear. "Did they teach you how to block? Or did you find a better way to interrogate our suspects without beating their fists with the side of your face?"

"Did you have fun playing house with Will Briscoe's ex-girlfriend?" I shot back.

"Parker," Mark said in that tone I hated, "I was just about to send a search team to find you. What happened after you got the axe?"

"I made a new friend. You always tell me to play nice, so I did."

Lucca made a choking sound in the background, but I ignored it while I filled the two of them in on Brad, Coker's money troubles and disdain for lawyers, and the possible dangers related to betting. Then I focused on the blown-up surveillance cam photo of our suspect.

"Are we sure the suspect is male? Some of those female fighters have musculatures resembling men. Linka's probably in the buck sixty or better range and around 5'10."

"It looks like a man to me," Lucca said, "on account of

an obvious lack of female breast development."

"Yeah, I'm not even going there." Mark shook his head. "We'll have the techs reconsider the possibilities, but my gut says our shooter's male. He was seen on courthouse surveillance going inside the men's room. Someone would have noticed." He checked the notes and witness statements, but no one had gotten a good look at the unsub. "What'd you discover on your outing, Lucca?"

"Will and his girl had a falling out. She enrolled in some classes at the city college and wanted him to follow her lead. He refused, but they stayed together for another six months before she broke it off."

"Are you sure she broke it off?" I asked, wondering if a scorned girlfriend might have had reason to want Will's dad dead. Maybe William Briscoe Sr. didn't approve of the relationship.

"That's what she said." Lucca shrugged. "But things get even more interesting. I asked her what Will did besides drop in and out of college and hang out with friends, and she said he was taking up boxing. That was the real reason she wanted him to stick with school, so he'd give up the fight scene and focus on a safer, more stable future. She couldn't take seeing him beaten up all the time. She said she spent more time dressing his wounds than getting dressed up."

I swallowed, hearing Martin's rendition of the same argument in my head. "Do you have her profile?"

"Cynthia Jackson, twenty. No priors. Made the dean's list last semester," Lucca read. "Were we aware Will Briscoe was following in his father's footsteps by participating in the sweet science?"

"He didn't mention it, and neither did Laura. From the way they made it sound, I thought they had no clue how involved their father was with boxing and coaching or any of the men he trained." The pieces were starting to come together. It explained how Will was able to recognize the fighters in the photos, and perhaps it even explained his extreme guilt and failed suicide attempt. "Earlier, Linka Greenwood mentioned a Cynthia being hysterical when her boyfriend was hurt at Coker's gym. I wonder if it's the same

Cynthia."

"Will Briscoe's our connecting piece. We need to speak to him. He must know who the shooter is," Lucca insisted, giving Jablonsky a desperate look. "Can't we get a judge to sign something to grant us access?"

"Go find out, kid." Mark dismissed him. Once Lucca was behind his desk, rapidly dialing, Mark snorted. "You and those damn hunches. It looks like you might be right again."

"Don't you hate it when that happens? Which hunch was right this time?"

"That there's a connection between Santos' death and the two courthouse killings. While you were gone, I spoke to Elias Facini and Gavin Levere. Facini's searching for new representation and isn't exactly being cooperative." He chewed on a hangnail. "Levere knows something, but he's scared. The police are keeping him for the time being with manslaughter and a possible homicide charge hanging over his head. The kid doesn't know which way to turn, but he knows what's going on, at least with the fight scene. The thing is, he mentioned William Briscoe's death in relation to Santos' death. It stands to reason everything's connected. No coincidences, like I always say."

"How do you propose we convince Levere to open up?"

"I'm working on it. In the meantime, you might as well get comfortable since we're working through the night on Will Briscoe Jr.'s connection to this shit."

I left the conference room, intent on changing back into regulation attire and making a quick phone call before settling in for another all-nighter. At least Martin couldn't say this was a lame excuse to avoid sharing a bed.

Once I was dressed, I returned to the conference room and took a seat. Lucca didn't look happy. I suspected it was because Will was still off-limits for the time being. Jablonsky was going over some things with Agent Lawson, our resident tech, so I turned my legal pad to a clean sheet and started sketching out the timeline for the rest of the week.

Tomorrow night, the money was supposed to be left inside the locker. Surely, the PD had some type of sting in place. However, I resisted the urge to call O'Connell and ask. We needed to question Linka and some of the guys from the gym to find out what they knew about Will Briscoe Jr. Since they all seemed to know Coach Willie, they were probably aware Will Jr. was his son.

As if reading my mind, Jablonsky announced, "I'll follow up with Laura Briscoe. The two of you can't seem to get the job done, so I will find out about William and Will. Damn, what is wrong with people naming their kids after themselves? Sheesh." Mark rolled his eyes. "Someone give the realtor lady a call and show her some photos of the fighters. Maybe she'll be able to identify one of Coker's trainees as the mystery man. Take a photo of Will Briscoe with you."

I noted the time. "She already left for the day."

"Then track her down." Mark focused on Lucca. "You should have a talk with the Greenwoods. Since Parker's out and the PD will be busting the gym tomorrow, we have to get our questions answered tonight. We'll reconvene in two hours and work through dinner."

Picking up my phone, I dialed Sylvia Britt's personal number. After three rings, she answered with a reluctant, "Hello."

"Mrs. Britt, this is Alex Parker, I'm sorry to bother you. I just need five minutes of your time. It's very important."

"I'm about to meet with a potential buyer. Can't this wait until morning? I have done nothing but cooperate, despite the fact you lied to me."

"I didn't lie. I am in the market for a new office." I figured it might just get her to open up. "Just five minutes, please. I can meet you at a house or office or bar, whatever you want."

"Fine. I'll be showing an apartment, but I'll probably grab a quick drink before going home. If you can get there before I leave, then I'll speak to you tonight. But only for five minutes. I'm a busy woman. I don't have time for this foolishness."

"Yes, ma'am." After writing down the address, I left the conference room, noticing Lucca a few steps behind me.

"I won't mention you or anything you discovered while

at Coker's gym," Lucca said as we rode the elevator to the garage together. "Since your new friend is connected to the gym, we might need you to speak to him again. I don't want to burn you faster than you burn yourself."

"Just don't piss them off. Linka's like a bear, and Ron has a hell of an uppercut."

"Thanks, but I'll be fine."

We parted ways, and I put on my game face, slipped back into the cool, impenetrable façade of a federal agent, drove to the bar, and went inside. Mrs. Britt was laughing and touching a woman's forearm. Even from this distance, I could tell it was an act. The couple she was speaking to looked antsy. Perhaps they were on the fence about renting an apartment or making a buy, so I gave them space. The last thing I needed was for Britt to be in a foul mood before asking her if she recognized anyone from the photo array I had stuffed in my bag.

Taking an unobtrusive seat a few stools away from Britt and her clients, I ordered a sparkling water and studied my surroundings. The place was reasonably crowded, but no one stood out as sinister. Frankly, everyone looked overworked and exhausted, unless I was projecting. Ten minutes later, the couple left, exchanging a round of handshakes and promises to follow up. I waited a polite fifteen seconds after they cleared the front door and then moved down to the unoccupied stool.

"Good evening, Mrs. Britt. Thanks for taking a moment out of your day."

She sighed dramatically. "What do you want?"

"Look, two people are dead, actually three, and you might be able to help us find the killer. It'll just take two minutes to go through these photos. Tell me if you recognize anyone, and I'll be on my way. Unless something else surfaces, we won't bother you again."

"That's what the agents said last time." She took the stack of glossies and flipped through the images. Her manicured nails came to rest on the third photo. She laid it on top of the bar and scanned the rest of the images before returning to the one she removed. "I don't know. He sort of looks familiar."

"From the open house?"

"No," she squinted, "I'm thinking we might have bumped into each other a different day."

"Where?"

"The office building where the open house was but before that." She bit her bottom lip and shook her head. "I don't know. People bump into me all the time. I could be wrong, or he could look like someone who was walking down the street that I passed today or something. I try to remember faces because that's a good business practice. However, worrying with strangers isn't one of my concerns."

"What about the others?"

"They aren't familiar." She gave the photo of Elias Facini one last look and put forty dollars on the bar. "Please make sure this is the last time I'm questioned. I'm far too busy to do my job and yours too." Haughtily, she walked out of the bar.

On the bright side, her generous tip covered my sparkling water. I went back to the car, wondering how Facini could keep popping up at every turn but without providing any evidence to use against him. Something was missing.

I was the first to return to the federal building, and I didn't see any reason why I couldn't ask Facini a few questions while I waited for my cohorts to arrive. Once Facini was settled into an interrogation room, I made sure the AV equipment was working properly and a technician was monitoring the feed. Then I stepped inside the room, closed the door, and took a seat across from the fighter.

"Do you want to call an attorney?" I asked.

"No." He leaned back. His hands were cuffed in front of him, which wasn't exactly protocol, but I didn't believe he planned to escape or harm me. "You were right."

"On the off chance that it happened more than once, do you think you can elaborate on which instance you're referencing?"

"Tim Coker paid for my former representation. Tim offered since he encouraged me and Gavin to scare off the man that stopped by. Since it was his fault we were being charged with assaulting some slimeball attorney, he provided us with a different slimeball attorney. His words, not mine. I didn't know anyone had been killed. I mean," he swallowed and scratched at his upper lip, "obviously, I heard about Hector. I'm not a bad guy. I don't want to be on the wrong side of things."

"What can you tell me about the office building across the street from the federal courthouse?"

"Parking's a bitch, and the damn chiropractor doesn't even validate."

"So you're familiar with the building and the area?" This wasn't going well for Facini, but he didn't seem to notice. Either he was brilliant, or he was an idiot. "Are you aware of any other office spaces inside that building?"

"I don't know. Lawyers, accountants, people in suits were always in the elevator whenever I had an appointment." He narrowed his eyes. "What? Is it some black site for the CIA or something?"

"I couldn't tell you. My clearance level isn't that high." Offering a smile, I figured it wouldn't hurt to play along. "Do you have back problems?"

"My shoulder mostly." He manipulated the left one around as best he could with the cuffs, and it made an audible popping sound. "I played baseball in high school. Boxing tends to aggravate an old injury. The guys at the gym suggested a chiropractor since it seems like something's misaligned."

"Has it helped?" I stretched, letting him hear my vertebrae emit a similar sound. "Ever since I bruised my spine, I creak and pop like a hundred-year-old house."

"Honestly, I can't tell the difference. I've been going to the same guy for the last six months. Sometimes, it feels like it's worse when I leave."

"Do you have a standing appointment?"

"I go Tuesday mornings on my lunch hour."

"What do you do for a living besides box, Mr. Facini?"

"I'm a consumer hotline representative which is the fancy way of saying I answer calls from disgruntled customers and take catalog orders from the few people left on the planet who don't know how to use the internet. It's not exactly glamorous, but it pays the bills."

"Where were you on Friday?" I consulted the file to make sure I had the correct date of the shooting, even though that was chiseled in my brain, along with the rest of the irrefutable facts we knew, which were few and far between.

"At work. You can check if you don't believe me. At least a dozen people saw me there. That other agent, the older guy, he said he would look into it."

"I'm sure he did." I rubbed my face. "Elias, why did you assault Mr. Fletcher? You don't seem like a violent man or a stupid man. What were you thinking?"

"I wasn't. It was a mistake. The gym is practically my second home. Those guys are my brothers. I didn't want someone to threaten my home or my family."

"Why did you think Mr. Fletcher was a threat? Did he say or do anything that led you to believe that?"

"He came inside and asked to see the place. I figured he was just another guy wanting to sign up to fight. A lot of corporate guys do. Tim showed him around. The next thing I know, the two of them are arguing, and Tim tells him that saying things like that could have drastic repercussions. As soon as the lawyer walked out, he called Gavin over and told him to make sure he didn't come back again. Then Gavin got me to help. Like I said, it was a stupid mistake. I really wish I could take it back." He looked sheepish. "You said you could have the assault charges dropped if I cooperated. Isn't this cooperating?"

"Yes."

"Then how come I'm in handcuffs?"

"Because you're still considered a suspect in a double homicide." I held up my palm before he could voice a protest. "I'm going to check your alibi, and if you're willing to have your chiropractor release your appointment schedule to us, I'll do my best to get you out of here by morning."

"Sure, I'll release whatever you want. If you want DNA and fingerprints, I'll hand those over to. Whatever you want. I just want this to be done."

"There's one other thing. You need to stay away from

Coker's gym and everyone affiliated with it for the rest of the week. Can you do that?"

"Sure, I guess."

"Okay. Let me check on some things. I'll be right back."

TWENTY-SEVEN

When Mark Jablonsky came into the conference room, he took one look at my note-covered whiteboard, put the Chinese takeout on the table, and said, "I thought I told you not to speak to Facini."

"Did you? It must have slipped my mind."

"You promised to cut him loose tomorrow. Any particular reason?"

"Fletcher dropped his complaint. The PD is willing to let it slide, and the DA doesn't seem to care one way or the other. If he's free and responsible for the extortion, O'Connell will bust him, and that'll be it." I turned, watching Mark dig into a container of lo mein.

He pointed his chopsticks at the container closest to me. "Orange chicken."

"You remembered, how sweet." I peeled the paper off a second set of chopsticks and opened the container. Until this moment, I didn't realize I was starving. "Get this, Facini's chiropractor is on the same floor as the office our shooter used. Too bad he has an alibi."

"I ran it myself, but maybe it's possible Facini slipped out when no one was looking. I'd say he looks good for the killings. He has the training and know-how. He had an excuse to scout the location, and we know he's capable of doing incredibly stupid things to protect his precious coach and gym. Beating up a guy is just a stone's throw away from murder."

"Yeah, but I'd say he'd bludgeon someone to death instead of using a high-powered rifle to shoot them."

"He shoots for sport. He might have rationalized it as target practice. It's one way to stave off a guilty conscience," Mark suggested.

"The only hitch is that Facini was at work, and he has a dozen co-workers vouching for him." I speared a piece of chicken with a chopstick and popped it into my mouth. Unfortunately, chewing only bought so much time to think, and with the way this case was going, I'd need at least a decade to sort it out. "If Facini isn't our shooter, and that's a big fucking if, then it's someone intimately aware of everything Elias does. Nothing else can possibly explain it."

"I'll get a list of his friends and family. In the meantime, try to punch some holes in his airtight alibi."

No matter how I spun it, there was no way Elias Facini magically transported himself from his job across town to the office building across the street from the courthouse, got inside a cab, took it to a different neighborhood, hopped the subway, and made it back to work without anyone noticing. The entire event would have taken at least two hours. Too many people saw him at work during that timeframe. He wasn't our guy. Every shred of evidence pointed to him, but it wasn't him.

"Here," Mark tossed a yellow legal pad on the table between us, "family, friends, co-workers, and everyone from his social media friends list."

"I hate social media." Thankfully, it looked like Elias did too since there were only thirty-eight names on the list.

"Our computer techs said the shooter is definitely male, so I took the liberty of crossing out half the names."

"Do we have a gym roster?" I assumed whoever killed Briscoe must have a boxing connection.

"Tim Coker wouldn't turn over the names, and there isn't enough to compel him to do so. Plus, we can't be positive the shooter is a boxer wannabe. I'd put my money on the killer being involved in the gambling scene."

"I hope you didn't spend too much time coming up with that one," I said. "O'Connell's looking into it since we have no basis. None of our evidence points to that. Hell, our evidence doesn't point to anything. We have a smoking gun, but we don't know who fired it."

"I'm gonna tell you what I think." He leaned back in the chair. "Will Briscoe Jr. was pissed at the old man. He was daddy's disappointment, and no matter what he did, he never felt good enough. So he takes up boxing because he wants to show the old man he's just as good as the fighters Briscoe's training. Obviously, the circuits overlap. Maybe Junior didn't make the cut to fight, or he had his ass royally kicked. Regardless, the kid couldn't hack it, and he quits."

"Making him an even bigger disappointment," I added.

"Which pisses Junior off even more, so he talks to some of the guys at the gym, tells them about his dad, the way his dad helps train the fighters, and wants someone to make sure Briscoe is humiliated as a coach."

"Depending on who Will Jr. spoke to, it could have compromised his father's coaching strategy and Hector Santos' fighting style. That could be the reason Santos was beaten so badly. Do you think the fights are fixed?"

"I don't know. But the coaches know their fighters' capabilities. Junior might have tipped the scales in Coker's favor."

"We've gone through Briscoe's financials. There's no indication he was betting on the fights."

"No, but Tim Coker has been having money troubles. I bet it's gotten worse since he lost Hector Santos to William Briscoe."

"That's why Tim made sure Santos was down for the count with the last fight." I inhaled deeply. "Coker bet on the fights. I wouldn't put it past him to have a fighter take a dive if he thought he was going to lose, but the only way we can even get close to proving that is to get someone to talk. Unfortunately, it still doesn't give us the shooter. Tim doesn't fit the bill. He's too short and stocky."

"It's just a theory," Mark muttered, "but it's the only one I have."

"Which means we need Will Briscoe to talk to us," Agent Lucca said from the doorway. I didn't notice when he came into the room, but he couldn't have been there that long. "I spoke to the Greenwoods. Wow, they really like to talk." He met my eyes. "You weren't being mean when you said Linka's like a bear. Although, I'd say she's more like a teddy bear and probably just as cuddly."

"Great, you can face off against her in the ring. However, I would like my teeth to remain in my mouth."

Lucca laughed. "Yeah, I can see how that could be an issue."

"What'd you learn, Eddie?" Mark asked, gesturing at an untouched takeout container which was probably cold by now.

"Coker's gym would be going under if it weren't for the Greenwoods. Tim has a strict coaching policy toward the men. Along with a strict training regimen, no girls are allowed to hang around. From what I gather, Coker's a misogynist."

"I could have told you that," I said.

"Which makes the situation pretty damn hilarious that the majority of his paying customers are women. The female fighters are keeping his business afloat, or rather, the female non-competitive fighters since they're the only ones paying membership fees at the gym. Most of the men are getting trained on contingency, and they haven't had any star fighters in a long time. Coker has three other coaches working for him. Each coach has three or four fighters, and seventy-five percent of those men train on contingency. A cut of the profits goes to the coach, and the rest goes to Coker." Lucca reached across the table for the plastic-wrapped flatware set. "It looks like an upside down pyramid scheme with the way the money flows from the bottom to the top. It's no wonder Coker can't make ends meet."

"We know he has money troubles," Mark said, hoping to cut the running commentary short.

"Sort of." Lucca opened the container and skewered his beef and broccoli with a fork. "His fighters can't hack it. The training routine is basic. The equipment is outdated.

Coker's old school, and it shows. According to Greenwood, a lot of fighters have jumped ship and moved to greener pastures. They much rather pay to fight well than train for free and have their asses kicked."

"Not to mention, Tim's new three strikes and you're no longer training on contingency policy," I said, considering the implications. "That means Santos should have won the fight, but Gavin Levere knew his moves because the two trained together. Even though Coker was calling out the combinations, Santos should've had a few new tricks up his sleeve. Dammit, we need to see the spread." I pulled out my phone and dialed Fletcher while Mark and Eddie stared as if I were speaking to an invisible third party.

"Hello," Fletcher said.

"Hey, do you remember the odds on the Santos versus Levere fight?"

"It's boxing. They use a moneyline instead of a spread." Fletcher explained the minus and plus system for the favorite and the underdog. "I can probably find the exact numbers somewhere, but Levere was the underdog. Whoever bet on him must have made a killing that night." He gulped into the phone. "Sorry, that was a poor choice of words."

"Thanks," I said, prepared to disconnect.

"Ms. Parker, that's why Detective O'Connell thinks I was blackmailed," he volunteered. "Have you reached the same conclusion?"

"What exactly does O'Connell think?" I asked, and Mark's ears perked up. "Hang on. I'm putting you on speaker." I hit a button. "Okay, go ahead."

"O'Connell thinks someone fixed the fight and that I might have overheard or caught them in the act due to my hasty exit," Fletcher said. "Honestly, I wasn't paying a bit of attention."

"You bet on Santos, right?" Mark asked.

"Yeah," Fletcher sounded uncertain about answering since he had no clue who was asking.

"Why would anyone think that you possessed knowledge about the fight being fixed?" Mark asked again.

"Go ahead, Mr. Fletcher," I said, hearing his hesitance

over the line. "That's my friend Mark asking the questions."

"Because after I left, the person I arrived with placed a substantial amount of money on Levere."

"How substantial?" I asked.

"Twenty thousand," Fletcher replied, "and the winnings were nearly triple that."

"Shit," Lucca said.

I took Fletcher off speaker before the attorney became too anxiety riddled. "They think you discovered what was going on, made a miniscule bet, and left in order to rip off the house, even though the house always wins."

"That's what the police think," Fletcher affirmed.

"With whom did you place your bet?"

"I don't know. The police hooked me up with a sketch artist, and they came up with a decent rendition. Please tell me you don't need anything else from me. We have eighteen hours until I drop off the money, and I'm getting the feeling you're not even close to figuring this out."

"The police will handle it. Don't worry, Jack. Just do whatever they say. I'll be in touch afterward. If not, give me a call tomorrow night and we'll discuss this further." I hung up and put the phone down.

"Why do you always have to steal my thunder?" Lucca asked, finishing his container of takeout. "May I continue?"

"Go ahead, boy scout. Impress me."

"As I was saying, if it weren't for the women the Greenwoods coach at night, Coker wouldn't be bringing in enough money to keep the place running. According to Linka, Tim records a larger net gain on the losing matches than he should. She knows what he makes because Ron is almost always at the fights with him, so they think he's doing something underhanded on the side. But they don't know what."

"Or so they say," Mark said. "How come they were willing to open up about their boss's practices to you?"

"I suggested Coker was being investigated for unrelated illegal activities, and in order to avoid the gym or anyone at the gym being implicated, it'd be in their best interest to cooperate." Lucca glanced in my direction before I could say anything about him misleading witnesses. "It's true. The police are looking at him as part of the extortion conspiracy and probably for illegal betting based upon that phone call."

"They'll probably warn Coker," Mark said.

"They're aware if they say a word, they'll be charged with obstruction of justice and possibly accessory after the fact," Lucca said. "I read people. They won't talk. They have too much to lose. From what Parker's said and what I've witnessed, they have far more to gain by letting Coker take the fall. Hell, they have enough paying clients and know-how to start their own gym."

"You better be right about this," Mark warned, pushing away from the table. "Make sure the police department is maintaining a visual on Coker tonight in case he makes a run for it. If you're wrong, you'll not only botch their op but the tiny shred of progress that we've made tonight too."

"Aye, sir," Lucca said, watching Mark leave the conference room.

"I'm only saying this once." I swiveled my chair to face Lucca. "You're probably right. The Greenwoods aren't in bed with Tim. However, that doesn't make them innocent bystanders or uninvolved."

"Neither of them fits the description of our shooter."

"No, but something else is going on with them. I've seen too many whispered words to think differently."

"Maybe they want to take over Tim's gym or take his client list and start fresh somewhere else. One of the hazards we face is seeing crime everywhere. You don't have to be so cynical and jaded, Parker. Not everyone is carrying a Mach 10 underneath their trench coats in order to commit a dozen homicides or something equally atrocious."

"That remains to be seen."

TWENTY-EIGHT

It was almost three a.m. by the time I made it back to Martin's. Damn, I really needed to start thinking of this as home instead of his place. After my epiphany in the conference room, I elected to stay at the office and try to piece more of this daunting puzzle together, but as the hours ticked by, my thoughts continued to unravel. Finally, I called it quits around two after Lucca insisted he'd call first thing in the morning to see what the verdict was on speaking with Will Briscoe or if any progress was made once Facini was released from custody. It was a mess, but for the next six hours or more, there was nothing I could do.

Grabbing my gym bag, I headed for the stairs. Unfortunately, late hours came with a price, and three lattes later, I was far too wired to sleep. When I spoke to Martin earlier, he said he was planning to turn in early, so there was no reason why I couldn't burn off some energy.

It had been a while since I'd gone for a long run on account of a few torn ligaments, but the treadmill held an undeniable appeal. After changing in the downstairs bathroom, I carefully stretched and stepped onto the exercise machine. After toying with the various settings, I discovered a marathon training program in the preset controls but stopped after four miles when my hip started to hurt. Checking my time, I wasn't exactly up to my norm, but thirty minutes wasn't too shabby.

After taking a five minute shower, I slipped into one of Martin's dress shirts that I typically slept in and silently climbed the steps to the bedroom. The room was pitch black. I inched my way to the closet, opening the door and flipping on the interior light in order to hang up my jacket from earlier. Just as I replaced the hanger, the room illuminated.

"I wasn't sure you'd even come home," Martin said, climbing out of bed, "but at least you called to tell me."

"We had to work late. I think we're actually making progress. Tonight, we made some headway on linking the extortion with the homicides, but I can't say much more than that."

"You must be exhausted."

"I've had far too much coffee in the last six hours to even entertain the idea of sleeping, but that doesn't mean I can't keep you company while you sleep. And this way, you'll realize how annoying it is to have someone watch you when you're unconscious."

He enveloped me in his arms and kissed along my collarbone. "Did you eat? You must have lost ten pounds since going back to the OIO. It's a miracle I can even kiss you like this without breaking a tooth. God, Alex, you're nothing but skin and bones." He exhaled against my neck. "I'll make you something for dinner."

"I already ate. Mark picked up Chinese."

"Of course, he did." Martin returned his lips to my clavicle while his free hand reached around and began unbuttoning my shirt. "Please tell me you didn't go back to your apartment to shower before coming home."

"I showered downstairs after testing out your treadmill. I didn't know it had marathon settings."

"And I didn't know you were supposed to be running distances yet," he retorted. "Are you positive you don't want to get some sleep or eat?"

"I'm fine. It's four a.m. Why don't you go back to sleep?"

"Because I already slept eight hours. These last few weeks finally caught up with me, but I'm awake now." He continued to work on the buttons.

"What are you doing?" I leaned against him, feeling some of the stress start to leave my body.

"You missed a button. Three actually." He undid the three that I had buttoned and ran his hands along my shoulders and down my arms, causing the shirt to fall to the floor. "God, you're so tense. You need to relax. How about I rub out those knots?"

"What did I do to deserve you?"

"Too many things to count," he nipped at my earlobe, "but if you insist on unnecessarily showing your gratitude, feel free to get creative."

*   *   *

I woke up with my face buried in Martin's pillow. I had the vaguest recollection of a whispered 'I love you' before he left for work, but almost everything else was a blur. The shrill ring of my cell phone sounded again. I reached across the nightstand to grab it.

"We're interviewing Will Briscoe in two hours. Nothing indicates Coker was tipped off. We have a surveillance team on Facini," Lucca said. "Other than that, Detective O'Connell called a few minutes ago to tell us not to botch the PD's operation tonight. It's going down around five. And lastly, I'm not your fucking secretary."

"Did you pick up breakfast?" I asked, reluctantly pulling myself out of bed.

"Screw you, Parker."

Yep, just another typical morning. I knew that strange quasi-friendliness we had wouldn't last. However, given that it was barely after eight, it was unlikely Lucca had slept at all, so I could overlook the bitchiness on account of his apparent sleep deprivation. Barely managing to force myself to resemble a living, breathing member of society, I found a pot of coffee already brewed downstairs in the kitchen. Thankfully, Martin was smart enough to realize caffeine was vital to life, and if I had to spend another morning fighting with his fancy single cup brewer, property damage would surely ensue. With coffee in hand, I drove to work.

Arriving on the OIO floor, I scanned the room, but there was no sign of Lucca. After reading the morning memos, I performed a final search for my supposed partner, but he wasn't around. SSA Jablonsky's office was dark, and the door was closed. I probably should have stayed home given how superb the day was already going.

Picking up my phone, I dialed Lucca's cell. "Where are you?"

"On my way to speak to Will Briscoe."

"Why didn't you wait for me?"

Conversation continued in the background, but I couldn't make out the words before Lucca finally responded, "Laura Briscoe made it very clear you are not to go near him again. She filed a complaint against you."

"That's ridiculous. I've been nothing but sympathetic. She even told Will that I was just doing my job. What changed?"

"I don't know. Jablonsky's with me. He said to stay away from her too. I'll let you know how the interview goes."

After we hung up, I drained the rest of my coffee in one gulp and resisted the urge to throw the cup across the room. Instead, I went upstairs to have a friendly chat with our crime techs. When I walked into the room, not a single person even bothered to turn around. Computer geeks tended to have a singular focus, and since I didn't have a monitor mounted to my face, I wasn't even a blip on their radar.

"How long has Facini been roaming free?" I asked, startling two of them.

Agent Lawson spun around. "My guess is he'll be taking the day off. I doubt he managed to get much sleep inside a holding cell." He pointed to a monitor. "Our surveillance team has eyes on him, but there hasn't been any movement since he arrived home twenty minutes ago."

"That's where he lives? Shit."

I raced out of the room and back to my desk, digging through the contents of the case file on Facini. His address and current location didn't match up. After a quick search, I realized the address listed on his driver's license was his parent's place, but that wasn't his home.

"Son of a bitch."

I typed in the location for information on the current occupant. The apartment was rented to Philip Dennison, and based on the driver's license photo, that was the same man who roomed with Brad. This realization floored me, and I remained momentarily dumbfounded.

Brad had two roommates, Philip Dennison and Elias Facini. After performing my due diligence on Philip Dennison, I found the information proved useless. The guy was a grad student and teaching assistant. He had no connection to the fight world or to either of our victims. As far as I could tell, he didn't own any weapons and had no criminal record. He was just an innocent bystander with at least one questionable roommate. I thought back to the uneasy feeling Brad's clinically clean room had provoked, and instantly, it was clear that he had tried to set Facini up to take the fall.

My phone rang, and I answered, "Parker."

"Will Briscoe's a bit wonky from the sedatives, but he had plenty to say. Apparently, he trained at Coker's gym and made quite a few friends, but he was kicked out or quit. The actual dynamics seem too elusive for him at the present, but after he gave up boxing and his girlfriend walked out on him, he blamed the old man. The kid was angry and confused."

"He still is."

"Yeah," Lucca exhaled, "but maybe mandatory counseling will help. Anyway, about a month ago, Will was hanging out with some of his boxing buddies, smoking pot, and shooting the shit. He said some things that he wishes he didn't. He didn't go into the specifics, but he's afraid that one of them made a move on his dad."

"Did you get names?"

"Half a dozen. Gavin Levere and Elias Facini were the only ones that stuck out though."

"Did he mention anyone named Brad?"

"Bradley Bellows," Lucca said. "How did you know

that?"

"Because Bellows was either feeling me out or trying to get into my pants. He's one of Elias Facini's roommates. That explains why Elias looked good for the shooting."

I heard shuffling and static as Lucca passed the information along to Jablonsky who must have grabbed the phone. "Wait there. Do not do anything until we get back. That's an order, Agent Parker."

"Yes, sir."

While I waited for the rest of the team to return, I compiled a profile on Bradley Bellows. The worst part was Bellows didn't exist until ten months ago. Rubbing my temples, I tried a few more search routes before filling out the requisition forms to run his photo through facial recognition, filed the paperwork, and brought the ID to our techs.

Agent Lawson narrowed his eyes at the printed driver's license photo. "I've seen him recently."

"Probably on the surveillance feed." I pointed to the monitor. "Is he home?"

Lawson picked up the radio and passed my question along to the surveillance team who provided a negative response. Brad had left the apartment an hour ago, and since they didn't have orders to follow him, they had no idea where he went. On the plus side, he didn't appear to be running since he left empty-handed.

"Fair warning, it'll probably be two days before he gets pinged, if he gets pinged," Lawson said.

That didn't seem too promising, but I thanked him anyway and returned to my desk, grabbed Brad's number, tried to perform a few reverse lookups, discovered the number traced back to a burner, and slammed my palms down in frustration. Who the hell are you, Bradley Bellows?

Entering the conference room, I flipped on the light, grabbed a marker, and started on our revised theory, feeling as if this was the twelfth time I'd performed the exact same task. I better not be doing this again tomorrow.

As I diagrammed the connection from Will Briscoe to Elias Facini to Bradley Bellows, or whatever the man's real name was, I still couldn't fathom why or how a kid's bitching could lead to a double homicide, especially one carried out with such precision and planning. If I hadn't chosen Brad as my mark yesterday, Elias would still be our primary suspect, even though his alibi was rock solid. Did Brad make me yesterday with all the talk about guns and gyms and betting? Was he suspicious, or did he think I was just some adrenaline-junkie? Regardless, the singular question that remained in my mind was what motive did Brad have for killing William Briscoe and Stan Weaver. We were missing a few vital pieces of the puzzle. I could only hope Lucca and Jablonsky had some answers. If not, perhaps Bradley Bellows' real identity could shed some light on the matter.

"Where did you come from?" I asked the photo.

"The psych ward," Lucca said, causing me to jump and nearly pull my nine millimeter. "I wanted to tell your friends you said hello, but there just wasn't enough time. They must miss you."

"Bite me."

"Now, now, I believe you know firsthand that behavior like that often leads to being restrained." He nodded at the board. "Jablonsky will be here in a second, and we're supposed to wait for him. But why didn't you tell me about Brad sooner?"

"I did. I just didn't realize his other roommate was Facini. The address we had didn't line up."

"Excuses."

"You're kidding me, right?"

Lucca dropped into a chair. "Sorry, Parker. I get a bit irritable when I haven't slept. I'm just ready for this to be done, so I can go home, get some sleep, and not have to think about a bunch of cyclic information that makes no sense and leads us back to where we began."

"Then you might want to change careers," Jablonsky said, joining us in the conference room, "because we're about to take another spin on the merry-go-round."

TWENTY-NINE

Laura Briscoe made it clear I was to stay away from her and her brother, particularly now that he was released into her care. Will had never been diagnosed with depression. The professionals determined the extreme circumstances surrounding his father's death were the cause of his contemplated suicide. And since I was the last person to question him, it was my fault he almost went over the edge. Maybe I brought him to the brink. At the moment, it was unclear if she planned to pursue any legal recourse against me or the OIO, but Jablonsky was running damage control in the meantime, hoping to avoid another debacle.

The effects of the sedatives hadn't completely worn off, and it made questioning Will Briscoe more difficult than necessary. On the plus side, he didn't hesitate to answer any of Jablonsky's or Lucca's questions, but his answers were anything but concise. From their account, Will was angry at his father for always neglecting him. When he tried to become a boxer to show the old man he could hack it just like Hector Santos, Will's efforts fell flat. He didn't last too long at the gym before Coker kicked him out. Will never participated in a single match, and when his girlfriend had stopped by to watch him train the day he'd gotten popped in the eye, Coker saw the kid as a liability.

During his time at the gym, Will had made several friends. They were his buddies who let him sleep on their couches. Almost a month ago, Elias had a party at his apartment. He invited the other fighters from Coker's gym, his roommates, and Will Briscoe. That was the night Will had gotten wasted and spent the evening telling every person there exactly how horrible his father was.

"He told them about his dad having to serve jury duty," Lucca said as I followed along with the briefing.

"Is that why he thinks his father's death is his fault?" I asked.

Lucca nodded.

By the end, it was obvious Will didn't kill his dad. Based on his actions, I didn't think he planned his father's death either. However, Will's story pointed to a few solid suspects, comprised of a group of men who we hadn't considered or barely considered until this morning. Now we just had to determine who had opportunity, access to an unregistered, illegal sniper rifle, and why a buddy's sob story was incentive to plan an almost perfect murder, execute it, and continue on as if nothing happened. It appeared we were dealing with a true psychopath.

"Bradley Bellows," Jablonsky said, focusing his gaze on me, "tell us everything you know."

"He's a fighter from Coker's gym. He shares an apartment with Elias Facini and Philip Dennison. The lease is in Dennison's name. Philip has no record or ties to the underground fight scene that I've found. He's a grad student at a nearby university."

"What's his area of study?" Lucca scribbled furiously on a pad of paper.

"Accounting," I replied. "He's an economics TA or something like that. It's on the university's website if you do a student search. Brad Bellows is one of Coker's fighters. He didn't involve himself in the fray that ensued when I confronted Tim about Santos' final match. Frankly, he was nothing but background noise. He never paid much attention to anything, kept to himself, and worked on the bags. I don't even know if he had a sparring partner.

Inside, there were a lot of half-naked guys knocking each other around. No one really stood out."

"Even though you noticed they were half-naked." Lucca chuckled.

I glared at him. "Brad left the gym alone, which is why I targeted him for an approach."

"What was your first impression?" Jablonsky asked.

"A bit cocky and self-assured. Probably a player. He had no problem inviting me to his place. He's also a neat freak, but his roommates are pigs. He made sure to tell me the mess was theirs. He probably smokes pot. There was a bong on the window sill."

"Then he can't be a competitor. They drug test, or at least they do at the sanctioned matches," Lucca said.

"It could be our way in. We've used less to bust a place." Mark contemplated our options. "What else?"

"We slapped each other around a bit. Literally. We were play-fighting. It was part of my spiel about being kicked out of the gym. It made sense at the time. Then he took me to his room."

"And you thought I had some hidden kinks," Lucca retorted. "I'd hate to see what you do with people you really like."

"Well, it's a good thing I really don't like you," I replied, and Mark slammed his palm on the table. "Anyway, he left me alone for five minutes, but I didn't discover anything incriminating."

"Not that you were illegally searching through his belongings," Mark added.

"Of course not. Before I left, he gave me a few dozen business cards to various gyms that he supposedly tried out."

"Do you still have them?" Lucca asked.

"They're at my desk, along with his phone number."

"Get them. See what you can run down, Lucca. Parker, update the boys in blue on these recent developments. Normally, I'm not one to share, but you brought them in, so make sure they don't fuck up our bust while we're busy making sure we aren't screwing with theirs. In the meantime, I'll get an update on where we stand with everything, and we'll reconvene in TacOps." Mark glanced at the two of us. "Really? I have to say dismissed? Jeez. Dismissed."

"Aye, sir." I crinkled my nose playfully and went to get the business cards for Lucca to analyze. I was relieved to pass the research aspect of the job off to someone else.

After Lucca was settled, I phoned O'Connell, who was out on a call. I tried Thompson's desk phone, but since they were partners, it yielded the same results. Deciding there was no point in remaining inside the federal building for the next few hours when there were endless opportunities beyond these walls just waiting to be discovered, I grabbed a set of keys and drove to the precinct. One of these days, they'd post my picture at the front desk in order to keep me out, but as of yet, that hadn't happened.

The squad room was bustling. I took a seat at O'Connell's desk and nonchalantly skimmed the sticky notes and files he had left out in the open. Knowing Nick, the sensitive materials were secured inside his desk or in the filing cabinet, but it never hurt to make sure something hadn't slipped past. It didn't.

"What the hell are you doing here?" Lieutenant Moretti asked. "You already dragged two of my detectives into some extortion bullshit. Now what do you want us to do for you, Agent Parker?"

"Actually, I'm here to see if there's something the OIO can do for you. We've made some progress on our double homicide, and a few key players and locations might overlap. Jablonsky wanted to make sure we weren't compromising any of your hard work."

"Tell Mark he owes me big for this one." Moretti narrowed his eyes. "How did a resigned federal agent turned private investigator end up back on the government payroll?"

"I'm not sure, but if you ever figure that one out, I'd love to hear it."

He chuckled. "You weren't a half bad police consultant. Too bad you're one of the idiots with the suits now. You had potential."

"Story of my life. Any idea when O'Connell or

Thompson will be back?"

"From the last radio call I heard, they should be on their way. Sit tight." He watched the way I swiveled at the desk. "Don't touch anything, and don't look at anything either. This is a police station. Everything on that desk is relevant to official police business. You are not." He walked away, leaving me alone and bored.

"It's about time you showed up. Do you really think I have nothing better to do than wait for the two of you to come back from a call?" I asked when Thompson and O'Connell entered the bullpen.

"Clearly, you don't have anything better to do." Thompson turned to his partner. "I'll get started on the paperwork and meet you in interrogation. Don't waste too much time with this one."

"See ya, Thompson," I called as he walked away. "He wasn't cop enough for me anyway."

"What does that even mean?" O'Connell asked, shooing me out of his chair. "And what do you want now?"

"Off-the-record?"

"Fine."

"Despite our current lack of evidence, it seems obvious our killer is one of the gym rats. He's using a fake name, and we're still working on motive. Suffice it to say, the wheels are turning, and while we haven't discovered an irrefutable connection between the two homicides that occurred on federal property and a particular member of Coker's gym, there might be some overlap in our investigations. What's your play tonight? We don't want to botch it."

"Unbelievable." He sat heavily in the chair. "You throw this extortion shit into my lap and beg that I help out one of Martin's friends or whatever Fletcher is, and now you want to know what we're doing about it because you're afraid you're gonna step on our toes. Dammit, Parker."

"Nick—" I began, but he cut me off with a wave of his hand.

"The police department will monitor the drop site. Fletcher is supposed to deliver the money to the locker promptly at five. He will be wired. The money will have a tracker. Undercovers will be stationed outside, prepared to move in as soon as the money changes hands, so stay away from the gym and the people inside until your office receives the all clear. Is that understood?"

"Sure, whatever you say."

"Hey, you're the one who asked for a favor." O'Connell muttered some inappropriate things that I pretended not to hear.

Some days, it didn't pay to get out of bed, but on the bright side, at least I knew where and when the PD's operation would commence. On the drive back to the federal building, I phoned Fletcher and wished him luck and ran through the basic tenets he needed to be aware of in order to avoid confrontation. The idea of dropping off the money didn't freak him out. The only thing he was worried about was showing up after being chased off the last time. If Tim was behind the blackmail, it made no sense why he'd want to scare away the golden goose, so I marked Tim's name off my mental list of potential extortionists and focused on tying our alleged killer to William Briscoe and Stan Weaver.

Just as I exited the elevator on the OIO level, Lucca looked up and waved me over. "Do you want the good news or the bad news first?" he asked.

"Surprise me." I pulled a chair over and sat down next to him.

"I know who Bradley Bellows is. I also know why he might have wanted to kill William Briscoe."

"I'm not getting any younger, so don't ask me to guess."

"Bradley Bellows, formerly Brad Holmes, might possibly be Tim Coker's bastard son, and since dear old dad was feuding with William Briscoe, Brad decided to take matters into his own hands to earn some of his daddy's love."

"And I thought I had abandonment issues." Clearing the cobwebs from my brain, I checked the copy of the birth certificate. No one was listed as being the father. No one had signed the birth certificate, and there was no paternity test to indicate if Lucca's assumption was even true. "Did you talk to Brad's mom? There must be a million Tim Coker's out there."

"A few dozen in the area, but what are the odds Brad found the wrong one?"

"It depends. That's why you ought to speak to his mother."

"She died a year ago. It's probably what made him seek out his father and change his name."

"So you think he found his father and then changed his name? Why the secrecy?" It didn't make sense, and it definitely didn't explain why Brad would shoot two men.

"I checked with the various gyms listed on those business cards. Brad asked a lot of questions about the coaches and fighters. A few of the other owners thought he was trying to track someone down. He asked about fighters from thirty years ago, and what happened to them. It makes sense. He lost his mom, who probably told him stories of his dad being a boxing coach or a fighter, so he went looking for the man he never knew."

"That's a hell of a lot of unsubstantiated conjecture for an analyst. Plus, he's thirty-two. Who would still care at this point?"

Lucca cocked an eyebrow and looked concerned by what he perceived to be my break from reality. "I can't tell if you're being serious, but on the off chance you are, it's normal for a person to wonder where they came from and seek out those answers."

"It's ridiculous, and we aren't dealing with a normal person. We're dealing with a cold-blooded killer. By definition, they aren't normal."

"Hey, at least we have a name." He scooped a file off his desk. "Here's his profile. There's not much to go on yet, but I'm working on it. Brad was arrested for aggravated assault and attempted murder three years ago, but the charges didn't stick. Before that, he had a few other assault charges related to a bar brawl, a domestic abuse call made by an ex-girlfriend which was also dropped, and a few instances of fighting as a kid which is part of his juvie record. Did he strike you as having anger issues?"

"Not really. Unless he was hiding something with that neatness factor, he didn't seem violent." I thought back to our slap fight and how he immediately backed off when he thought I was hurt. "Are you sure we're talking about the same guy?"

"Yeah. It's right here in black and white. Perhaps you're just unable to recognize anger issues."

"Or perhaps you screwed up somewhere, and these records belong to someone else."

"Why would a non-violent man suddenly execute two people in cold-blood, assuming Brad is our shooter?" Lucca's point resonated in my gut.

"You're right. I must have missed it." I took the folder back to my desk, wondering why my radar was on the fritz.

THIRTY

After reviewing the information Lucca had procured, it appeared Brad was involved. He had a history of violence, just like his alleged father. From the number of gyms he researched, he was intent on finding Coker. But my mind and body were not one over this fact. There was no evidence to support Tim Coker being Brad's father. Just because he settled in at Coker's gym didn't mean he was searching for his dad. Didn't we already have enough people involved in this double homicide who had daddy issues?

At three, Lucca and I met Jablonsky in Tactical Operations where Mark proceeded to tell us Brad hadn't returned home from his morning outing. However, assuming Brad had a day job, that didn't seem suspicious or surprising to me. Facini hadn't left the apartment, and Philip had come and gone twice already. Will Briscoe's statement was supposed to be the nail in our shooter's coffin, but that didn't work. Frankly, we were no closer now than when we started.

Lucca shared his theory about Brad searching for his father. When he was finished, Mark sent him to make copies of the information. Once we were alone, Mark's face morphed into that knowing look.

"You think it's bullshit," he said.

"I'm not an analyst, and I already spent twenty minutes arguing with Lucca that Brad isn't our shooter, even though he has a history of violence, a baseball cap that matches the one our shooter wore, and he's the right build. So let's not go with my gut instincts today."

"Eddie's a brilliant analyst, or so everyone kept telling me when they forced him on me last year, but he still has a lot to learn. Hoofbeats aren't always horses. Sometimes, they aren't even from hooves."

"Wow, aren't you insightful?" I rested my hips against the edge of the table. "Didn't you warn me not to go on a safari? At this point, you can't honestly believe we're going to identify our shooter and have enough to charge him, so what's the point? We should be focusing our efforts on the dozens of open cases and ongoing operations, not on something that will never be resolved."

Jablonsky's jaw went slack, but before he could respond, Lucca returned with copies of the information. After skimming the files and asking for a more thorough breakdown that would explain why Lucca thought Brad was searching for his unknown father, Mark eyed me.

"Brad made a few dozen inquiries to the hospital where he was born for information about his father prior to his gym search," Mark said, committing to Lucca's theory. "One plus one equals two, right?" He exhaled. "Okay, let's see if we can put a gun in Brad's hands. Then we'll check into Philip Dennison and any other known acquaintances to see if anyone is on record as purchasing a Remington or ammunition. Someone has to question Brad and the rest of the fighters at Coker's gym but not until the PD finishes dealing with the blackmailer." Mark met my eyes. "Parker, go home for the night. You've been burning the candle from both ends, and it's impairing your work."

"Mark," I protested but clamped my mouth shut when I was met with a glower.

"You've done an excellent job today, Lucca. Finish gathering that information and go home to your wife. She's probably forgotten what you look like by now. I'll see you both back here at seven a.m."

*   *   *

"God, I need a drink." I searched the wet bar, sighing. "Crap."

"What's wrong?" Martin asked, continuing to prepare dinner. "You're actually home early. Isn't that a good thing?"

"It would be if we had evidence to support our theory of who the shooter is. We're not gonna find him. I know it, and when I said as much to Mark, he sent me home. Isn't that ridiculous?"

"Mark's an asshole."

I spun a few more bottles, not finding what I wanted. "I must have left the Stoli in my liquor cabinet at home. I mean at my apartment. My old apartment."

Thankfully, Martin let my verbal blunder go. "What's a matter with Grey Goose?"

"You're out."

"It's in the freezer. When you moved in, I started keeping it there since lemon drops are your drink of choice. I thought you'd prefer them cold."

Opening the freezer, I found the bottle behind the ice cream and frozen mixed berries. "C'mon, confess, you were hiding the good stuff."

An amused smirk lit up his face. "That's what I did last night." His eyes twinkled with mischievous glee.

"You and those damn glow-in-the-dark condoms." I shook my head and busied myself with finding a shaker to hide the blush on my face. "Pervert."

"I prefer the term creative genius."

"And I prefer non-glowing latex."

"Fine, but that means we'll have to leave the lights on until we finish the box."

"I like keeping the lights on."

"Now who's the pervert?" He kissed my cheek as he went by. "For the record, I like keeping the lights on too, unless it's the middle of the night and there's the possibility we might actually sleep at some point. Then

- 236 -

again, if the last few weeks are any indication, our chances of ever getting a good night's sleep are probably slim to none."

"Tell me why getting sloshed right now and going to bed is a bad idea." I poured a shot and drank it straight before measuring out the contents for my martini. "Do you want one?"

"So I can get sloshed too?"

"Sure. Why not?"

He capped the bottle and stuck it back in the freezer, answering my question. "You're not drinking your dinner." He pressed his lips together, watching as I took a sip. "Alexis, what's wrong?"

"I just told you." I tapped the rim of the glass. "Is this thing on?" He didn't laugh at my joke.

"You have to talk to me. The last time you didn't tell me what was going on, you ended up moving in. Next time, we'll have to get engaged or something. At this rate, you'll run out of grand gestures and escape routes pretty fast."

"It's nothing. I'm just frustrated, confused, and annoyed. I hate being those things." My phone rang, and I swore again. Checking the ID, I saw it was O'Connell. "Don't wait on dinner. This might take a while. I promised a client I'd look into something for him."

"A client?" Martin raised an eyebrow. He found this tidbit of news pleasing. "Are you planning on returning to the private sector?"

"No. It's a favor for an acquaintance, and it somehow relates back to the OIO case. Therefore, I can't discuss it."

"Fine. I'll be upstairs in my office, analyzing MT's new marketing objectives. Come find me when you're done, and we'll eat then."

"We don't have to eat together," I said while simultaneously answering the call.

Martin shrugged, turned off the oven, and went up the stairs.

"What do you mean we don't have to eat together?" Nick asked. "The only reason I called is so I don't have to eat alone since Jenny's still at work."

"Ha ha. Why don't you come over and eat with Martin?

That way the two of you can leave me alone."

"Someone's bitchy." He cleared his throat. "Am I supposed to apologize for snapping at you earlier today?"

"No."

"Good. I really didn't want to."

"Is there a point to this call?"

"You might want to grab a pen and sit down."

Fletcher delivered an envelope of cash to the locker at precisely five o'clock. He wasn't stopped by anyone inside the gym. That feat was made easier since Tim Coker had to run an errand and was conveniently out of the gym for a few minutes. The other fighters didn't pay the attorney any attention, and Jack was in and out within three minutes. However, it was now after eight p.m., and no one had made a move to collect the envelope of cash from the locker. The police were still monitoring the area. They had even planted a tiny recording device inside the envelope, so if the locker was opened or the light pattern changed, a signal would be sent to the officers keeping watch. Frankly, it looked like the operation was tanking, which explained why O'Connell was calling.

"Do you think the surveillance teams have been made?" I asked.

"I don't know. If they were, no one noticed it happening."

"Please tell me a bunch of overzealous officers weren't speaking cryptically into their sleeves."

"We train our people better than that. It's not like we have those earpieces with the curlicue wires running down the side of our necks and into the back of our collars."

"That's the Secret Service, not the FBI." I rolled my eyes. Our fight was moot. This conversation was moot. Hell, the entire case was fucking moot. "Has Fletcher received any other communications?"

"I was about to ask you the same thing. As far as I know, our blackmailer has gone radio silent. However, our digging into this matter has turned up some interesting facts that you might find enlightening. Do you recall Fletcher saying his friend placed a winning bet that night?"

"Uh-huh."

"Well, it turns out we're dealing with the exact same amount. The blackmail demand was precisely what his pal won. Odd coincidence, isn't it?"

"So it's possible Fletcher was just an innocent bystander, and the blackmail was intended for his co-worker."

"Could be, or it could have just been a random amount that happened to coincide with his friend's winnings. However, if it's not a coincidence, that means either the house or a bookie is our blackmailer. Do you happen to know anyone good with numbers who also has access to the locker room?"

"I might know a guy." I bit my lip, deep in thought. Dennison was an accounting major. Was he at the fight? Would Fletcher recognize him?

"Does this guy have a name?" O'Connell asked.

"Yes, but I can't hand him over to you. I need to check with Fletcher first and reevaluate the fight videos. I gotta go. Thanks, Nick."

"You're just gonna leave me hanging?"

"Murder trumps blackmail, but in the event I'm wrong, you might want to start your own investigation into identifying the blackmailer."

"Without a pick-up, I don't think we have enough evidence. Fletcher received anonymous communications. We can't just pin it on someone. The LT said I have a day to put this together. You could have at least bought me dinner before screwing me."

He hung up, and I went into my makeshift office and turned on my laptop, already dialing Fletcher. When he answered, I said, "I'm e-mailing you a photo. Tell me if you recognize this man."

"What happened with the drop? Is someone in custody?" Fletcher asked.

"No. The cash hasn't been picked up yet, but this could be the break we've been waiting for. Detective O'Connell might have connected the blackmail to the OIO investigation. Just look at the photo." I hit send and waited for Fletcher to speak.

"That's the man who took our bets, but he was much

more discreet. He wore a ball cap and windbreaker. At the other events, he had sunglasses, but that night, he took off the glasses because the lights were low."

"You're sure it's him?"

"I'm positive." Fletcher sighed unhappily. "This means I'll have to testify, and this won't be brushed under the rug." He swore a few times. "I'll turn my resignation in tomorrow morning."

"Don't do that yet. This isn't a fire sale. Everything doesn't have to go."

"It'll look better if I resign instead of being asked or forced to leave."

"Look, I have enough of my own problems, Mr. Fletcher, but you should wait this out until we have someone in custody. Who knows what charges or what evidence might come to light."

"Is that your legal opinion?"

"No, I don't have a legal opinion, but I do have knowledge of pending federal charges that are unrelated to gambling."

"Okay. Will you give me a call when this turns into a fire sale?"

"You have my word."

After speaking to O'Connell, I spent the next four hours rewatching the fight footage to make certain Philip Dennison was present at the fights. Since Fletcher said Dennison was at the other bouts taking bets, I watched those videos too, marking down timestamps for the techs. Then I called Mark to relay my findings.

"I know this might sound crazy, but Philip Dennison is the blackmailer," I said.

"Do the police have him in custody?"

"No, the cash hasn't been picked up. There's no proof, but circumstances dictate that he's our guy."

"Okay, I'll bite. Is he also our shooter? What reason would he have to kill William Briscoe?"

"I don't know the answer to either of those questions. What did Lucca find after I left? Did he discover anything related to Dennison that might point to a smoking gun?"

"Nothing conclusive." An awkward pause filled the air

between us. "Parker, I'm worried about you."

"You always worry about me. That's nothing new."

"But you throwing in the towel is new. What the hell was today's conversation about? You don't give up. What's wrong?"

"Nothing. I'm being realistic."

"Bullshit. I'm not asking this question as your boss. I'm asking as your friend."

"Things have to be different this time, or I have to be different this time. So I'm prioritizing my efforts."

"Did Marty say something about you working too much? Because he's one to talk."

"Martin has nothing to do with this." I paused, wondering why there was such animosity on both sides. "What's going on with the two of you? You're supposed to be friends. Did I miss something?"

"You should ask him." Mark cleared his throat. "Look, since you're prioritizing, whatever that means, we'll work on a solution tomorrow. Maybe Dennison will grab the cash in the morning, and the PD will nab him. Then we'll just hit him with a phonebook until he confesses."

"That wouldn't be admissible in court."

"It was a joke, Parker. Get some sleep. I want to see the optimistic version of you in the morning."

"I'm pretty sure there's never been an optimistic version of me."

"Well, consider throwing the realist out the window so we can get back to the status quo. I miss the pain in the ass who refuses to give up."

Sometimes, I did too.

THIRTY-ONE

"Why would anyone ask for thousands of dollars and leave it in an unsecured location?" Lucca asked.

The three of us were positioned around the conference table, sipping coffee and attempting to remain in an upright position. At least, that's what I was doing. From the dark rings underneath Lucca's eyes, I couldn't be positive I wasn't staring into a mirror.

"Lucca, I want you to pull Dennison's class schedule and wait for him at the university. Let's give the tree a nice shake and see what happens. I'm guessing that he'll make a grab for the cash if we scare him," Mark said.

"What should I question him about?" Lucca asked, sitting up straighter.

"Ask about Facini. They're roommates, and that way, Dennison won't necessarily think we're on to him. Throw in a question or two about Bellows and ask if he knows Will Briscoe Jr. Don't let on what we know or what we're investigating. Keep it brief. Scattershot."

"Aye, sir." Lucca's eyes darted to the conference room door.

"You don't have to wait to be dismissed," I whispered loud enough that Mark heard. "Jablonsky said that yesterday. Weren't you paying attention?"

"Parker," Mark's full attention was on me, but I caught the amused look that he was doing his best to hide, "it seems you've changed your tune since yesterday. Any particular reason for it?"

I waited for Lucca to leave before I said, "I threw rationality out the window this morning. You wanted crazy, reckless Alexis Parker, so you got her."

"That's not what I meant." He flipped through the file again. "If the bait doesn't work, we'll have to run a Hail Mary play. Facini knows us, so you can't go near the apartment."

"I'm guessing I'll be stopping by the gym again tonight." I snorted. "Damn, I shouldn't have left my boxing gloves at home."

I worked from my desk the rest of the day. Lucca's attempt to spook Dennison didn't yield the results we wanted, so he was hanging out with the surveillance team to see if anything exciting happened at the apartment. At four, O'Connell called to say the PD was pulling units off the gym in another two hours. Our day was up. If no one came to collect the blackmail money, they probably never would.

After I voiced this update to Jablonsky, he phoned Lt. Moretti and asked for another few hours. It was possible the pick-up might be made during class change when the men were clearing out. Unfortunately, the PD was only willing to wait around until eight before washing their hands of this mess.

"Parker," Mark hollered, and I stepped into his office, "get down there and see if you can accidentally bump into Brad."

"Why don't I just call him and make a date?"

"All right. See if you can get him on the hook, just make sure you don't run into Facini. And be careful, he has a temper."

"So do I."

"Yes, but you didn't kill two men because you were pissed about a boxing match."

"We don't even know our shooter's motive. What have

we been doing for the last two weeks?"

Mark ignored my question, and I returned to my desk to attempt to make a date.

"Hello?" Brad answered on the second ring.

"Hey, Brad. It's Alex, the troublemaker from the gym."

"Hey, yourself. What's up?"

"I've had a long day at work, and since I can't exactly blow off steam at the gym anymore, I wondered if I could interest you in meeting for drinks. Maybe afterward we could work on some close quarters maneuvers."

"I don't know." Despite his words, he sounded interested.

"Oh, right, you'll probably be worn out from working out. I guess I'll just have to call someone else. Another time, then?"

"No, I can make tonight work. How does seven sound?"

It sounds like you're desperate. "Great. Shall we hit that tavern near your place?"

"Sure. I'll see you there."

Returning to Mark's office, I relayed the news. Since the PD was pulling their surveillance teams at eight, our seven p.m. rendezvous would encourage someone at Brad's apartment to pick up the money before our date. If not, there was a fine line between coercion, entrapment, and having someone willingly commit a crime right in front of my face, but I was willing to make it work. It's not like anything else had, and Jablonsky said it was time for a Hail Mary. Too bad I left my rosary beads at home with my boxing gloves.

After endless hours of research that failed to result in anything substantially incriminating, I went into the women's locker room to prepare for my date. Shellacking on the makeup and clipping my hair into a loose bun, I gave my reflection a final glance and hoped for the best. I slipped my nine millimeter into my purse with my credentials, removed my shoulder holster, and traded out the government-issued vehicle for my car. I fired off a text to Lucca to tell him and our surveillance team that I'd be in the neighborhood and not to blow my cover. His reply wasn't exactly professional, but they had my back.

I arrived at the destination thirty minutes early and circled the neighborhood, looking for a decent parking space and checking to see if I could spot the police surveillance vehicles. A nondescript white van was parked near the gym, and a few men in cheap suits sat stiffly at the window of a coffeeshop. They could be the reason Dennison hadn't picked up the money. Our own surveillance team was still keeping watch on the apartment, but they were in an SUV parked a block away. It wasn't exactly clandestine, but it was better than the PD's version. Damn, when did I buy into the us versus them mentality?

Stepping out of my car, I locked the doors and gave my reflection another look, tucking a strand of hair behind my ear and opening another button on my blouse. The white dress shirt I wore with black slacks was fundamental to most business professions, so hopefully, Brad wouldn't think too hard about it. Then again, if I kept opening buttons, he wouldn't be thinking about much of anything. Snorting at the sudden conceitedness, I sauntered into the tavern and selected a table in the middle of the room.

A waitress appeared, and I ordered a glass of white wine to sell my cover and waited for Brad. When she stopped by again to ask if I needed anything else, I asked for a bowl of pretzels. By the time I had made a slight dent, Brad appeared, freshly showered and dressed in a t-shirt and jeans. He waved before joining me at the table.

"Hey," he leaned in close, "did I keep you waiting?"

"It's not your fault. I was early."

"Sucky day?"

"I have a lot of those."

"Me too." He motioned to the waitress for a beer. "I was surprised you called."

"Why? You gave me your number for a reason, didn't you?" I smiled like I had a secret. "Or was that only to be used to arrange going to a fight together?"

"You can use it any time you want." He returned the smile, his eyes never leaving mine, even as the waitress placed his beer on the table.

"How was the gym?" I broke eye contact and sipped my

wine. "Did Coker bitch about chicks being a pain in the ass?"

He laughed. "No. Apparently, there was only one pain, but she's gone now. The rest of the crew was pretty docile. Damn, what a firebrand, stirring up trouble." He drank a third of his beer and grinned.

"I wish I had kept my mouth shut. I get so annoyed at work that the only thing I want to do is haul off and hit something."

"Have you ever considered anger management?"

"Why would I need anger management if I have a heavy bag to hit or a willing sparring partner?"

"Because it helps. They should call it stress management instead." He looked away and took another healthy sip.

"I'm sorry. I didn't realize. You should probably know I have an innate talent of putting my foot in my mouth." I licked my lips, slipping into interrogation mode. "What made you go to anger management?"

"Let's just say I didn't have a choice," he shrugged, looking in my direction but not quite at me, "but it was a turning point. It put a lot of things into perspective and made me realize I shouldn't lash out, especially toward people who don't deserve it." He shook his head. "I'm probably scaring you away. Don't worry, I promise my baggage has been checked and has gone through security, so it's safe to board."

"Aren't you cocky?"

He chuckled, reddening slightly. "That wasn't exactly what I meant, but I'm game if you are."

"Are your roommates home?" I wanted to delve deeper into what sounded like court-appointed anger management and exactly who he felt deserved his wrath.

"Yeah, it's retro game night." He looked embarrassed. "I don't understand how I ended up rooming with a math geek and a closeted computer nerd."

"What do you do?"

"Mostly, I try to avoid them."

"I meant for work."

"Right now, I'm a cook. Long-term, I'm not sure."

"No aspirations to be a boxing champ?"

"Nah. I'm past my prime, but it's a good way to keep in shape and meet people. Plus, the fight scene's a blast." He reached into his pocket and pulled out two tickets. "You were serious about going, right?"

"If I say I'm busy, will you be heartbroken?"

He clutched his chest. "Most certainly. But Philip will be there, so the extra ticket won't be a total waste." He held it out. "Are you seriously busy, or is that just a line in case you want an out after you see where the evening leads?"

"You're too clever for your own good."

"C'mon," he pulled a twenty from his pocket and put it on the table, "let's go have some fun. By the time I'm finished with you, you'll be begging to spend the weekend with me."

"What exactly did you have in mind?" His place was definitely off-limits because of Facini.

"You'll like it. Trust me."

"Why should I trust you? I barely know you."

"It'll be fun and exactly what an adrenaline-junkie like you will love."

THIRTY-TWO

"What are we doing here?" I asked, feeling a little panicked as he opened the rear door to Coker's gym and led the way inside.

"You'll see." He took my hand and gave it a squeeze.

It was after eight. The women's boxing class had wrapped up a few minutes ago. Brad flipped on the lights and led the way from the back of the gym to the main room, walking past the locker room without even the slightest stumble. Since he knew how to get in after hours, it probably meant he could pick up the money any time, without anyone ever being the wiser.

He led the way to the front desk, dropping my hand as he ducked into the office on the side. "I just want to make sure everyone's gone. Sometimes, Ron and Linka hang out for a while."

"I don't understand. Why did you bring me here?" My eyes darted around the room, but we were alone.

"You said you wanted to blow off some steam by hitting things, so let's hit things."

He grabbed the shoulder strap on my purse, taking it and tucking it into a compartment beneath the front desk. Then he glanced around the room, finding two pairs of training gloves hanging from a peg on the wall.

"Isn't this illegal? We're trespassing or breaking and entering or something."

"Does that turn you on?" he asked, a teasing quality to his voice "Because if it does, then yes, we're doing all kinds of illegal things, but if it freaks you out, then Coach Coker gave me a key so I can practice whenever I want."

"Why would he do that?"

"He and my pops were friends from way back." A dark cloud settled over Brad's features. "Coker has a lot to make up for. This is the least he can do." He put on a pair of gloves and ran through a ten hit combo on the closest heavy bag, making it swing easily from side to side. "Your turn," he rasped, inhaling and making sure he was back in control. After an outburst like that, I wasn't positive those anger management sessions worked.

I slipped on a pair of gloves and danced around the bag, taking easy swipes that barely made it move. The fact that I was alone with a murder suspect who had an aggressive streak was slightly unsettling, particularly since my gun and badge were across the room.

Brad leaned against the ropes of the center ring, watching the way I moved. When I stopped, he smiled and clapped, the relaxed, laidback exterior once again in place.

"Step into the ring." He pried open a space between the top two cords so I could slink through. "No one's around. Let's play."

We circled each other, feigning punches and landing a few taps. Thankfully, Brad had no intention of hurting me, but that might change if he found out who I was. He stepped forward, throwing a right cross. I ducked down. He danced around, circling and launching himself in my direction. I slid to the right, and he threw his arm out, wrapping it around my waist and taking us down to the mat.

Immediately, I rolled on top of him, pinning him to the floor using a self-defense hold. He snickered, thinking it was part of the game, and I eased the pressure, unlocking my knees from his sides. I dropped down to his chest and rolled off of him.

"Sorry, I tend to get carried away."

"I'll bet." He brushed my hair behind my ear. "Are you feeling less stressed out now?"

"Yeah."

"Good." He climbed to his feet and offered his hand. "Do you want to go another round?"

"Not really." I raised an eyebrow. "Did you have something else in mind?"

"We do have the entire gym to ourselves." He adopted a mischievous grin and dragged me away from the ring and into Coker's office.

"We shouldn't be in here," I said, but my words sounded hollow since I wouldn't get an opportunity to search the place again.

"I know. That's what makes this fun." He took a seat in Coker's chair and swiveled back and forth. "What do you think he keeps in here besides dozens of shattered dreams and the broken hearts of failed fighters?"

"Cognac." I nodded at the bottle on a shelf above the trophy case.

"Figures." Brad opened the desk drawer, finding Coker's ledger. "Damn, business isn't what it used to be. Clearly, he shouldn't have kicked you out. He can't afford it." He flipped through a few more pages. "I'm one of the only idiots paying to attend. Do you seriously think he makes enough on contingency?" Brad's questions were making me suspicious.

"We shouldn't be looking at this."

"What's the harm?" He replaced the ledger and continued going through the drawers. "Do you think he makes enough to keep this place open, or do you think he's doing something under the table? Most of his fighters are crappy." He looked over his shoulder at me. "Didn't you ask if he was betting on the fights? How would we find out?"

"I don't know. Didn't you say that was none of our business?"

"Maybe I changed my mind." The wheels were turning in his head. Had I been made?

"Do you think he bets on the side?" I asked, hoping to

derail whatever suspicion was circling through his head by making this seem like his idea. After all, his roommate would know.

"I don't know. Like you said, this isn't any of my business." His gaze came to rest on the framed photo above the trophy case. "What a joke." The photo upset him, so he crossed the room to get a closer look. "Can you believe this?" He pointed an accusatory finger at the frame and corresponding newspaper article. "That fucking bastard." Without warning, he slammed his fist into the glass, shattering the frame. "He's proud of it. Of that night." He swallowed and fought against tears, his voice cracking when he spoke again. "He killed my dad."

"What?"

"Coker fought him in the ring, and he died the next day from a brain bleed. I never even had a chance to know my father." He wiped his eyes, noticing the shards of glass stuck to his bloody knuckles. He took an unsteady breath and let out a nervous laugh. "I guess I don't quite have that baggage checked just yet."

"I'm so sorry, Brad." Lucca had been wrong, which didn't seem that surprising. "How can you come here every day and see the man who did that to your father?"

"I'm trying to learn forgiveness."

"Is it working?" Or did you possibly lose it and go on a shooting rampage? In which case, Coker should have been your only target.

"It was until today." He stared at the glass shards. "I should clean this up."

"Go clean your hand first. You don't need to bleed on everything. Why did you bring me here if this place is so difficult for you?"

"I've never been in here alone. I...I didn't have the nerve to look by myself. But you wanted to hit something, and I wanted to see what else Tim's hiding." He wiped his nose with the back of his undamaged hand. "You must think I'm crazy."

"Sanity is overrated. I'm a little crazy myself."

He went into the men's room, and I took the opportunity to check the office for something that might lead to our shooter. I wasn't positive Brad wasn't crazy enough to open fire on the courthouse, but the targets didn't coincide with his sob story, unless he was covering his tracks. Facini could have told him what was going on, or he heard about Lucca confronting Philip earlier. My call for a date might have seemed just as suspicious.

There was a thud and then a clang. Brad opened the bathroom door and looked in the direction of the sound. His neck rotated around like an owl, making sure I was still in the office.

"Did you hear that, or am I really losing it?" he asked.

"No, I heard it too." I stepped toward my purse, but Brad was already halfway toward the locker room.

"Hello?" he called.

"Hey, man. It's just me," Facini said. Immediately, I ducked back into Coker's office. "What are you doing here?"

"I'm hanging out with a friend, and you freaked her out."

"You're such a dog," Facini replied. "I'll see you back at the apartment."

"Wait. What are you doing here?"

"I forgot something in my locker. It's no big deal. But I had a problem getting the door to open. Can you give me a hand real quick? It'll take two seconds." There was a pause. "She can wait a minute."

"Yeah, okay." Brad raised his voice and said, "Alex, it's okay. It's just my nerdy roommate. I'll be back in a minute."

"Sure," I called back, uncertain if Facini would make the connection. Mainly, I wanted to get into the locker room and see if he just picked up the blackmail. If he did, I'd make the arrest since the PD couldn't be bothered.

Before I could step into the locker room, Philip Dennison stepped out. He was tucking the envelope into his back pocket, when he froze like a deer in headlights. He'd been caught, and he knew it.

"Philip, right?" I put on a friendly smile. "Alex, from the other night. Y'know, with Brad."

"Oh, yeah. What are you guys up to?"

"Not much. Sparring, drinking the coach's cognac, things like that." I nonchalantly edged backward toward my purse which contained my gun and credentials. "What are you doing here? I didn't know you were into boxing. Brad made it sound like you only watched the fights."

"I do a bit more than that." He moved closer. From the way his jacket fell, he was armed. "I'm guessing you already know that."

I made a move for my purse, and he rushed forward, knocking me into the office and against the trophy case. I kneed him in the groin, but the bastard was wearing a cup. Who shows up that prepared? He barely flinched and slammed me harder into the wall. I got my knee between us and pulled it to my chest, digging my heel into his stomach. For a future accountant, he was built.

His hand went for his gun. Both of my hands wrapped around his, shoving the gun upward. It fired into the ceiling, covering us with drywall and plaster. He backhanded me, but I didn't let go. Instead, I kicked his shin. His grip on the gun loosened. He went to one knee. The gun fell on top of the trophy case behind me. I didn't dare turn my back on him, but I clawed behind me, feeling for it.

My fingers brushed against it, but it clattered to the floor behind the case. He blocked my next kick which would have broken his jaw. Getting back to his feet, he grabbed me in a bear hug and lifted me off the ground.

"Freeze, FBI." The words echoed in the room. I shook away the tunnel vision to find Lucca in the doorway. "Let her go," my partner ordered.

Philip squeezed harder, forcing the air from my lungs and slamming his shoulder into my sternum as he tried to flip our positions in order to use me as a shield. I locked eyes with Lucca, encouraging him to fire, but he hesitated. Philip tried to spin us. Then the world seized as waves of fire shot through my nerve endings. The burning ebbed, only to hit with renewed vigor. When it finally calmed, I was staring at the hole in the ceiling.

"Easy, Parker. Stay there. Don't move." Lucca knelt on the ground next to me. "Shit." He pulled the radio from his pocket. "Agent down. We need an additional support team and paramedics. The suspects are subdued." He pressed his palm beneath my sternum, pushing gently until my muscles stopped spasming and I was no longer hyperventilating.

I turned my head to see Philip on the ground, cuffed and barely conscious. One of the darts from Lucca's stun gun was lodged in Philip's back. The other was stuck in my arm. Lucca pulled it out, but my nerve endings were too busy misfiring to register.

"I'm going to fucking kill you," I growled.

"It was just a stun gun. You'll be fine." His eyes focused on the area beneath me. "Seriously, Parker, you need to lie still." He took his jacket off and brushed some of the broken glass away from the edges. "Are you in pain?"

He practically lit my nerve endings on fire. "You're kidding, right?" I realized I'd crashed through the trophy case. Something warm and wet was on my back. If my bladder released because of the electrical shock, I'd shoot Lucca before we even made it out of the building.

He lined the edges with his jacket and lifted me out of the trophy case, laying me against the floor and pushing me onto my side. The warmth on my back was blood. He placed a gentle hand against my arm as my synapses randomly fired, igniting another wave of fire inside my body that made me gasp. On the bright side, Philip Dennison was handcuffed and appeared to be down for the count.

THIRTY-THREE

"This is a place of business, not a brothel," Jablonsky said, approaching my desk. I was practically lying on top of it with my shirt off while a medic dug shards of glass out of my back.

"Isn't a brothel a place of business?" I asked, unable to lift my head to look at him.

"Shush. How do you feel?"

"Like I ran two full marathons after spending eight hours lifting weights."

"Your shirt took the brunt of the impact with the glass, but your nervous system needs to reboot. The stun gun disrupted your muscle function, and the sudden seizing formed an automatic build-up of lactic acid, which is why you feel like you worked out too hard," the medic offered. "Luckily, you don't have any large pieces of glass lodged in your back. There are just a few cuts and nicks, but nothing that requires stitches."

"Oh, I know exactly where to lodge a piece of glass." My body tingled with the occasional shooting pain. The adrenaline surge only made it worse. I felt jittery and exhausted at the same time. No amount of caffeine could combat the muscle fatigue.

"How's your heart?" Mark asked, sounding fatherly.

"They hooked me up to a monitor inside the rig, but everything looked normal. That's why I came back to work." I closed my eyes, trying to focus.

"I need to check on our suspects and get an update on Brad. Stay here."

"That's basically all I can do."

The medic finished and handed back my shirt. Instead of regulation white, it was now polka-dot red. Whatever. It would suffice. I struggled to sit up and clumsily shoved my arms through the sleeves. My thumb was twitching, so I gave up on the buttons and propped myself sideways in the chair in order to rest my head against the backrest.

"Parker," Lucca approached my desk, "are you okay? I didn't realize with the glass that—"

"Where was your gun?"

"I couldn't shoot the suspect. The bullet would have gone through him and into you."

"I didn't need your help. I had things under control, but you could have shot him. I'd rather get hit with a piece of lead than be zapped. You hesitated. You were in the doorway, and you hesitated, which is why both darts didn't go into Philip. How many times have I told you that you can't hesitate?"

"Parker—"

"Dammit, Michael."

His face darkened. "Eddie."

"What?"

"My name's Eddie. I can't believe you don't even know my first name."

"I know your first name."

"Then why the hell did you call me Michael?"

"Agent Lucca, go wait in my office and stay there until I tell you otherwise," Jablonsky ordered, appearing from behind. I bit my lip and fought back tears. "Alex, you need to go home after an ordeal like that. I'll drive you. There's a ton of shit that has to get sorted tomorrow, so I need you back here early in the morning." Without another word he helped me out of the chair and looped my arm around his shoulders as we went to the elevator. "You should have gone to the hospital given your history."

"Don't bring up Paris. Stun guns are supposedly safe, so it's not a problem."

"If they're so safe, why are you exempt from the qualification process? Are you sure you're okay?" He had heard my outburst, but he didn't mention it. At least getting zapped meant my neurosis had a free pass.

"I just need to shutdown and restart." I closed my eyes and drifted on the edge of consciousness until the car stopped.

"I'll see you tomorrow." Mark parked near the garage entrance to Martin's compound.

"I hate to break it to you, but the likelihood that I can make it up the steps on my own is pretty slim." Noting the lack of town car, I added, "Martin's not home yet."

"Fine, but for the record, you're the only reason I'm setting foot inside this house." Mark helped me up the steps and into the living room. "Are you good?"

"Perfect." I slumped sideways onto the sofa, barely aware of his departure.

I woke up a few hours later to the sound of Martin's voice on the stairs. I was sore but far less twitchy. My hands had a slight tremor, and my arm ached from being the epicenter of the shockwave. Feeling in charge of my faculties, I no longer wanted to kill Lucca. Instead, I wanted to use him for taser practice.

"You'll coordinate the deliveries tomorrow. You know what's coming in and where it goes," Martin said, opening the door to the second floor. "Thanks, Marcal. I'll see you in the morning."

"Hey," I said, knowing the first thing Martin would notice was the blood on the back of my shirt, "today wasn't one of my better days, but I'm okay."

"Why are you lying on the couch in the dark?" Martin flipped on the light.

"I took some friendly fire and went through a trophy case. How was your day, darling?"

He stared at me for a long time. The muscles in his jaw clenched, and he pressed his lips together. He went to the wet bar, poured a scotch, and sat on the coffee table in front of me, not speaking while he drank. Then he put the empty glass down and kissed me.

"What do you need?" he finally asked.

"Nothing, just some sleep."

*   *   *

"Parker, in my office," Mark barked before I was even out of the elevator. I did as he commanded, closing the door behind me. "Before we get started, how are you?"

"A little sore and pissed at Lucca."

"Are you planning to file a complaint against him?"

"I don't know yet." I blew out a breath and took a seat on the couch in the corner of the office instead of in front of Mark's desk. "I have to write everything up first. I'm not entirely clear on what happened yesterday. A lot of things aren't making sense, so I need more facts before I can give you an answer."

"We need your account before you access everyone else's report. You know how this works."

"Yep." I stood, heading for the door.

"There's one more thing. I told Eddie about what happened to you in Paris and why you reacted so harshly to the stun gun."

"That was none of his business."

"Probably not, but he deserved to know why you're ready to use him for target practice, especially if he's facing a reprimand because of it."

"Stop making it sound like I'm the unreasonable one. He shot me." I reached for the door handle, sensing there was something else. "Did you tell him who Michael is...was?"

"He knows not to ask you about it again."

"Damn you." I spun, finding the look on Mark's face sympathetic but not contrite. "You'll have my report in an hour."

"Good."

I went to my desk and put my head in my hands. Weren't there laws against hostile work environments? Getting shocked by your own teammate and having your dirty laundry aired by your boss seemed pretty damn hostile to me. Perhaps anger management wouldn't be a bad idea. Instead, I pushed through, typing out my report from yesterday to include everything, but I put a nice PR spin on the stun gun incident since I wasn't sure what to make of it yet. There was no reason why I couldn't be professional while I determined if heads would roll. Then I printed a few copies, threw one of them into Jablonsky's lap, and returned to my work area.

Lucca glanced up, offering an uncertain smile. "Good morning."

"I want your report and the case file."

"Philip Dennison and Elias Facini are in holding cells. So far, they've only gone through some preliminary questioning. The state also has quite a few charges pending against them, but the police department is holding off until we finish our investigation. It's a good thing you have friends in blue."

"Yeah." I took the folders from him without making eye contact, but he continued to linger near my desk. "Is there something else?"

"Alex, I didn't realize. You haven't exactly shared many details from your past or your life. Anyway, I'm sorry."

"Why are you sorry? I don't want your pity, and you've been doing this long enough to know that apologizing is basically asking for official action to be taken against you. So why are you sorry?" Admittedly, I was looking for a fight. Self-destructive behavior was part of my charm, and the gloves had just come off. But Lucca didn't take the bait.

"I just am. If you need something else, let me know."

"Jackass," I muttered under my breath. He wasn't supposed to be nice.

After I calmed down, I read the official incident report and Lucca's account. Approximately thirty minutes after Brad and I entered the gym, Philip Dennison and Elias Facini left the apartment. They walked the two blocks to the gym, unaware of the surveillance team watching their every move. They entered through the rear door. Two minutes later, the sensor inside the envelope was triggered.

The PD had decided to share with our team,

unbeknownst to me, and since we had eyes in the vicinity, they decided we could monitor the blackmail drop ourselves. When Dennison and Facini entered, Lucca made his approach. For some reason, Agent Lucca had the misguided belief that I needed his help. He didn't understand I was not some damsel in distress.

Facini was speaking to Brad outside the gym, when Lucca appeared. Facini must have recognized Lucca because he took off. One of the other agents from the surveillance van apprehended him a block from the gym. Brad surrendered on-site. However, their involvement in the blackmail scheme was questionable at best. Currently, they could be considered accessories, and Facini could be charged with resisting arrest.

Philip Dennison was a different story. He was carrying an unregistered firearm. He assaulted a federal agent and was caught red-handed with the blackmail money. Jack Fletcher identified him as taking bets, so Mr. Accountant wouldn't be getting his CPA in this lifetime. If he was really lucky, he could manage his fellow convicts' prison wages.

"Where did you leave your white horse?" I asked, swiveling to face Lucca's desk.

His brow furrowed, confused. "What?"

"Since you rode in to save the day, where'd you leave your horse?"

"Funny." He went back to whatever he was doing.

"So we've solved the police department's blackmail case. Hurray for us. What about the double homicide? Is anyone talking?" I stood up, tapping the folders into a neat stack on the edge of the desk. "Where did Dennison get his unregistered handgun? Did Facini teach him how to shoot? Oh, and before I forget, you were completely off the mark about Brad Bellows. Have we discovered anything that puts him near the courthouse or the extortion scheme?"

"Nothing conclusive yet. We have a warrant to search their apartment and offices at work. We're going through their life histories with a fine tooth comb. Jablonsky said once we have something solid, we'll go at them with both barrels in the interrogation rooms and put this to bed. Until then, we're keeping them on ice."

"I want to talk to Brad."

"That's not a good idea, Parker."

"We'll see." I scooped up the files and went to Mark's office to ask permission.

THIRTY-FOUR

"That was the worst first date I've ever been on." Brad laughed and ran a hand through his hair awkwardly.

"Don't blame yourself. I'm an awful date. Last night doesn't even make it onto my top ten list." I sat sideways, scooting closer to the table and pulling my knees to my chest on the small folding chair. "You can ask for a lawyer at any time."

"I don't need one. I didn't do anything wrong." He leaned back. "Weren't you wearing that yesterday?"

"No, that shirt has bloodstains on it."

"Because of Philip?" he asked, and I nodded. "Asshole." He white-knuckled the edge of the table in order to keep his anger in check. "Are you okay?"

"I'm fine. So you mean to tell me you've never hit a woman or hurt anyone?" I slid his file across the table, opened to his rap sheet. "Why'd you change your name, Brad?"

"I wanted to make a clean break and start fresh. Haven't you ever wanted that?"

"Yes, but it didn't work out the way I planned." He saw the sincerity in my eyes. "Tell me what's going on."

"First, I want you to know that I didn't hit her." He

poked the paper. "I shoved her and smashed a few dozen glasses with a baseball bat. I'm not denying I was wrong to do it, but you already know I have anger issues." He read the rest, but he didn't refute any other details from his record. "This is the reason I changed my name. As you know, I've been going to therapy, but that doesn't mean anyone wants to hire a guy with a record, recovering or not. This was my chance at a fresh start. A new name. A new place. A new beginning."

"Why'd you go looking for Tim Coker?"

"I needed to face him. Originally, I hoped to forgive him and let him make amends for the things he did, but there's a lot of shit going on at that gym."

"I need you to elaborate. We went there last night because you were looking for something. What was it? Why were you there?" I didn't believe it was the cash, but the evidence was inconclusive.

"I don't know. I just wanted to see what Tim's hiding. You know what he did to my dad, and that fucker has it framed in his office. Just imagine what else he's done. I needed to see for myself. Tim is nothing but a two-faced snake. He acts like he's doing me some huge favor by apologizing, but he has shit like that on the wall."

Brad pushed away from the table and stormed toward the corner of the room. I expected him to lash out and break his hand on the cinderblock. Instead, he huffed and puffed for a few moments before returning to the table. I didn't think he was dangerous and had removed his handcuffs in order to make him more comfortable. He didn't harbor any animosity toward me, nor did he fight back when he was arrested last night, so I had a hunch he was innocent.

Lucca opened the door and glanced inside. "Do you want me to sit in, Parker?"

I knew damn well he had been watching from the other side of the two-way mirror. "It's under control. Why don't you get us some water?"

When the door closed, Brad asked, "Is he the reason you have so many bad days at work?"

"Mostly." It didn't hurt to have a friendly conversation.

This rapport we had was keeping Brad talking, and the more he said, the better off we'd be. "Do you know why Philip and Elias crashed our date?"

"I didn't even know they were there." He cocked his head to the side. "You believe me, right? I mean you were there. We were in Coker's office talking, and then," he licked his lips, seeing a flaw in his logic, "I broke the picture frame."

"So?"

"It wasn't a distraction. I didn't take you into the office so they could sneak in." He was starting to panic.

"I know, Brad." I reached for his hand, running my thumb along the bandage covering his knuckles. "It's okay. No one said you were involved. I just wondered if they mentioned they'd be stopping by the gym. You guys are roommates. Hell, Philip borrowed your baseball cap, so clearly, you're friendly with them."

"I didn't know. Elias never mentioned Coker let him go after hours, and Philip wasn't a fighter. He just liked to watch the fights."

"Is that all he did?" I asked, but Brad looked torn. "Whatever you say to me can only help you. Do you trust me?"

"Philip was taking bets. He has an entire system worked out. The guy is a numbers genius. I don't even understand it, but he'd come home every week with thousands of dollars. I did my best to ignore it." He looked down at his record. "I've been involved in enough crap to last a lifetime. They were nice enough to let me room with them, despite my record and shitty job, so I didn't want to cause trouble."

"How'd you meet them?"

"I met Elias at the gym when I first came to town. I had been trying to track down Tim, and when I found his gym, I started hanging around there. At the time, I was living out of a motel room, looking for work and a place to live. Elias said they had an extra room, and for a couple hundred dollars, it was mine for the taking."

"Before that, you never met Elias Facini or Philip Dennison?"

"No."

"What about Will Briscoe Jr.?"

"He started at the gym around the same time I did. A little after, I think. He's a friendly kid. He was taking some classes at the same college as Philip, except he was a freshman or sophomore and Philip's a grad student. He stayed on our couch a few times and came to parties at our house. He and Elias seemed to hit it off. They'd hang out a lot after our training sessions and on the weekends." Brad chuckled. "I always figured if I moved out, Will would be the first one they'd ask to move in with them."

"Did you ever meet Will's father?"

"No, but I heard stories he was another coach. Tim didn't like him. I'd hear him griping to Ron that their best fighters were being snatched away, and if it kept up, the gym would be forced to raise rates, cut the contingency training, and possibly shut down. Frankly, it couldn't happen to a nicer person."

Before I could ask anything else, the door opened, and Lucca came in with a bottle of water for Brad. "Jablonsky wants to see you," Lucca insisted, but I didn't budge. "Now, Parker."

"I'm not finished. Can't you see we're in the middle of a conversation?"

"That wasn't a request." Lucca jerked his chin at the door. It was obvious I was getting pulled for some reason. "I'll take it from here."

"I'll see you later," I said to Brad. Moving toward the door, I brushed against Lucca and whispered, "Don't ruin this. He'll talk to me."

Jablonsky was waiting outside the interrogation room. "We're sweeping their apartment now. You ought to be there." He saw the uncertain look on my face. "What? You'd rather stay here and play with your new boy toy?"

"He was opening up. If I leave now, I'll have to start over from the beginning in order to get him comfortable enough to talk to me again."

"Are you sure you're playing him? It seems to me he could be playing you."

"Maybe we're just having an honest conversation."

"Since when do you take a suspect at face value,

particularly one with a questionable history, fake name, ties to other known criminals, and our best bet for two murders?"

"That doesn't mean he's a liar."

"And right now, your distaste for Lucca is clouding your judgment. You need to take a step back. Go check the apartment and oversee the evidence collection. You must have a theory. Go find the smoking gun."

"Why don't you send Lucca?"

"He might be a liability."

I sighed. "I'm not pursuing any official action against him, but the next time he has to re-qualify on that damn stun gun, I'm volunteering to help." I turned on my heel and headed down the corridor. "And until then, he owes me." I stepped into the elevator. "Make sure he doesn't screw up my interrogation. Brad better be talking when I get back."

When I arrived at the apartment, a team had already begun cataloging evidence. I flashed my credentials at the man in charge and made it clear that each room in the apartment was to be treated as a separate unit. No one was pleased by that instruction, but it was my investigation. I didn't want evidence from one room contaminating the entire apartment.

I circled through the living room, kitchen, and bathroom, giving everything a quick sweep. The bong from the window sill had already been bagged and tagged, but so far, no other drugs or drug paraphernalia had been discovered. The weaponry that decorated the walls was being dismantled with notations to test for blood.

Not seeing any need to hover over the techs diligently doing their jobs, I went into Brad's bedroom. It looked just like it did a few days ago. The bed was made, and everything was neat and tidy. I performed a much slower, methodical search, working from corner to corner. Tucked in the bottom of his closet was a shoebox. Inside were newspaper articles, photos, and other keepsakes concerning his dad. Other than that, the personal effects were few and far between.

"Who lives like this?" one of the crime scene guys asked

from the doorway. "No photographs or mementos to clutter the place. He's gotta be hiding something."

"Take extra care with the contents of this box and make it a priority. As soon as you're through cataloging it, I want it sent to my desk."

"Yes, ma'am."

I moved past him and into the next room. From the boxing gear in the corner, I figured it was probably Facini's room. Amazingly, the pizza box had been removed from the floor, but the place reeked. Opening the closet resulted in a tidal wave of random items pouring out. After carefully picking my way through the mess, I decided to let the professionals deal with it. It would take me a week to sort through it, and I'd want to wear a hazmat suit before remaining in such close proximity to whatever toxic chemicals might be lurking within the confines of Facini's personal space.

The only remaining room was Philip's. Paperwork cluttered the desk and dresser. Textbooks were piled in a corner, next to the overrun bookshelf. The walls were covered with posters of mostly naked women, some from prominent video games. Wow, this is what it looked like for a teenage boy to be trapped in a man's body. Beneath the bed was a pile of worn *Playboys* and *Maxims*. Inside the closet was another dresser and a few storage containers. Something useful was here. The problem was finding it.

Opening a few dresser drawers, I found nothing but clothing. If this dresser contained clothes, what was in the other one? I went across the room and opened the top drawer. There was a pile of socks, and beneath that was a ledger. The next drawer resulted in similar results. How many books did this guy have? Feeling overwhelmed, I closed the drawers and went to the window.

The building that housed Coker's gym was visible, but from this distance, it'd be impossible to see who was coming and going. I didn't think Philip or Elias knew for certain Brad and I were inside last night when they crashed our date, particularly after seeing the look on Philip's face before he attacked, but he had a gun and was wearing a cup. He was either extremely cautious or expected to run into trouble. Where did he get the gun?

I spun, searching the room with renewed vigor for a different lead. After another two hours of ripping the furniture apart and discovering numerous hidden items and compartments, something shiny caught my eye. With the help of a few of the crime techs, who photographed and removed the grate from the vent, I found an opened Chinese food container inside. The metal handle had reflected the light, catching my attention. Stowed inside was a handful of bullets. Some went to a handgun. The others corresponded with the caliber used in a high velocity rifle.

"Put a rush on this place. If you need additional units, call for reinforcements. Jablonsky will sign off on it." I clicked a photo using my phone and headed for the door. "Don't leave a single nook or cranny unchecked. I want these bastards, and I want to know precisely which ones are involved with what illegal activities."

THIRTY-FIVE

"Did you have anger issues before you moved in with Elias and Philip?" I asked, studying Brad from across the table. The evidence collection was still underway, but progress was rapidly being made. "Living with those two slobs would make me want to kill someone."

"Unfortunately, I can't blame them for that. We're supposed to own up to our mistakes. Can I ask what you're hoping to find? Why am I being detained? Last night, it was for extortion, but that guy that makes you grimace, Agent Lucas, he said this is a murder investigation."

"Lucca," I corrected. "He's an idiot." *Great, tell our best asset and potential suspect he's about to be charged with murder and see how quickly he shuts up and asks for a lawyer.* "A lot of bad shit's surrounding Tim Coker and his gym. Unfortunately, it appears your roommates might be involved, so we can't let you go until we're certain you're not helping them. The more you tell us, the faster we'll get you out of here."

"I'll tell you everything I know. I have nothing to hide." He stared into my eyes. "The pot's not mine. I was just joking around about it because you acted like you were into edgy bad boys."

"Your record makes you a bad boy."

"Yeah, but not the kind of bad boy any sane woman would want to spend time with, particularly alone in an unfamiliar apartment with a strange man who has a history of violence. It was my pathetic attempt at flirting, but they do random drug testing at work, probably because it's a diner and we're responsible for preparing people's meals. You can test me now. I'm clean."

"Okay." I tossed a glance at the mirror behind me, knowing someone would be showing up momentarily to perform a blood draw. Brad just gave us permission. Who knew when or if his DNA might come in handy. "Let's talk about your roommates. Besides the pot, are there any other illegal substances inside the apartment?"

"Not that I know of."

"What about weapons?"

"You saw my collection on the living room wall, but you're not asking about that. Are you still hung up on guns?"

"Philip was armed last night. He fired on me. Did you know he had a gun?"

"What?" Brad sounded surprised. "Is this a trick?"

"No tricks. Do you remember either of them talking about firearms? Handguns, rifles, shotguns, whatever? Maybe going to the range or buying ammunition?"

He exhaled, rubbing his five o'clock shadow. "Elias goes to the shooting range every week. He said he trained at the police academy, but I didn't believe him. He likes to blow smoke. They both do. I guess they've talked about shooting stuff, but I just assumed they were talking about their stupid video games or paintball."

"Have you ever seen either of them with a weapon or ammunition?"

"No."

Lucca entered the room with one of the lab techs. "Parker, you've been at this all day. Why don't you give Mr. Bellows a break? Maybe some quiet time will help jog his memory."

"I am kinda hungry," Brad said, understanding we were done for the night. "Are you guys gonna feed me, or is starvation the method you use to get me to talk?"

"Agent Lucca will get you whatever you want," I promised, "and I'll try to expedite your release. Thanks for cooperating."

"Whatever I can do, Alex," Brad replied.

Leaving the room, I went to my desk to see how much progress had been made on the evidence collection. While I was interviewing Brad, Lucca and Jablonsky questioned Facini and Dennison multiple times. Reading those transcripts might lead to something useful. Settling into my chair with a cup of coffee, I set to work.

"The two of you seem pretty cozy." Jablonsky sifted through the files that had collected on my desk. "Bellows won't shut up when you're in the room. He thinks he's controlling the situation."

"By answering everything I ask?" I gave Mark a skeptical look. "I doubt that."

"You think he's innocent."

"I don't think anything. I simply follow the evidence." I began ticking points off on my fingers. "Dennison has been positively identified as partaking in illegal betting. He was carrying an unregistered, illegal firearm. He assaulted a federal agent, which we can trump up to attempted murder, and inside his bedroom, we found a hidden container with various types of bullets, one of which will probably match the sniper rifle used to kill AUSA Weaver and William Briscoe." I picked up a transcript. "How come you haven't beaten a confession out of him yet?"

"His attorney won't let us."

"Who's representing him?"

"Thomas Harper."

"What is going on? Why would Coker pay for Dennison's attorney too?"

"I don't know who's paying Harper. We can't get access to those records. It falls under attorney-client privilege. There's no way we'll get a court order to access them."

"Is Facini using Harper? When he was being detained by the police department, he supposedly kicked Harper to the curb."

"No, Facini's on his own for now, but he's stonewalling

us. I get the distinct impression he has no earthly idea what to do to get out of this mess. We'll crack him eventually. In the meantime, we're keeping a unit on the gym. The Greenwoods are supposed to come in tomorrow afternoon, and Laura and Will are coming in to answer some more questions first thing in the morning."

"What about ballistics? Have they matched the bullets inside the apartment with the same type they pulled out of Weaver's skull?"

"We're making progress, but everything takes time. The reports should be back tomorrow. The problem with everything inside that apartment is, regardless of location, it could belong to any of the occupants."

"Blame it on Dennison. His name is the only one on the lease."

"He'll just pass the blame onto Facini and Bellows, even if they aren't behind it." Jablonsky smiled, understanding my point. "And when he gives details that no one else is privy to, we'll have him for murder."

"Facini alibied out, so did Brad. They have day jobs, but Dennison's a TA. Maybe he has office hours, but unless he has a meeting scheduled, he could slip out without anyone noticing."

Mark looked at his watch. "It's Friday night. We'll pull campus records first thing Monday morning. Finish up, leave your notes in my office, and call it a night." He turned to leave. "Oh, and don't show up too early tomorrow. We don't want to fuel the fire with the Briscoes."

*　　*　　*

"You're late," Martin said when I stepped foot inside the house. "We're supposed to meet Jen and Nick in an hour."

"The engine on your town car is still warm, so don't act like I'm the only one running late." I went up the stairs to the bedroom with Martin at my heels. "Can I have a raincheck for this weekend?"

"Alexis, you promised."

"Really? That's the argument you're making?" I opened the closet door, searching for something backless. The stiff cotton from my dress shirt had been pulling at the band-aids, causing the adhesive to irritate my skin. "We finally have a break in the case. Today, we uncovered a stockpile of evidence. Three suspects are in custody, and two interviews are scheduled for tomorrow. I have to be there. Work first, remember?"

"Work's not supposed to be on the table for this weekend." He sighed. "Fine, but when you're here, you're actually focused on us." He put his fingers underneath my chin and forced me to look at him. "Agreed?"

"Deal."

He selected a garment bag and went into the bathroom while I changed in the bedroom, carefully freed my hair from the braid it had been in, and let the loose waves fall against my naked back. It wasn't exactly glamorous, but it'd work for tonight. I smoothed the dress and lay sideways on the bed to keep from wrinkling it. Truth be told, I was tired. Today had been interminable. My muscles were a little sore from the previous night. At least I had gotten to spend most of the day sitting inside an interrogation room and talking with someone who actually wanted to cooperate. I could count the number of times that happened on one hand.

Martin opened the bathroom door and stood in front of the full-length mirror to adjust his tie.

"Hello, sailor." I whistled, watching him give his appearance the once-over. "Is that a new suit?"

"It is. I'm glad you like it." He eyed me through the mirror. "I had to replace the one that didn't make it out of the shower."

"You're ridiculous."

"Ridiculously handsome." He turned to face me, buttoning his vest and the jacket. "You look particularly comfortable. Are you trying to seduce me?"

I sat up and reached for his wrist, pulling him closer before he could walk away. "Where do you think you're going?"

"Come on, Alex. You know we're meeting the O'Connells tonight. Don't make this harder than it has to be." He winked. "Did you want Cristal or Dom? I figured we'd get bottle service, and I want to know what you're in the mood for, besides me."

"A pitcher of beer."

Ignoring the exasperated look on his face, I climbed off the bed and ran my palms along the expensive material. I could have bought half a car for what that suit cost, but damn, he made it look good. Too good for a casual evening with civil servants and the working class. Carefully, I started on the top button, but he grasped my hands in his.

"You can undress me later. This weekend is about us, and it starts the moment we get home."

"I hate to break it to you, but I'm not trying to get in your pants. You just can't wear that tonight."

"Why not?" He raised an eyebrow, spinning to check his reflection in the mirror. "What's wrong? Is there a tear or snag?" Martin's forehead creased when he failed to find a defect in his attire. He shook his head ever so slightly. "You've never dictated my wardrobe before. Did Nick say something?"

"No, but—"

"But suddenly the wealth disparity is an issue because we live together." He laughed, choosing to roll with the punches instead of arguing. "You keep looking for reasons why this won't work or problems that don't exist. When will you admit this is working? And the things that aren't, we'll figure out." He went into the bathroom to grab his watch. "I have a surprise for you, but since you're working this weekend, it'll have to wait."

"Martin, I don't like surprises." I glanced around the room, noting an additional matching dresser on the other side. Great, now he was in the middle of redecorating. Why was he wasting his time? And I realized that I didn't expect this to last. "What if I'm the problem?" I asked quietly, but he didn't hear the question.

He came back into the bedroom, looking a million different kinds of sexy and impatient to get going. "Are you ready?"

"I guess."

He grinned. "Perhaps you were right about the suit. It's a shame no one will even notice it because they'll be focused on how stunningly beautiful you are."

"Somehow, I doubt it." I grabbed a pair of strappy heels and carried them down the steps.

When we arrived at the bar, Jenny and Nick were waiting out front. Martin insisted on taking us somewhere elegant and quiet, probably since last date night Nick and I spent thirty minutes debating if we should bust the drug dealer in the corner of the room. By the time we'd come to an agreement, the guy was gone. So tonight, we were on the guest list of a members only club. Martin held the naïve belief that illegal activity would be at a minimum in a place like this, and I didn't have the heart to burst his bubble. Nick and I would just have to be on our best behavior.

Jen was impressed, staring at every fixture and the lavish furnishings while Nick caught my eye and made a face. *Fancy*, he mouthed to me. Despite the fact that this setting was supposed to force us to forget about work, we had plenty to discuss, particularly since the blackmail envelope was picked up the previous evening. Thankfully, privacy was one of the key features of swanky, exclusive clubs.

THIRTY-SIX

"I'm unclear who gets the collar," Nick said. "The blackmail is local jurisdiction, but Agent Lucca took over the surveillance when we pulled out. And now you have three suspects in custody?"

"Yes, but since I was on a date with one of them, I'm not entirely sure how suspect he is. We're detaining him the full forty-eight. Jablonsky thinks he's involved, but I'm not so sure. He has a history of violence, and he's changed his name. But he's working the program. He's alibied out for the potentially connected homicides that actually are within our jurisdiction."

"Let me get this straight, you think the blackmailer is also the murder suspect."

"I hope so because we're out of leads. Oh, and before I forget, guess who's representing the blackmailer."

Nick's jaw dropped. "There's no fucking way." He shook his head in disbelief. "That alone should be enough of a smoking gun." He screwed his eyes shut, deep in thought. When he opened them, I saw the light bulb click on. "The gym owner, he's the common denominator. He's probably your shooter."

"He doesn't fit the profile. We have a basic physical

description from the office surveillance footage. He isn't a match." I pressed my lips together, halting the conversation. Even though I wasn't supposed to discuss an ongoing case, Nick was the exception to the rule since he was a police detective for the major crimes division and I dropped this in his lap. But it was hard to talk shop when Jen and Martin lingering nearby. Luckily, Martin had gone to get another round of drinks since the bottle of champagne was empty and Jen had gone to the ladies' room. However, she was on her way back to the table, so Nick and I fell silent.

"I'm not fooled. You always do this." Jen glared, first at her husband and then at me. "Our double dates were never intended to be events for the two of you to discuss work."

"I'm sorry, honey," Nick said. "Alex is a pain in the ass. I keep telling you we need to stop associating with the uncouth."

I stuck my tongue out at him. "Do you even know what that word means?"

"No, but there's a dictionary app on my phone. It really helps when I'm interrogating clever suspects."

"Ooh, you'll have to send me a link. They get so annoyed when I'm flipping through pages, trying to find the definition for smartass."

Jen laughed, covering her mouth to hide the amusement that escaped. "Fine, you win. Discuss away." She turned, searching the room. "Where's James? If I have to spend another minute listening to this comedy routine, I'm going to need a drink."

I glanced up, zeroing in on Martin. "The chances of getting that drink are decreasing by the minute." The bartender practically had her tongue hanging out of her mouth as she flirted with him. "I told him not to wear that suit."

"It's not the suit," Jen replied.

Nick rolled his eyes. "I am sitting right here. Have some dignity, woman."

She laughed and kissed him on the cheek. "You know I'm only kidding."

"Uh-huh." He gave her a skeptical look. "Do you want

me to intervene?"

"That's okay. He can handle himself," I replied.

Jen gave me an odd look. "How are the new living arrangements?"

"Brutal. It's trench warfare. There might not be any survivors," I joked, but she sensed the truth to my words. I cautioned another glance in Martin's direction and leaned across the table. "You're a nurse. What can you tell me about PTSD?"

"Alexis," she looked wholly sympathetic, "what's wrong?"

"Nothing. I'm just curious."

"Trouble sleeping, nightmares, reliving the event, constantly thinking about it and the outcome, reimaging ways it could have been different, anxiety, depression, and sleep disturbances are just some of the symptoms."

"What about violent outbursts?"

"Like anger issues?" she asked. "Sure, that could happen too."

"That's not what I meant." Before I could clarify, Martin returned with a round of drinks, barely managing to balance the glasses.

"What did I miss?" He slid a drink in front of me.

"These two pretending they weren't talking about a case while we were gone," Jen replied, "and just now, Alex was telling us how great it is that the two of you are living together."

"Should I grab a knife to cut the sarcasm?" Martin picked up his glass and put an arm around my shoulders. "It's been an adjustment." He focused his full attention on me. "I haven't asked if you like our new living arrangement."

"What's not to like?" I took a sip and snuggled closer in the hopes of distracting him from realizing I provided a non-answer. "Are you hoping I'll move out so the bartender can move in? She seems ready, willing, and able."

"Probably, but she works weekends. I'm in the market for someone who will actually take a weekend off."

"Well, if you're gonna move out, do it by next week," Nick interjected, "or I'm gonna owe Thompson."

"Gee, thanks," I said. "I'm really feeling the love here."

"Hey, I love the Mets, but I'm not putting money on them to stick it out until the end either," Nick said, hoping to defuse the tension.

"Shush, Nick," Jen snapped. "They'll figure it out." She turned to face us. "The two of you will be fine. I bet it'll last, and I only pick winners."

"That's it. Maybe someone was making it difficult to pick a winner. That could be our motive." I looked to Nick, hoping he'd agree with my assessment.

"You'd need to find a ledger to prove it. How do your victims even fit into that theory?"

"The shooter's target was Santos' coach, and the other was collateral damage."

"Do you think the fighters were supposed to take a dive?"

"From what I know, our victim was a man of honor, so maybe he coached Santos too well. He must have refused to let his boy throw the fight. Since Hector died after the bout, I bet his coach would have wanted someone to investigate precisely how that happened. It could have brought the gambling and fixed matches to light and caused the entire fight circuit to shut down. That's why he had to be eliminated."

"That sounds reasonable, but can you prove it?"

"I'll find out tomorrow."

*   *   *

"I didn't think you'd be here this early," Jablonsky said when he found me inside the conference room. "The Briscoes haven't shown up yet, so you'll have to make yourself scarce." He glanced down at the photocopies of Dennison's ledger. "What do you hope to find?"

"A connection. I'm working under the assumption Philip Dennison is our shooter. So far, nothing contradicts that. Our ballistics expert matched the caliber of bullets to the gun. Dennison's build is spot on. He has motive, hundreds of thousands of dollars worth of motive."

"We need to put the gun in his hands, and we have to

make sure he can't alibi out either."

"We've eliminated everyone else. It's either Dennison or a random act of violence."

"You sound certain."

"Process of elimination and we have the proof." I gestured at the paperwork. "We just have to pin it down."

"All right. Keep at it."

Four hours later, I pushed away from the table. Every joint in my body ached from sitting for so long. My legal pad was covered in notes that we could use when interrogating Dennison. Also, I'd placed enough phone calls to determine that Philip had been at the shooting range with Elias Facini on numerous occasions. If we could get Facini to flip, we'd be one step closer. Thomas Harper was the only remaining point of contention in my brain. I made a note to drag Levere in for another interview.

"Hey, Lucca, do you have a minute?" I called into the bullpen. He dropped whatever he was doing and came inside. "Have you spoken to any of our suspects today?"

"Dennison's not talking. Facini's getting edgy. The last time I checked, he was searching for new legal representation and hoping to qualify for a public defender. Bellows sent me to fetch steak and eggs for his breakfast."

"And you didn't bring anything back for me? Some personal assistant you are."

He ignored the dig. "Jablonsky plans to kick Brad loose by dinnertime. We have a unit prepared to keep watch on him. He'll be prohibited from returning to his apartment on account that it's part of our investigation. Are you going to let him crash with you?"

"Ha ha."

"You spent yesterday with him. He's the future Mr. Parker, right?"

"Don't be jealous." I flipped to a blank sheet. "How did your interview with the Briscoes turn out?"

"Will spoke extensively about his time with Facini, corroborating what Brad told you. We asked about Dennison, and he admitted to spilling his guts about his dad's training methods to them. William Briscoe believed in Hector Santos and wanted the kid to succeed. Will Jr.

hated him for that. He thinks his friends might have done something because of it. Unfortunately, he has no proof."

"But Will believed that possibility so strongly he was willing to throw himself off a roof because of it. That'll speak volumes to a jury," I insisted.

"It will, but unless we can put Dennison inside the office building at the time of the shooting or put the gun in his hand, I don't know that there's enough to prosecute for murder."

"Then we better make damn sure we have him for illegal gambling and every other thing we can come up with. He's going down for something. I don't give a shit what it is." I glanced at my watch. It was a little after twelve. I could easily spend the entire day reviewing the cataloged evidence, but it wouldn't put us any closer to discovering the truth. Our best bet was convincing someone to cooperate. Bellows would tell me whatever I wanted to know, but he wasn't privy to the information we needed. It would have to be Facini, and he wasn't talking until he had independent representation. "Call me if something changes." I pulled out my card and scribbled Martin's home phone number on the back. "If I don't answer my cell, use that number instead. If nothing else occurs, I'll see you Monday."

"What makes you think I'm working the weekend?"

"You owe me, Eddie." I stood up, grabbing my files to take home. "I didn't report you for misconduct, so isn't this a better alternative?"

At the mention of his first name, he softened, swallowing whatever retort he planned to utter. "Did you pick up blackmailing tips from the men we have in holding?"

"It's not blackmail. It's a quid pro quo. If you didn't owe me, I'd be asking for a favor instead of demanding payback. That's how things work around here. You should get used to it."

"I don't know that I'll ever get used to you, Parker."

"It's better if you don't."

On my way home, I stopped at the precinct to have a word with Detective O'Connell. Since the police department had made the original arrest, I wanted to clue him in on what was happening on our end. After last night, I wanted to keep Nick in the loop. If for some reason we dropped the ball, the police department ought to be in a position to pick it up and run with it.

Then I detoured to my favorite pizza joint, hoping Martin wasn't planning to renege on his promise of pizza and TV since I carved out a chunk of our weekend together for work. Arriving back at his house, I parked in the garage and took the two pies out of my car. The blaring music was a dead giveaway that he was in the middle of a workout, so I brought the pizza upstairs and returned to the ground floor and entered his spacious home gym.

"Hey," I yelled over the music, but he didn't respond. I went to the stereo and turned the volume down. "Honey, I'm home."

He finished a set of bench presses and secured the bar, pulling himself up. "Is it Sunday evening already?" he asked, beginning on a set of inverted crunches.

"I said I'd cut my workday short, and I meant it."

"Amazing." He continued his reps. "Jenny called this morning. She said you were asking about post-traumatic stress. Is there something you want to tell me?"

"Can you stop doing that? Watching you is making me dizzy."

Once he got to fifty, he moved on to the freestanding punching bag in the center of the ring. "It's this house. You can't stay here because of what happened two years ago." He hit the bag hard. "But I don't understand it. You've been staying here on and off for over a year, so I asked Jen what might be causing the problem." He laughed bitterly. "She thought I was having issues, so I had to explain that you've been having nightmares more frequently."

"What did she say? That I'm crazy?"

"Yes." Martin stopped hitting the bag. "The last time you actually lived here, you were my bodyguard, which was one of the worst decisions I ever made, but Jen thinks that subconsciously it's why you have the need to protect me in your sleep. Basically, stress adds up. Exhaustion doesn't help. The less you sleep and the more stressed you are, the more it affects your nightmares. It'll lead to these relapses. The fact that you went back to the OIO has a lot to do with it. You have a new job, a new living arrangement, more stress than you can handle, and you spent the week not sleeping. That'll make anyone crazy."

"And this hostility is supposed to make it better?" I moved into the ring with him.

"No," he hit the bag a few more times, "but I'm helpless to fix this for you, and it pisses me off."

I had a feeling something else was pissing him off, but I let it go. Instead, I moved in front of him. "We need to have another lesson in self-defense."

"Alex, we've gone through the basics. Bruiser and I spar once a week. It's not like I'm completely incompetent. I'm pretty certain I can protect myself against an attacker."

"That's great," I peeled my shirt off and pressed my fingers against my side until I found that sore spot Brad hit the other day when we were play-fighting, "but we're not talking about someone random." I reached for his hand and placed it against my ribs. "Right here. Do you feel that bump?"

"No, it feels the same."

"Then you'll just have to remember this spot. I don't think it ever healed properly after the last time I was hurt. It gets sore whenever I sit too long or lift weights or when it rains, and it hurts like a bitch whenever I take a hit." I saw the question on his face. "I want you to remember this," I pressed his hand harder into my flesh, "because if I ever lose control or do something violent in my sleep, I have to know that you'll stop me from hurting you again. So hit me as hard as you can, right here. It should put me down and wake me up if nothing else works. "

He tugged his hand free. "I won't do it. I refuse to hurt you. How can you even suggest such a thing? God," he looked utterly appalled, "you know what you're asking is insane."

"Don't you get it?" I looked away, putting my shirt back on and forcing my voice to remain even. "That disgusted feeling in the pit of your stomach is the same one I have every night we go to bed because I am scared to death that

I will do something to you because I'm dreaming about some psycho. I've done things, Martin. I've seen so much. I don't trust myself around you." I moved away from him. "The worst part is that I've realized the only way I can get a good night's sleep is when I'm close enough to feel you breathing or hear your heart beating, and that's too close. That's close enough to strangle you or shoot you or," I shrugged and stepped away, "I don't even want to think of all the possibilities. So if I'm going to stay here, you have to promise me that you will not let that happen because I cannot bear to live with the thought that I hurt you."

"That won't happen," he insisted.

"If you're so sure that my violent nightmares will never turn physically violent, this will never be an issue. Therefore, promise me that you'll incapacitate me before I hurt you." He reached for me, but I stepped closer to the stairs. "Promise me, Martin."

"This is pointless. Your dreams are just that—dreams. They aren't real. You won't act on them."

"Say it anyway."

"I promise I won't let you hurt me."

THIRTY-SEVEN

"Morning, beautiful," Martin whispered, running his fingers along my arm. "How did you sleep?"

"Great. How about you? Any contusions, bruises, scrapes, or gunshots to report?"

"None of the above, and it seems you haven't shoved a knife in my back lately either." He pressed his lips against my forehead. "How about I bring you breakfast in bed?"

"It's a crime to bribe a federal agent."

"It's only a bribe if there is an agreed upon exchange. I don't recall you offering to compensate me." He cocked an eyebrow up suggestively, and I slapped his arm. "I thought you were afraid of hurting me." It was obvious he intended to use our conversation and my ultimatum from yesterday as fodder for his rhetoric. "To be on the safe side, let's call in a few attorneys and have a contract drafted, expressing exactly what types of physical contact are considered acceptable and what is unduly burdensome or unwanted and what forms of contact would warrant the reaction you so adamantly requested yesterday because I'm not happy with the terms and would like to renegotiate."

"Don't you think you already have enough lawsuits to worry about?" My words were scathing, but he wasn't prepared to back down.

"I'd also argue that I was coerced to agree, thus nullifying our contract."

"We don't have a contract." I rolled onto my back. "Nothing was bargained for. There's no consideration."

"That's right." He propped himself up on his elbow and stared at me. "You have absolutely no consideration for anyone except yourself." Although his tone remained playful, truth resonated just below the surface.

I studied his features, searching his green eyes for some indication of his emotional barometer. "Talk to me."

"Like you talk to me?"

"I suck at communicating. You don't. You could sell ice to penguins in Antarctica. What's wrong?"

"The polar ice caps are melting. The penguins could use some additional ice."

"You're gonna make me work for it?"

"That sounds like a bribe. Could that be construed as entrapment?" he teased.

"Martin."

"I miss you. I miss this." He sat up, collecting his thoughts. "Can you even remember the last time you talked to me?"

"I talk to you all the time. We live together."

"We live together because you stopped talking to me. We live together because, somewhere along the way, you stopped telling me what was happening in your life. You went back to the OIO, and the only reason I even found out was because the guy you were investigating came to your apartment to get revenge. If I hadn't been there, you'd be dead, and I would have never known why because you didn't tell me."

"I told you I wanted to go back. You encouraged it. You said you'd support that decision."

"I would have, but you didn't give me the chance. You didn't trust me enough to tell me."

"That's not true. It happened so fast. Mark brought me back in." I stopped mid-argument. "This is why you aren't speaking to him. I'm the reason you lost your best friend." I sat up. "It's not his fault. Since you want to be angry with someone, be angry with me."

"I can't be angry with you." Martin looked to be in utter agony. "Mark knew better than anyone how destroyed you were when you left the OIO. You spent months adamantly opposed to returning. Being inside that building is torture, at least that's what you said. But he's been wheedling his way inside your brain, manipulating you, slowly convincing you that you have to go back, and it worked because as soon as they rejected you, it was the only thing you wanted. And once you were back on the job, it damn near killed you."

"I am not malleable. You make it sound like I'm a brain dead nincompoop. I'm not."

"No, you're not. But there's a reason you didn't tell me, and it's not because of some sworn to secrecy bullshit. It's because deep down you know I'm right, and you don't want to think about it because Mark is the closest thing you have to family. But he betrayed you by putting his needs above yours." Before I could voice a protest, Martin made a final concluding point that I just couldn't shake. "It's painfully obvious how devastating you find the job by the physical manifestations that you've been experiencing ever since."

"You arrogant bastard." I fought the urge to storm out of the room. "You don't know what it's like."

"Because you don't talk to me," he said calmly. "Is this a mistake? Be honest. Do you want to live together, or did you agree to this because you didn't want to fight anymore?"

"That's not it." I blinked a few times, wishing Martin wasn't a morning person. Arguments and discussions should only occur after noon and numerous cups of coffee. Not before. "Everything's different, but it's the same. I can't get out of the quicksand. The harder I try, the faster I sink."

"What?" My metaphor confused him.

"I thought by moving in I could keep you safe." I swallowed and tugged on the sleeve of his t-shirt, exposing the faded bruise and his scar. "That's because of me. All of this shit is because of me. I convinced myself that things would be different once I moved in, but they aren't. At some point, something horrible will happen again, and I don't know how to stop it. That's why I started sleeping downstairs, but you ruined that, which is why you had to promise that you wouldn't let me hurt you."

"Alex," he sighed, "I get it."

Biting my lip, I struggled to come up with a response. "Then what's the solution?"

"I don't know." He opened his arms, beckoning, and I hugged him as a sort of quasi-apology. "I wish you never left Martin Technologies."

"Too late now."

"We'll have to figure out some way to make this work. You've been stuck in this uncomfortable state of flux for too long. It's making us both miserable."

"Misery loves company," I mumbled. "But right now, we need to go back to sleep because this is a horrible start to our day together, and I want a redo."

When I woke up again, I wasn't sure if our fight actually happened or if it was a dream. Most of our fights involved screaming and property damage, so this was tame. Maybe I dreamt it. Either way, I was capable of being more compassionate and understanding. Talking wasn't one of my strong suits, but I was willing to work on it.

"Morning, sleepyhead," Martin said when I turned to face him.

"Please tell me we aren't moving on to round two. I would like to be conscious for part of the day, but I'll stay asleep to avoid another confrontation."

"I said my piece." He brushed his lips against mine. "Where did we land on breakfast in bed?"

"I'm not opposed."

"Great. I'll be right back."

"I'll be here." When he returned a few minutes later, I eyed the tray suspiciously. "Is that banana bread?"

"And fruit salad." He put the tray on top of the bed and sat down.

I picked up the glass and took a sip. "That's not orange juice."

"Why would I put orange juice in a champagne flute?" He took a sip of his own mimosa and stabbed a slice of grapefruit. "What would you like to do today?"

"Apparently go into a sugar coma." I nibbled on the bread. "Oh my god, this alone is enough to ensure that I'll never leave again."

"I'm choosing to take that as a compliment rather than an insult."

I made a show of looking around the room. "Well, since you didn't fulfill my request for a TV, I guess we'll have to talk." By the time I shut up, we'd finished breakfast, the entire bottle of champagne, had a light lunch, and it was getting dark out. Everything that hadn't been said, regardless of how insignificant, was out there, and Martin looked like a kid in a candy store. "Are you happy now?"

"Yes." He grinned. "I know I said I wanted a weekend in bed, but I feel like celebrating. It isn't every day that I win my girlfriend back from the U.S. government, even if it's only for the next twelve hours."

Martin made a few calls and strongly suggested that I wear something elegant. Then we spent a few hours taking a private tour of an art gallery and enjoying a privately catered dinner on a rooftop overlooking the city. It was breathtaking and the most extravagant thing we'd done in quite some time. Close to midnight, we returned home.

While Martin puttered around the kitchen, I went into the second floor guest suite, planning to give my notes the quick once-over before showing up at the federal building tomorrow. Inside, the room had been transformed into almost an exact replica of my living room. In fact, it was so precise, the furniture even matched, down to the scuff mark on my coffee table.

"Martin," I called.

He appeared behind me. "Surprise," he said, sounding sheepish. "Before you freak out, I can move it back if you don't like it."

"You stole my furniture?" I went into the adjoining room, expecting to find my bedroom set shoved in the corner with my dining room table on the opposite side. Instead, the bed that had already been in the suite was moved. The main area was arranged in the exact same order with all of my belongings where they were at home.

"Why would you do this?"

"Since you love your apartment and didn't want to make this your home, I brought your apartment here. Your dresser didn't match mine, so I left it and your bed. However, we can redo our bedroom if you want." He looked at the bed that had been in the room. "I left that here just in case you ever need a break from the fourth floor."

"I always knew your guest suite was bigger than my place." I sat down on my couch, feeling strangely at home and in the *Twilight Zone* at the same time. "I'm still keeping my place for my own sanity and for when I have a dangerous assignment, so where am I going to sit or work when I'm there?"

"I bought new stuff for your place. Well, originally I bought it for us to use here, but I thought you'd like this better. Do you?"

I stood and went into the bathroom. Thankfully, he hadn't ripped out my vanity or cabinet, and the towels and toiletries were the same as what was in here the last time I checked. "When did you do this?"

"Friday. Marcal's been overseeing the move. It's why I wanted to keep you upstairs this weekend."

"Where are my notes? My work is sensitive."

"I know." He led the way into the office. "I moved everything in here during the move. It's in the same order. It's just in a different location. I was going to move it back sometime today, but we were reconnecting. No pun intended." He grinned. "Say something, Alex."

"You love me." I sounded dumbfounded on account of being completely awestruck.

"You just figured that out? Obviously, I don't say it enough." He enveloped me in his arms. "Do you like it, or do I call the movers to replace everything tomorrow?"

"I can't believe you did this. Everything," I went back into the guest suite, "is in the same place where I had it. It's incredible." I sat on the couch, grabbing his wrist and pulling him down next to me. "You'll do anything to get invited to my place, won't you?" I reached for the remote and flipped on the television. "The TV even works."

"Speaking of TV, I have something else to show you upstairs."

"Oh, I have something to show you, right here," I purred.

"Upstairs first." He dragged me off the couch and up the steps. "I couldn't figure out why you wanted a TV in the bedroom when you didn't even have one in your bedroom at home, and then I figured it was for one of two reasons. Either it was because you can't sleep when I'm working late or away, or it was so you could monitor my home security system." He had left a gift box on the dresser. Inside was a tablet and stand. It was preloaded with my favorite movies, television shows, and every streaming subscription service available. It also connected directly to the home security system, which was the real reason I wanted a television in the bedroom. "This way, you can watch whatever you want, any time you want, and it won't disturb me if I'm asleep beside you."

"Thank you." There was so much I wanted to say, but the words wouldn't come.

"Say you'll stay. Say that moving in together wasn't a mistake."

"How can I possibly leave now? My apartment's downstairs, and you've given me all kinds of neat toys to play with." I shook my head. "It's too much. You can't keep spoiling me like this. I haven't given you anything."

"That's not true. You spent the day reintroducing me to my girlfriend. I've missed her. But don't disappear again because I'm out of romantic gestures."

THIRTY-EIGHT

"Good morning," I greeted when Agent Lucca stepped into the conference room. "I've been thinking, and I'm positive we can get Facini to crack. Also, I phoned the district attorney's office to see what they planned to do with Gavin Levere. Once the PD concludes its investigation, they're considering bringing him up on manslaughter charges, but they're willing to cut him a deal if he can provide valuable testimony to us for the murder of Assistant U.S. Attorney Weaver. And after reviewing everything and speaking with Detective O'Connell, we've concluded that Tim Coker's involved. He has to be. He's the only connecting piece." I flipped through the ballistics and forensic reports. "I like Philip Dennison for the shooting. The forensics doesn't necessarily lead to him, but it doesn't disprove he's our killer either. We need a confession or some damning corroboration from the other involved parties."

"Someone's in a good mood." Lucca leaned over my shoulder and scanned the papers. "Is this what happens when you make me work on a Sunday while you stay home?"

"Yep. Oh, and I checked in with our surveillance units. Brad's been hanging out at a cheap motel and going to work. He looks clean. The unit on the Greenwoods hasn't noticed any unusual activity either. We might be able to get them to turn on Coker if your assessment's accurate."

"My assessments normally are. The Greenwoods want to take over Coker's gym or his client base, so if they aren't involved in blackmail or murder, there's no reason not to reward them."

"Fine, you wave the carrot around. I'll carry the stick. It's obvious you shouldn't possess any type of weaponry, regardless of how rudimentary." I cracked a smile. "So that's my agenda for the day. Where do you want to start?"

"I want to start by asking what you've done with Agent Parker." He lifted my coffee cup, finding it filled. "How many of these have you had?"

"One." I jerked my chin toward the mug near the empty chair. "Yours is over there."

"Um, thanks." He took a seat. "Let's start by getting Levere down here. We'll talk to him about the gambling and any instructions he was given concerning his fight with Santos. With any luck, he'll be able to point a finger at Dennison and maybe Coker. Then we'll move on to Facini. Depending on how things go, we'll either bring in the Greenwoods at that point or go straight for the big dog, and we'll end by making our move against Dennison."

"The only snag is Mr. Harper. He'll see what we're doing and keep his clients quiet."

"Not if Levere and Facini have someone else representing them."

"Do they?"

"You'd know the answer to that if you had been here yesterday." He collected the files and went to the door. "I'll phone for a transfer and meet you inside the interrogation room."

Maybe hell had frozen over because Lucca and I were actually on the same page. More accurately, I was through screwing around and getting screwed in the process. Since this case started, I'd been saying it needed to end. The pieces were spread out on the table. The only thing left to do was assemble them into the perfect picture.

On my way to the conference room, I passed Jablonsky

in the hallway. He offered a good morning as he continued to his destination. I brushed Martin's warning aside for the moment. I had too much to think about without his paranoia getting inside my head. I knew Mark. I had trusted him with my life on numerous occasions. He wasn't the antichrist, despite what Martin might think.

While I arranged the interrogation room and made sure the recording equipment was functioning, Lucca made the transfer request. Gavin Levere had been in police custody since Jack Fletcher's assault. Even though Fletcher planned to drop the charges, the police department had every reason to hold Levere while they concluded Hector Santos' autopsy. While Santos' death did not appear to be caused by premeditated murder, the blunt force trauma Levere delivered during the fight might be directly linked.

"Mr. Levere," I nodded at the agent who escorted him into the room, "we meet again."

"This is bullshit," Levere snapped. "I didn't kill Hector. I was told the assault charges were being dropped. What is any of this about?"

"Do you have that carrot handy?" I asked Lucca. "Or should I hit him with the big stick?"

"You are aware of your rights, Mr. Levere," Lucca said, probably wondering if I'd really hit Levere, "so I'm not gonna waste your time reminding you what they are and what penalties you might be facing. Here's the truth. We're in a bind. Three people have died because of these fights. I'm not talking about what went on inside the ring. If you have any knowledge of why these deaths might have occurred, you should come clean now. I'm prepared to petition the district attorney's office to drop all charges against you, but that's only if you help us."

"This is another trick." He focused on me. "You offered a deal before, but I've been stuck in custody ever since."

"Are you aware that placing bets and gambling is illegal without the proper licensing?" I asked, refusing to let his accusations goad me. I held up my hand before he could protest that he never partook in any such activity. "Having established this fact, are you aware of any illegal activity that may have occurred at the boxing matches or outside the boxing matches?"

"It's a sport. People wager. That has nothing to do with me," Levere insisted.

"It might. Were you ever asked to take a dive?" Lucca asked. Levere looked incredibly uncomfortable. "Did your coach ever ask you to take a dive?"

"You aren't supposed to be speaking to me without my attorney present," Levere said, apparently having earned his law degree while in central booking.

"Do you really want Mr. Harper here for this?" I circled the table. "His interests reside with the man paying his fee, and I'm positive that he wouldn't want you to implicate that person."

Levere looked at Lucca. "What's in it for me? Are you serious about having the charges dropped? I didn't kill Hector. We fought. I never meant to hurt him that badly."

"Except you did," I muttered.

Lucca tossed a warning look in my direction and sat in front of Levere. "I watched the fight, and I've read your stats. You should have lost."

"I didn't want to lose. I'm tired of losing." Levere sighed. "I want the deal in writing and signed by the district attorney himself before I say anything else."

"How do we know you have anything we want to hear?" I challenged.

"Coach Coker wanted me to throw the fight. I can name two other people who heard him say it. Hector wasn't expecting what he got. I don't think he knew the matches were rigged. Even Coach started calling out the combos to give Hector a fighting chance, but he wasn't listening." He sniffed and looked away. "Hector and I were supposed to go out for burgers afterward, but we never got the chance." Levere looked into my eyes. "We weren't enemies. That was just hype. We trained together. We were buddies. I never meant for him to get hurt like that."

Finally, some remorse and honesty. It was what I'd been waiting for since this started. I nodded to Lucca, and he pulled the paperwork out of his breast pocket. The deal had already been signed. We just had to make sure we had a willing party.

When Gavin Levere was finished spilling his guts, a junior agent accompanied him back to central booking. He'd be free soon enough, which meant we had to get the rest of our ducks in a row before word spread. Lucca radioed the surveillance unit to bring in Ron and Linka Greenwood, the two witnesses present when Coker instructed Levere to throw the fight.

"I feel like I need a shower," I said, heading back to the conference room, "but it'd be pointless since the sleaze factor is about to get worse."

"You realize this doesn't put us any closer to identifying the shooter, which is the entire point of our investigation," Lucca said. "The killer is still seven moves ahead."

"It'll work out. We're playing dominos, not chess. It doesn't matter how far ahead he is. When the pieces start falling, there's no way he can avoid getting crushed."

"Are you certain Philip Dennison is our shooter?"

"I'd stake my reputation on it."

"That isn't saying much." Lucca looked like he regretted the dig. "Sorry, I was out of line. You actually have a stellar reputation, Parker. Commendations, meritorious service award, your work speaks for itself. Anyone would be lucky to work with you."

I shoved Lucca into the wall of the empty conference room. "Whatever you think you know, you don't. Whatever Jablonsky said to you or let you read on Thursday, just pretend that didn't happen. You don't like me. I don't like you. We bitch at one another, and somehow, we get the case solved. You do your thing, and I do mine. Don't be a pussy. I don't want or need your pity." I let go of his shirt front and stalked across the room. "You just had to ruin my good mood, didn't you? Next, you'll probably pull out your taser and shock me again for the hell of it."

"That could be fun."

"If you're so keen on shocking someone, go surprise Facini with our newfound knowledge. He needs to pave the way to Dennison. I'll talk to the Greenwoods when they get here. We'll share our knowledge at lunchtime, and you're buying."

Lucca opened his mouth like he wanted to say

something, but instead, he bowed his head and went out the door and down the hall. Taking a deep breath, I glanced at my scribbles and went to wait for Ron and Linka. In the interim, I phoned the precinct. Detective Thompson answered, so I updated him on the fight and Levere's pending release.

"You give us a collar, and then you take it away. Remind me again why we always work with you."

"Hell if I know. Did you make any progress on determining what happened to Hector Santos from the time he left the fight until he died in the emergency room?" I asked.

"No, but even if we did, I'm not positive I'd tell you. You'd probably destroy our progress there too."

"So there is progress."

"Goodbye, Parker." Thompson hung up, and I considered the possibilities and any potential ramifications it could have on our case. But I didn't see a connection.

My goal was to illustrate that the gambling was motive for murder. I knew we'd get there. The hidden bullets we discovered practically put the gun in Dennison's hands, and the ledgers and books we found in his room made it obvious he was in charge of the wagers and the payouts. He had hundreds of thousands of dollars worth of motive. The only problem was Levere was supposed to throw the match, so why was he alive when Hector Santos and William Briscoe were dead? It was the same hang-up that I still couldn't explain.

When Ron and Linka arrived, escorted by the two agents who had been surveilling them, it was clear neither expected to see me. Linka looked uneasy and fidgeted while Ron went straight into friendly mode. After getting them situated in an empty conference room, I took a seat at the head of the table.

"First off, I'd like to apologize for the deception and thank you for agreeing to speak to us. I'm sure you're aware we've been investigating events and persons related to Tim Coker's gym." Being diplomatic was normally the best route to take, and it gave them the opportunity to open up without being forced to show my hand.

"Yeah," Ron said, "another agent spoke to us a few nights ago. We haven't said anything to Tim or anyone."

"That's good to hear. It's rare anyone willingly cooperates." Now I was laying it on thick, but they didn't seem to care. "My colleagues and I have spoken to numerous fighters under Tim Coker's tutelage, and it has come to our attention that these bouts aren't exactly on the up and up. Can you elaborate?"

"We don't know anything about it," Ron replied.

I shifted my focus to Linka. "You work on Tim's books. You know they don't balance. The buy-in for the fights, the payouts to the winners, what Tim's making on contingency, and what he charges in monthly fees don't equal out. You know what he's doing."

"He bets on the fights." The words burst from her mouth.

"What did he tell Gavin Levere before his fight with Hector Santos?" I asked.

"Gavin was supposed to throw the match. Tim wanted Gavin to go down in the second round, but Hector was shooting off his mouth, bragging about how great Coach Willie was."

"William Briscoe?" I asked.

"Yeah," Ron said, looking displeased his wife was blabbing.

I looked at Linka. "What did Gavin do?"

"He fought hard, hoping to prove he was a better fighter, despite his coach's shortcomings. He hoped to piss Tim off and get kicked out so he could start over somewhere else. You did the same thing." Suddenly, a thought crossed her mind. "That's why you confronted Tim and why you showed up early. It was because you wanted information."

Perhaps she was a bit slow, or maybe she'd been hit one too many times, but I simply shrugged. "Did Gavin intend to kill Hector?"

"No," Ron interrupted, "Gavin had nothing to do with that. I've seen a lot of fights. A lot of fighters take worse hits. Hector might have had a few fractures and definitely plenty of bumps and scrapes, but he should have been able to walk away."

"Who kept him from walking away?" I was an expert at reading between the lines. He shrugged, clasping his wife's hand, and they both fell silent. "You were there. You work for Tim Coker. It wouldn't be that difficult to charge you as an accessory."

"I don't want to say anything. It's not right. It's not my place," Ron insisted. "You can charge me if you want, but I'm not guilty. There isn't any proof that I've done anything wrong or that I'm involved, so I'll take my chances."

"Ron," Linka chastised, shifting her gaze from her husband to me, "just tell Alex what she wants to know." He didn't budge, and she sighed dramatically. "I'll tell you what happened, but you can't let anyone know where it came from."

"I can't promise that," I said.

"If you want to know who killed Hector, you have to."

THIRTY-NINE

"Fine. Deal's on the table." I put the paperwork in front of the Greenwoods. After Linka's insistence, I phoned Thompson with an update. He arrived at the federal building with an ADA and a tape recorder. "Tell us what happened after the fight."

"Tim was pissed. I've never seen him that angry in all the years that I've known him. He marched out of the arena right after Hector left," Linka began, but Ron clasped her hand to silence her.

"They were fighting. I heard them screaming at each other. Tim was saying how ungrateful Hector was to abandon the gym, and that if he couldn't figure out how to defend himself when the combos were being called out, then he had no business being in the ring. Hector said something about Tim being a washed-up loser who didn't give a shit about anyone but himself." Ron stopped, taking a sip of water. "I had to pull Tim off of Hector. He was going postal, slamming Hector up against the wall and pummeling the crap out of the poor kid. While Tim cooled down, we put Hector in a cab, but we didn't find out until the news broke the next day what happened. The original article said it was due to trauma sustained during the bout, and I had no proof that it wasn't true."

Detective Thompson opened his mouth to ask a question, but I cleared my throat. He wanted to work Santos' murder, but I needed to get to the bottom of the gambling scheme in order to solve my two murders. Thankfully, Thompson didn't request a round of rock, paper, scissors to determine who was going to ask the next question.

"Why did Tim go after Hector? Shouldn't he have been pissed at Gavin instead?" I asked.

"He was. He is. He kicked Gavin out of the gym and off the training roster," Linka said.

"Why didn't he attack Gavin instead of Hector?" I asked, and the two exchanged a look. "You agreed to provide information, so someone better start talking."

"Gavin won the fight, so that made him valuable. You wouldn't break a winning racehorse's leg," Ron replied.

"But you might do that to a loser in order to collect the insurance," Thompson said. "What was Tim hoping to collect by injuring Hector?" Neither of the Greenwoods spoke, and Thompson redirected his line of questioning. "Coker was betting on the fights, which is why he was fixing the fights. How much did he lose because Santos didn't win?"

"Fifty thousand," Linka said. "He thought he could recover that by attracting new fighters to his gym by boasting about his success, training Gavin. Tim finally turned out a winner."

Ron cleared his throat. "I don't believe Tim ever intended to kill Hector. It was an accident. He was angry. He made a bad call."

"It doesn't matter. He intended to harm him, and it resulted in Hector Santos' death." Thompson glanced back at the ADA and received a head nod in response. "I need an official statement and an agreement that you'll testify," Thompson said, ready to hijack my interrogation.

"First, I need a detailed account of Tim Coker's betting and anything else you might know about the wager system set up at these fights," I insisted.

*   *   *

By lunchtime, I was back in the conference room, battling a migraine and hoping the Greenwoods had provided us with enough usable information. Something about their behavior bothered me. I had difficulty believing they were nothing more than innocent bystanders. I also had issues stomaching how they could continue to work in such close proximity to someone who for all intents and purposes murdered a man because he didn't win a boxing match. However, that was for the police department to determine.

Lucca came into the room with a couple of Styrofoam containers and put them on the table. He picked up the signed statements and read Ron and Linka's account of the illegal gambling. When he was finished, he watched me eat a few fries.

"Tim Coker was involved in betting and fixing the fights. The Greenwoods backed Levere's story and provided additional information. Did you send someone to pick up Coker?" he asked.

"No, the police department had an arrest warrant signed before the Greenwoods even left the building. The PD's bringing Coker in for murdering Hector Santos." I picked up the burger, considered taking a bite, decided against it, and put it back in the box. "What did you get out of Facini?"

"Nothing yet. He wants full immunity."

"What is up with everyone? Do they air *Law & Order* nonstop at the gym or something? The only reason anyone needs immunity is if they did something illegal." Pausing, I rubbed my eyes and scoffed. "What did Elias Facini do? His coach is a murderer. His roommate probably is too. Let me guess, he capped a little old lady because she crossed the street in front of him."

"It wouldn't surprise me. Nothing would surprise me at this point." He bit into his sandwich. "Jablonsky's speaking to him and his counsel."

"Not Harper."

"No, some second year associate from one of those ambulance chaser firms."

"That might be the only thing we have going for us."

"Yeah, well, Dennison doesn't know that."

I wiped my mouth and grabbed one of the folders. "No, he doesn't, and Harper will be too busy dealing with Coker's arrest. How are your poker skills, Lucca?" Before he could answer, I flipped the lid closed on his lunch container. "That's right, you read people, so it's about time you show me how well you play people. Let's go, boy scout."

"He could shut us down in a second since we have no right to talk to him by himself."

"Watch and learn." I went down the hallway to the interrogation room and pushed open the door hard enough that it slammed into the wall. Philip Dennison jumped, surprised by the abrupt entry. "Mr. Dennison, I have a few questions for you."

"My attorney isn't here, so I'm not talking."

"Mr. Harper's at the police station. He's busy trying to get the death penalty taken off the table. It seems another one of his clients has been arrested for murder." I spun to face Lucca. "Did he say how long it would take to negotiate that deal for Tim Coker?" Lucca stared silently at me, so I turned back to Dennison. "If you want us to wait for him to get here, we can. Coker said he had a lot to give up, so it shouldn't take Harper that long to negotiate a deal. Once that's done, we'll talk to you." I sat down and put my feet up on the edge of the table. "Do you care if I wait in here? If I go back out there, someone will want me to do something. Monday afternoons are always the worst. Filing, ugh."

"Parker," Lucca warned.

"C'mon, Eddie, you hate the paperwork too." I flipped through the folder I had carried inside. "We have the Greenwoods testimony to go through. Then Facini's. Coker's. Bellows'. And don't get me started on Briscoe's autopsy report and the ballistics. Shit, did I tell you the forensic team pulled a latent print from the elevator? Crap, I was supposed to turn in the requisition form for the university's security cam footage too. Remind me to do that before I go home." I sighed, pretending Dennison wasn't in the room. "How come the secretarial staff only works for the supervisory agents? We have ten times the amount of paperwork to get through, which explains why it takes so long to finish the evidence collection and compiling our cases. It'd be more efficient if the secretaries and assistants worked for us. I don't even want to think about the amount of time it will take to catalog every item we found in Mr. Dennison's apartment. We need our own assistants."

"Why don't you tell that to Director Kendall?" Lucca suggested.

"Good idea."

"Coker's making a deal?" Philip licked at the layer of sweat that coated his upper lip. My rambling made him nervous. Granted, I hit every possible location where we might have discovered evidence and every person who could point a finger at him. Now he was afraid he missed something.

"Yep."

"What kind of deal?" Philip asked, trying too hard to sound disinterested.

"We can't really talk about it. From what I gather, it's one of those first come, first served things. Y'see, three people are dead. One of them is a nobody kid from the wrong side of the tracks that no one gives a shit about. That's the one Coker popped. But one of the other two victims was an Assistant United States Attorney with a stellar conviction record, so his colleagues are out for blood. We found the sniper rifle used to kill him. We found the bullets. And Coker might know who did it."

"I thought the attorney's murder was an accident," Lucca said, finally joining the game. "They can't pursue the maximum penalty unless we have intent."

"You don't think Coker will say whatever they want him to in order to get the best deal possible?" I asked.

Lucca chuckled. "Coker would give up his own grandmother."

"He can't." Philip slammed his fist into the table. "He doesn't know anything. He's not entitled to a deal. Just because he thinks he has clout in the boxing world doesn't mean he has any real influence anywhere else."

"Do you want to set the record straight?" I asked.

Philip's eyes darted around the room. "I'm not an idiot. That's what you want. I'm not saying a word."

"Good. I'd hate to go through another internal review because a confession was made under suspicious circumstances. I can't really afford that with my record." I went back to flipping through the folder. "Plus, Coker's deal will close this case, and I don't get paid enough to care." I sat upright, letting my chair legs slam forward. "Do you honestly believe I get paid enough to let some son of a bitch like you try to shoot me?" I jerked my chin at Lucca. "And I sure as hell don't make enough to let an asshole like him hit me with the same fucking stun gun he shot you with. So honestly, Philip, I'm only sitting inside this room to make sure you keep your damn mouth shut until Coker's deal is finalized because if you start running your mouth now, everything's gonna go to shit. Stay quiet, or I'll make sure you can't speak. Have you ever had your jaw wired shut? It's not fun."

"Agent Parker," Lucca snapped, hiding the surprise from my sudden personality shift, "do you want to be reprimanded?"

"You didn't hear a word, or I will file a complaint against you." I climbed out of the chair and approached Lucca. "You realized if you'd pulled your actual gun and shot this bastard, we wouldn't be dealing with this bullshit right now."

"This isn't my fault."

"Of course not. Nothing ever is." I stormed to the door. "I'll give the precinct a call and see if Harper's on his way. Make sure he stays quiet."

I left the interrogation room and stepped into the attached observation room. Through the two-way glass, I watched Lucca take a seat at the table. He didn't say anything but sat with his arms crossed, glaring menacingly at Philip Dennison. I didn't know if he'd crack or not, but there was a chance. I waited another minute and then went to find Jablonsky.

Mark was the final piece. Either it'd work and Philip would confess, or we'd reset the board and try again with actual questions once his attorney showed up. Philip was smart. He was a numbers guy and a business genius, but that didn't mean he possessed common sense. He was scared. That would impair his judgment. I led him to believe if he admitted Stan Weaver's death was an accident, things would go easier for him.

Once Mark was up to speed, he went into the interrogation room and pulled Lucca out to deal with a more pressing matter. Before the door even closed, Jablonsky began apologizing for our behavior, assuring Mr. Dennison that anything he said to us would not be used against him and asking again if he would be willing to answer some questions without his attorney present.

"Do you think Philip believed you?" Lucca asked, joining me in the observation room.

"We'll find out."

After a minute of utter silence, Mark made his way to the door, promising to send Mr. Harper in as soon as he arrived. Before the door closed, Philip cleared his throat, stopping Mark in his tracks.

"Is it true that Tim Coker is making a deal?" Philip asked.

"I'm not at liberty to say. That business involves the police department. It doesn't involve me."

"But you give people deals, right?"

"It depends on what the prosecutor's office wants to do, but I'll put in a good word if a suspect has valuable information." He reached back to pull the door closed.

"What about confessions?" Dennison asked. "Does that mean there's leniency? And what about intent? What happens if a crime was committed accidentally?"

"It depends. Charges are sometimes dropped. Other times, they might be lessened. Did Agent Parker say something? She isn't authorized to offer a deal," Jablonsky said.

"She didn't want to make a deal," Philip said, the wheels in his head turning. "That's the last thing she wanted to give me."

"Based on her report, you tried to kill her, and she tends to hold a grudge. She can be dramatic. Your lawyer will have to deal with those allegations." Mark flipped through the folder. "Although based on the evidence, that will be the least of your worries, pal."

"What if the attorney's death was an accident and someone else plotted and conspired to eliminate the other boxing coach?" Dennison asked.

"Then I'd say it's your word against theirs, and whoever can prove the allegations will get the better deal." Mark looked into the hallway. "But I'm sure you want to wait for your attorney."

"Actually, I don't."

FORTY

"I don't get it." Lucca read the transcript again. "Most of what we had was circumstantial. If Dennison kept his mouth shut, we might not have had enough for a jury to find him guilty of murder."

"The prosecutor's office would have tried anyway. Not to mention, we would have buried him with the gambling. For the number of bets he took, he'd be facing decades in prison," I said.

"But two counts of murder will still lead to decades in prison."

"Yeah, but he took Tim Coker down with him. Philip produced the recording he made the night Tim went to the apartment and offered to pay him to eliminate William Briscoe. After Hector's death, Tim was scared shitless that Briscoe knew what happened to his fighter. Not to mention, Briscoe was coaching Hector for free, which flew in the face of Tim's business. In exchange for Philip pulling the trigger, Tim promised to rig a dozen or more fights in order to ensure he and Dennison walked away with a ton of cash. The fifty thousand they hoped to extort from Jack Fletcher was just the tip of the iceberg."

"I don't understand why the prosecutor was willing to give Dennison immunity on the gambling charges when that was a slam dunk."

"A murder confession is also a slam dunk, and it was about loyalty to their fallen comrade. It makes sense to me. They wanted the murderer caught with no doubt left in anyone's mind. It sends a message. You can't kill one of ours and get away with it. Plus, once we got a hold of Dennison's credit card history, we were able to trace the illegal gun sale to an online entity, so we finally found our smoking gun. And this way, Tim gets charged with manslaughter and the illegal gambling, racking up the years on his potential sentence too."

"The Greenwoods testimony wouldn't have been enough to take Coker down since they had every reason to lie," Lucca said, "but Philip Dennison didn't know that. Apparently, it came out in the wash."

"Be thankful. It got Will Briscoe Jr. off the hook for feeling guilty about his dad's death. Maybe that family will finally find some peace." I pulled the printed glossies off the board. "Coker's arrest will bring Brad some peace too. From what Detective O'Connell said, Brad's hoping they'll investigate his father's death to determine if it was indeed an accident. I doubt they'll prove otherwise, but Brad's happy Tim's finally getting what he deserves."

"It's a good thing Dennison had the foresight to make that recording as an insurance policy." Lucca studied me for a moment, a question forming on his lips. "You were the only one who thought Brad was innocent. How'd you figure that out?"

"Despite the fact that he had owned up to his previous indiscretions, the anger never went away. If he killed someone, he wouldn't have been angry."

"That's the most convoluted thought process ever."

"When you kill someone, you feel guilty. You might feel remorse. Hell, maybe even relief. If you're angry about the kill, it's focused internally. He wasn't our killer. He had no reason to be."

"You scare me sometimes."

"Only sometimes?" I cocked an eyebrow in his direction.

"I think Elias Facini had more to do with this than we've discovered, but Philip didn't implicate him. And he alibied out." I sucked air in through my teeth. "Something just doesn't sit right. He went to the gym with Philip to pick up the blackmail money."

"He was the enabler," Lucca said, closing the box. "He took Philip to the shooting range, taught him about sharpshooting, and introduced all the affected parties. Without him, Dennison wouldn't have known how to conduct the murder, nor would he have met Will Briscoe Jr. and discovered where William Briscoe would be at a specific time and date. He might not have even gotten involved in the small-scale boxing scene or started the underground betting. Facini provided him the resources to do all of that, but it can't be proven. The best we can hope for is that the accessory charges stick."

"The Briscoes could pursue damages against him in civil court."

"For what? Some kind of tort with that 'but for' bullshit?"

I shrugged. "I just hate that he's practically walking away unscathed."

"He could be innocent."

"Yeah, sure."

Lucca scanned the room to make sure he had everything. We were alone, and the case was finally closed. "Alexis, sit down. I need a moment of your time, and I want you to listen to what I have to say."

"You have one minute." I dropped into a chair and studied my watch. Whatever he was about to say, I didn't want to hear it.

"Jablonsky asked if I'd be willing to work with you in the future. I told him yes."

"That was a mistake. Do I get a say in the matter?"

"Why is it a mistake?"

"You know why. Jablonsky let you read the report." I blinked and looked away. "I told you when this case began that you should stay the hell away from me. Nothing's changed."

"You didn't kill them. Those two agents died because of

a booby trap, not because you made a bad call."

"They're dead. Don't tell me that's not on me." I stormed toward the door, but Lucca blocked the exit.

"If you believed that, you wouldn't be here right now. So what the hell are you afraid of?"

"I do believe it, but I've come to terms with it. I just don't want it to happen again."

"I remind you of him. Of Michael," Lucca said softly.

"You're nothing like him." I squeezed my eyes shut. When I opened them, I hoped Lucca would be gone. Unfortunately, he wasn't.

"You called me Michael." He stared back at me, but I didn't deem his comment worthy of a response. "Why don't you want to work together?" he asked, adopting a new tactic.

"It has nothing to do with you. I don't want to work with anyone. I've lost enough. I can't be responsible for losing someone else."

"So you're not a heartless bitch? Damn, you had me fooled."

"And you're a shitty liar. Now get out of my way so I can talk to Mark and correct your mistake."

"I didn't make a mistake. Today proved we balance each other." He leaned against the door and folded his arms across his chest. "You didn't pursue any official recourse to taking friendly fire. Obviously, you would have done that if you wanted to keep me away from you."

"Whatever you have to tell yourself, boy scout, but we're not working together again. I work alone." I pushed him out of the way. "If you ever bring up my past again, I'll show you precisely what a stun gun is capable of doing to male genitalia."

Stopping in the ladies' room, I splashed some cold water on my face. Today was a win. The case was closed. Lucca's little speech had sullied my otherwise good mood, but it was five o'clock. After I turned in my final report, I'd be on my way home. The thought of Martin and my living room furniture situated inside the second floor guest suite helped to combat the dark clouds that settled over me.

Knocking on Jablonsky's door, I entered and dropped

the file on his desk. He picked it up, gesturing to the chair. I sat while he skimmed it.

"That was a risky move you pulled with Dennison. It easily could have backfired," Mark scolded.

"It was worth it, and honestly, we were out of options."

"Next time, give me the heads-up before you implement another doomsday scheme."

"Sure, no problem." I took a deep breath and fidgeted in the chair.

"That was it." Mark looked up. "Do I have to say dismissed? I thought that was just Lucca's hang-up."

"I don't want to work with him again. I don't want to work with anyone."

"It doesn't really matter. You're not in charge, Parker. This is a hierarchy. It isn't a democracy. You aren't your own boss anymore. You're lucky I buried the stuff from Fletcher, or Director Kendall might have wanted to have a word with you."

"Right, you're saving me." Martin's words came back into my mind. "How come you didn't suggest that I tell Martin I was getting reinstated?"

"We discussed that. You didn't want to tell him, remember? It was a security issue for both of you. You and I agreed it'd be best to keep him out of the loop." Mark dropped the folder back on his desk and blew out a breath. "I take it you spoke to Marty about this."

"I can be overprotective. You know this. As my friend, you're supposed to tell me when what I'm doing is ridiculous. But you agreed with me instead."

"We made the right call."

"No, we were wrong. He should have known. If our positions were reversed, I would have wanted to know. I would have wanted my best friend to tell me. You should apologize to him."

"Why? He's not always right. He's being a stubborn jackass."

"Perhaps. But he made quite a few valid points, and there is no reason in the world why it should have taken as long as it did for the background check to clear once I decided that I wanted to tell him. We're the fucking FBI.

We run background checks on a daily basis, but his was stuck in limbo for weeks. Regardless of who's right, just say you're sorry and fix this. It's hard enough to be here every day without having to worry about my boss getting along with my boyfriend, particularly when the two of you were friends before I even came into the picture."

"Fine, but I'm only doing this for you, Alex."

"And I'm only back here because of you, so I guess that makes us even." I walked out of his office, even more confused as to whether Martin's assessment held any truth.

On my way home, Jack Fletcher phoned. He wanted to thank me for keeping his name out of the investigation. Apparently, it was no longer necessary that he testify, and since the blackmailer was caught, he felt safe and protected. However, in a strange turn of events, he was called into a meeting this afternoon and offered a position as senior partner.

"Last week, you wanted to resign. It's a good thing someone talked you out of that," I said.

"Thank you, Ms. Parker." He lowered his voice. "Do you think they knew about the blackmail?"

"I don't know. Why would they offer you the position if they thought you posed a danger to their good name?"

"Maybe it was a test of my loyalty or my ethical code."

"You must have passed. Congratulations on the promotion. I just have one request."

"Name it."

"Don't do anything illegal again. I don't even want to hear that you got a speeding ticket, okay?"

"Yes." He laughed. "I'll be a straight shooter from here on out."

"Excellent. Good night, Mr. Fletcher."

"Good night."

"Oh, and don't turn into a pompous douche bag either."

"I'll do my best, but that might be a requirement to getting my name on the door."

We disconnected just as I pulled my car into the garage. Martin's town car was parked on the end, and I went up the stairs, glad to see him. It was nice to be home.

Intended Target

DON'T MISS ALEX'S NEXT ADVENTURE.

MUFFLED ECHOES IS NOW AVAILABLE IN PAPERBACK AND AS AN E-BOOK

ABOUT THE AUTHOR

G.K. Parks is the author of the Alexis Parker series. The first novel, *Likely Suspects,* tells the story of Alexis' first foray into the private sector.

G.K. Parks received a Bachelor of Arts in Political Science and History. After spending some time in law school, G.K. changed paths and earned a Master of Arts in Criminology/Criminal Justice. Now all that education is being put to use creating a fictional world based upon years of study and research.

You can find additional information on G.K. Parks and the Alexis Parker series by visiting our website at
www.alexisparkerseries.com